ALSO BY PETER DELACORTE

Levantine

Games of Chance

TIME

ON MY

HANDS

A NOVEL

PETER DELACORTE

SCRIBNER

SCRIBNER
1230 Avenue of the Americas
New York, NY 10020

SCRIBNER and design are trademarks of Simon & Schuster Inc.

DESIGN BY DIANE AND ERICH HOBBING

Set in Electra

Manufactured in the United States of America

1   3   5   7   9   10   8   6   4   2

Library of Congress Cataloging-in-Publication Data is available.

Delacorte, Peter.
Time on my hands: a novel/Peter Delacorte
p.   cm.
1. Reagan, Ronald—Fiction. 2. Motion picture actors and actresses—California—
Los Angeles—Fiction. I. Title.
PS3554.E433T56   1997
813'.54—dc21   96–53316
CIP

ISBN 0-684-82651-8

Photo credits appear on page 399.

For Bonnie

ACKNOWLEDGMENTS

Immeasurable thanks to Jim Glenn, who knew where Schroedinger kept the cat.

Just barely measurable thanks to Anne Salenger, who knew Malibu. And to all those who helped in one way or another: Solange Bocchino, Eve Goldin, Don and Dianne Heiny, Fred Hill, John Koethe, Kate Kretzmann, Michael Lesser, Judy Mason, Curtis Mayfield, Ernest Marquez, Joe and Lolita Metscher, Cynni Murphy, David and Mona Nelson, Stuart Ng, Joan Osborne, Harry Redmond, Judy Stone, Justine and Molly Underhill, Carol Walter, and Barry Weiss.

PART I

THE
ERRAND

1

I have some time on my hands. There is no better way to describe my situation. As I write these words—whose writing may turn out to be an act of utter self-indulgence—I sit at a rustic table in a primitive cabin in the woods outside Corvallis. Having spent virtually every day of my life in one city or another, I must tell you it is strange and quite lonely here, that I feel utterly out of place, that my only solace is in knowing soon, one way or another, I'll be leaving.

I should tell you an important thing about myself. I don't wish at this early juncture of the story to seem ostentatious, but as a child I had a very clear sense that I was destined to do something exceptional. There was never a specific vision: I didn't daydream about becoming president or discovering a cure for cancer. I was just a well-balanced boy who had (considering that I had no parents) a fairly normal, happy childhood, during which I strongly felt something singular was in store for me.

A memory has come bouncing into my head this minute, a moment I hadn't recalled in twenty years at least, and now it's such a vivid picture that it gives me chills. I see myself at age ten, the one summer I spent at camp, in Maine, and the eight of us in my cabin, plus two counselors, were on a three-day canoe trip. We paddled like galley slaves up one lake and down another, what seemed like sixteen hours a day. We paddled through rainstorms and blazing hot August afternoons. Wherever it was we were trying to reach, we got there, and on our third night we spread our sleeping bags on an island some-where close to Canada, under a sky that contained far more than the usual contingent of stars. We city boys ravenously consumed our canned swill, after which the traditional swapping of ghost stories around the campfire was supplanted by an epidemic of falling asleep.

I did not sleep. I had found a strength in myself. I had never complained during this little ordeal, unlike my fellows. I had taken extra shifts at the bow position in my canoe, had found myself growing stronger as we'd glided toward the twilight. Now, filled with exhilaration, I walked among the fallen, the seven boys and the two adolescents, under that magnificent chandelier of a sky, and I realized that *I alone was seeing what I saw.* In this recognition I did not exclude only the nine unconscious human beings nearby, but all the rest of the world. I was at that solipsistic instant the absolute center of the universe, aged ten.

To call the moment an epiphany would be to understate. To recall it merely as solipsism would be to do my ten-year-old self an injustice. I did not, after all, suspect even for a second that I was God, or even related to God. I had simply discovered the fact that if some beast came out of the woods and did away with me, or if by any other means I suddenly ceased to exist, then so too would all I surveyed. I had stumbled across my importance.

It was not a thing I dwelt upon over the years, nor was it something I chose to tell anyone, especially not the aunts who raised me rather diffidently. It was something I suspected other children, at least those of my acquaintance, had not experienced. I did quite well in school, went away when I was sixteen to a boarding school whose reputation far outstripped its proficiency at educating, but nonetheless I made the progression to the next level, to a famous university in New Jersey. Here again I did well, although not spectacularly.

I was never terribly popular, which I like to think was a phenomenon of my own choosing. I could be charming and ingratiating when I needed to be, but I seldom needed to be. I was content with a small circle of friends. I had no trouble getting dates, and when I wanted to sleep with a woman it was usually only a matter of time before we did. If I never sustained a relationship, it was again because I chose not to.

What difference does any of this make to you? I suppose that if you're to have any understanding of what's to follow, you should possess at least a minimal portrait of its author. My urge is to gather up everything we might loosely call exposition, to make it as succinct as possible, and set it down right at the start. But do I have the time? Do I have the space? Even if so, will you ever see it?

It is better, I think, to jump forward (quite a ways forward, from my present perspective) to a more pertinent moment in my story.

I was in Paris. It was the first week of May, 1994. I was working. There is a man in Seattle named Harvey Wells Greenglass who some years ago devised a sort of new-age guidebook. If you've traveled to any number of cities in Europe and the United States and if you're of a certain class and sensibility, you're probably familiar with the Greenglass *Entrée* series. Greenglass books are small and good-looking, they cover traditional touristic attractions minimally, often with some irony, but they excel in taking the visitor to all manner of places he won't find in other guidebooks. To a church almost as spectacular as the one everyone else is gawking at, but off the beaten track. To restaurants every bit as good as Michelin's latest pet, but not nearly as expensive or crowded. To bistros, bars, stores, neighborhoods, nightclubs, zoos, theaters, subway stops that offer something out of the ordinary.

Greenglass came up with the *Entrée* concept. He has relied on others to do all the research, all the writing, all the editing, all the production. You will find Greenglass's name in quite conspicuous print on the front of every *Entrée* book. You will find the names of people who've done all the work in the very back of the book, in tiny print. You will find my name—or shall I say that one used to be able to find my name—in the back of the original *Entrée to Paris* and in all three updates.

Thousands of Americans and other English-speaking travelers have carried that little book around Paris for days or weeks, have paid homages to Harvey Wells Greenglass at every eccentric little shop, every out-of-the-way outdoor market they would otherwise have missed, while the fat old philistine himself has probably never seen more of Paris than his suite at the Ritz.

I don't intend to seem bitter. If there is a strong element of injustice here, I can't dwell on it terribly long when I consider the positive aspects of my association with *Entrée*: they paid me generously, they reimbursed my expenses promptly, down to the last centime, they edited my work minimally, diligently. And of course every other year they sent me to Paris for a couple of months.

Had you been able to see my *Entrée to Paris*, you'd know the love I have for the city. I lived there briefly, in my twenties. I imagined I would stay there forever. Each day was a new discovery: new places to eat, to browse, to shop, to stop and stare in astonishment at some beauty, physical or metaphysical. I found after six months that I was getting nothing done. It was as if I had set myself the task of organizing my room, and I proceeded to do so with vigor and passion until everything was in fine shape, and then the following week I took it apart and started over again. Much room organizing. Terrific ideas. But once the room is done, there must come a time to *use* it.

I am goal oriented. Is it altogether fatuous to say that? Is it unnecessary, superfluous, redundant? I was so extraordinarily happy, and yet at odd moments I would be overcome by attacks of piercing anxiety, thinking *My God, if I stay here I'll never get anything done!*

So I left Paris, moved back to New York, became an editor, lived my life, got things done, to no great satisfaction. I quit my job, left New York when I was twenty-nine, moved to Los Angeles in part because there was a woman who fascinated me. That did not last. Lovelorn, I took a long trip to Turkey and Bulgaria, wrote some pieces about it that grew into a book. The book did not do particularly well commercially, but it found a certain audience that eventually included Harvey Wells Greenglass. And nine years after I left Paris, I was back—doing precisely what I'd done as a directionless twenty-four-year-old, but getting paid for it now.

Let me then duly note the passage of another nine years. The Paris *Entrées* weren't all I did in that period. A book on Australia, emphasis on vegetation and beer; a book on Quebec, a curious mixture of *gourmandise* and politics, the latter perhaps because I spent much of my Canadian spring and summer in the apartment of Marie-Laure, exquisite epicurean daughter of a separatist icon. She accompanied me to the West Coast: to Vancouver, to Seattle, where she charmed Greenglass out of his Birkenstocks. In my house in Santa Monica I told her I loved her. I'd never said those words to anyone. I was forty-two years old.

She said, "Why do you love me?"

It was not the response I'd anticipated, certainly not the one I'd hoped for. For what seemed like a geological era I said nothing, and then I stammered and halted and lurched. What I said, if I can recall with any definitude, was that I knew I loved her because she was the first woman I'd ever needed to tell I loved.

I recall her next words exactly. I have such a clear picture of us in my kitchen, her leaning against the dishwasher. She said, "Well, then I love you too."

This is of course not the "pertinent moment" I referred to some pages ago, although it is undeniably a moment that *leads* to that moment. Because if Marie-Laure had not accompanied me to Paris, this rather unlikely series of events would never have occurred, and instead of writing an ante-memoir for you, I would probably be sitting in a seedy hotel in Vladivostok, or the only European restaurant on Madagascar.

She came with me, and for a time we were in heaven. It's still not clear to me when things started to go wrong. We bustled from one side of Paris to the next, from arrondissement to arrondissement. She participated in the process; more than once we had a meal or a drink in some unlikely establishment simply because Marie-Laure had noticed it. For my part, I wondered how I'd managed all those hundreds of previous Parisian sorties on my own. How many times had I sat in the corner of a new bistro, at a table for one, subsisting on interior conversation? How much more pleasurable was it to eat the same meal, to share the same discovery, with someone I loved?

The alteration of my social life was considerable. I had been in the habit of looking up three or four American acquaintances during my visits to Paris. Now I was visiting fifth-floor walk-ups off Boulevard St. Michel, taking part in earnest discussions of philosophical ethics and the relative skills of Jean Renoir and Steven Spielberg until four in the morning, waking up at eight to discover my only clean set of reconnoitering clothes still stinking of stale marijuana smoke. It was exciting. It was rather like being back at college. Marie-Laure, of course, was only eight or so years removed from college.

The difference in our ages was not something that concerned me a great deal. For one thing, these evenings were attended by plenty of graybeards, so it wasn't as if I stood out. For another, I have always looked uncommonly young. It was a mild but flattering inconvenience, on the infrequent occasions that I found myself buying alcohol, to be asked for proof of age well into my thirties. At forty-two, I think I could easily have passed for thirty-five.

I would say I am a good-looking man: slightly under six feet tall, with light brown hair and blue eyes, with modest, well-formed facial features. I keep myself in good condition. I weigh, I believe, a pound or two less than when I entered college.

Marie-Laure struck me at first as being only beautiful. The more time I spent with her, the more I became convinced she was the most beautiful woman I had ever seen. She had inherited from her swarthy father brown eyes and a permanently tan skin tone, from her Nordic mother luminous blond hair. Perhaps three inches shorter than I, she was exquisitely proportioned, with the sort of figure that caused men to stop and stare abjectly.

Jean-Luc Mouchard was an academic and a small-time critic, a major figure in Marie-Laure's group, which I came to think of as the Moveable Snack. He was lean and balding, with a pitted face and an irritating manner, strident and self-righteous. It was my impression that Mouchard shaved about every third day, that he bathed about half as often as he shaved, and experienced a lucid thought a third as often as that. Here was the man who took Marie-Laure away from me.

I will not bore you with vignettes of her duplicity. I believed her when she began begging out of our midday meals because she was "gaining weight." I accepted each excuse when she was twenty, thirty, forty minutes late for our afternoon appointments. Until finally she did not appear at all, and I was forced to confront her, and she confessed to me the whole sordid matter. Mouchard, on top of everything else, was married, was father to three children. This, Marie-Laure whispered to me in depressed, penitent tones, was of great concern to her.

She moved out of our room, into the love nest she shared with her

scrawny freak. I had barely uttered a word. I had three weeks remaining in Paris, three weeks of all-expenses-paid investigation, three weeks anticipated as pure pleasure, and suddenly I was in shock, deserted, devastated, sleepless, torn asunder, miserable.

— ◦ —

I spent the following morning as if heavily anesthetized, sitting in my room with the television playing a succession of otherworldly programs, including an American situation comedy that, judging from the bell-bottoms and the excessive hairdos, dated from the mid-1970s. Whatever it was, I had managed to miss it during its currency, and now this unattractive ensemble was murmuring to me, twenty years later, in badly synchronized French. I drank cup after cup of room-service coffee, trying to propel myself out of the funk. I made occasional attempts to read my daily copies of *Le Monde* and the *Herald Tribune*, but my concentration span seemed limited to about five seconds.

Trips to the window revealed a gruesome day, a regression toward winter: a gray sky, a steady rain, pedestrians bundled and huddled against the wind. I had already missed my morning visit to the Musée de Cristal, a fairly long Métro ride away. Given the circumstances, I decided that departing from my schedule might be therapeutic, that diverging from my frugal pattern this once wouldn't put too large a dent in the Greenglass pocketbook. I had the concierge call a taxi.

Lunch at a beloved café on the Rue St. Martin hardly cheered me up; I could think only of how much Marie-Laure would have enjoyed the place. When the rain briefly abated to drizzle, I walked several blocks up the street to the Musée National des Techniques, my favorite of all of Paris's little museums. I use the word "little" simply to differentiate these places from the Louvre and the Musée d'Orsay and the other monsters. The Musée des Techniques (the National Technical Museum) is fairly spacious, just the proper size to provide an afternoon's pleasant survey, or several days getting a true sense of the place.

It is a cornucopia of machines. It is as if someone with a few screws loose had been handed a few million francs, had been assigned the job of accumulating a certain number of machines that would (first) fill the space provided in a proper esthetic manner, and (second) illustrate the history, the development, the evolution of machinery in a properly *French* manner. Thus there seems as much emphasis on the

wrong turns of technology, on various baroque solutions to eigh-
teenth- and nineteenth-century agricultural and industrial problems,
as there is on their more efficient and recognizable brethren. This
museum could not exist in Germany.

On the main floor one is invited to weigh oneself on a scale that is
connected to a laughably out-of-date computer/printer. One may
then discover, by pressing the requisite buttons, how much he would
have weighed in various European cities four hundred years ago, when
each had a very different notion of what a "pound" was. Thus you may
have weighed 150 in Bologna, but 175 in Berlin. The point is to show
how much clearer things have become by virtue of standardization, of
the metric system. But one gets the impression, holding the faint dot-
matrix printout, that the Musée des Techniques is more than a little
wistful about progress.

So I had for the fifth time in twelve years completed my chronological tour of mechanical history, and I was beginning to dread the conclusion of my visit, wondering where I was bound next, and how I
would see myself through a second post-Marie-Laure night. But I
knew I had the basement still to go. The basement, in the best depart-
ment-store tradition, is where the Musée des Techniques keeps all the
bargain stuff, everything it doesn't know what to do with. There are all
sorts of ancient bicycles and motorcycles and a few automobiles, a racing car, and other means of propulsion gone by the wayside.

Near closing time, I wandered toward the end of my final aisle,
coming across a final assortment of undocumented pieces, evidently
new arrivals. A tall, gaunt man who appeared to be in his late sixties or
early seventies was raptly examining one of these objects. His appearance was striking: he was perhaps six feet six, his ivory hair arranged in
a ponytail. He wore a brown leather jacket that looked as if it had survived the Battle of Britain, black jeans, and green cowboy boots. He
caught my eye. "Ce truc là," he said with a distinctly American accent,
"à votre avis, c'est quoi?"

He had asked me what I thought the unlabeled object was. His
French, but for the accent, was colloquial and right on the money. I
was much more intrigued by him than by the curious machine in
question. I said, "I'd taken you for a local."

"As opposed to what? An express?" He guffawed, and the sound
echoed through the enormous room. He took a step toward me then,

and I took a reflexive step backward, wondering if I'd encountered a madman. "I'm sorry," he said. "What made you think I was French?"

"The look," I said. "Especially the boots."

He grinned at me. "What could be more American than cowboy boots?"

"Yes, exactly," I said.

"Ah, I see." He nodded. "We're talking paradoxes here, aren't we? You took me for a Frenchman because I'm wearing American shoes. I took you for a Frenchman because you're wearing French shoes." Indeed I was: French loafers, in a gray suede, chosen by Marie-Laure. "It just shows you how deceiving the simplest things can be, doesn't it? Which brings me back to this machine. What do you suppose it is?"

I took my first good look at the thing on the floor. What sprang to my mind was that it was a device for gliding across water. It was about three feet long, two feet wide at its broadest, with what was definitely a seat, a padded leather (or synthetic) seat projected up from its center. It was rather generally wing shaped, broad at the front, tapering off at the back. There was what appeared to be a set of controls at the front, just below an area roughly analogous to the dashboard of an automobile, and on the dashboard itself were several little protrusions that might have been gauges of some sort. It seemed, above all, neither new nor old. Other than the leather or vinyl seat cover and the glass or plastic gauges, it was difficult to discern what this thing was made of. It appeared to be metal, but it might well have been something else—fiberglass, or some higher-tech equivalent.

I said, "It looks like a miniature boat, a jet-ski with its skis removed."

"Not bad." He grinned again. "Quite ingenious. Yes, I could see that. But it's sort of top-heavy, isn't it? Don't you suppose it would tend to flop over on itself?"

"I have no idea," I said. "I know absolutely nothing about seaworthiness, or aerodynamics. Or physics, for that matter."

"You've been here quite a while, though," the old man said. "There must be something about science that interests you."

How did he know how long I'd been in the museum? If he'd been aware of me, how could I possibly have missed him? I said, "You've been watching me?"

He gave a short burst of laughter. "Hardly, my friend. I've been *aware* of you. I'm always impressed by someone who takes notes in a place like this. There's so much to learn, so much to know, but most people experience it as a freak show, an entertainment."

"It is, after all . . ."

"Of course it is. But it shouldn't be treated like a television show. What do you think most of them . . ." He made a sweeping gesture with his right hand, apparently referring to our fellow museumgoers, when in fact we were virtually alone here in the basement. "What do you think they'll recall from this visit—Foucault's Pendulum, or how much they would have weighed in Strasbourg in 1714?"

In my case, undoubtedly the latter. "I'm sure it depends entirely on the individual visitor."

The old man nodded. His nod, as everything else about him, was quite intense. "All right, then," he said, "what are you doing here? Why are you walking around with that notebook?"

"Because it's my job. I'm doing a Paris guidebook update."

"Ah," he said, "a tastemaker. A trailblazer."

"To a degree." He must have been moving gradually closer to me, because I kept craning my neck until I must have resembled an open Pez dispenser.

"And I would venture to say, a despondent trailblazer. Am I right?"

It struck me as unnecessarily cruel that having lost Marie-Laure to the ungainly Mouchard, I should immediately afterward be waylaid by a preposterously tall psychic madman. But I had no power to resist. "You could say that."

He said, "Let's get out of here. Let a concerned countryman buy you a drink. What do you say?"

Indeed, what could I say?

— ◦ —

At the corner of Rue de Réaumur and Avénue de Sébastopol was a café called Le Capitole. I remember thinking at the time how strange it seemed to sit down in a place that wasn't on my list, that hadn't been recommended by a friend, an acquaintance, or a reader. I made a note to myself that I must still maintain a fraction of my critical eye, just in case there was something remarkable about the Le Capitole. There was not, save that it was the location to the most important conversation of my life.

His name was Hudnut. Jasper Hudnut, formerly of Oregon State

University, formerly of the Max Planck Institute, formerly of the California Polytechnic Institute at San Luis Obispo, among other places. He was, nominally, a quantum physicist. He was seventy-two years old, and a single man. He had no children and virtually no possessions. Once he'd gotten this far in his biography, he inquired as to my politics.

The rain had stopped, and most of the café's patrons occupied several sidewalk tables under the blue-gray late afternoon sky. Hudnut and I had the inside all to ourselves. "My politics?" I responded.

"It's not a difficult question, is it?"

"Rather general, though. I mean, what do you want to know?"

"Do you vote?"

"Yes. Always."

"Good. Tell me, if you would, how you voted in the presidential elections of 1980 through '88."

I had to calculate for a moment. "Carter," I said. "Then Mondale, then Dukakis."

Hudnut took a small drink from his enormous mug of beer. "If you had to sum up the presidency of Ronald Reagan in a few words," he said, "how would you do it?"

"How few?"

"Twenty seconds' worth."

"Well, I suppose I'd quote François Mitterrand. He and Pierre Trudeau were meeting with Reagan, God knows what year, God knows what occasion, and Reagan told Mitterrand some daffy anecdote, some fantasy from his past. And afterward Mitterrand, who was of course nearly as old as Reagan but quite a bit more together, came up to Trudeau and said, 'What *planet* is that man from?' "

Hudnut burst into laughter—great spasms of laughter, until tears poured down his cheeks. Eventually he got control of himself and he said, "Oh, that's wonderful. I'd never heard that one before."

"What's this about?" I said.

"I think my favorite moment," Hudnut said, as if he hadn't heard my question, "was the business with the president of Liberia. His name was Samuel Doe, and Reagan's introducing him at a dinner or some such, and he refers to him as 'Chairman Moe.' It's such an extraordinary, profound moment, because it brings so many things into play. I mean, here's Reagan with *his* kind of African leader—a dictator who's killing people left and right, the only reason we love him is he's not a Communist—and not only can't he get Doe's name right, but he confuses him with a Chinese guy who happens to be *synonymous* with Communism. So what can you make of that? We know that all black people looked alike to Reagan, but apparently black people and Chinese people were completely interchangeable."

"Mr. Hudnut . . ." I began.

"Call me Jasper," he said.

"Why are we sitting here in Paris, trading Ronald Reagan stories? What's the point? What do you care about my politics?"

"Gabriel," he said, "could I suggest that you lighten up? Maybe I'm just making conversation, and not doing such a bad job of it. We've discovered a fertile common ground, I'd say. Or maybe if you weren't so damned depressed you wouldn't even be asking a question like that. Why shouldn't I be interested in your politics? You're a well-educated, talented man who's been all over the world. People depend on your wisdom for the two most important weeks of their year."

"Not on my politics."

"It's all of a piece, though, isn't it?"

Was it? Hudnut's flattery was sinking in, abetted by my second Pernod. I said, "I have no idea what you mean by that."

"Gabriel, please. I have to admit I'm not familiar with your books, but I do firmly believe that a certain mentality speaks to a certain mentality. I'm not saying there are absolutely *no* dull-witted right-wing Americans carrying your book around Paris, but I'd bet they're in a distinct minority."

"Of course. But that's a cultural phenomenon that has nothing to do with me. I was hired to write a book for a specific audience . . ."

"And what kind of audience is that?"

"Well-educated, sophisticated. People interested in broadening their horizons a bit, people who might not be attracted to the usual touristic crap."

"There you go," said Hudnut. "I rest my case."

I was not altogether sure what he was talking about. There didn't seem to be a great deal of logic involved, but for the moment it didn't matter. The old man's rather odd charm was doing its job: I was aware that he was working on me, trying to elevate me from my funk, and I didn't care.

"I think it's truly propitious that we met today," he said. "It's the sort of thing that almost makes one believe in a Higher Force."

"You're getting a little carried away, aren't you?"

"Not at all. I'm thinking how marvelous it is that I've found myself a travel expert who seems to be footloose and fancy-free."

"Footloose, perhaps," I replied, "but I'm not so sure about fancy-free. And why is it so marvelous that you've found a travel expert in the first place?"

"Now that you mention it, I've always wondered about that. Wouldn't 'fancy-free' mean lacking fancy, devoid of fancy? That's to say, wouldn't 'fancy-free' tend to be the exact opposite of 'footloose?' "

"Yes, except I don't believe it means one is free of fancies. It's the other way around, isn't it? 'Fancy' modifies 'free,' so it's a way of saying one is particularly free."

"But that would hardly be you," Hudnut said. "At this very moment you are undoubtedly footloose, but you're utterly without fancy, am I correct?"

"Yes, I suppose. Or close to it. But please tell me why it's so important that you've found me."

Hudnut raised both his hands, urging patience on my part. "Let me provide you with a fancy. Does the name Arturo Toscanini mean anything to you?"

"Of course. One of the great virtuoso conductors. Led every famous orchestra at one point or another."

"Excellent," Hudnut said. "Now, did you know that when he was quite young, Toscanini killed a man in Italy?"

"I didn't know that," I said, "and I don't believe it's true. I know a fair amount about Toscanini, and I'd suspect that you've been misinformed."

"It was a crime of passion," Hudnut said. "There was a scandal. Toscanini was put on trial for murder—"

I interrupted. "Where was this?"

"Parma, of course."

I knew that Parma was Toscanini's birthplace. Hudnut resumed: "He was put on trial, and he was found guilty. He was sentenced to death—"

"This is nonsense," I said.

"It happened that the means of execution in Italy was a very primitive form of electrocution—"

"*Please,*" I said, "this would have been sometime in the eighteen eighties."

Hudnut brushed aside my objection without losing his rhythm. "A very *primitive* form of electrocution. They would lay you down in a shallow bed of water, with electrodes attached to you, and pull the lever. When it worked, when it went smoothly, it was very humane, very efficient, you got sizzled right up. But this was Italy, of course, so the technology was a lot more ambitious than it was competent. They put Toscanini in this contraption, pulled the switch, and nothing happened. They tried it again, and they singed his eyebrows a little. They sent him back to his cell, gave him a meal, zapped him again a few hours later, no luck. Finally they just let him go. Word had got around, of course, so Toscanini was besieged by the press when he got out, and everyone was asking him what happened, how had he survived several thousand volts surging through his body. And Toscanini said, 'Well, I must not be a very good conductor.' "

"That's awful," I said. "That's terrible."

Hudnut grinned at me. "But a fancy nevertheless."

— —

I had always had mixed feelings about the hotel named L'Hôtel. It was in my favorite section of Paris, in the sixth arrondissement, where I always stayed unless testing a hotel elsewhere. It was five minutes from the Seine on a swank little street called Rue des Beaux Arts, a brisk walk from my lodging of the moment. I had never actually stayed there because, at somewhere between a hundred fifty and two hundred fifty dollars per night, its rooms were well beyond my readers' budgets, and had I had the audacity to put such an extravagance on my expense account, Harvey Wells Greenglass would certainly have underlined it in blue pencil and written WHY? in the margin. Over the years I had spent five or six evenings in L'Hôtel's bar, however, and invariably espied at least one, often several young show business types, American or British, male or female, sometimes with entourage, sometimes without. It was an excellent place to be seen.

It was also, to my bemusement, Hudnut's hotel. When he'd invited me for lunch after our third drink the evening before, I'd said, "You feel the need to mingle with the jet set?" And Hudnut had replied, "I've been staying there for thirty years, before any of the goddamn Rolling Stones ever heard of the place."

His room was on the fifth floor, triple the size of my ninety-dollar-a-

night postage stamp. He was as hearty and effusive as earlier, and I must say I was feeling quite a bit more chipper, in part because I'd just had a stimulating twenty-minute walk along Parisian streets on a bright spring day, but mainly and undeniably because Hudnut had cheered me up.

We sat across from each other at a small table made of some lustrous hardwood. L'Hôtel did not to my knowledge have room service, but Hudnut had somehow managed to provide us with an elaborate salad of crisp greens, bits of marinated chicken, and tomatoes as fresh and luscious as if we were in the height of summer. He said, "Of course you know Oscar Wilde died here."

"Of course I do. Manet was born across the street, and if you were to draw a three-hundred-meter radius from this spot, you'd create an area lived in or visited by about every great artist, writer, or composer since the middle of the seventeenth century."

"You don't miss a trick."

"I don't. It's my job."

"You absolutely love all this stuff, don't you?"

"Which stuff? Paris? History?"

"Both of those. But I guess I'm mainly thinking about travel. What is there about travel that fascinates you so much?"

"I don't think I'm that different from everyone else. Why are there hotels all over the world? Why do the airlines and the cruise ships stay in business?"

"But not everyone's a fanatic," Hudnut said. "Not everyone devotes his life to wandering around the world."

To be sure, this was something to which I'd given a fair amount of thought over the years. I said, "I suppose I'm the sort of person who's never done terribly well staying at home. I suppose I'm happiest when I'm on the move, when I'm taking in new sights, when I'm learning."

"Always moving forward?"

"Not always. I think I'm happiest when I come back here. The combination of the familiar and the exotic. I probably know more about Paris than a lot of natives, but I'll always be an outsider here, a visitor, as often as I come. In a sort of perverse way, that appeals to me."

Hudnut impaled a final wedge of tomato on his fork, waved it briefly as if it were a tiny flag, and devoured it. "Gabriel," he said, "there's something we need to discuss."

2

We were in the bowels of L'Hôtel, in a storage room in the basement, to which Hudnut had a key. "You're obviously an important man around here," I said.

"Just an old and valued customer," he replied, and he switched on the overhead light, a fluorescent bulb that flickered slowly to life. He pointed to a large object against the dusty brick wall. "You recognize it?"

It was the top-heavy jet-ski Hudnut had been admiring at the Musée des Techniques. "What's it doing here?" I asked.

"I acquired it," Hudnut smiled.

"How did you acquire it?"

"What difference does it make?"

"Look," I said. "I really don't care how you got the thing. It just seems odd to me that one day something's in a museum and the next day it's sitting in the basement of a ritzy little hotel."

"They had no use for it," Hudnut said. "They didn't know what to do with it. They didn't know what it is."

"Neither do I," I reminded him.

During an extended moment of silence Hudnut stared at me so intensely that I felt as if I were going through some kind of last-minute test, as if he were looking into my soul, searching for impediments. Finally, he said, "It's a time machine."

I laughed. I assumed he was putting me on, as he had quite successfully with the Toscanini business. After a good while (let us say ten seconds), during which his expression remained fixed, I changed my mind, and came to the alternative conclusion that "time machine" was a metaphor. I said, "And in what sense is it a time machine?"

"In the sense," Hudnut said, "that you will sit in it, you will activate it, and it will transport you back in time."

— —

Was I skeptical? Of course I was, much as I'm sure you would have been. The next thing Hudnut did was ask me the time. By my watch it was 2:47. "Take good note of that," Hudnut said. "Remember it."

He proceeded to tell me a story. He had, as a younger man, as a thirty-year-old assistant professor of physics, come across a machine quite a lot like this one. Wasn't it a bit much—I interrupted—that he, a physicist, should be the one to stumble across the time machine? In point of fact someone else, a scruffy pre-hippie (this was 1952), had found the thing in the vast wilderness of central Oregon, had been directed to Hudnut at Oregon State, and had brought him to it. Hudnut's benefactor had been bewildered that this object, which he first assumed to be a boat, should be sitting at the very top of a hill, ensconced in scrub fir, in the middle of nowhere, and had sought a scientist's confirmation that he'd come across a spaceship. Hudnut had quickly disabused the man of that notion, then spent many hours experimenting privately with the machine before he discovered a combination of commands that made it work.

And that had not been in the manner of a great, rational, scientific deduction—which is to say he did not at first realize anything had happened. He was aware only that he was overcome by a profound feeling of well-being. After a time it struck him that something quite strange had occurred: although his watch told him it was noon, that some twelve minutes had elapsed since he'd checked the time before his sudden change of mood, the sun seemed actually to have receded to the point in the sky it would occupy at eleven o'clock.

In a state of considerable elation Hudnut had descended the hill, found his car, switched on the radio all atremble, just in time for the 11:30 time check, at which point his watch told him it was 12:25. He knew then that he had traveled back in time about fifty-five minutes.

He had reclimbed the hill, duplicated his previous routine, save for a slight increase in what he assumed to be the time setting. Again he had sat himself down and set himself off, and indeed this time he had completed his moment's journey at about 10:30 in the morning, or slightly less than three hours from his departure. His watch still read 1:26.

He had then immediately set the controls to reverse his second journey—to go back to 1:26. The routine had been the same: elation, visual confirmation that his mission was successful; and soon afterward the onset of a headache, which grew to such epic proportions that he wondered if his brief excursions through time had caused the accelerated development of a brain tumor. He had spent the rest of the day immobile in the back seat of his car, had eventually driven back to Corvallis late that night, had returned to the hill two mornings later—and to his horror discovered the machine missing. He had located its finder, the pre-hippie, at his shack, and questioned him subtly but extensively, until Hudnut was convinced that the man's professed ignorance was credible. He had returned to the site and searched for clues, found none. He had concluded eventually that the machine's owner, perhaps a tourist from the future, had reclaimed it and moved on, perhaps back whence he came.

I had plenty of questions. Which should come first? "You said this was a machine that would transport me back in time. But evidently the first one could go forward as well."

"Not exactly," Hudnut said. "From what I understood of the controls, from my interpretation of the machine's disappearance, I assumed that it could go forward only to the point of its departure. So if you'd left at noon, you could return to noon. If you'd left in 1980, you could return to 1980. It seemed rather silly to invent a machine that could take you somewhere far away but couldn't bring you back."

"Why do you say 'far away,' " I asked, "if you never went back more than three hours?"

"Another assumption. My interpretation of the dials. My next experiment would have been to go back a day, then see if I could use the machine to come back."

"What about the headache? What caused it?"

"I don't know," Hudnut said. "Maybe it's something that inevitably follows use of the machine by a couple of hours. Maybe it only happens when you use the machine twice in short order. Maybe it's a price you pay for returning to your departure point by machine instead of in real time. I can't say. All I know is that I've never had a headache like that since, and I hope I never have one again."

Well then, I thought, what am I to make of all this? There was always the possibility that Hudnut was a complete fraud, that he was setting me up for some sort of scam. He certainly didn't act or look like a bunco artist, but then, I supposed, a good one wouldn't. I said, "How many people have you told about this?"

"Not a soul."

"Why me?"

Hudnut did not reply immediately, but his eyes remained fixed upon mine. After several seconds he said, "Do you believe me?"

"I don't *dis*believe you," I said. "But I think I find the whole thing preposterous. It doesn't make any sense to me—that there would exist such a thing as a time machine, or that you'd be showing it to someone you just ran into, or that I'd be standing next to it in the basement of a hotel on the Rue des Beaux Arts."

Hudnut grinned. "Do you want to try it out?"

"Take it for a spin, you mean? A test drive?"

"If you like."

"Not if I'm going to get one of those headaches."

"I doubt very much that you will."

"But you're not a hundred percent sure?"

"Not a hundred percent, no."

"No other ill effects?"

"In all probability, no."

I said, "What if you were to try it out, while I observed?"

"It wouldn't be the same."

There was Hudnut, there was the machine, sitting there looking sleek and futuristic in the dim fluorescent light, and here was I. Hudnut said, "Live a little, Gabriel."

I sat down. The seat was firm but well cushioned, with excellent lumbar support. Hudnut said, "What time have you got?" I looked at my watch. "Three eleven."

"Me too," Hudnut said. "Hold on a minute." There was a small canister by the brick wall; he picked it up and began spray-painting on the wall. He wrote: VOUS NE VERREZ PAS.

"What won't I see?" I asked him.

"Don't worry about it," he said. "On the control panel in front of you, on the bottom left, there's a button. It's not easy to see, but you can feel it. I want you to press that."

I felt for the button, found a small ovoid section that was smoother than the rest of the black plastic panel. Assuming this was to be the first stage in a series of actions, I pressed it. Immediately I felt as if someone had injected an ounce or two of strong vodka directly into my veins. I was dizzy and euphoric. This lasted at most a second or two, during which I was conscious of no movement, of no change in light, of nothing olfactory or aural. I was aware of nothing at all until Hudnut said, "How are you?"

"I'm fine," I said.

"What time is it?"

I looked at my watch. "Three thirteen." He showed me his watch, which read 2:49. I was in that giddy, punchy state one occupies after getting off a roller coaster. "You set it back," I said.

Hudnut said, "Look at the wall."

My head still spinning a bit, I looked. "What about it?"

"Is anything written on it?"

The wall was bare of spray paint. Hudnut couldn't possibly have removed it during my very brief time of intoxication. "Where did it go?" I said.

"I haven't painted anything on the wall yet," Hudnut told me.

I could hear myself giggle. "Of course you have. I saw you do it, just before I pressed the damn button."

Hudnut approached the machine and put a hand on my right shoulder. "Try to concentrate, Gabriel. It was three thirteen when you pressed the button. Now it's two forty-nine. You've retrogressed twenty-four minutes."

"What about you?" I said. "You weren't on the machine, and you've gone back twenty-four minutes too."

"No, I haven't. I haven't written on the wall yet. I haven't done any of the things I did between the original two forty-nine and three thirteen."

"How do you know what you did, then? How do you know you wrote on the wall?"

"I had planned a certain succession of events, ending with spray-painting the wall, but they haven't occurred."

My euphoria wasn't fading. Far from it. But I felt as if I was starting to think extremely clearly. I wondered if this was an illusion, a product of the euphoria. I said, "All right, let's get back to this notion of the original two forty-nine. When two forty-nine first happened, I wasn't sitting in this machine, and we weren't having this conversation. Am I right?"

"Entirely."

"You and I were in this room together for twenty-four minutes. We had a discussion that I remember vividly, but as far as you're concerned, that never took place."

"Quite so."

"Very good. But what about *your* transition? Let's say at the original two forty-eight and fifty-nine seconds you were standing over there by the wall, talking to me. Now, boom!, all of a sudden I retrogress twenty-four minutes from three thirteen, we've got a *new* two forty-nine, and you're transported twelve feet across the room. How does that affect *you?*"

"It's seamless," Hudnut said. "I have no idea how it works, but there's an illusion of continuity. I believe the present's a lot roomier than the conscious scene we're always assembling from it. Do you understand what I'm saying?"

"I'm not sure."

He resumed: "Apart from the mental aspect of it—that I expected all this to happen, so it didn't surprise me—the physical aspect is seamless. I did not feel myself being moved across the room. My memory doesn't contain the jump cut."

The jump cut, indeed. I, in combination with the machine I was sitting upon, had served as Hudnut's film editor. I had deleted twenty-four minutes from his life and spliced in this new present without so much as a dissolve. And, to my growing delight, I seemed to understand what was happening. "I've actually changed history," I said.

"In a very small way."

"Nothing that occurred during the original twenty-four minutes will necessarily repeat itself." I spotted the spray-paint can sitting against the wall. "That's not going to get up on its own power and paint VOUS NE VERREZ PAS on the wall."

"That's right," Hudnut said. "But outside this room, everything is happening just as it did. We haven't affected things one bit."

I digested that. I said, "But we could."

"Yes, I think we could," Hudnut concurred.

"I didn't mean to suggest that we *should*," I said. "I wanted to make that clear."

"Why not?"

I took this to be a Socratic question. "Well, because then we'd run the risk of really screwing things up, turning things upside down, upsetting the order of things."

"Gabriel, my dear fellow," Hudnut said, "don't you *want* to?"

3

It would be very much an understatement if I said my state of mind that evening was oscillatory. The euphoria I'd felt after my little journey receded gradually into a mild giddiness in time for me to go about my rounds, to keep my dinner appointment at a bistro a few blocks from the Place de la Bastille. It had been recommended by an acquaintance, a peripheral member of the group that hung around Mouchard, my nemesis. The man himself had been a perfectly agreeable academic, who actually knew a couple of obscure favorite places of mine in San Francisco and spoke so enthusiastically of this favorite of his that I'd added it to my list.

It was worse than ordinary. The word *lentille* can mean either "lentil" or "contact lens," and I hardly exaggerate when I tell you that either might have been the principal ingredient of their featured soup. The service was friendly and efficient, the house red was passable, and I finished my half liter therapeutically as my thoughts fluctuated among the vagaries of taste, the misery of loss, the thrill of discovery.

I knew Marie-Laure was gone, but I would have welcomed her back in a second. Her absence was so new to me that it was still routine for me to think, after my third spoonful of the dreadful soup, "Wait till I tell Marie-Laure about this," and then to experience the attendant plunge, the roller-coaster dip, when I recalled that I wouldn't be telling Marie-Laure about the soup or anything else. My mind would thence set out on its quest for refuge, for comfort, for diversion, and have to search back only four hours or so to my adventure in the basement of L'Hôtel, the recollection of which would propel me just as hastily to a state of precarious exaltation.

In those moments I felt as one does after waking from a dream in which one has performed the physically impossible, while the dream still holds sway, before hard, practical wakefulness has resumed control, and the sensations of flight, or of superhuman speed or strength, are still vivid. I felt transcendent and privileged. *I had traveled in time.*

As evening progressed into night, I realized that my roller coaster was gradually losing its dips, that I was starting to dwell less and less on Marie-Laure, more and more on Hudnut and the machine. As I transcribed my notes and went over my itinerary for the next several days, I began asking myself questions: Was there any possibility that this afternoon's demonstration had been some kind of trick? If so, why on earth would Hudnut have chosen me as its object? On the other hand, if the machine were real, why had Hudnut chosen me to share his secret? Simply because I was a professional and inveterate traveler? What did he have in store for me? If he were indeed planning some ambitious trip to the past, would I have any say in its destination?

As I lay in bed, well past midnight, it did of course occur to me that I could use Hudnut's machine to regain Marie-Laure—that I could take myself back to a point just before our departure for Paris, that I could call Harvey Wells Greenglass and tell him to get himself another boy, so Marie-Laure would never even meet Mouchard. Then I could rejoin Hudnut at a date and place of his choosing and make myself gratefully available to his project, whatever it might be.

This excited me. I saw myself proposing it to Hudnut, saw myself insisting on it. Obviously you want me for whatever you've got planned, I would say, and I'll be happy to participate on the condition that I first go back to February 24, three days before we stepped onto the airplane, and I keep Marie-Laure from ever setting eyes on the man who stole her.

I fell asleep. I awoke just before dawn. I should tell you that I am not the sort of person who can thrive on just a few hours' sleep, that normally I am filled with anxiety and apprehension when unintentionally conscious during the hour of the wolf. But this morning, perhaps as the last hangover symptom of the previous afternoon's adventure, I was at once stuporous and gifted with clear thought, permitted to see my life as if with some supernally radiant light, and I suddenly perceived that Mouchard had been incidental, a bit player, a patsy, a device—that Marie-Laure would have run off. . . . No, that if I were to travel back to a happier time she *would* run off no matter what we did, where we went—with a scruffy Italian in Rome, a corrupt Togolese in Lome, an amoral Eskimo in Nome.

— —

I did not go back to sleep. I wrote down every question that occurred to me regarding Hudnut's machine and all its ramifications. I listed them in order of importance. I vowed to be direct and efficient with Hudnut, to confront him as to my role in his plans at the earliest occasion.

When I called him at nine o'clock—a decent hour, I thought—I was informed that M. Hudnut was not in. No further information was offered. I went about my morning rounds, which took me to a coffee bar (I've had better cappuccino in Southern California, but the pastries were delicious) and a sandwich shop (very tasty, but overpriced) on Rue St. Honoré. At noon I found myself only a few blocks from L'Hôtel, so I stopped by. The extremely polite functionary, a slim man with slicked-back hair, told me that M. Hudnut had checked out. My heart sank. Had M. Hudnut left a message for M. Prince? No, regrettably, he had not. Had he left a forwarding address? Indeed he had. The slim man handed me a slip of paper and I read:

Jasper Hudnut
Heartbreak Hotel
Lonely Street
Anytown, USA

"It's a strange address." The desk man spoke to me in French.

"Yes," I replied, wondering if Hudnut was playing some sort of game, or simply laughing in my face.

"It's like a song, isn't it? And there's a city, but no state." I handed him back the paper. He said, "There were two men here before you, perhaps twenty minutes ago, very rude, very angry." He glanced at the paper. "They didn't like this at all."

I rode the Métro back to my hotel in a state of shock, having made an instantaneous transition from exhilarated fatigue to bewildered exhaustion. I knew almost nothing about Hudnut. I wondered if I had misinterpreted everything he'd said and done, assuming quite brazenly and incorrectly that I was to play some sort of major part in his plans. I had no idea where to find him, either in France or the United States.

The cherubic woman at the front desk of my hotel handed me an envelope along with my key. When I asked from whom had it come, she gave me a cherubic French shrug and told me it had arrived during her husband's shift. I ripped open the envelope right there.

My Dear Gabriel:

I hope that my abrupt departure has not alarmed you. It has entered your mind, I am sure, that I am some sort of charlatan or madman who tempted you with superhuman powers and then fled like a thief in the night. This is of course not the case. Actually, I shall deny only the char-latan part. As to the rest, you are capable of making up your own mind.

As to mine, I felt it necessary to leave as quickly as possible. It is always possible that others might be aware of and interested in acquir-ing the object I showed you. Assuming you're reading this in the early afternoon, I can say with confidence that I and it are together (although in different compartments of the aircraft) about midway over the Atlantic.

Am I correct in recalling that you return to California in about ten days? I'll be in touch.

Jasper Hudnut

Was I relieved? I was just this side of ecstatic. Evidently my emotion showed. The cherubic woman, who had wondered on several occa-sions what had become of my beautiful friend who spoke French like a native, asked me, "*C'est de votre petite amie?*" No, I told her, the note was not from my girlfriend, but it contained good news nevertheless.

—▪—

I will not bore you, then, with details of my final week and a half in Paris. Let me simply say how strange it was to perform my daily sam-pling in this garden of earthly delights, for the first time, as if it were nothing more than a job. It was not that I had become jaded. No, far from it. It was as if I'd had a small sampling of an exotic drug that came to dominate my consciousness. While the notion of traveling in time beguiled me, while the idea of visiting places forbidden to the rest of my generation fascinated me, it was that tingling, giddy feeling that had stayed with me, that taste of euphoria I'd experienced after my tiny trip backward.

Back in Santa Monica, I virtually locked myself in my study, working at least fifteen hours a day on the text for the new Paris *Entrée*, suspecting that I might have to wrap it up at a moment's notice.

The days passed. I was a whirlwind of efficiency. Hudnut did not call. I was reluctant to leave the house, lest my answering machine fail. When I did go out, I called the machine myself, left messages to make sure it was working. A week went by. I was done with my jet lag, almost done with my work. I had seldom worked this quickly or this well, and yet I was beginning to despair. Perhaps Hudnut had found a better qualified pilot for his machine; perhaps he'd decided to take the job himself.

What did I know about him? He'd taught physics at Oregon State in 1952, forty-two years ago. Later, he'd worked at the Max Planck Institute, which I assumed to be somewhere in Germany. Still later, he'd taught physics at Cal Poly in San Luis Obispo.

On my eighth day back in the United States, at nine o'clock in the morning, I placed a call to Oregon State, maneuvered through voice mail, identified myself to the female human who eventually came on the line as a journalist seeking information about a long-ago professor at the university. She asked me if I could hold. Moments later, another female human. I repeated my request, gave her Hudnut's name and the date. She too asked me if I could hold. Moments later, she was back. "I found him," she said. "Jasper Hudnut, doctorate in physics from the University of Chicago, came here as an assistant professor in 1949, stayed until 1955."

"Do you know where he went after that?"

"Nope. Sorry. That's all we've got."

Now what? I could attempt to locate the Max Planck Institute, then try to converse with someone there, but jumping directly to San Luis Obispo seemed a more sensible course. Indeed, after three calls and a minimum of cautious explaining, I found myself on the telephone with a secretary at the Physics Department, a woman who had worked at the university since 1960 and remembered Jasper Hudnut quite well.

"Was there anything unusual about him?" She repeated my question. "Well, I should say. He was a very outspoken man, very vocal about his politics, which was unusual then, in the early sixties, at least here. I would say he was the first faculty member to speak out against the Vietnam War. That would have been in . . . sixty-four or sixty-five. It didn't make him very popular with his colleagues. Not that they were necessarily in favor of the war, just that they didn't think it was proper to go public with ideas the administration might consider controversial. There were some members of the department who resented Professor Hudnut because of his family money. He didn't have to live in faculty housing, and he always drove a very nice car. And I suppose they felt he could afford to jeopardize his job because he didn't really need it."

I asked if she recalled the circumstances of his leaving the university. "He resigned. That much I'm sure about. It was in the early seventies, maybe seventy-three. There was a woman in the mathematics department who was denied tenure. She was young and very political, and I think there may have been something between her and Professor Hudnut. I can't think of her name, but I wouldn't be surprised if there was a connection between her going and his going."

If Hudnut had left Cal Poly in 1973, how had he spent the ensuing twenty years? Was there any purpose in my trying to identify the mystery woman? And if Hudnut had lost interest in me, of course all this was academic.

4

The call came precisely ten days after my return. The connection was excellent; it sounded as if he were just down the street. "Where are you?" I asked, not at all sure that he'd tell me.

"Pacific Coast Highway," Hudnut said. "Do you know where the Malibu Colony is?"

He *was* just down the street.

In a manner of speaking. My house was about three minutes from the Pacific Coast Highway, whence a right turn took me quickly into Malibu. In moderate traffic I cruised along the six-lane highway, realized I hadn't been here since September's great fire. Between work and Marie-Laure, I'd hardly been home at all since September. The fire had evidently been both lethal and capricious, wiping out great clusters of homes on the hills to my right, north of the highway. Often within a complex of bare foundations, blackened trees, new construction barely under way, I would spot a house or two the flames had entirely ignored.

Hudnut's place was twenty-two minutes from mine. It was a beach house, not terribly imposing from the outside, but a beach house in the most exclusive corner of Malibu just the same, not the sort of place physics professors generally retire to. It seemed to me I'd recently read that one film star or another had recently bought one of these houses for three or four million.

"It's not mine," Hudnut said, standing next to me on the deck. It was a dazzlingly beautiful day, temperature in the high seventies, not a cloud in the sky, the bit of smog that had been evident in Santa Monica nonexistent here. The ocean was gentle, as if in deference to our conversation. "It's not *all* mine, to be precise. It belongs to my family."

"It never occurred to me that you'd have a family."

"Of course I do," Hudnut said. He wore overalls, a Hawaiian shirt, and Topsiders, no socks. "We've all got families, don't we? Why should it surprise you that I've got a family?"

I laughed. "There's just a certain incongruity between you and this house."

"What sort of house should I be in?"

"Something out in the woods. Something very rustic, with solar heat and unfinished wood."

"Outdoor plumbing?"

"I wouldn't go that far."

"I spent five years in Oregon in a house with outdoor plumbing," Hudnut said. "You've got to have the courage of your convictions, Gabriel. Go all the way."

I said, "Why did you leave San Luis Obispo?"

He grinned at me, either not taken aback or not showing it. "Been doing some research, have we?"

"It's my job."

"All right, then. I left because of love and principle."

"The person I spoke to said you'd been involved with a woman in the math department. She was denied tenure, and you quit."

"Annabel Kinnamon," Hudnut said. "She was fired. She'd been a teaching assistant, a graduate student, at Wisconsin when those idiots blew up the building in the middle of the night, and a janitor along with it. Annabel was very political. Everybody loved her at Cal Poly. But someone in Sacramento was doing background checks and found out she'd been the head of the Madison SDS chapter for about five minutes. This is when Reagan was governor, of course. And she was gone."

"You quit in sympathy?"

"Not exactly. She was an assistant professor, I was the head of the physics department. I figured they'd think twice if I threatened to quit. They didn't, and I couldn't really back down in good faith."

"A pretty impressive thing to do, just the same."

"Not really." Hudnut shrugged. "It didn't do either of us a lot of good. I was out of a job, and Annabel felt guilty and depressed. Generally miserable. We lasted about three months after all that. She married an engineer and they both got jobs at NASA. Life's funny, isn't it?"

"Is the machine here?" I asked.

"It is."

Waves lapped. In the southward distance, a volleyball game occurred among young men and women dressed in small bathing suits. In the foreground, the house's patch of private beach sat empty under the noontime sun, save for a small group of sandpipers searching in formation for tidbits of seafood. I said, "What was all that about? Leaving, without saying a word. Waiting all this time to get in touch."

"All this time? How long have you been back? A week?"

"Ten days."

"Oh, sorry. That *is* a long time, isn't it?"

"It is when something's important to you. When you're anxious about something. And you haven't answered my question. What was the 'Heartbreak Hotel' business?"

"You'd know right off it was a joke. Somebody else might be thrown off for a little while."

"Someone French?"

He nodded. "Or someone from an altogether different culture."

"What are you talking about? Someone from the future?"

"Possibly. I had a call the night before I left that bothered me, from my friend at the museum. Someone else, evidently, had been interested in the machine."

"I looked for you at L'Hôtel the day you left. The desk man told me two men had been there just before I was."

"Looking for me?" Hudnut laughed. "Then about now, they're probably trying to find Anytown."

"They know your name," I said.

"Sure they do. But I haven't had a listed telephone number or address in twenty years, and there must be five thousand Hudnuts in the United States, give or take. Whoever they are, they won't find me for a while."

An immense gull flew in our direction and briefly coasted overhead, peering down at us as if doing reconnaissance for some higher power, then was swept away by an updraft and disappeared. Hudnut grinned. "What's important to you—the way you feel after you've used the machine, or the idea of what you could do with the machine?"

"Why should I have to differentiate?"

"Don't worry about it." Hudnut sat on the end of a chaise longue; I remained standing. "When I went back for that machine forty-two years ago and it was gone, God, what a sinking feeling that was. I'll never forget it."

"You must have had slightly mixed feelings, at least. After that headache."

"Of course. The headache scared the hell out of me. I was afraid I was going to die. But I didn't. I spent the next couple of days making plans, trying to figure out how to avoid the headache, how to remedy it if it occurred again. Imagining how far I could go, where I could go. And then the thing was gone." He looked up at me with his arms spread wide, palms upturned.

"To some small degree," I said, "I know the feeling."

"Tremendous sense of loss," Hudnut said.

"Yes."

"You were afraid I'd disappeared for good, maybe I'd found some-one else to take charge of the machine?"

"Exactly."

"Good. I don't want anything halfhearted on your part."

Now I sat on a deck chair facing him, so our eyes were on a level. "If it meant so much to you forty-two years ago, and now wonder of won-ders you've come across another machine, how can you not just use it yourself?"

He grinned again. "The past three weeks, let us say I've reac-quainted myself with the high."

"You've used it?"

"I've made some small experiments. Nothing very extensive because if the thing has a finite power supply I don't want it to run out. What I've got in mind for you is something I'm not cut out for."

"Tell me, please."

Hudnut took a deep breath, appearing as he did so infinitely wise and grandfatherly. "I want you to go well into the past."

"How far?"

"Fifty years, let's say. More or less."

This set me atingle. "Before we go any further, I have questions."

"By all means."

"Why are you involving me in this? Whatever you've got in mind, why aren't you cut out for it?"

"Too old," he said matter-of-factly. "Too old, and I think not as tal-ented in certain respects as you."

I could only hope that was a compliment. "If I did this, I take it I'd be a guinea pig of sorts."

"You would be."

"Can you regulate it? Can you fix it, set it, whatever, so you're sure how far back I'm going?"

"I think so. I'm not sure I can be absolutely precise."

I took a deep breath. "What about getting back?"

Hudnut gave me a broad smile. "If you live long enough, you should be back in about fifty years."

"You know what I mean."

"Yes, and I wish I could be more definitive. Theoretically, forward time travel should be easier than backward time travel. Do you want me to explain that?"

"Would I understand the explanation?"

"I doubt it."

"Then just answer my question."

"It's complicated, Gabriel. Have some patience, please. I assume that wherever this thing came from they have machines that are just as capable of traveling to the future. I assume that since I was able to make a short round trip with the first machine, you'll be able to make a long round trip with this machine."

"And what about the headache?"

Hudnut frowned. Moments passed. "The headache could be a problem," Hudnut said, "if it's caused by coming back."

"Let me sum this up as I understand it. I can probably use the machine to go forward, but just to my point of departure. If I do that, there's a good chance I'll have a terrible headache—"

"Worse than terrible."

"But transitory."

"Yes. Mine lasted five hours, I'd say. There's always the possibility that the duration of the pain could be linked to the length of the passage."

"So my headache could last . . ."

"Forever, more or less," Hudnut said.

"That's encouraging."

"But of course it's entirely possible the pain has nothing to do with returning. If it's the result of using the machine at overly short intervals, then you'd have nothing to worry about."

I stood for a moment staring vaguely in the direction of the volleyball game, picturing myself stranded somewhere in the past, eight years or so before my birth date, trying to deal with a terminal headache. I said, "This gets more appealing by the minute."

"I thought," Hudnut said, "that this would excite you—you in particular—because you obviously have a sense of adventure. Because you're someone who lives to travel, and there could be no more exotic form of travel than this. I would say, Gabriel—I would emphasize—that if you feel a strong attachment to the here and now, if it means terribly much to you to get back to 1994, then perhaps you're not right for the job."

I did a quick evaluation of my life. It was half done, more or less. I had no immediate family, no one who depended upon me, no ties to close friends, organizations, anything. Harvey Wells Greenglass would never find a writer-researcher half as good as I'd been, but I imagined it would make little difference. Was there something about the 1990s, other than a general sense of orientation, that was indispensable to me? There was not.

I did a quick evaluation of Jasper Hudnut. Did I know anything about him? Not much. Did I trust him? Yes, although that trust seemed utterly irrational. Did I have any idea what was transpiring? "Why do you want me involved in this?"

"Because you're perfect for it."

"Why are you too old? Does this involve athletics? I haven't exactly been working out."

"No athletics. Gabriel, if I were thirty years younger, if I had to choose between you and me, I'd probably choose you. In my own way I'm too cautious, and I tend to compensate by doing something really courageous that turns out just to be irrational."

This was ever so flattering, especially from a man so cautious that he'd just acquired a time machine and shipped it eight thousand miles. Myriad small concerns flitted about my head, as did one huge one. "Jasper"—I used his given name for the first time—"I have the feeling that you don't want to send me back just for the sake of it. I have the feeling there's some sort of mission involved here."

"Yes," Hudnut said, "an errand of sorts. But before we get to that, have you ever played the horses?"

5

The beach house had a garage big enough for two small cars or, in this case, one shiny Porsche 911 that didn't look its years and one machine hypothetically capable of transporting me to a time well before the Porsche existed.

One moment I was watching Hudnut set the series of dials on the control panel, the next I was alone in the garage. I imagined for an instant that Hudnut had somehow managed to move behind me; then I felt the first suggestion of that tingling I recalled so well, and I knew what was happening. I pressed a button on the wall and the door rolled open. My car was not in the driveway. I had just retrogressed slightly more than a day and my car was parked safely on the street outside my house a few miles away.

With each small movement I made, the warm blanket of well-being spread over me. I took a few steps onto the driveway and looked at the sky: the sun was almost directly overhead, so I had gone back to yesterday noon, as planned. I walked back into the garage and opened the Porsche's door; the keys, as Hudnut had said they would be, were in the ignition. Pulling onto the Pacific Coast Highway, it was almost as if I could isolate and caress each individual endorphin.

With a copy of tomorrow's sports section in my pocket and forty dollars in my wallet, I drove the Porsche to Santa Anita. I was there in time for the fourth race, which would be won by thirty-to-one Portsider. I bet four dollars on the favorite, Clem's Gal, to show. Clem's Gal finished third, as I knew she would, and paid $2.40. I picked up my $4.80 at the window, bet two dollars to win on Dangerous Ned in the fifth, and bought myself a Polish sausage and a cup of Budweiser. The sausage was grilled, quite decently cooked, and with a fair amount of spicy brown mustard it was not bad. The beer was thin and bitter, rich in carbon dioxide. Dangerous Ned paid $15.20. I felt terrific.

I checked the official results of each race against tomorrow's *Times*, and there was no deviation.

I bet on the winners of the sixth, seventh, and eighth races. In the eighth, I wondered briefly if I might have disarranged history, because the horse who according to the *Times* would win by a head and pay $6.80 was dead last going into the stretch. But Speedo Elsie made up ground on the outside and caught the leader at the wire.

I was a little over forty dollars ahead. I bet it all on Dest-A-Knee in the ninth, who went off at fifty-seven to one, just as the *Times* had said he would, and won by a length, just as the *Times* had said he would. My instinct was to head for the pari-mutuel window directly and beat the crowd, but I sat and watched the tote board until the numbers were posted. Dest-A-Knee paid $116.60 to win. I checked tomorrow's *Times* to confirm what I knew: when Dest-A-Knee originally won this race, before I was here to add forty dollars to the pool, he had paid $116.80.

Such giddiness. It was almost as if I could float above the freeway traffic and fly home. I parked the Porsche next to my car. I turned on my computer; the tremendous amount of work I'd done the first time I traversed this day was, of course, nowhere to be seen. I rewrote it in half the time it had taken me originally, partially because I was writing from memory, partially because I felt so absurdly sure of myself. It flowed. I cooked myself an improvement on my original dinner, adding some lemon and tarragon to the chicken sauce. I opened a much better bottle of wine. I worked again, until midnight, then slept as soundly as I had since childhood.

Waking, I took accounts. There was nearly twenty-four hundred dollars in my wallet; there was a Porsche parked outside, behind my car; the morning's sports section was identical to the creased and smeared one taken from my jacket pocket, save for one figure, one digit. This version of this morning, I had changed history to the tune of twenty cents.

— —

"When do you want me back here?" I'd asked Hudnut before departing on my joyride, and we'd proceeded to have a little semantic imbroglio trying to communicate a simple concept for which words didn't exist: Come back around this time on what will feel like tomorrow to you but will really be today again.

Had he meant the same time I'd arrived, or the same time I'd departed? To be on the safe side, and because I couldn't think of anything else to do and was still feeling the vestiges of my rapture, I got to the house in Malibu around eleven-thirty, a good hour earlier than my previous arrival. When there was no response to several repetitions of bell ringing and a couple of brisk raps, I tried the door. It opened.

Within, I called Hudnut's name. There was no response. Was he on the deck, its thick sliding glass doors shut? He was not. Was he on the beach below? Not a trace of him. Back in the house, I opened myself a bottle of imported fizzy water and decided to have a look around. Thus far I was acquainted only with the foyer, the kitchen, the living room, the deck.

Upstairs there were four good-sized bedrooms, each with its own bath. Two looked out on the ocean, two on the coastal hills to the east. The Colony, I knew, had been leased in the mid-1920s from the family that owned the twenty-six-mile narrow strip of beachfront called Malibu. At the time—other than the family's own holdings—its buildings were the only substantial evidence of civilization on this long sliver of coast. They were set back from what was then a two-lane road. Now there was a shopping center between the Colony and the six-lane Pacific Coast Highway.

No bedroom showed signs of occupancy except the northeastern one, whose bed was unmade, whose closet door was open. On the wall above a small bedside table was a black-and-white photograph of four people. Three of them were quite tall: one appeared to be a teenaged Hudnut, two others quite probably were his parents; all looked rather dour. The fourth was a considerably shorter young woman, perhaps in her early twenties, strikingly beautiful, smiling broadly.

The three other bathrooms contained fairly modern plumbing and what appeared to be recently installed, mass-produced ceramic tile. This one's fixtures seemed at least half a century old, and the tile—covering both the floor and the four walls—was wildly colorful, vertiginously Moorish.

Back downstairs, off the kitchen was a sizable room I had not seen before. It contained a long, dark hardwood table capable of seating ten or twelve. The table was old and elegant, inconsistent (as Hudnut's bathroom) with the house's predominantly contemporary decor. A closer inspection revealed that the entire dining room was a sort of family museum. The long east-west walls were covered with photographs, fifty or sixty of them, all black and white, all expensively framed.

I did my viewing in reverse chronological order. The photographer, or photographers, had evidently died off or lost interest in the late 1960s or early 1970s, judging by the appearance of my only frame of reference. Here was Hudnut probably in his mid-forties, with hair down to his shoulders. Here he was several years earlier, still definably bohemian but far less hirsute. His relatives were for the most part tall and hearty, good-looking and toothsome.

It was not difficult to spot him in pictures from the fifties, the forties. Here was Hudnut in uniform, an enlisted man from the looks of him, and very young, no more than twenty. Here he was as a teenager, already tall, towering over the beautiful young woman previously seen in the photograph upstairs. Who was *she*? They stood on the beach; Hudnut, in a droopy black bathing suit, scowling at the camera, his arm draped around his companion. She wore shorts and a modest short-sleeved shirt; her hair, short and upcurled in the back with bangs in the front, might have been light brown or dark blond; her cheekbones were intriguingly high, her lips full, smiling.

I reversed my direction, heading back into the war years and slightly beyond, wondering how I could have missed her the first time through. I had not: there were no later pictures of this nymph, unless she had abruptly lost her looks and grown six inches. There were in fact only two other photographs of her—slightly younger, looking smallish and a little shy surrounded by all the lofty Hudnuts.

I heard the front door shut, and Hudnut called my name. "In here," I called back.

He appeared in the doorway. "You've found the family tree?"

"Quite a vivid one, I'd say."

"How do you feel?" Hudnut asked.

"How do *you* feel?" I replied.

"Just fine, thank you," Hudnut said, "although I don't really think that's at issue."

"Isn't it, though? I've got a sense of continuity about all this, but it must be fairly weird for you. I mean, you spoke to me a few minutes ago on the telephone, am I right?"

Hudnut shook his head. "Actually, I haven't done that yet, won't be doing it this time around. I can only assume I did it originally because I know I didn't park the Porsche outside. So either someone stole it from the garage, thought better of it, and left it parked outside the house, or else I called you"—he looked at his watch.—"about twenty minutes from now and started the chain of events that led to your being here now."

"If I were in your position I'd be awfully confused."

"Gabriel, please, don't be concerned about me. I've told you, from my point of view it's all quite seamless, and as long as you do more or less what we agree upon, I have a sort of synthetic knowledge of what you've done. Do you understand?"

"Of course."

"Then how are you?"

"Wonderful. I feel great. But before we get started, could you identify some of these people for me?"

"I'm flattered that you're interested in my family, but couldn't we do that some other time?"

"Just one, then?"

Hudnut strode across the oak floor and joined me by the picture of his teenaged self and the mystery sylph. "My cousin Lorna," he said.

"She's only around for a couple of years, then she disappears."

"She was my father's older sister's daughter. They lived in Massachusetts, we were in Connecticut. The rest of the family all lived out here. My uncle Charles bought the place from some actor in 1929, after a fire jumped the highway—it was only two lanes then—and burned the whole Colony down. Bought it for a song, and then all the siblings chipped in and became equal partners, built this house. Here's Charles." Hudnut pointed to a tall man (who bore a considerable resemblance to him) in a photograph that featured what I presumed to be the rest of Charles's family. "That's Sally, who was a six-footer, and their kids, the two girls. . . . This must be 1938, I'd guess, so the girls are nine and ten, and there's Charlie, who's twelve here. He was closest to me in age among the male cousins. Very bright, but kind of a nasty kid."

"What about Lorna?"

"I met her when I was . . . ten, I imagine. That would have made her seventeen. The first erotic thoughts I ever had were about Lorna. In this picture I was fourteen. She was in college then, at Smith. She lived here full-time for a while after she graduated. She was in a few movies—nothing you've ever come across, I'm sure."

"Under what name?"

"Her own. Lorna Fairchild."

"And what became of her? Why does she disappear?"

"She died."

"How?"

"An accident." Hudnut's tone had been quite neutral, informational, but now I began to detect a hint of emotion. "It was a little eerie. There was a huge storm in the winter of '38, and I remember everyone was concerned about Lorna. Hundreds of people were killed, bridges washed out, houses destroyed. The phones were out all over Southern California. The eastern Hudnuts couldn't communicate with the western Hudnuts for a few days, and then we could, but Malibu was still cut off. Lorna was out here alone and for all we knew the whole Colony could have been washed into the sea."

"So she drowned?"

"No, not at all. It turned out this house survived the storm just fine. Charles managed to get out here and found everything in good shape; he called us and gave us the news. But then another couple of days went by and we still didn't hear from Lorna. Charles called the studio she worked for—I can't remember which one, offhand—they hadn't heard from her. For about a week she was considered missing. And then finally they found her body. She'd been driving to work in her little sports car, and she'd been buried in a slide, an avalanche, just up the highway."

— —

We walked to the deck, where I recognized with a certain queasiness that the volleyball game down the beach was exactly the same as the volleyball game I'd watched twenty-four hours earlier. Hudnut said, "So you feel wonderful?"

"Omnipotent. Completely on top of things."

"Have you felt this way before?"

"I have. Not often."

Hudnut stared out at the sea; it was at least a minute before he spoke. "Do you think it's . . . legitimate to feel so good now?"

"Legitimate? How do you mean?"

He paused again. "Do you think the time travel has served as a drug?"

"I'm sure it has—but as the kind of drug that enhances emotions, not one that brings them on."

"Good," Hudnut said. "Now then, I gave you a sports section, I believe."

I handed it to him. He turned and laid the wrinkled swatch of newspaper next to its near-twin on a glass-topped table, and let out a discreet chuckle when his eyes found the figures I knew so well. He clapped me on the back. "This is fantastic, Gabriel!"

"You don't have to tell me that."

"But the *significance* of it . . . I mean, that you've achieved a sort of temporal autonomy. On two counts. One, you've gone back and done something of which we have evidence. Two, if you've got the money you won . . ."

"I've got it."

". . . you've brought something *back* from the past."

"You didn't expect everything would happen this way?"

"I can't exactly say I expected it. I hoped everything would happen this way."

I gazed off at the volleyball game. "I think it's right here that the guy in the blue shirt makes a great spike." Two seconds later the guy in the blue shirt made a great spike. Hudnut was oblivious. He said, "Gabriel, I don't want to jump to any conclusions, and I certainly don't want to start confusing myself with the Supreme Being, but I think this means we've pretty much got carte blanche."

I said, "I've got more questions."

"By all means."

"Is this machine identical to the one you found in Oregon?"

"It would appear to be."

"And you assume that both of them were left by people who traveled back here from the future?"

"Yes. There could be hundreds of these machines scattered around the world at any given moment. Or these could be the only two. That doesn't make much sense, in terms of probability, but I've got some thoughts about it."

"But the first one you found—you assume that its rightful owner came back and reclaimed it, right?"

"That's one explanation for its disappearance, yes."

"What if that happens again? What if that happens with this one?"

Hudnut nodded, and took a deep breath. "Then we'd be without a time machine. That's all the more reason to act quickly."

"To go back fifty years?"

"Give or take."

"And why couldn't the owner find his machine there?"

"Why couldn't he find his machine fifty years from where he left it? Because he wouldn't have the machine. He'd be stuck here."

"What if he's got a friend in Burbank, or Kansas City, or Ulan Bator, with a time machine? What if his society has some sort of temporal tracking system? What am I going to do if I find myself in the year three thousand looking at a five-year stretch for grand theft time machine?"

"Good questions," Hudnut said. "I'm afraid I don't know the answers. Does that concern you?"

"Of course it concerns me."

"Does it give you second thoughts?"

"Obviously it gives me second thoughts."

"Does it make you want to forget about the whole thing?"

"No," I said. "At least not until I find out what you've got in mind."

Several seconds passed in silence. "Do you want to talk about that now?"

"Yes, of course," I said. "The sooner the better."

"Let's go inside," Hudnut said. "Out of the sun."

—◦—

"We have a fabulous instrument at our disposal," Hudnut said. "I'm of the opinion that when someone hands me a tool like this, I should use it."

We sat across from each other in the spacious living room of this rather grand house. It was tastefully done, with bleached hardwood floors and unpretentious but probably very expensive modernistic Italian furniture. "What do you mean, 'hands you a machine'?"

Hudnut's facial expression, usually suggestive of irony, was changing, taking on a beatific cast. "I don't think things like this happen by accident. Whether it's fate, whether it's synchronicity, whether it's intentional on the part of someone or some group from the future . . . I mean, Gabriel, the fact that in my lifetime I should stumble across *two* of these machines . . ."

My chair was covered in a supple gray suede. The lumbar support was impressive. "Are you suggesting that someone from the future wants you to take care of something?"

"I think it's altogether possible." Hudnut was beaming.

"Wouldn't it be a lot simpler if he or they just took care of it on their own, instead of leaving time machines around for you to find?"

"Perhaps there's some sort of constraint involved, or some fear of being detected."

"I don't think I know what you're talking about."

"Just look at the information you have in front of you. If you win the grand prize in the California lottery, it's a freak occurrence, a twenty-million-to-one shot, something like that. Winning it twice just doesn't happen, unless someone's fixed the game . . ."

"I know. I understand that part. You're saying that in terms of pure probability, it's pretty much impossible for you to have found two time machines. I think there's a big flaw in your reasoning, in that once you found the first you knew what to look for, and then you started searching for a second."

Hudnut had begun frantically shaking his head. "No, please, Gabriel, let's not play intellectual games. Just tell me whether or not it's extraordinary that I've come across two of these things."

"Yes, it is. It's super-extraordinary. Mega-extraordinary. What I don't get is the part about constraints and fear of being detected."

"Just a theory. I'm just trying to find a fairly logical explanation for something extremely improbable. And the conclusion I keep reaching is that someone, some group, some organization, God knows how many years in the future, is for some reason prevented from coming back here and taking care of something terribly important."

"Like what, Jasper?"

Hudnut got to his feet and began pacing. "Here's one thought I had. Let's imagine these machines come from—pick a number—three hundred years in the future. Let's say the operator can only go back a certain number of years. . . . Maybe it's analogous to deep-sea diving. Maybe if you go back more than—pick a number—seventy years, it's like diving too deep and risking the bends. Maybe you have to go back in stages: fifty years, and then you wait five months, or five years, and recharge your physical batteries, and then fifty years more . . ."

I interrupted. "So in that scenario, you happened on the machine in Oregon just before the operator was ready to embark on the next stage, and he happened to come back a few days later . . ."

"Yes!" Hudnut nodded enthusiastically. "Or, quite possibly, there was some sort of alarm attached to that machine, and whoever left *that* one there didn't want me to take it. *Or*—and this is the thought that really makes sense to me—that one *was* left for me, but they determined that I wasn't ready for it yet, that I couldn't yet have enough information to understand what my mission would be."

I leaned back in my sleek suede chair, trying to decide whether this very tall old man gangling above me, who had been a paragon of reason until now, until the second coming of a beautiful May afternoon in Malibu, had gone nuts. I said, "What do you suppose that mission is, Jasper?"

Hudnut stopped pacing abruptly; he loomed over me. "I'll put it to you. If you could use the machine to go back—say to the beginning of this century—and make any reasonable change, anything that would alter the course of the century, what would you do?"

Without much hesitation I said, "I think I'd eliminate Adolf Hitler before he had the opportunity to do much damage."

"Yes! That was precisely the thought I had when I found the first machine. But I didn't particularly like the logistics. I didn't speak German. I'd be very much a stranger in a strange land, no matter what period of the man's life I chose, not even taking into account whether I could set the machine accurately. The easiest thing would be to locate Hitler when he was a child. But could I murder a child, even when I knew he was going to develop into the greatest monster in history? Then of course it occurred to me that I could achieve my effect just by handicapping him—cutting out his tongue, for instance. But I couldn't imagine myself doing that, either. I thought of going after him in Munich in the twenties, when I'd be able to find him easily, but when he'd already be surrounded by plenty of thugs, much more difficult to get to."

I had experienced a little chill imagining myself cutting out young Hitler's tongue. I said, "I suppose I should be clear about something. Are we talking about hypothetical situations, or are we talking about something you expect me to *do?*"

"The latter," Hudnut replied.

"Because I'm not going to kill anybody," I said. "I think it might in fact be an excellent idea for someone to go back in time and eliminate Hitler, or Stalin, or any number of other people, but I'm not the guy."

"You're way off base, Gabriel."

I created a quick list of other possibilities: Joseph McCarthy, J. Edgar Hoover, Richard Nixon, Charles Manson, Lawrence Welk, Oliver Stone. *Anything that would alter the course of the century.* I said, "We're obviously not thinking along the same lines."

"But we *do*. Don't you remember our conversation in Paris, at the Capitole?"

I pictured us sitting at the café, ran through the dialogue. After a minute I said, "Are you talking about Ronald Reagan?"

"Precisely." His grin bordered on the maniacal.

"Jasper . . . I'd have to say, if you asked me to put ten, even *twenty* people on my list of evil twentieth-century personages, I don't think Reagan would make it."

"Recall the situation," he said. "Somebody, some people, some organization, has placed two time machines in my path. They want me to take care of something. I ask myself: if they've gone to such great lengths to choose *me*, what is it that they want me to do, and the answer I come up with again and again is: Reagan."

Eventually I spoke. "So you want me to knock off Ronald Reagan?"

"I wouldn't put it so harshly," Hudnut replied. "I want you to go back and take care of things so he doesn't become president. The method's up to you."

My brain was so awash with objections that it was terribly difficult to find the most apposite, so I plucked one at random. "Look, if ever there was a world leader who wasn't self-generated it was Reagan. The man was a shell, a charming automaton with lots of rich, nasty people standing over him, pulling the strings."

Hudnut's grin disappeared. "Then who did generate all that vulgarity, all that hypocrisy, all that banality, that occurred between 1980 and 1988?"

"All of Reagan's friends," I said, surprised at the rancor in my own voice. "All the greedy, plutocratic sociopaths who were really running the country when Reagan was president."

The grin flickered back. "Do you suppose, Gabriel, that if Reagan never existed, or if his existence were interrupted well before he got involved in the politics of wealth, all those plutocratic sociopaths could ever find a replacement?"

It was an intriguing question, but one I didn't much want to consider, so I shook my head and said nothing, and Hudnut resumed. "Look, I've scoured the sources. I've watched the old movies, read the old magazines, the rosters of the Screen Actors Guild. God knows there were plenty of conservative actors, plenty of George Murphys. But Ronald Reagan was unique. No one else possessed that terrible combination of attributes. He was smart enough, quick enough, to give the impression of substance, when of course there was no substance. He was good-looking and likable. He reacted so well. He ad-libbed like a performer. He could do thoroughly profane, illegal things and no one cared. No one *noticed*. The crucial element was that he didn't *know* he was doing evil things. He didn't conceive them, nor did he think them through. He did, essentially, just what he was told."

"Look," I said, "I have no argument with any of that. You already know I don't have a very high regard for Reagan as president. But I don't think you've really answered your own question, Jasper."

"Which question was that?"

"The one about the plutocratic sociopaths. Aren't you narrowing your field a bit too much? I mean, maybe Reagan *was* the only movie actor of his era who could have grown into a political monster, but how significant is that? Think back to the 1980 election, for God's sake. Nobody had any respect for Carter. The Iranians were holding the entire U.S. embassy hostage in Tehran, and Carter couldn't do a thing about it. Any strong Republican would have beaten Carter easily. And after Nixon and Ford, the right wing had taken over the Republican Party, so even if Reagan didn't exist the nominee would have been someone from the right, with the same agenda Reagan had."

Hudnut's smile returned, full force. "Yes, Gabriel, the same agenda, but not the same personality. Not the same *presence*."

I got to my feet. The sudden rise left me slightly dizzy. I was no longer in the state of good feeling that had enveloped me when I entered this house perhaps forty minutes earlier. Far from it. I was consumed by the sort of agitation one feels in a miserable traffic jam when one needs desperately to reach a destination. I wondered briefly if this were a delayed reaction to my twenty-four-hour retrogression, or if it were simply attributable to Hudnut and the "errand" he evidently had in mind for me. The latter, all things considered, seemed sufficient cause for my condition, if indeed I would soon have to choose between an act I could not possibly commit and an activity I could not imaginably abandon. I said, "This doesn't have anything to do with what happened in San Luis Obispo?"

"With Annabel? Of course it does, in the sense that she was Reagan's victim, indirectly, like millions of other people."

"But that personal element doesn't bother you? It's not as if I'm your avenging angel?"

"Please, Gabriel. Don't I deserve more credit than that?"

"Yes. Probably you do, but it's all too much for me. It doesn't add up, and I don't think I'm your man."

Hudnut towered over me. "Gabriel, please think about this. Fine, possibly some conservative Republican would have defeated Carter. Maybe a career politician. Maybe a game-show host. Maybe a baseball player. Who knows? But in the darkest Mephistophelian right-wing fantasy could you *imagine* what Reagan brought upon us? James Watt. Edwin Meese. Elliot Abrams. All those horrible, incompetent people he nominated to the Supreme Court. The Contras. Iran-Contra. Oliver North. The welfare Cadillac anecdote, over and over. Visiting the SS cemetery in Bitburg. Star Wars. Trickle-down economics. The national debt goes up by a gazillion percent, and the taxpayers have to come up with God knows how many billions because those crooks deregulated the savings and loans. Sending a goddamn army to invade a Caribbean island smaller than this room! And I'm just scratching the surface. I'm talking about someone who was the most powerful man in the world, and he didn't know the difference between Grover Cleveland and Grover Cleveland Alexander!"

Searching my pockets for keys, I remembered that my car was still parked against a curb in Santa Monica. I said, "Is it all right if I borrow that Porsche again?"

— ▬ ◂

I had never been good at lying, so it was something I almost never did. I am in no position to defend that statement, of course, or to prove it. You, I'm afraid, must accept it (like everything else you read here) at face value, or not. (Given that there is much in these pages that could be interpreted as fantasy, I suppose it is my obligation to make my presentation as believable as possible.)

It has quite probably occurred to you that I could simply have *pretended* that I found Hudnut's scheme agreeable. I could have said,

"Sure, I'll take care of Reagan for you," then zoomed back to 1940-something and gone about my merry way—thus not only seizing the machine for myself, but keeping Hudnut from finding someone else to do his job.

But I could not lie. There was something fundamentally satisfying, something enriching, about the truth. I believed that if I stuck to it I was invariably better off in the end.

So I tried to focus my attention on the Paris *Entrée* as I had in the days before Hudnut's call, but I'd lost the ability to concentrate for more than ten minutes at a time. As I paced around my little house, picturing myself on the machine, I tried to re-create just a shade of the giddiness I'd felt after traveling, but it proved a pointless exercise. What was worse, before a day had gone by, Hudnut started sending me faxes.

I didn't know how he got my fax number. I didn't believe I'd even told him I had a machine. Later, when I asked him, he told me he'd simply assumed I had a fax machine, had looked up my name in the telephone book, found a second number listed there, and begun faxing away. In retrospect, I felt stupid. I had attributed to Hudnut some kind of clairvoyance.

Anyway, the faxes. Evidently Hudnut had kept a scrapbook, and that scrapbook covered every minute and every detail of the Reagan years and their tawdry sequel, the Bush administration. At first I supposed they were random: an Iran-Contra highlight here, a gruesome presidential faux pas there, a fatuous remark by some cabinet member here, an outright lie by a State Department toadie there. After a succession of short pieces that painted Reagan as a clown or an oaf, the gruesomely fascinating, book-length magazine story about an entire Salvadoran village massacred by U.S.–trained troops. After several days I began to realize this had all been organized with real genius, that Hudnut was creating for me a vast and comprehensive electronic diorama of decadence and extraordinary corruption.

At this juncture I think I must put things in the clearest possible perspective—lest you have any misapprehensions at all about your correspondent. I have made every effort to be evenhanded in my recollections of conversations with Jasper Hudnut. Of course not every exchange between us has been reported verbatim, merely because that would have resulted in a tedious volume as thick as the Manhattan white pages. But

I believe that in recording the *gist* of our conversations I have been absolutely fair and accurate. In going over what I've written, I discover a portrait of Hudnut as a man of intelligence, whimsy, irony, purpose, obsession. And perhaps the slightest implication of madness.

As to my self-portrait, it has been thus far comparatively lacking in detail and, perhaps by reason of the same understatement, potentially misleading. If I had the time to reconstruct this I would, for instance, expunge or at least abridge my little canoe memoir because its purpose could easily be misinterpreted. And I would beseech you not to make the assumptions Hudnut evidently did that first afternoon in Paris. Yes, I had voted Democratic in every presidential election for which I was eligible, and yes, I thought Ronald Reagan was way beyond his depth as president, but at the same time I never *disliked* the man. I never felt a personal enmity toward him, as I had toward Nixon, who seemed evil incarnate. I considered Reagan a figurehead of sorts, as if he were the daffy old king of America.

I was no more distressed when Reagan won his second term than when he'd won his first, in part because neither time did I care much for his opponent. While many of my more leftist friends saw the very fabric of the nation rapidly unraveling, I suppose that from the beginning I saw Reagan's presidency as an exercise in surrealism, ultimately a fantastically bad piece of art.

I knew no air traffic controllers, no Central American peasants, no inner-city black youths—no one who belonged, in the words of one of my more politically involved friends, "to any of the myriad, disparate, and huge collections of people devastated by the absurd and inexplicable acts of an administration that appears to consist almost entirely of arch-pragmatists and sociopaths." While I would never have considered my friend's description inaccurate, my own attitude was decidedly more dispassionate.

After five days of Hudnut's barrage—during which he never once otherwise made contact with me, nor I with him, although *twice* I enabled him to continue by putting a new roll of paper in the machine—I had been stripped of much of my veneer. Was it because of the brilliance of Hudnut's collage, or because all the banality originally spread out over twelve years had now been compressed into a little less than a week? Or was it because I'd spent five nights having vivid, ardent dreams about the time machine?

Just before 1 A.M. on the fifth night, as I sat in my study wondering whether I could sleep, wondering whether I should shut off the fax machine, I took a look at its latest issue, in progress. It was a profile of Margaret Tutwiler, clipped from a magazine I'd never heard of. This glowing little piece about the woman whose monotone had caused me to change channels a thousand times did not break the camel's back. Rather, it was the scrawled addendum at the bottom that did: YOU WOULDN'T HAVE TO <u>KILL</u> HIM, FOR GOD'S SAKE.

6

I finished the *Entrée* copy and composed the usual cordial little note to my editor, a woman in Seattle whom I'd never seen and knew almost nothing about. Unless she were to take violent exception to something I'd written, I wouldn't be corresponding with her again until the arrival of galley proofs a couple of months hence. I had to resist adding a postscript about the galleys. I wanted to write something like, "I may be incommunicado for a while, but don't be alarmed . . ."

This was the sort of concept that started my head spinning. If I disappeared, or *when* I disappeared from the present, would the world—as far as I was concerned—simply stop and wait for me to return, or would it go on without me? Was there perhaps a seamlessness in this sense too? Inasmuch as I was a small but integral part of a certain continuity, what would that continuity make of my sudden absence?

"I'm not sure," Hudnut offered. "Not at all sure."

"Well, I can't imagine that everything would come to a dead halt just because I'm gone."

"No. Well, it wouldn't really be that way, in any case. I mean, time's going to proceed. It's just a question of how it's going to close up the little hole you cause when you go."

"All right," I said. "Here's a very practical example. I send off my manuscript. Then I go. Two weeks later my editor finds some big problem in the copy. Not that that's ever actually happened, but just hypothetically. She picks up the phone to call me. What happens? Does she get my machine, because I'm visiting 1942? Or is she somehow prevented from making that call until I'm back in 1994?"

"You don't even want to think about it," Hudnut said.

"You're the physicist, for God's sake. Don't you have any theories?"

"Plenty."

"But I wouldn't understand?"

"Fine. Let's leave it at that."

We were sitting by the beach several miles up the Pacific Coast Highway from the Colony. It was another beautiful day in Southern California. I said, "My God, Jasper, you're not exactly filling me with confidence."

"Look, ninety-seven percent of physicists believe time travel is impossible. This is all theoretical. It's all guesswork. I'd love to tell you exactly what's going to happen, but I can't." Hudnut was shirtless, shoeless. Over the past couple of weeks he'd developed an excellent tan. I regretted not having worn a long-sleeved shirt. What if I found myself stranded in 1944 with skin cancer, fifty years removed from my health plan? I said, "I've been assuming from the start that you had a pretty good idea how all this works."

"Keep in mind, please, that we're dealing with technology miles beyond anything that exists today. Imagine how astonishing something like a computer, even a pocket calculator, say, would be if it popped into the hands of some extremely learned person in the year 1890."

My forearms were already turning pink. "I'm sure he wouldn't have the slightest idea what it was. That doesn't make me feel any better."

"He'd experiment with the keys. Figure out the power comes from that little round battery. Figure out those tiny chips permit the thing to do what it does. He'd *use* the damned thing and figure out how it works."

I imagined retrieving my jacket from the car, a hundred yards or so away. I imagined that if I'd come across a pocket calculator in 1890 I'd have set it aside after a few minutes' fruitless analysis. "What about this machine, then? You know what it does, or some of what it does. Do you know how it works?"

Hudnut chuckled, dug his feet into the sand. "If I had two of them at once, I'd take one apart. I don't have two, so all I can do is guess. Do you understand circuit boards?"

"No. And please don't try to make me understand."

"All you need to know is that circuit boards are vital to the operation of computers, and at the same time they're what limits the potentialities of today's computers. Because circuit boards have to be laid out with parallel paths. Open up a transistor radio, a calculator, a computer, anything electronic, and you see the same circuit-board grid. The more sophisticated the machine, the more extensive the grid. Mainframe computers have gigantic circuit boards."

Hudnut turned and gave me that intense, impassioned look. "Someone in the future, Gabriel, someone forty or eighty or a hundred years from now, has figured out how to make those paths run *over* each other. Someone's figured out how to make three-dimensional circuit boards—which means you could take the most gargantuan supercomputer today and put it in a box nine inches square. Do you get the concept?"

"I do."

"Good. Now, our machine may be the product of still another century's worth of sophistication, may represent leaps in technology we can't even imagine. The brain, the engine, the heart—whatever you want to call it—of that machine is to our most powerful computer today as that computer is to an abacus."

This much was not terribly difficult to understand. The time machine was a really smart computer. But how did it *work*? What sort of computing did it do in order to transport its jockey back in time? Here I must confess that I fail you—or rather that I fear you would have found Hudnut's explanation, his "guesswork," frustrating even had you been better disposed than I to understand it, so the failure is not entirely mine. Hudnut spent the next thirty or forty minutes methodically explaining various concepts to me—trying, for instance, to communicate the essence of quantum physics, as well as notions like the Copenhagen School and Minkowski Geometry, not to mention the interesting tale of Schroedinger's Cat. It was rather like watching a movie whose dialogue was in a language tantalizingly close to one I knew—Portuguese, for instance. There was the occasional word that made sense, sometimes even a sentence, but by and large even a vague gist was more than I could expect.

I suggested an image to Hudnut. I said, "Let's say that I'm sitting at the peak of a hill. In front of me is some very powerful vehicle. Normally this vehicle and I sit there, juxtaposed, and nothing happens. Then you show up and hand me the time machine. I get on it and activate it. For some reason, this causes the very powerful vehicle to start moving forward. As it moves forward, it creates exhaust. So not only does the vehicle begin moving away from me, ultimately its exhaust causes me to slide backwards down the hill."

I recall Hudnut's response precisely. "That's not a bad analogy, Gabriel. Not bad at all." Should I have interpreted his tone of voice as mildly patronizing or ironically complimentary? Perhaps both.

— —

What an odd shopping expedition. I wouldn't be bringing any luggage, of course, so all I'd need would be on my back or in my pockets. I suggested that I could balance a small overnight bag on my knees, but Hudnut shook his head and grimaced. We went first to a shop off Sunset in Hollywood that specialized in period clothing. (I could give you the addresses of three such stores in Paris.) Hudnut picked several suits— all in remarkably good condition—off various racks and handed them to me. I would pop out of the dressing room—increasingly self-conscious with each new change, wondering what management and other customers must make of this odd couple—get a thorough examination from my haberdasher, and head back to the dressing room. A double-breasted blue serge was "too thick—you look like something out of Eric Ambler." A dusky flannel was "Madison Avenue—you'd never wear something like that in Southern California," although evidently someone had. My sixth attempt was a white linen suit, again double-breasted. It fit as if it had been made for me. To my surprise, Hudnut made a little nod as he caught sight of me. He said, "What do you think?"

"I like it."

"Is it comfortable? You may have to wear it for a while before you can pick up more clothing."

"It's fine."

Hudnut fingered the material, looked me up and down again. "Might be a bit heavy on a very hot day, but you wouldn't want to be in cotton if you set down on a cold night in January."

That made sense to me. We chose a white Oxford shirt and found blue boxer shorts with a button fly, a pair of thick gray woolen socks, and black wing tips that would have seemed as appropriate for a contemporary Century City lawyer as to a 1940s visitor without portfolio. My wardrobe cost me $425—a fraction of the cash earlier provided by Dest-A-Knee.

Well off the beaten track in West Hollywood was a coin shop where for slightly more than face value I bought two hundred dollars' worth of bills printed between 1936 and 1940, and for considerably more than face value a pocketful of buffalo nickels, liberty dimes, Standing Liberty and early Washington quarters.

"That's enough money?" I asked my counselor.

"More than enough. With two hundred dollars you can live like a king for a week. You'll need more to set yourself up, but that's not going to be any problem." Hudnut then conferred briefly with the proprietor, a chubby and sallow fellow who, in baggy pleated trousers supported by gray suspenders, seemed prepared to join me in the past.

Hudnut returned to where I stood, at the end of the counter. "Give the man another two hundred, Gabriel."

"For what?"

"Your document."

"What document?"

"Just give him the money."

My additional two hundred dollars had paid for a blank, authentic, vintage-1900 California birth certificate. "It's not legal to sell those, you know," Hudnut had told me en route back to Malibu, explaining the outrageous price. "Besides, what difference does it make how much money you spend? You can't take it with you."

"It's the principle of the thing," I said. "I don't imagine ninety-year-old birth certificates are exactly a hot item."

"Don't begrudge the man his profit, Gabriel. It's a valuable document to have, and it wasn't an easy one to find."

— • —

"I assume you'll want to keep your name?"

"Any reason I shouldn't?"

Hudnut had inserted the birth certificate in a Royal upright anachronistic by a good forty years, but who was counting? "You have a middle name?"

"No."

He typed. "Born where?"

"Old Saybrook, Connecticut."

"Perfect. Far away, obscure. We'll use it. Born when? Let's see . . . say you set down in 1941. How old are you?"

"Now, you mean?"

"I mean your actual age."

"I'm forty-two."

He looked askance. "That'll never do. You look much younger. Let's make you thirty-six, born in 1905. Birthday?"

"January ten."

He typed. "Excellent," he said. "See, this has already taken years off you." He got to his feet. He said, "Now, Gabriel, for a little leap in technology."

I had no idea what he was talking about. He'd been sitting at a small desk in the master bedroom, I at the foot of the bed. Hudnut slid open the closet door and reached in. He turned and showed me a stack of three-and-a-half-inch computer disks. "These," he said, "are your ace in the hole."

I counted them. "What am I going to do with eight floppy disks in 1941?"

"You've got a little laptop, right?"

"Of course I do. But I don't understand what's happening here. We've just made a substantial effort to make me look like a legitimate citizen of 1941, and now it seems I'm going to be arriving there with something that won't exist until fifty years later."

"Just keep it to yourself."

"It's kind of a big risk, isn't it?"

"The advantages vastly outweigh the dangers."

"Tell me about the advantages."

"You're going to need a means of making money. I don't want you wasting your time wandering around unfamiliar territory looking for a job. If one comes your way, fine. But if not, I've taken the sports section trick a step further. Those disks contain the results of every race at every track in Southern California between nineteen thirty-eight and forty-five, plus weekly New York Stock Exchange quotations for the same period. You'll have easy access to the future."

"My God, Jasper, that must have taken you months."

He shook his head. "Didn't take long at all. I paid some kid a few bucks to transfer most of it from microfilm."

"What about power? How long can the battery last?"

"You've got an AC adapter, right? We had electricity back then, too. Just plug it into the wall."

"How do I transport it? You snorted when I suggested putting the overnight bag on my knees."

"Inside your shirt."

It made sense, at least in that my computer was small and light enough to fit. "What about my camera?" I said.

"What about it?"

"I could wear it around my neck."

He issued a sigh of impatience. "Look, you're going to be using the computer in private. Unless your camera's an antique, it's probably not the sort of thing you want to be seen with. If you need a camera, you can buy one when you get there."

Two days after our shopping trip, just past midnight, Hudnut and I sat in the living room of the beach house, sharing a bowl of popcorn and watching a videotape of *Kings Row*. Previously we'd sat through *Knute Rockne, All American*; *Brother Rat*; and *Dark Victory*. (The tapes hadn't been at all easy to find. We'd ransacked the specialty video stores, ended up borrowing *Brother Rat* from a collector friend of Hudnut's.) I was trying to absorb as much period Ronald Reagan as possible; it was difficult because Hudnut kept hooting at the television screen. Not, for the most part, that I could blame him.

As George Gipp, Reagan hadn't had much to do except give his bathetic and I'm sure completely apocryphal deathbed entreaty to his mates. In *Dark Victory*—not an entirely bad movie—he was really nothing more than a piece of scenery, the rest of which was devoured by Bette Davis. In *Brother Rat* he showed a borderline aptitude for comedy, a kind of genial presence that nearly compensated for an utter lack of timing. But *Kings Row* proved to be something else again. I knew that it was Reagan's favorite among his own films, knew that it was the first time he'd been treated as a serious actor by Warner Brothers and the critics, knew that a line from the movie (when his character awakens from anesthesia and discovers both his legs have been amputated he screams, "Where's the rest of me?") had become the title of Reagan's first autobiography.

I should tell you that between the ages of fifteen and twenty-five I'd probably watched a thousand black-and-white Hollywood movies on television. And in recent years, as specialization had brought the "oldies" concept to cable TV, I'd added a few hundred more. Indeed, I'd seen both *Dark Victory* and *Knute Rockne* before, the latter several times. But nothing had prepared me for the majestic (and virtually endless) mixed metaphor of *Kings Row*.

Bucolic small-town America, at the turn of the century, yet. The studious, dedicated boy grows up to be Robert Cummings, while his carefree, adventurous pal turns into Reagan. Intimations of cryptic evil are constantly played off against acts of good. Implications of incest develop into mere psychosis. While Cummings goes off to Vienna to become a psychiatrist (in 1904, more or less), Reagan stays home and is cheated of his inheritance by an amoral, unseen bank manager. Forced by circumstance to work on the railroad, Reagan has his legs chopped off by the town doctor (whose pronounced sadistic streak has somehow gone unnoticed all these years), and seems headed for terminal depression until Cummings forsakes a good job under the master (Freud himself?), returns to Kings Row, and cures his old pal by way of very basic reverse psychology.

Whereupon legless Reagan beams beatifically, turns to Ann Sheridan, and says, "For Pete's sake, let's give a party! I feel swell!" And there's the movie.

"Great God!" Hudnut shouted. "Don't you see it? That's Reagan's vision! All the little subcontexts in there, all that unsophisticated crap about the evil that lurks just below the surface, about hypocrisy and corruption—that was way over Ronald Reagan's head! What he *got* out of this movie was the goddamn small town, the big shingled houses. The redemption! Who cares if some malevolent bastard cut my legs off? I feel swell! Let's give a party!"

"He wasn't bad, I thought."

Hudnut chortled. "*Please*, Gabriel! Is that all you can say? After we've just witnessed two insipid hours of weird foreshadowing, you look at me with a straight face and you say *he wasn't bad?*"

"I found the movie quite entertaining."

"Good grief," Hudnut snarled. "Maybe we'd better just forget the whole thing."

"I don't disagree with a thing you've said, Jasper. I'm simply observing that Reagan probably felt at home in that role. He did it rather well."

"He's just playing himself, for God's sake."

"Is he, though? Don't you think it's possible he arrived in Hollywood as a kind of blank slate? That the movies formed a large part of his personality? How many instances were there during his presidency when he'd refer to something that happened onscreen as if it had been real life? We made fun of him for that."

"As well we should have."

"But we appreciate actors who become their roles—who gain fifty pounds or shave their heads, who stay in character the whole time a film's in production."

"You're talking about *actors*, Gabriel. Not hacks like Ronald Reagan. And what's more, if there's separation of church and state, there sure as hell should be separation of screen and state, don't you think?"

"But couldn't you say that Reagan actually did the consummate job of becoming his role? He got sucked into that black-and-white image of small-town America, with himself as the good Joe who works for a living and takes care of problems when he sees them, and ultimately he imposed that image on the country for eight years. And the really terrible thing is that the country, or enough important parts of the country, didn't mind it a bit."

Hudnut sat silent for a good minute. Then he looked at me with the slightest of smiles. "Yes, I suppose you could say that."

The television was off. I was ready to leave and there were things we still hadn't discussed. I said, "You're going to have to go over that control panel with me one more time." We adjourned to the garage.

"A child could master this," Hudnut said as we stood on either side of the machine. Perhaps Hudnut as a child could have mastered it; I as a child would doubtless have been just as intimidated by this abstruse row of gauges as I was now. "First," he said, "you set the dials." There were four circular protrusions, each about four inches in diameter, each containing a silvery needle visible through tinted glass, or glasslike plastic. The dials, like certain modish clocks and wristwatches, contained no numerals, but a succession of gradations. One turned the needle with a tiny, anomalously primitive plastic knob in the center of the dial. "Left to right," Hudnut continued, "minutes, then hours, then days, then years."

"How did you know that when you found the first machine? What if you'd pressed the wrong buttons and gone back fifty years?"

"I didn't know it. I didn't adjust the dials at all. I just pressed the "go" button. The machine had been set for me, I'm convinced."

"Tell me this, then. We know from experience that the first two dials are minutes and hours. How can we be sure the next two are days and years?"

"Logically, what else would they be?"

"How about weeks and months?"

"We know the third dial is days. I put it at its first setting when you went to Santa Anita."

"So I've already been a guinea pig. That's reassuring."

"And we'll find out in a few hours if the fourth dial is for years. If it isn't, all you've got to do is come back."

"Coming back, as I recall, is what almost killed you."

"Look, Gabriel, there's an element of risk in all of this. That's something we're taking as a given, right?"

"Of course," I said. "Tell me how I return."

"This switch." It was almost as unnoticeable as the "go" button: a tiny toggle on the far left of the panel. "Up takes you back in time, down brings you forward. That's it. That's all there is to know about the controls."

I felt informed, but hardly confident. I said, "What's my departure site? How do I know I'm not going to arrive in the middle of someone's garden party, or dental appointment?"

"This house," Hudnut said.

"Why?"

"Because it was empty virtually throughout the war years. Occupied maybe for a week, total, between forty-one and forty-five. People came to clean, things like that. But let's say the odds would be about a thousand to one against there being anyone here when you set down."

"What if I set down before the war? After the war?"

"Look," Hudnut said, "the alternative is to go way the hell out in the middle of the Mojave or way the hell up in the middle of the Tehachapis. You set down in the middle of nowhere, there's a good chance you'll burn up or freeze to death. And you've got to find your way back to the machine if you need to use it again. This way, you take off from the garage, you set down in the garage, you can always get back to the garage. Besides, if we're aiming for forty-one, we shouldn't be off by more than a year or two, and even if you come down in thirty-nine, say, this house would only be inhabited weekends, so the odds would still be five to two in your favor."

"All right. It makes sense."

▄ ▄

So it was that I stood on the threshold of the past. I was saturated with the emotions one feels before embarking on a trip to the unknown: excitement and apprehension, giddy anticipation invaded by the occasional wave of dread. I felt, ultimately, like one of Columbus's sailors: I had to depend entirely on my captain's interpretation of a voyage for which there were no maps, no guidebooks. Except, of course, that the captain wouldn't be coming along on this voyage.

Regarding my mission, the captain had said precious little since I caved in under his avalanche of faxes. That night, long after *Kings Row* had rolled to its inane denouement, Hudnut asked me, "You're not getting to like him, are you?"

"I'm not *getting* to anything. I don't feel any different from yesterday, or five years ago. This is a man who's responsible for a lot of really awful stuff, but it's still hard to associate him directly with everything that happened."

"But you know, Gabriel, that he hired all those people. All those Meeses and Abramses. Without him, they'd have been applying their nasty characters to something much less pertinent to the state of the world. They'd have been lobbyists for the tobacco industry, they'd have been point men for corporations looking for places to dump their toxic waste."

"I know."

He gave me a weary and earnest look. "Now I'm starting to think I was kidding myself before. Maybe if I were twenty years younger— hell, *ten* years younger—I'd do it myself. I don't know how, but God knows I'd figure out some way of getting the bastard off track."

"Yes. I'm sure."

"You'll take care of it, then? For all of us? For the world?"

"I'll do my best, Jasper." As I spoke the words I recognized that I was using the wrong tense. To be accurate, though, I would have needed some sort of subjunctive preterite, something we don't have. The future would have to suffice. "I'll do something," I said.

"Good." He got to his feet, a broad, exhausted smile on his face. He leaned over and massaged my shoulders. "I believe you will."

7

How would I know when I had arrived, or where I had arrived? There had been no discernible difference between my first voyage, in Paris, when I went back a few minutes, and my second, when I retrogressed a full day. Each had taken, to my perception, an instant. But I had assumed (and Hudnut had concurred) that since this trip would involve a destination some eighteen thousand times more distant than its predecessor, I might expect to find myself in some kind of suspension, some kind of limbo, for a while.

We had a final session with the control panel, and evidently I passed. I recall saying to Hudnut, "Well, here we go," touching the button, and before I could draw another breath, or at least seemingly before I could draw another breath, I had arrived.

I knew this because the Porsche that had been three feet away from me was no longer there, and because—thank God—that familiar glow of well-being, no more or less intense after this long voyage than it had been after the shorter ones, quickly and voluptuously embraced me.

I swung my feet out of the machine and stood up. Surely I had retrogressed, but for all I knew I had traveled to 1972, or to the previous Thursday. I took the little computer from my midsection, unzipped its sturdy canvas carrying case, and examined it. It appeared intact; I removed the floppy disks from my jacket and slipped them into the pocket of the carrying case. There was resistance. I set the floppies aside, dipped into the pocket, and found a packet of photographs from my final week in Paris. I'd neglected to send them off to Seattle, and now they'd joined me in the past. No matter.

The Porscheless garage was an elder cousin of the one I'd left behind. That one had been inhabited principally by cardboard storage boxes and a coiled garden hose. This one contained storage items

73

tending more to trunks and wooden boxes, a hose of approximately the same length as its descendant, and several bicycles. Adult bicycles—thick-tired and clumsy looking, a pair of them, and children's bikes, three of them, one perhaps having belonged to, or been ridden by, the young Jasper Hudnut. And there was the atmosphere. When I left, the most identifiable odor in the garage had been of sea air. Now it was as if I'd been transported into my own childhood garage—suffused with the smells of motor oil, gasoline, and fresh rubber mingling in an enclosed space.

There was no car but there were little oil spots on the concrete floor, indicating that something had been parked here recently. The caretaker's vehicle? Or perhaps I'd come down in 1939, in which case I'd better hope I hadn't landed on a weekend.

Feeling as I did, feeling high and confident and ready for anything, I had to force myself to stop and take stock. What did I know about where I was? Judging from my surroundings, I'd probably hit somewhere within Hudnut's target range. Judging from the temperature in the garage, it was probably spring or fall, or a cool summer day, or a warm winter day. In any case, it was daylight.

Just to be safe, I knocked on the door that connected the garage to the house, and waited a full minute before letting myself in.

I headed first for the kitchen, which provided a couple of surprises. It bore absolutely no resemblance to the kitchen I'd been in hours earlier. That was the first of many things I'd expected and yet been completely unprepared for. No microwave, no toaster oven, no dishwasher, no electric clock, no Formica-topped counters.

I'd been conscious of a dull electrical hum and I realized that it emanated from the pearl-white, ovoid-peaked refrigerator. I took a look inside: three eggs, a half-empty bottle of ketchup, some oranges (perhaps tangerines) that could well have dated from the Peloponnesian War. If anyone was staying here, he certainly wasn't a big eater.

Where I was accustomed to sliding glass doors and a panorama of beach and ocean there stood a wall with a modest window looking out on the beach, and a standard wooden door, which I opened. The deck had lost (had not yet gained) two thirds of its depth, so really it was more a back porch, with a couple of wicker chairs and a glider suspended from the overhang of the second story. The beach was unpopulated, the tide low, the sun high enough to suggest that it was either a summer midafternoon or a nonsummer early afternoon. A clear, sunny afternoon in any case, the temperature perhaps seventy, with a cool breeze off the Pacific. It felt like spring to me, like March or April. In my condition, of course, thirty-mile-an-hour winds and a downpour would have felt like spring.

I was full of energy, ready for challenges. I found a two-piece telephone in precisely the place its modern equivalent had been, in a nook off the living room. There was no accompanying phone book. I put the receiver to my ear and dialed 0.

"Operator." The voice enunciated each syllable clearly.

"Could you possibly tell me what time it is?"

"Certainly, sir. It's . . . twelve-sixteen P.M."

"And the date?"

"The date, sir?"

"Yes, if you would."

"It's Saturday the twenty-sixth, sir."

"The twenty-sixth of what?"

"Of *February*, sir."

I thanked her and hung up, truly hanging up for the first time in my life. If I remembered correctly, the winter meeting at Santa Anita ended in mid-March, so I'd arrived in plenty of time to establish my nest egg at the track. I returned to the garage, opened the little computer and switched it on, inserted the disk named SANTA ANITA into the floppy drive. Where to start? I'd neglected to push my luck and ask the operator what year it was, but that shouldn't be too hard to figure out.

I called up the directory marked 1941 and scrolled to February 26, which my race data told me had fallen on a Wednesday. Today, unless the operator had lied to me, was Saturday. So I'd missed my target, but by how much? I scrolled forward to 1942, in which February 26 was a Thursday. Of *course*—each 365-day year has fifty-two weeks and one extra day, so in 1943 February 26 would be a Friday, and in 1944 . . . a Saturday.

Nineteen forty-four. An inauspicious year to have arrived. Ronald Reagan would be in the army, not fighting in Europe but making military training films in California, married to Jane Wyman. Should I take it upon myself to reset the dials and try again for 1941? Hudnut had given himself the insufferable headache by using the machine twice in quick succession, so I'd be best to wait, to get the lay of the land, to go to Santa Anita.

I began scribbling race results in my notepad, writing win, place, and show horses identified by numbers, along with their payoffs. Halfway done, I was startled by the sound of an approaching car, then a slight squealing of brakes; was it directly outside the house? I held my breath. The rough-idling engine shut off, and three seconds later a door slammed. Now I heard footsteps, and a key in the front door.

I stuffed the computer into a box, crept to the garage door, turned the latch, and slid the door upward on its evidently well-oiled mechanism. It didn't make a sound. I closed it just as silently and now stood outside, in the driveway, my heart beating like a ferret's.

What to do now? I could begin wandering down Pacific Coast Highway toward Santa Monica; presumably I would come across a public phone eventually, call a taxi, and either head for Santa Anita or begin to get myself situated. But it hardly seemed sensible to leave the machine—and my computer—sitting in the garage. Fortunately I was rather well stocked in confidence.

The vehicle at the curb was a low-slung little roadster, its black hood as shiny as the chrome grid of its grille. Was it a Jaguar? An MG? I noticed the letters SS in the middle of the front bumper and realized this was a pre-Jaguar, a Stanley Swallow, due for a name change in the very near future when its initials would be co-opted by a more sinister organization.

I could assume, in any case, that this SS didn't belong to a maid or a workman, that its owner was someone who enjoyed driving around with the top down, someone without much in the way of family responsibilities, since the car was a two-seater. I stood at the front door for perhaps a minute, constructing a little scenario, and then I pressed the bell.

It was a young woman in white who opened the door. She was in her early twenties, she was strikingly beautiful, and I had the odd sense that I knew her. She looked me over, and in a not unpleasant voice she said, "Yes?"

I struggled to keep hold of my mise-en-scène as things began to clarify. If this was who I thought it was, the year wasn't 1944. I began calculating, counting backward, subtracting two days for leap year, concluding that the previous February 26 to fall on a Saturday was . . . 1938.

In color, in three dimensions, she was far lovelier than she'd been in the photographs on the dining room wall. She had died in the Great Storm of 1938, which clearly had not yet occurred. I said, "You must be Lorna."

She was about five and a half feet tall. Her hair, as I had guessed from the pictures, was dark blond. She wore a knee-length white skirt and a long-sleeved, translucent white blouse. Her feet were bare. "Must I, then? And what about you?"

I began wondering when that Great Storm was scheduled to arrive. Judging by this moment's weather, not anytime soon. I found my place in the script: "My name is Gabriel Prince, and I'm a friend of your cousins, the Hudnuts."

"Which Hudnuts?" Her eyes were more blue than green.

Which Hudnuts, indeed? If Jasper had ever told me his parents' names I certainly didn't remember them. "Actually I was Jasper's teacher," I said. In my state of invincibility it seemed the perfect solution. I was fascinated by her eyes.

"At Lawrenceville?"

Why not? "At Lawrenceville. I'm here because there's this sort of experimental boat they wanted brought out here . . ."

"They being?"

"The Hudnuts . . . well, specifically, Jasper's father . . ."

77

"Edgar wanted you to bring some sort of boat out here?"

"Yes. For Jasper."

Her lapis lazuli eyes darted left and right. "So you've brought a boat, but it's not here yet. I didn't think Edgar and Grace were even coming out this summer."

"Actually, it is here. I got here a while ago, and I dropped it off. Put it in the garage."

She looked at me with what I interpreted as benign suspicion. "How did you get in the garage?"

"It was open."

"I could have sworn I'd locked it." She gave another look around. "How did you get here? How did you get the boat here?"

"A truck," I said. "Friend with a truck, dropped me off, and here I am."

"So, you let yourself into the garage, dropped off your boat, and here you are. Listen, you're not some kind of criminal, are you? I understand criminals in snappy white suits are all the rage."

"I am the personification of innocence," I said.

She smiled, and so did I, exuding credibility. "Well, I guess I should ask you in, then. I have absolutely no reason to believe anything you've told me, so I suppose I should. If you'll show me the boat."

"My pleasure," I said, and I walked through the front door.

She led me to the garage and opened the door. She examined the instrument of my delivery. "Well," she said, "I'd never have guessed *that* was a boat. What's it made of?"

"A kind of plastic."

She stroked the machine's body. "How smooth it is. Why in God's name would anyone want to make a boat out of plastic?"

"It's light and it moves well through the water," I said. "Less drag." I imagined at this point that she could ask me anything and I could supply a plausible answer.

"Ah," she said. "Less drag. I see. It still doesn't look like any kind of boat to me. You're Jasper's physics teacher, then? What are you doing in California when you should be back in New Jersey teaching all those boys about drag?"

"English teacher, actually."

"And you quit to go into the boat business?"

"No, to concentrate on writing."

"Writing," she said, giving me a look that I interpreted as a bit sardonic. "And you've come out here to try your hand in the movies, I'll bet."

It seemed as reasonable an ulterior motive as any for my trip from New Jersey to California. "Thought I'd give it a try," I said.

"Well, you might just be in luck. A good friend of mine is a writer at Warners, and I could put in a word in for you. Have you published anything?"

"Quite a lot," I said. "Travel books, mostly."

"I'm afraid Warners might not be terribly impressed by travel books. Don't you have any scripts?"

How long could it take me to knock off a script or two? "I do, as a matter of fact. Do you work at Warners?"

"I do, as a matter of fact," she said. "Under contract. Did you happen to see *Love on a Shoestring*?"

"Don't think I did."

"Then I'm afraid you've missed my career so far, which isn't to say you've missed much."

"So you've just started?"

"Came out here a year ago. We've just wrapped one up that should be released in a couple of months, and I'm shooting another one now. Got to be on the lot at six every morning, which is no fun for someone who likes to stay up."

"But you get your weekends off?" She nodded. Things were proceeding awfully well. I said, "Perhaps you'd like to join me, if you don't have any plans for the rest of the day?"

"It depends on what you've got in mind."

"I thought Santa Anita."

She laughed. "Gabriel, you've just dropped off your boat, you've been in Los Angeles for about five minutes, and you're heading for the racetrack. Are you a hopeless gambler?"

"I'm quite good at it, actually. I was thinking that if we left right now we could catch the last four or five races."

"And how were you planning to get there?"

"I was thinking we'd take your car."

She laughed again. "Oh, this is terrific. Well, I certainly can't fault you for timidity."

When she went upstairs to change I retrieved the computer and got myself to 1938 in a hurry. Copying today's race results in my

notepad took a little longer than it might have because I was somewhat preoccupied. Lorna worked at Warner Brothers; Ronald Reagan
worked at Warner Brothers. Had Hudnut indeed sent me to 1938 by
accident, or did he have a motive other than the mere alteration of
history? Was I here to save Lorna's life as well? In which case, why
wouldn't he simply have told me, and wouldn't he have given me
more information than he did?

As it turned out, I had just enough time to get the results down before
Lorna descended. She wore shoes now; she was no less beautiful.

— —

I cannot begin to describe the exquisite torture of our passage from Malibu to Arcadia. I had made the same trip days earlier by taking the Pacific
Coast Highway to the Santa Monica Freeway, thence to the Pasadena
Freeway, ultimately to Colorado Boulevard for the last several miles. In
light traffic, I'd done it in about forty minutes, most of them spent driving seventy miles per hour. In my current version of greater Los Angeles, freeways did not exist. Here was something else I knew full well—yet
for which, in the circumstances, I was completely unprepared.

Imagine if you will first the exhilaration attendant to being in the
presence of someone you've just met and find immensely attractive.
Imagine next the fascination one might experience traveling through
a succession of streets and avenues and boulevards, covering a total of
perhaps forty miles, of territory quite familiar yet totally different:
from the relatively narrow Roosevelt Highway (which would evolve into
the six-lane PCH) running along Malibu beachfront—much of it simply vacant, not yet built upon—through the unfamiliar heart of my
most recent hometown, Santa Monica, along the edges of a scaled-
down Hollywood, glancing south toward a downtown devoid of high-
rises, it was as if I'd been deposited in a weird virtual reality hybrid, a
travelogue with a little colorized 1938 newsreel footage edited in.

One wishes to spend each second in appreciation of one's companion. One wishes almost equally to spend each second in appreciation
of a geography that existed only before one was born. And all the
while, in conversation, one must be assembling one's identity, manu-
facturing it from a mixture of backdated history, personal half-truths,
utter spur-of-the-moment fantasies, keeping in mind that one had
better be awfully careful to remember everything one spouts if one

wishes to maintain credibility with the extremely desirable woman driving the car.

Imagine, finally, that the woman drives her fast and tiny car like a maniac. Even in this state of euphoria one must struggle to put one's mind at ease: there is far less traffic than what I am accustomed to; this car is so maneuverable and her reflexes so fast that we probably won't hit anything very hard. One's instincts compel one, perhaps fifty times during the excursion, to reach for the seat belt, which—like the freeways—has not yet been created.

Lorna Fairchild turned to me when we were stopped at a red light, perhaps halfway to Santa Anita, and said, "I hope my driving doesn't upset you."

"Only slightly," I replied.

"I've never had an accident, if that's any comfort. I don't think I *intend* to drive aggressively, it just seems to me that if you're going someplace to enjoy yourself, or to get something done, well then, the point is to get there. Doesn't that make sense to you?"

"Perfect sense."

The light became green and we lurched forward, cut in between a huge Buick and a Chevrolet coupe in the left lane so we might overtake a slow-moving panel truck in the right lane, then veered right and sped into the open field. We had so far talked almost exclusively about me. I had fabricated a youth more or less parallel to my actual one, based on my having been born (by Hudnut's whim) in 1905, which made me thirty-three. It worried me that while I might have passed for thirty-six (my ostensible age in 1941), pretending to be *nine* years younger than I really was might be stretching things a bit. That would turn out to be the least of my troubles. For example, I would have graduated from college in 1927. . . .

"Where did you go?" she'd asked.

Was I to make something up, get caught in my lie in some unexpectable circumstance later on? "Princeton," I answered.

"What class?"

"Twenty-seven."

"Twenty-seven? Oh, then you would have been there the same time as my friend at Warners. You must have known him—Bill Wadsworth?"

"No. Afraid not. I kept to myself pretty much. Hardly knew anybody."

"Which club were you in?"

"No club, actually."

"I thought everybody at Princeton *had* to be in a club."

"Not so. There were a few of us who weren't."

"A matter of principle?" she'd asked, giving me an earnest look.

"Economics," I'd replied. "I just couldn't afford it."

After my imagined solitary existence at Princeton I'd gone searching for an editorial job in New York, hadn't found one to my liking, begun teaching English in the public school system, interviewed two years later for the job at Lawrenceville, got it. The wonderful thing about teaching for a living was that I could travel in the summer. Thus the sideline of travel books. Where had I been? All over the world, I began to tell Lorna, then recalled that my ten fictional postcollegiate summers had occurred in an era when steamships were the means of getting from one continent to another, and I wouldn't have had the time to go to all the places my real self had been. All over Europe, was my scaled-down revision.

"I would so *love* to go to Europe," she'd said, to my considerable relief. As she hadn't yet been, there would be no cautious comparing of notes, no danger of casual references to buildings not yet built, train stations not yet converted to museums.

Now, some twenty minutes (at Lorna's pace) from Santa Anita, I asked her how she'd found her way to Hollywood. She told me she'd found college (Smith) dreadfully boring except for the dramatic club. At her parents' insistence she'd hung on and graduated. She'd spent summers at the Provincetown Playhouse on Cape Cod, not terribly far from her house in Brookline, and become convinced the theater was to be her life. Everyone who'd directed her at Smith and Province-town had told her she had talent, so she'd gone down to New York immediately after graduation, not exactly with her parents' blessing, found an apartment with two Smithie friends (one a fellow actress, one a would-be editor), spent a promising summer (small parts in several radio plays, Cressida in an obscure company's production of *Troilus and Cressida*) followed by a tedious autumn and a depressing winter, in the midst of which her acting roommate was offered (through family connections) a bit part in DeMille's *The Plainsman*, and on a whim Lorna accompanied her west.

The roommate, whose career had begun and ended with *The Plainsman*, whose scenes had in fact not made the final cut, had since returned to the East Coast and married a lawyer. Lorna had visited her West Coast relatives, spent lots of time at the beach, done screen tests at Metro and Warners without any expectations. To her considerable surprise, Warners had offered her a contract. The money wasn't great, but it was more than a living wage, especially because she stayed rent free at the family beach house, and she figured that if Warners in particular or Hollywood in general ever became oppressive, she could simply get in her car (the first material dividend of her craft) and drive back to the East Coast.

It struck me that during the length of Lorna's monologue (four minutes? Five?), I hadn't taken my eyes off her. She had unquestionably taken precedence over the landscape.

— —

Santa Anita. How astonishing it was suddenly to be in the midst of thousands of people, thousands of extras from a 1938 movie, a racetrack movie. Whose protagonist was obviously the man in the white linen suit, the man without a hat. Neither Hudnut nor I, both of us keen observers of style and history (Hudnut as well someone who had been alive during all of 1938 and awake for perhaps two thirds of it), had thought to get me a hat.

Instead of general admission I'd bought us clubhouse tickets, for a dollar apiece. A pair of programs cost me another twenty cents. We'd arrived a few minutes before the third race, and I sat down and had a look at my program. It seemed, since I was about to have a very successful afternoon, that I should at least go through the motions of handicapping. "Look," Lorna said, pointing to her own program, "Seabiscuit's running in the sixth race."

Could it be? One of the great horses of history at Santa Anita on an ordinary Saturday afternoon in February? My computer had given no names, only numbers. I flipped a couple of pages and discovered that Seabiscuit would be the number five horse, and he was destined to finish . . . second. All the better for me: the way the races stacked up, I could bet fairly conservatively, certainly not conspicuously, and still earn enough to set myself up for the next few months.

Eighth in line at the ten-dollar window, I took the crib sheet from my pocket for a confirmative peek. I heard Lorna's voice say, "Big spender."

"I thought you were getting sandwiches," I said.

"I just wanted to tell you you were in the ten-dollar line."

"I've got some good information on this race." Indeed, my information could not have been better.

"Tell me, then."

"Why don't I just bet for both of us?"

"Not at these prices," she said.

Should I simply offer her a piece of my bet, or would that set a precedent that might prove awkward? I whispered to her, "The eight horse. His name is Phlox."

"Phlox? Are you kidding me?" She looked at her program. "My God, there it is. Phlox. Five to one. I'm not sure I could bet on a horse named Phlox."

"I would if I were you. He's six to one now."

She stood on tiptoes and whispered back to me, "Thanks for the tip." She took two steps backward, waved, and trotted off in the direction of the two-dollar windows. Phlox would pay $14.60 in a matter of minutes. I resisted the urge to bet my entire two-hundred-dollar bankroll; I'd have to experience one race at least to make sure this business actually worked. I handed the man a twenty and a ten—bills that had for one reason or another survived into the nineteen-nineties and now come home to die. I said, "Eight to win, three times."

Phlox broke well, took the lead almost immediately. Lorna began chanting, "Come on, Phlox" in a normal voice. Her pitch rose gradually until, when Phlox ran neck-and-neck with Galmica in the stretch, she was screaming, clutching my hand.

She hugged me when Phlox reached the finish a head in front of Galmica. She smelled of sunlight and something else terribly familiar. Her body had the same suppleness as Marie-Laure's. I was not averse to hugging reciprocally; it was in fact awfully difficult to let go. I said, "How much did you bet?"

"Just two dollars." She beamed. "But I don't think I've ever won anything before. How much is it going to pay?"

"He was six to one on the board, so at least fourteen dollars."

"My God," Lorna gasped, "so I've won twelve dollars! Maybe *more* than twelve dollars." She was silent a moment, thinking. "And Gabriel, you've won even more! A ten-dollar bet, five times fourteen, minus your bet—am I right? Sixty dollars!"

In fact, Phlox would pay $14.60 and I'd won $189, but it didn't seem strategic to tell Lorna that. She said, "How can we celebrate?"

"By betting on the next race," I said. "I've got a good feeling about that one, too."

"A good feeling, or good information?" She alluded to my remark before the previous race.

"Here, I'll show you." The fourth race would go to a horse named Torchy, about whom I knew absolutely nothing. I studied his line in the program for about three seconds. "Look," I put my arm around her and pointed to her program, "Torchy's been recording better times each race—"

"Except for the last one. He finished seventh."

"But see here, it was a muddy track. The previous race, on a fast track, he was second by a nose." All at once I recognized the other fragrance: it was Breck shampoo. Tina Ogilvie, the light of my life when I was seventeen, had always smelled of Breck shampoo. While the sexual revolution was in its early glory days we had swum naked, had long and earnest conversations about William Burroughs and Henry Miller, nearly sneaked off to Woodstock, never slept together.

"But this horse, Kumreigh, won his last race, also on a fast track."

"Fine. Except Torchy's going to win."

"I think I'll bet him to show," she said. I withdrew my arm, sliding it along the fabric—cotton, most certainly—of her flowered skirt.

I said, "I like the way your hair smells."

"How sweet of you," she replied.

I watched Lorna collect her winnings, then quickly picked mine up from the adjacent cashier. While Lorna stood in a long line at the two-dollar window, I got to the ten-dollar man in a couple of minutes. "Five to win, ten times," I said.

This time, although Torchy had all he could do to hold off the redoubtable Kumreigh at the finish, and won by a head, the element of suspense was not nearly as great. For me, that is. Lorna was on her feet in the stretch, virtually levitating when our horse reached the finish. This time we engaged in a genuine embrace. My arms around her waist, I lifted her two feet off the ground, placed her down gently, gazed into those extraordinary eyes. I said, "How much did you bet?"

"Two dollars to show . . ." she paused dramatically, "and two dollars to win!"

"You're such a fox!" I took for granted that the word had no connotation beyond cleverness.

"And you?" Her eyes were constellations.

"My winnings from the last race, plus a little more."

"My God, Gabriel, you're going to get rich at this rate."

My intention, of course, was not to get rich but to make myself money to live on for a time. I had anticipated doing so in discreet solitude, but this way was much more enjoyable.

We studied the program for the fifth race. "Look," Lorna pointed, "Clean Out has just the sort of record Torchy did, see?"

Indeed Clean Out did, but Clean Out was going to finish third. "The problem is," I said, "he's coming up in class."

"What does that mean?"

"He's running against better horses. He won't be able to compete with Lithorome."

"Lithorome? Lithorome's fifteen to one! Lithorome hasn't finished in the money in any of these races."

"But he's coming down in class."

"How do you know that, Gabriel?"

"I told you I had good information."

She paused, looking at me, wondering (I guessed) whether to ask the nature of my information. She said, "Well, information or not, I'm not going to bet on Lithorome. What if I bet Clean Out to show?"

"Might work. But if I were you, I'd stick with Lithorome."

Again I waited for her to collect before I visited the cashier, who handed me three crisp hundred-dollar bills and a twenty. Back at the ten-dollar window, I put one of my new hundreds on Lithorome's nose.

Lorna said, "I think I'm getting carried away." There was an edge of excitement in her voice.

"What did you do?"

"I couldn't make up my mind. I bet Clean Out to show, and I walked away from the window. I figured he'd pay about three dollars, and that wouldn't be much fun. So I went back and bet him twice more." Now she grinned. "Then I bet two dollars on Lithorome to win."

"You'll be pleased you did."

"I can afford it," she said. "I've won seventeen dollars, after all."

Lorna got her money's worth. Clean Out was near the lead from the beginning, seized it at the turn, and seemed prepared to keep it.

He led through the stretch, by which time Lorna was again on her feet, bouncing as if on an invisible pogo stick. But two horses were coming up fast on the outside; the first edged by Clean Out with thirty yards to go. Lorna stopped and sagged. I shouted, "You're all right." The second horse, Lieutenant Greenock, passed Clean Out as Lorna turned to look at me. "Of course!" she shouted back, her face brightening. "He's still going to show!"

"And look who's just won," I yelled.

Lorna's head swiveled back just as the first horse crossed the finish line. "Number seven!" Lorna screamed. "My God, Gabriel, that's your horse, that's Lithorome!" This time it seemed our celebratory embrace was just a little bit more intimate.

Her profit was exactly thirty dollars, putting her $47.80 ahead for the day. Mine was $2,660, bringing my winnings to a little over three thousand 1938 dollars. Lorna said, "Maybe we should get out of here before Santa Anita turns into a giant pumpkin."

"I think you're supposed to play a winning streak until it ends," I said.

"But that way you always lose your last bet," Lorna observed— rather sagely, I thought.

"All right, then. Let's make the sixth race our last bet, win or lose."

"Fine with me," she said. "I think this is the most money I've ever had at once. What should I do? Bet half of it on Seabiscuit? He probably won't pay even a dollar on a two-dollar bet."

"No. I wouldn't bet on Seabiscuit at all. Not to win, anyway."

She gave me a look of theatrical astonishment. "Isn't he the most famous horse in the world? Isn't he the *fastest*?"

"Not always," I said.

There were only a couple of big plungers at the hundred-dollar window. Out of Lorna's sight, I bet two hundred even on Aneroid, a horse I had never heard of before today. His victory would put me slightly over six thousand dollars for the day, enough to buy myself a car, find an apartment, assemble a wardrobe, enough to keep me solvent for quite a while—so among other things I wouldn't have to come back here and abuse the statistical applecart for the foreseeable future.

It was quite a race. Aneroid immediately took the lead, with Seabiscuit well back in the pack. While Aneroid set a brisk pace, Seabiscuit's jockey encountered nothing but frustration trying to move his mount between horses. The huge crowd, much of which had bet on the favorite, grew restive. As the leaders rounded the turn, a horse began making up ground rapidly on the outside, and the track announcer called out, "Here comes Seabiscuit!" But my eyes had been riveted on Seabiscuit, who had just freed himself from traffic and now stood fourth. This object of mistaken identity, I discovered with a quick glance at my program, was a horse named Time Supply!

Lorna was once again in motion, yelling, "Come on, Aneroid! Hold on, Aneroid!" Our horse appeared to have lost none of its stamina, but in the stretch Seabiscuit began to make his move, as if he had suddenly found traction, zooming past Time Supply and then Indian Broom, finding himself still a length and a half behind Aneroid with twenty yards to run. Lorna bounced and beseeched, vaulted and implored, as the great horse Seabiscuit threatened to lunge past our favorite.

The finish line was at precisely the right spot, so Aneroid's nose reached it first. Had it been ten feet farther down the course, Seabiscuit would have won by a nostril. Had it been fifty feet farther down, Seabiscuit would have won by two lengths.

Lorna had wrapped an arm around my waist at the midpoint of Seabiscuit's charge and pressed more of herself against me until the finish, after which we took a small step beyond enthusiastic congratulation. Holding her as tightly as I could without risk of injury, lifting her once again, I brushed my lips against hers as her head was moving left, mine right. On the return trip, she seemed to make an effort to kiss me.

I held her for how long? Ten seconds? Fifteen? Certainly no longer than that. The hatless man and the nascent contract actress creating a tableau in the clubhouse at Santa Anita. I set her down. She said, with a little sigh, "My God, I hardly know you."

But I knew all too much about her.

8

She had no idea of the magnitude of my winnings. I did not wish to overshadow her own very successful afternoon. Nor, in making my first impression, did I want to appear omnipotent or freakish. I should not neglect to mention something else here. My own calculations prior to the fifth race had been a little off because it hadn't occurred to me that a hundred-dollar bet on a long shot like Lithorome might cause a tiny wrinkle in the pari-mutuel pool. According to my floppy disk, in that other 1938 Lithorome had paid $27.80 to win; this time around he paid $27.60. I had an anxious moment—not for the twenty dollars uncollected; that I knew I could recoup anytime. Rather I worried whether, like Godzilla lumbering obliviously through Tokyo, I might not have stepped on someone else's life. I'd cost an unknown number of bettors a tiny percentage of their winnings. Had I deprived someone of the extra money he needed to pay his mortgage, buy an engagement ring, settle with his bookie?

Probably not, I decided.

— —

Lorna took not nearly as many chances on the way back to Malibu, perhaps having filled her risk quota at the track. It was thus a most pleasant drive: two very happy people cruising through bucolic, semi-urban Southern California on a splendid early evening. Two very happy people also quite interested in each other, wondering what was in store. To be accurate, I can only speak for myself. I assumed that at least some of the growing ardor I felt for her was reciprocated, but there were other concerns: one cultural, one purely utilitarian.

Where I'd come from, even the sort of minor intimacy Lorna and I had shared at the racetrack might lead to consummation in a brief matter of time. But here, thirty years or so before mores would be turned on their heads, I had no idea what to expect. Not that I felt any great urgency. I was, for the moment at least, content to proceed at whichever pace seemed appropriate.

The cultural led to the utilitarian. Dusk was gathering, and I was a stranger in a quasi-familiar land. Should I ask Lorna to recommend a hotel? Thanks to my afternoon's labors I could afford the best, but did I want to attract attention to myself, wandering into the Beverly Hills Hotel with neither luggage nor a hat? Did the Beverly Hills Hotel yet exist? The neatest solution would be to spend my first night at the Hudnut beach house, but here I saw the potential for another Godzilla step. I didn't even know whether Lorna was the only family member staying at the house. I could be sure that other family members would disapprove of a young woman's being joined, even for a night, by some boat deliveryman and racetrack habitué from the east. Why jeopardize the safety of my machine, not to mention the future of my relationship with Lorna, for the sake of convenience?

As we approached Hollywood, Lorna turned to me. "Where have you left your things?"

"My things?"

"You know, your luggage. Your clothes. Whatever you brought with you."

"Ah. Don't have any, actually. It's being shipped out."

She raised her eyebrows. "Gabriel—don't tell you've been wearing that nice white suit for the last week. It certainly doesn't look as if you have."

"No, of course not," I said. My mind wasn't working quite as fast or creatively as it had been earlier, but I still had a gift for the plausible. "I had a suitcase in the truck. I completely forgot about it, left it in the back when we got the boat out. I'm sure Ralph will drop it off before he goes back."

"Ralph is your friend with the truck?"

"Right. He's picking up a load in Long Beach and going back to New York."

"Whatever do they make in Long Beach that people would want in New York?"

"I have no idea," I said.

"Then you don't have your writing, either?"

I was caught off balance. "My writing?"

"Your books. Your scripts."

"That's right!" I whacked my right thigh for emphasis. "In the suit-case."

"That's terrible, Gabriel. And you have no way of getting in touch with this man Ralph?"

"No way at all, I'm afraid." Lorna seemed genuinely horrified that my *oeuvre* was parked outside some warehouse in Long Beach, thence to proceed back to the East Coast. "It's not that important," I said. "Really. I have copies."

"But I was hoping you could show your work to my friend at Warn-ers tomorrow."

"Even if Ralph doesn't come by it shouldn't take me more than a few days to put together some treatments," I said. "I'm sure I can sur-vive till then."

We drove several blocks in silence before she turned to me again. "So that's all you've got? Your beautiful white suit? No toothbrush? No clean underwear?"

"Lots of money," I said with a big smile. "Enough for a good hotel, anyway."

"But what's the point?" She touched my knee with her right hand. "Why don't you just spend the night at the house? We've got extras of everything, I'm sure. You could still come with me to the studio in the morning. I'll introduce you around. And we can go shopping in the afternoon—that is if Ralph doesn't come by."

"It's very kind of you to offer," I said, "but I don't want to get you into any trouble. I can't imagine your family would approve of some stranger spending the night . . ."

Lorna squinted at me, and grinned. "Gabriel, my gosh! How mar-velously Victorian of you! This is 1938, after all, and I'm over twenty-one."

—•—

"I'm afraid I don't have anything to eat at the house," she said. There were three eggs and some ketchup, I knew. She asked me if I liked Ital-ian food, then caught herself. "Of course you do," she said. "You've *been* there."

At the ocean we turned left instead of right. Unlike Malibu, the

stretch between Santa Monica and Venice was nearly as built up and congested as I'd left it. We parked by the Venice Pier and walked a hundred feet to Jack's at the Beach. For the time and place Jack's was . . . debonair, I suppose, with black-coated, white-aproned waiters treading on a floor of glossy white tiles. "It's expensive here," Lorna said, "but it's very good."

I ordered the chicken cacciatore ($1.50), a green salad (35¢) and a glass of the house white (50¢). Lorna had veal scallopine (also $1.50), salad, and a glass of the house red. The salads were tasty but overdressed, crunchy fresh lettuce and ripe tomatoes bathing in a surfeit of well-mixed oil and vinegar. The chicken likewise was overcooked and over-spiced. Lorna said her veal was quite good. The wines were passable.

Lorna said, "Is it all right? I'm sure it's not exactly Rome, but does it pass muster?"

"Very satisfying," I said. "A fine ending for a perfect day."

Lorna drank the last of her wine. "Are you seeing anyone?"

Seeing anyone? "I've only been here a few hours."

"At home, Gabriel. I've been assuming there's no Mrs. Prince."

"None at all. Never has been. Actually, I've recently broken up with someoné."

"Broken off?"

"Broken off."

"A girl in New York?"

"She was from Canada, as a matter of fact." The last subject I wanted to get onto was Marie-Laure. I said, "What about you? Are you seeing anyone?"

"I suppose I am," she shrugged.

"You suppose?"

"My Warners friend. Bill Wadsworth. He was a class ahead of you at Princeton. Remember?"

"Right. You don't seem awfully passionate about Bill."

"He's very nice. Very talented. Good for me, I suppose. He's got his feet on the ground. But he's so . . ."

She seemed unwilling to finish the sentence. "So ugly?" I suggested. "So fat?"

"So *old*," she said, and she reached across the table to touch my hand. "I know you're just a little bit younger than he is, but I guess I'm not talking about chronological age. He's just so . . . stodgy. Not like you. I can't imagine sitting with Bill at the racetrack."

If Wadsworth had graduated from college in 1926, that would make him thirty-three or thirty-four now. How old was I? According to one birth certificate I was thirty-three; according to the more legitimate one I'd left behind I was either forty-two or negative fourteen, depending upon which direction you counted in. Given that much ambiguity, I'd say I committed no great impropriety in keeping my mouth shut when Lorna, by implication, celebrated my youthfulness.

— • —

We walked on the beach. I had left my suit jacket and my shoes at the house, rolled up the cuffs of my trousers; Lorna had exchanged a pair of white shorts for her skirt. The night was warm and breezy, the moon either just about to be or just past being full. She said, "Are you as good a writer as you are a horse player?"

"I'm really not that good a horse player. I had a very lucky day," I protested, not at all untruthfully.

She gave me a gentle poke in the ribs. "That didn't look like luck to me." We proceeded a few steps. "Tell me about one of your scripts."

"I'd much rather talk about you," I said, again not being in the least dishonest.

."What's there to talk about? I've already told you my life story. I'm a second-rate actress at a second-rate studio."

"Second-rate? Warners has James Cagney, right? Bette Davis? Errol Flynn and Olivia de Havilland? Humphrey Bogart?"

"Sure," she said, "they've got some stars. But Jack Warner is dead set against spending any money for anything. So you take a picture like *Angels with Dirty Faces*. It's got a great cast, very competent director, but the sets are so cheap, so obvious. I think he's stuck in the twenties, back before talkies, when you could stick a street sign in the foreground and the Statue of Liberty or something in the background, and that was New York. People are getting more sophisticated. You can't get away with things like that anymore."

"It's a big hit just the same, though, isn't it?"

"It hasn't even been released yet, Gabriel."

"Ah," I said.

We took several steps in silence. I wondered if my error had been of any consequence. She said, "Why did you mention Humphrey Bogart?"

"Because he's a good actor."

"He's a terrific actor. One of the best at Warners. But he's not a star, like Cagney and Flynn and Robinson."

I don't know whether you can imagine the disorder in my brain at that moment, as I sensed restraint was the judicious path, as I knew this was a condition I would doubtless face many more times than once—finding myself in conversation with someone who assumed she knew far more than I about our subject, when in fact it was I who knew far more than she ever could. "I'm sure it's just a matter of time," I said.

"Well, possibly, but he's almost forty. I understand he talks a lot about going back to Broadway. He's sick and tired of all the gangster roles they stick him with."

We proceeded along the beach in silence. In part to make conversation, in part because it seemed as good a time as any, I asked, "Do you know an actor named Ronald Reagan?"

"Reagan? Dutch Reagan?" Although somewhere in the back of my mind I knew better, I had pronounced the name "Ragan," as it had been spoken during the entire political career of the fortieth president of the United States. Lorna was correcting me, saying "Reegan," as the young actor pronounced his name.

"Yes," I said, "Dutch Reagan," regretting my small mistake, wondering, given her tone of voice, whether I should have asked the question in the first place.

"Sure, I know who he is. I probably know every actor on the lot. But how would *you* ever have heard of Dutch Reagan?"

"Why not?"

"He's a hick! He's from Iowa or someplace, and he's only been in a couple of pictures that came and went."

"He's a friend of a friend," I said. And then, recalling my earlier wild card, I embellished. "A friend of a friend of a truckdriver, actually. Ralph, who drove me out here, had a pal who wanted him to look up an actor at Warners named Ronald Reagan, just to say hello."

"Well," Lorna said, "that shouldn't be any problem. And if Ralph ever brings your suitcase, we'll take him to the studio and introduce him to Dutch Reagan."

— —

Back in the house we had a glass of wine and Lorna warned me that she'd be going to bed soon. She would be spending Sunday with her friend Wadsworth at his family's house in Beverly Hills. She was accustomed to getting to bed by ten because her weekdays began shortly before 5 A.M., since she had to be in Burbank, on the set of *Love*

Honor and Behave (a comedy starring Wayne Morris) at six. I was welcome, incidentally, to join her and watch Monday morning's activity,
and I should feel free to spend Sunday here in the house, as well as
Sunday night, if I wished.

"Maybe I should spend tomorrow looking for a place to stay."

"Why? You can just relax tomorrow, then start taking care of things
on Monday. It makes sense."

"You've twisted my arm," I said. "I don't suppose there's a typewriter anywhere in the house?"

There was a massive Underwood in the garage, in the first box
Lorna checked, jet black and heavy as a bowling ball. I carried it
upstairs as she led me to my bedroom. "This is the kids' room, Jasper's
room when he's here. He's outgrown the bed, I'm afraid."

It was the same room Hudnut had occupied—*would* occupy, I suppose—in 1994, with most of the same furnishings. Notably absent
were the photograph of himself, his parents, and Lorna, and of course
the shopping center between the narrow road outside and the highway. She brought me clean towels and a stack of typing paper. The
medicine cabinet in my bathroom contained everything else I might
need. I said, "Will I keep you up if I type on this thing?"

"I can sleep through anything," she said. She stood in the doorway,
still barefooted, wearing her white shorts and loose-fitting, gauzy
white blouse, looking for all the world like a gorgeous photograph
from *Life*, the ingenue at her leisure, something I might have stumbled across as a boy in the attic, something that would have stopped
me in my tracks even then.

I stood four feet from her, a bath towel, a hand towel, a washcloth
draped across my arm in ascending order. "Thanks for everything," I
said. "I'm very grateful for all this."

"It's nothing," she replied. "I enjoyed spending the day with you."

She took a step toward me, I a step toward her. We embraced, and
our lips touched lightly. I suspected this might be one of those
moments when assertiveness is rewarded—and I can think of few
times in my life when I have been so excited to be in the presence of
someone—yet there was no question in my mind that I should stand
back, and wait.

—·—

I had of course never written a screenplay, never written an outline for a screenplay, never had the remotest idea of writing a screenplay. But I had *read* a number of screenplays, so I was familiar enough with the form. And I had the benefit of a fairly comprehensive knowledge of the upcoming fifty-six years' worth of filmic achievement. I did not particularly relish what I was about to do, but I could hardly be accused of plagiarizing works that hadn't yet been written. I would of course be very much aware of my own deceit, but I reasoned that my pledge to Hudnut took precedence, that the ultimate purpose of my actions served a greater morality than any minor fraud I might commit, and—perhaps most pertinently—that the prospect of my sabotaging a future masterpiece by creating some half-assed premature synthesis of it was about nil, because certainly nothing I wrote would ever make it to the screen.

So I stayed up until midnight tapping out several two- and three-page treatments, some of them quite good, I thought. I went downstairs then and stood briefly on the attenuated deck, listening to the docile surf, feeling no longer euphoric, but as if I'd put in an extremely good day, and looking forward to the next one.

I stood at the top of the stairs, listened to Lorna turn and murmur in her sleep. In the bathroom, with its great complex of Moorish tiles, I brushed my teeth warily with a dollop of odd-tasting pink Squibb dentifrice on a stiff-bristled wooden toothbrush, washed my hands and face with a bar of Ivory that looked and smelled exactly like the one I'd used two days ago in my bathroom, in 1994, and crawled into my bed in the Hudnut summer house. The mattress was a bit on the soft side, the pillow slightly bulbous, but I could not have been cozier.

In the cool stillness of the very early morning, I wondered about Lorna's future. Had Hudnut told me anything more about the Great Storm? I had a computer full of race results, but nary a 1938 weather report. It was not quite March, but judging by today's weather the Southern California winter had passed, and Lorna would be in no danger until November, by which time I might know her well enough to take her far away from Malibu.

Drifting toward sleep, I thought I heard distant thunder.

9

When I awoke Sunday morning it was raining and Lorna was gone. There was a note in the kitchen: she'd left me some eggs, a loaf of bread, a quart of milk; she would be back past dinnertime. The rain was steady but not at all ominous. It gave me a little thrill that Lorna had gone shopping for me.

I spent the day expanding my portfolio, polishing my work, until I had eight treatments to be reckoned with. I waited for the rain to stop, but it continued. At three o'clock I called a cab and had it drive me into Santa Monica.

Any frequent traveler knows well what might be called the Phenomenon of Slight Difference—of water heaters suspended over kitchen sinks, latches instead of doorknobs, coffee cups without handles—all the details that, as much as language and politics, define the foreignness of a culture not quite the same as one's own. I had been so high my first day here, so much had been happening, so much of my attention had been focused on Lorna, that I had forestalled the queasiness that seasons one's awareness of being far away from home.

Had I been expecting a yellow late-model sedan with an electronic meter and a driver recently arrived from Qatar? No, but still the huge Ford surprised me. In the persistent rain the cabbie held the door open for me. He carried an umbrella and wore a badge on his cap. The taxi's interior was big enough for a dinner party, with a long, felt-covered seat and two jump seats for passengers who didn't mind riding backwards.

Then under a gray sky I spent an hour and a half walking streets I'd prowled off and on for the past five years. But the huge taxi had taken me to a Santa Monica as alien, in its way, as Lisbon or Prague. The removal of fifty-six years had erased everything I knew. As I wandered through the central business district, walking up Third Street and then back along Fourth, there was nothing—no market, no restaurant, no gas station, no doorway, no street sign, no mailbox, no fire hydrant—that I recognized. In all my years of travel I had never felt quite so far from home.

By early evening the rain had become quite heavy. In my grim state, I found an umbrella and took an uneasy walk on the beach, where the surf had begun to pound impressively, and the wind to gust sufficiently to cause me concern for the sake of the borrowed umbrella.

I tried again to recall the details of my brief conversation with Hudnut regarding the storm. No one heard from Lorna for days, because the telephone was out. Then Cousin Someone drove out here and discovered the house was intact, but still no word from Lorna.

I tried the telephone; it appeared to be in perfect working order. Seconds after I'd replaced the receiver, the phone rang. What was I to do? Possibly it was Lorna calling me, more likely it was someone calling Lorna. I wasn't supposed to be here. I stood frozen in the little alcove, wondering what to do as the phone rang six, seven times, and finally stopped.

She came home at about nine. She'd had a tedious day in Beverly Hills, then a miserable drive back to Malibu; the top of her SS didn't shut tightly and as a result she was quite moist from the waist up. She was gorgeous, as well.

I found myself lifted from my Slough of Despond. I suggested that perhaps she would be well advised to take a cab to work in the morning. Alas, that was a luxury she could not afford. Perhaps she and I could share a cab, then, and I would pay? That she would consider.

By ten she'd gone to bed, having promised to wake me in the morning. Probably my concern was unwarranted. Probably this would not become the Great Storm of 1938. If it did, might not Lorna perish in the back seat of a taxi just as readily as in the front seat of her SS? How flexible was history? What sort of difference could I make? These were thoughts I thought my second night in Jasper Hudnut's childhood bed.

—▬ ▬—

She did not wake me. On the kitchen table there was a note:

Gabriel—

Couldn't bring myself to disturb you. Anyway, what would you have done all morning in Burbank? Why don't you meet me there for lunch? Commissary at noon! I'll introduce you to Bill. See you then.

L.

All the way to Burbank I listened to the driver's complaints about the weather. "They said it was gonna rain, they didn't say nothing about rain like *this*. Jesus Christ, this is like Noah's Ark, the way it's coming down." Indeed, by now the rain was constant and prolific. Ill-conformed intersections were flooded, backing up traffic for blocks. Aftermaths of accidents were everywhere. The Malibu-Burbank journey took an hour and a half. I'd given myself what I thought was ample extra time, but still I was twenty minutes late.

The guard just inside the Olive Avenue gate scanned his list. Yes, Miss Fairchild had left a pass for Gabriel Prince. In the pouring rain, my taxi was permitted to take me directly to the commissary, centrally located in a vast complex of office buildings and soundstages.

I peeked into a large room that resembled a fairly snazzy restaurant: lots of white linen, many tables for four—and plenty of faces I was accustomed to seeing in black and white. The immediate effect was breathtaking. If you've ever come face-to-face with a celebrity in a supermarket aisle or on a streetcorner you know the peculiar succession of perceptions: your brain tells you that you've just encountered someone you know, but there's a moment of confusion as you realize it's someone you're accustomed to seeing in two dimensions, or on a stage very far away. In this case I was a few feet away from a complex of tables whose occupants included Errol Flynn, Olivia de Havilland, Basil Rathbone, Claude Rains, and, yes, Eugene Pallette, all in costume, looking like refugees from a Robin Hood movie, which is precisely what they were. Scanning the room, I saw Edward G. Robinson sitting with Claire Trevor and Donald Crisp, Bette Davis sharing a table with George Brent and Spring Byington. And where was Lorna?

Behind me, as it turned out. "Hi," she said. "I was afraid you weren't going to make it." She too was in costume; she looked as if she were about to attend a cocktail party, circa 1938. In her black, low-cut evening gown she leaned toward me and carefully kissed my left cheek. "Gabriel, you're soaking wet."

"I wouldn't have missed it," I said. "But I'd always imagined the commissary as something a little less elegant than this."

"You were right," she said. "This one isn't for the likes of us." She led me across the hall. "Technically, I'm allowed to eat over there with the swells because I'm a contract actress, but it's a lot cheaper over here."

We entered a much bigger room, with a cafeteria-style service line in the foreground. One acquired one's lunch, evidently, and then made one's way to any point along a complex of connected, semicircular counters with stationary diner stools. Lorna said, "The food here isn't great, but it won't kill you." She rubbed at my cheek with three fingers. "I've gotten makeup all over you. Listen, you've just missed Bill. He was looking forward to seeing you, but he had to go to a meeting. Have you eaten? Would you like some lunch? I'm afraid they don't have very much in the way of breakfast . . ."

"I'd love some lunch," I said. Standing in the short line at the

counter, I noticed that the only black faces in the second-class commissary were gathered together at the far end of the room. Beyond that bit of segregation, the commissary bespoke a sort of theatrical egalitarianism. There were people in costume here and there—some B actors, some extras. And of course one needed to look carefully to tell whether the workmen seated at the semicircle just to our right were in fact actors dressed as workmen.

In my damp and slightly rumpled white suit I might just barely have been admitted to the same cocktail party as Lorna. We were not an altogether incongruous couple. I selected a piece of broiled chicken, a portion of tired-looking peas and carrots, a fairly spry lettuce-and-tomato salad, a roll with the heft of a paperweight, and a glass of iced tea. Lorna said, "I've got to be back on the set in about ten minutes, but I'll be done at three. I told Bill all about our adventures at the track. He's dying to meet you. I told him you were up until all hours trying to re-create some of your scripts. Oh, how did that go, Gabriel?"

"Just great. I brought them with me."

"Oh, fabulous! So listen, I thought maybe after you finish your lunch—of course I'm not sure when Bill's going to be out of his meeting—you could just walk over to his office and wait for him. . . . Might as well be comfortable, right?"

We found two vacant stools. "I hope you don't mind, I told him you were at Princeton. He said he didn't remember your name, maybe he'd remember your face."

Not terribly likely. "That would be wonderful," I said, wondering just how delighted Bill could be about the sudden arrival of a mystery man in the life of his intended, regretting that I hadn't chosen to say I'd gone to Yale, or better the University of Irkutsk.

My first commissary meal was barely edible, but my companion was radiant in her evening gown, and so happy to be with me, so apologetic when it was time to leave. "I've got to go." She got to her feet. "Oh, I almost forgot . . . I assume you haven't heard from Ralph?"

"Not a word."

"Well, his friend Dutch is right over there . . ." She pointed to the western extreme of the room, at farthest remove from the black section. I stood up and turned around, and suffered a moment's tachycardia. There he was, accompanied not by Jane Wyman, as one might have expected, but by a more exotic young actress in costume. There he was, young and handsome, his hair a natural reddish brown, slicked down. Was he in the midst of an anecdote? The blond actress, all ears as he declaimed and gestured, burst into laughter when he stopped.

It was as if I had plunged deep into the Amazonian jungle in a quest for some scarce fauna, prepared to spend months or years searching, and discovered my prey behind the first jacaranda. I had been here under two days and I stood no more than thirty feet from Ronald Reagan. My heart raced, I felt a tremor in my knees.

Lorna said, "Would you like me to introduce you?"

"No, you're in a hurry," I replied. "It's not important."

— —

The writers' building was quite a hike from the commissary, tucked away amidst a grove of tall pines. Bill Wadsworth's office indicated that he was probably a rising star among Warners' stable of young writers: it was fairly spacious (perhaps twelve feet by twelve), it was carpeted (a bluish wool dhurrie), it had a fairly large window that looked out onto the parking lot. Further, the office was well kept and well furnished, unquestionably the space of someone with good taste and more than a little money. Wadsworth's desk was good-sized without being huge, attractive without being ostentatious. It was constructed of a dark hardwood, and everything upon it blended into a functional harmony, from the modernistic low-slung lamp to the neat stack of scripts to the chestnut telephone. I had presumed that all telephones of this era would be black; I wondered if Wadsworth had had his specially made, or if he'd painted it himself.

The wall across from the windows (the wall he faced when behind his desk) was dominated by a painting of Venice—late nineteenth century, I assumed—a view of San Marco on a blustery day. The wall one first encountered when entering was decorated with various framed images and documents: the Princeton diploma (he'd graduated *cum laude*), the M.A. from the University of Maryland (indicating a little postgraduate indecision), some literary prize I'd never heard of, photographs of himself with members of his family (I guessed; they looked alike, all pink-faced and sandy-haired), a photograph of himself with Lorna, both dressed casually in white, Wadsworth beaming, Lorna looking constrained and beautiful.

On the wall across from that were three shelves of books. Chaucer, Shakespeare, Marlowe, Milton, Fielding, lots of British drama, Thackeray, Dickens. So far, a survey course or two. Hawthorne, Jack London, Edna Ferber, Dos Passos, Sinclair Lewis, Hemingway. Fitzgerald: a pristine, jacketed first edition of *Tender Is the Night*. I opened it. On the title page, in black ink: "To my friend Bill, who one day may bring it to the screen. Fondly, Scott." Well, we knew that wasn't going to happen.

On the top shelf, at about the level of my shoulders, were the oversized books: a set of *Encyclopaedia Britannica*, a row of bound scripts, and a mother lode of Princetoniana. Wadsworth had his *Freshman Herald*, his *Nassau Heralds*, his *Bric-a-Bracs*, nine books in all, arranged in order. Why did Wadsworth keep these yearbooks in his office instead of his home? Perhaps because—with the other books and accoutrements—they composed a rather strident advertisement for himself. In any case, I was grateful for their presence. As it turned out, Wadsworth's meeting lasted long enough that I could relax on the plush armchair across from his desk, virtually memorize the 1926 *Bric-a-Brac*, replace it on the shelf, and be immersed in "The Wife of Bath's Tale" when he walked in.

He was a tall man, solidly built, his blond hair short and receding. He wore khaki pants, white shoes and shirt, a blue cotton jacket with a gray necktie. The tie was loosened, the collar button of his shirt undone. Espying me he stopped and grinned. "So this is Lorna's mystery man!" he said.

I got to my feet, *Canterbury Tales* in my left hand, my right outstretched. He gave my hand a death grip and said, "Bill Wadsworth, Gabriel. Pleasure to meet you!" He glanced at the book. "Well, I'm impressed! Not too often I walk in here and find someone reading Chaucer! Have a seat, Gabriel. Make yourself comfortable. Hope you haven't gotten too waterlogged." He let go my hand and moved behind his desk, took off his jacket, hung it on the chair back, sat down, leaned forward, and said, "So! Lorna tells me you'd like to write for the movies."

Back in the armchair. "I think."

"She tells me that's not all we have in common. You were at Princeton? I'm afraid I don't recognize the name or the face. Which class?"

"Twenty-seven," I said.

"Such a small campus. You'd think I'd have run into you some-where or other, three years in common. She said you didn't bicker?"

"Right. Couldn't afford a club."

"God!" Wadsworth shook his head. "I can't imagine two and a half years of Princeton without a club. Just about my fondest memories have to do with Cap and Gown. Must have been boring as hell, taking your meals in town. Where'd you eat, mainly?"

There'd been nothing in the *Bric* about the restaurants on Nassau Street, and I could be pretty sure the ones I knew circa 1973 hadn't been there forty-some years earlier. "Mostly I'd just eat in my room. I got to be very creative with sandwiches."

Wadsworth chortled. "Good for you!" He shook his head again, and gave a little shrug. "But I just can't imagine that, not having a club to go to." He tilted his head slightly and looked at me quite intensely, as if he were trying to peer inside me, but his affable expression never changed. "Lorna says you've got a gift for picking horses."

"Not really," I said, at once feigning modesty and telling the absolute truth, "I just had a spectacular day."

"I'll say you did! I wish I had a head for that kind of calculation, for gambling in general. It's all just a mystery to me. Lorna thinks I'm a stick-in-the-mud, of course. She's got a bit of a wild streak, you may have noticed."

I smiled and shook my head. "I've hardly met her."

"But you've driven with her?"

I laughed, spontaneously. "Yes, I suppose I have."

"God!" Wadsworth pounded his desk. "Can you *believe* what that girl does behind the wheel? She's not exactly a *bad* driver, truth be told. I mean, making moves like that, she'd be dead if she didn't have a talent for it. It's gotten to the point where I won't let her drive when we're together." He gave me another of those penetrating looks, and I wondered if they weren't just his way of gathering his thoughts. "But she's a great girl, Gabriel. I don't know what I'd do without her."

"I like her a lot," I said, sensing it was my turn to say something.

"So," Wadsworth resumed after a moment, "you were Jasper's Eng-lish teacher at Lawrenceville?"

Had Wadsworth gone to Lawrenceville, too? The thought hadn't previously entered my mind. I had never set foot on the campus of the school where I'd supposedly taught for eight years. My game could be up awfully soon. "I often thought Jasper was the teacher and I was the student."

"I know what you mean," Wadsworth took the bait. "He's a damn clever kid, isn't he. Scientific genius. And I couldn't believe it when I saw him last year. They don't come west every summer, I guess you know. Three years ago his nose was on a level with my chest. Last summer I walk in that house and there's a six-three kid towering over me . . ."

"He's grown since then," I said.

Wadsworth nodded and grinned. "You've brought some kind of boat out for the Hudnuts?"

"An experimental boat," I said.

"And you're . . . connected with the firm that makes the boat?"

"No, actually I know very little about the boat. Jasper's father knew I was coming out here and asked me to take care of it, paid my way out here, plus a little extra."

"I guess prep school English isn't the world's best-paid profession, is it? But Lorna tells me you've written some books. Travel books?"

"Right." Best to get off this subject as quickly as possible, I reasoned. "But I'm done with that. I'd really like to concentrate on writing for the movies from now on. . . ."

"You've written some scripts, Lorna told me, but evidently they've been hijacked to Long Beach?"

"I've spent a few hours doing outlines, treatments . . ."

"I'd love to see them," Wadsworth said. "I'm just a writer here myself, don't have anything to do with hiring. But I'm on a pretty friendly basis with a couple of the contract producers, and they're always looking for good material. I can put in a good word for you, and who knows?"

I handed him my two days' work. He glanced at the top page, put the whole stack down on his desk. "Just as a matter of curiosity, Gabriel, did you major in English at Princeton?"

"Yes, Bill, I did."

"God, isn't it strange? I realize we were a year apart, but we must have had a class or two together. Who was your adviser?"

I chose a name from my research. "Professor Sidney."

"Yes, of course. Young man. Expert on Thackeray and all that stuff. He your thesis adviser too?"

"He was."

"Just as a matter of interest, what was your thesis topic?"

Here, I supposed, I could tell the truth without risk of damage. "Henry James," I said. "*Turn of the Screw.*"

"Really? They let you get away with something that recent? And I'd have thought James was much too modern for Sidney. Must have been a lot of fun to write, though. Tell me, Gabriel, as an expert on the subject: were the ghosts real, or were they products of what's-her-name's imagination?"

"She has no name," I said. "Did you realize that? James was so smooth, I don't think I even noticed it the first time I read the book. I mean, usually a first-person narrator goes out of his way to let us know who he is. But she never tells us her name, and none of the other characters ever speak it."

"I didn't realize that," Wadsworth said.

"But there's no doubt in my mind that the ghosts don't exist. The governess is a very eloquent nut case."

"A *what?*"

"A nut case. She's out of her mind."

"A nut case," Wadsworth repeated. "I've never heard that before. Very clever term."

We chatted on for another hour or so, more of the same. It got so I could anticipate a rhythm. Wadsworth was polite, delighted to tell me about himself, to emphasize again and again the depth of his affection and appreciation for Lorna, and then every few minutes would come a significant question. He must have gotten around eventually to every aspect of our mutual alma mater. He'd drop a name, I'd respond. He'd ask what was the name of that building, that old dormitory across from Dod? And I'd casually supply the answer. He'd ask me if I'd taken a certain course, and I'd generally reply in the negative, but I had to have taken *some* courses, so once in a while I'd say oh, of course, that one, and Wadsworth would ask me if I took it in '25, when so-and-so was the lecturer, and I'd nod emphatically, hoping to God I wasn't walking into a trap. My memory of my education may have been a bit sketchy to Wadsworth's perception, but I certainly knew enough about the campus to indicate a thorough familiarity.

As the hour of my rendezvous with Lorna grew near, I recall deciding during a brief intermission in our conversation that if *I* were in Wadsworth's shoes, if *I* were trying to figure out what to make of me,

I'd have concluded that I was a fairly well-practiced poseur—a townie, or a dormitory janitor who'd taken on airs and decided to pass himself off as an alumnus. If that proved to be the case, I thought, it would probably pose no great threat to me.

— —

I am not an accomplished clothing shopper. I am unsure of myself, do not trust my sense of style. As a result my wardrobe has tended to be conservative and monotonous, except when I've shopped with women. The great frustration of my pre-Mouchard days in Paris with Marie-Laure was that I couldn't afford to buy most of the things she picked out for me. Our hotel was a block from a Daniel Hechter shop, for instance, with whose changing rooms I became intimate. There was a suede jacket, sort of a taupe color, snugly cut, whose material was so supple and fragrant that I couldn't stop touching it, stroking it. Marie-Laure and the salesgirl, who was a dead ringer for Marlène Jobert circa *Rider on the Rain,* both assured me that if God had ever intended me to have a garment, this was the one. My heart was pounding, my American Express card at the ready. I stroked the suede one more time, thought to ask Marlène *c'est combien?* Three thousand francs, about $525, at that day's rate of exchange. I caught my breath. Ah, I regretted, it was too much. Marie-Laure suggested that perhaps I was being just a bit penurious, that certainly Harvey Wells Greenglass wouldn't notice if I padded my expenses ever so slightly to buy a jacket that had been fabricated just for me. But I could not.

Now here I was with Lorna at Alexander Oviatt in Beverly Hills. She had chosen the place because I told her I needed a couple of good tailored suits, price to be no object, and my initial reaction when we walked in was that this was Daniel Hechter all over again. If anything—in its own way, in its own time—Oviatt's was more elegant than the Hechter shop. But upon discreetly examining a price tag or two, I suddenly possessed great insight into the psyche of the sheik who manages to get away from Jidda for one long weekend, walks into Harrod's, and buys everything he sees. I had so much money in my pocket that I wouldn't have thought twice about the $525 suede jacket, but here it was as if someone had meticulously moved the decimal point one digit to the left on every item in the store.

"You'd look marvelous in this," Lorna told me, fingering the sleeve of a navy blue gabardine suit, "but it's very expensive." How much? I asked. She sucked in a breath, raised her eyebrows, and whispered, "Eighty-five dollars." I did my best to appear impressed. I tried on the jacket. Lorna said, "It's gorgeous on you. But it's too much, isn't it?"

"It's courtesy of Santa Anita," I said.

I chose three suits, two pairs of shoes, three dress shirts and three casual shirts, two sport coats, four pairs of casual pants, five neckties, a box of linen handkerchiefs, and a supply of socks and underwear. Lorna said, "My God, Gabriel, I'm just adding this up in my head, but I'd say you're over five hundred dollars. Why don't you just get the suits here, and we can find the other things much cheaper somewhere else?"

That was precisely what I'd intended, but this was awfully good stuff and my pockets were full of Monopoly money. I assured Lorna I wasn't overextending myself. I reminded her I'd come west with just one suitcase, I'd been prepared to outfit myself. And besides, I could afford all this thanks to Lithorome and Aneroid.

"You didn't win *that* much," she said.

"It's all right," I assured her.

As the afternoon wore on I acquired my personal tailor, a small round man who followed me with his tape measure and chalk, and an assistant manager who periodically suggested that I might be interested in yet another area of the store. "You're going to have to deliver most of this," Lorna told him. "I couldn't possibly fit it in the trunk of my car."

"Certainly, Miss."

"To Malibu Beach."

He was unfazed. "We can have it to you day after tomorrow. No charge for the delivery, of course."

Of course. Two pairs of pants and one sport coat were altered while we waited. We took what little we could fit into Lorna's SS, or rather a couple of Oviatt lackeys carried it out, while sheltering us under a pair of oversized umbrellas through the pouring rain.

Just down the street was a camera shop, a broad expanse of open curb in front of it. I told Lorna to stop the car, told her I'd be just a minute.

I knew Leica had already begun marketing its sleek, compact 35-millimeter cameras. I asked a startled salesman what was the best he carried, and how much did it cost. He reached inside a glass display and brought out a silver-and-black jewel. "This," he said, "is the Three B with the fifty-millimeter lens. For two hundred and sixty dollars I'll throw in the leather case and two rolls of film."

Dashing back out to the car, I felt like a million dollars.

———

As it approaches the coast, Sunset Boulevard narrows and winds downward, enshrouded at various stretches by high canyon walls. When the walls become saturated, large chunks of them tumble down onto the roadway. Lorna cruised now down Sunset, driving perhaps five miles an hour faster than I would in such a heavy rain, but positively crawling compared to yesterday's pace. I suspected that the cliffs above us were nowhere near the point of collapse; I knew that Lorna and her SS had in the previous 1938 been buried by falling rocks and soil not here but on the oceanside Roosevelt Highway. I wondered just how elastic history was, or just how steadfast. While it was by no means certain that this *was* the Great Storm of 1938, the evidence was mounting. Would I save Lorna's life simply by accompanying her everywhere she went, because she was destined to die alone in her car? Was it only that great hunk of earth above the PCH that lay in wait for her, or did all the coastal cliffs conspire, just in case she happened to be elsewhere at the appointed moment?

10

The Laurie Smith Market on Fourth Street in Santa Monica stayed open late. I bought a good-sized chicken, some string beans, a head of lettuce, and two ripe tomatoes. I searched briefly for olive oil, was about to note the curiosity of its absence when I realized it wouldn't become a mainstream American consumer product for several decades. Gritting my teeth, I bought a small container of Wesson, some vinegar, some butter, some lemons. Back at the house, I pan-fried the string beans and much of the chicken in the interest of time. Lorna, who claimed not to know how to cook, mixed a decent salad. She asked me if I'd learned to cook in Europe.

She said, "Tell me what you thought of Bill." This was four hours after I'd left his office.

"He struck me as very friendly, very bright."

"But why do you suppose he gave you the third degree?"

"I think he's genuinely puzzled that he didn't know me at Princeton. He's trying to figure out how we could have missed each other."

"There must have been all sorts of people he didn't know."

"But we had the same major, took some of the same courses." I wondered what to say next. Fifty-four hours after my arrival, I was well past my time-travel euphoria; I had undergone a brief depression that might simply have been a product of miserable weather and disorientation. I felt at this moment, on the wet and windy last day of February 1938, quite the same as I had felt, let us say, seventy-two hours earlier, on a beautiful afternoon in May 1994. But I was already beginning to grow weary of my deception. I had probably told more outright lies since my arrival than during my entire previous life. There was a fundamental problem, of course, in that my very presence here was, if not a lie, an anomaly, a gross deviation from the proper order of things. In order to extend, to sustain, my existence here, I would have to perpetuate the deception. What was it that worried me more: that under the spell of yesterday's euphoria I had lied so easily, or that deprived of it today I found lying so difficult?

I said to Lorna, "Maybe Bill wants to find out as much as possible about me because he's concerned about me and you."

"Well, he's got no right to be," Lorna said, with an inscrutable shake of her exquisitely featured head.

The wind rattled windows and the surf sounded as if it were ten feet at most from the back porch. We listened to storm reports on the Crosley table radio, but electrical interference was so pervasive and annoying that after a few minutes Lorna switched it off.

She asked me about my work, about the outlines I'd handed over to Wadsworth. I was not terribly eager to discuss them. I think "ambivalent" would be an accurate, perhaps even a generous term to describe my feelings about them. I have already communicated my misgivings concerning the fraudulent nature of that work, which was done for the most part while I was still in a state of mild elation, and which I rationalized as morally tolerable because of my pledge to Hudnut. To be sure, I'd been enthusiastic about the outlines even earlier today, when I presented them to Wadsworth and when I mentioned them to Lorna, but now I was beginning to consider the gravity of what I'd done.

I did my best to change the subject, but Lorna insisted. "Just tell me the plot, Gabriel. Just one."

I chose my western, called *Four O'Clock*. "It's about a U.S. marshal in a frontier town, sometime after the Civil War, say 1880. He's just gotten married and he's about to leave town, take up farming. The day of his wedding he discovers that a man he sent to jail has been released and is coming back to settle the score. This is a very bad man and he's traveling with several other very bad men. They're due on the four o'clock train, thus the title."

"Wonderful," Lorna said. "I love it so far." We were sitting on a huge maroon sofa; Lorna edged closer to me.

"There are problems," I continued. "The wife is a Quaker, or some sort of pacifist. She'd agreed to marry the marshal only if he'd quit his job. Now she wants him to leave with her, to avoid the confrontation.

He thinks that would be cowardly, and not very strategic. The bad men would just hunt him down."

"It's fabulous, Gabriel. It's such a different kind of western. It's so *modern!*" Lorna had been perhaps eighteen inches from me when we initially sat down. Now her left leg was touching my right, and as she spoke the word "modern" she stroked my thigh with her fingertips—quite unconsciously, I thought.

"So he risks losing his wife, but worse than that, as the day progresses it becomes clear that very few people in the town are willing to stand by him. The odds keep getting worse and worse, until finally it looks as if he may be taking on these four very bad customers all by himself."

"I'll bet the wife changes her mind . . ."

"Exactly. There's a great scene: he takes her to the station, she sees the henchman standing there, waiting for the train. She's going to be taking the same train, after they get off, as it continues east—"

"Oh, my *God*, Gabriel, it's beautiful! So she makes her way back into town and together they take care of the bad men?"

"Right." Was the denouement that easy to figure out, or was I giving it away in my presentation? "The key moment is when the wife decides that she has to cast aside her principles because there's a higher good involved."

"I love it. I simply love it."

I was now in no position to repudiate this story, to convince Lorna that it *wasn't* really a great idea. It occurred to me that I'd felt these conflicting emotions many times before, as when doing a particularly good job of repeating an exciting anecdote, perhaps adding a few of my own details, before a rapt audience, or hearing bursts of spontaneous laughter when retelling a joke. All art is common domain, in a sense. No plot is unique, no story truly original.

Lorna said, "Gabriel, do you see me as the wife? Am I too young? It could be such a wonderful part."

"You'd be perfect," I said, without guile or flattery. I hadn't yet seen her on the screen, but she certainly had the looks and the presence to match Grace Kelly.

"I can't believe how exciting this is," she said. "I know you're going to get a job. If Warners won't hire you, I'm sure you could sell this picture to anyone, Gabriel. It's such a marvelous idea!"

What does one do at such a moment? It *was* a marvelous idea, I knew, but it wasn't mine. There was no way I could begin to communicate my feelings, my situation, to Lorna. So I did what my instincts told me to do, what they had in fact been telling me to do since this time last night, and what was now extraordinarily easy—almost mandatory, really—because our legs were touching from hip to knee, our sides virtually attached. I kissed her, and this time there was no victory acknowledgment involved, no ambiguity of any sort. I kissed her, and she kissed me in return. Neither kiss possessed great passion, to be sure, but as last night I suspected we could easily be headed toward something far more intense.

I had not taken into account the telephone, which rang once, then twice. Lorna pulled away ever so slightly. She said, "Oh, God." I could still feel her heartbeat as distinctly as I could my own; both were beyond brisk. She said, "It could be important. It could be the studio, about shooting tomorrow."

"There won't be shooting tomorrow," I said.

"We don't *know* that. Maybe they're calling to tell me not to come in. Anyway, I should get it."

I released her. She embraced me quickly and forcefully, as if telling me to stay exactly where I was, then stood up and moved swiftly to the alcove by the door, where she answered the phone as it was in the midst of its seventh ring. "Oh, hi," she said, and proceeded to listen for a few seconds, pacing uneasily, not looking at me. "No, I was upstairs. I had to run for the phone." She listened again. "No, I'm fine. Just a little out of breath." Again. "Yes, he's here. We went shopping. We went to Oviatt's." And again. "No, the man with the truck never came by. He's just about given up on him." Now, as she listened, she looked at me. "No, he's wide awake. I'm sure he'd love to speak to you."

She called me in a raised voice, as if I were farther away than just across the room, "Gabriel, Bill's on the telephone."

I got to my feet, thankful that the loose-fitting cut of my new trousers made my physical condition more discreet. Lorna cupped the mouthpiece with her right hand. "I'm sorry about this," she whispered to me.

If Wadsworth had any notion of what he'd interrupted, I couldn't detect it. "Gabriel, listen, I hope I didn't get you out of bed."

"Not at all."

"I was just looking at the material you gave me this afternoon, and I'll be completely frank with you: a lot of writers come here with the same sort of illusions as all the beauty queens who imagine they'll become movie stars overnight, and I had no reason to suspect you'd be any different. But some of this stuff is really very good."

"Thanks, Bill. Thanks a lot. Coming from you, that's a real compliment."

"You've got great a cinematic sense, you know. I can picture some of these so vividly. And there's something so . . . *new* about them. I'd say ninety percent of the hacks out here spend their time cannibalizing each other's stuff, but these outlines you gave me are so refreshing, so original, they're so full of energy. Some of them, to tell you the truth, some of them would be pearls before swine in Hollywood, sad to say. This melodrama of yours, for instance, the one set on the New York waterfront . . ."

"The Contender," I reminded him.

"Right. The tension in that is just excellent, the way you play off the two brothers, the moment when the girl discovers that this ex-boxer was actually the one who got her brother up on the roof the night he was killed. I love the way you build it, love the way you resolve it. But I don't think Warners is ready for that kind of realism, don't think anybody here is. I wonder, have you thought about writing it for the stage?"

Lorna stood by the little window over the porch, her back to me. "I hadn't, actually."

"Well, I could introduce you to some people here, although obviously New York would be the place for something like this. I mean, if you can write dialogue as well as you create plots and characters, this could put you in Odets territory. . . ."

"You're too kind, Bill. Really, I . . ." Really, I wanted to get off the telephone as quickly as possible.

"But Gabriel, let's get to what I *know* I can do. Just on the strength of your western—*Four O'Clock*, although I must say that title's a little prosaic—I can get you in to see Bernie Wiseman, who's one of the two or three most powerful producers on the lot. If he likes the cut of your jib, you're hired. I don't want to get your hopes up, but if I were Wiseman I wouldn't let you get away."

"That's wonderful to hear," I said. "Just wonderful." My gaze remained on Lorna's back; was she feeling the same strange mixture of intense sexual excitement and guilt as I? Of course she wasn't being festooned with compliments by the man she'd been betraying. And I? Had my ardor been dampened by this call from the nearly wronged swain, the man who a few hours earlier had been cautiously trying to find holes in my biography and now was lauding my ingenious synopses of the great films of the 1950s?

Not substantially, I would say. But I could not in all decency simply hang up on him, or tell him the bathtub was overflowing or the dog had eaten poison. I could not tell him I had suddenly become very tired, or remembered that I had to go out to fill a prescription. I could not tell him that, wonder of wonders, the truck had just pulled up outside and Ralph was beeping for me to come out and retrieve my suitcase, my books, my scripts. No, I was bound to see this conversation to its end, until Wadsworth was done talking. And he had a great deal more to say, as it turned out. He wanted me to know something about the pecking order among the writers at Warners, in which he saw himself as someone who pecked a great deal more than he got pecked. He wanted to tell me certain things about Bernie Wiseman, and how to impress him in an interview. He wanted to discuss my treatments other than *Four O'Clock* and *The Contender*, their relative strengths and weaknesses, and which ones I should show Wiseman. My participation largely comprised variations on "yes" and "uh-huh" and "oh, really?" until Lorna, after a good five minutes at the window, turned and shrugged at me. I shrugged in return, and she placed her palms together in what I first assumed was a symbol of prayer. But when she completed the pantomime by closing her eyes and resting her cheek against her hands, I realized this meant "sleep."

And I took advantage of a nearly simultaneous pause on Wadsworth's part to say, "Bill, Lorna's telling me that she's going up to bed," hoping that he'd ask to speak to her, and *she* might be able to suggest that he and I continue our conversation in the morning. But it was not to be. "Tell her goodnight for me, would you?" Wadsworth said.

"Bill says good night," I told Lorna. She nodded and approached me, and for a moment I expected she was going to take the telephone and rescue me. But instead she kissed my cheek and departed, leaving me with what must have been another thirty minutes on the phone—

most of it spent with half a mind listening to Wadsworth, half a mind contemplating that kiss just before the telephone rang.

It occurred to me at about a quarter after ten, some twenty minutes after Lorna had gone upstairs, that this might be a scheme on Wadsworth's part: if he called me every night shortly before her bedtime, nothing could ever happen between us. To be sure, he said nothing between 9:40 and 10:20 that couldn't have waited until the following day, and only at the very end of the conversation did he suggest a specific strategy—that he would show *Four O'Clock* to Wiseman tomorrow, or at least put it on his desk, that I should come to the studio around noon for lunch. I expressed my gratitude for the sixtieth time, and Wadsworth said, "Oh, my gosh, would you look at the time! I'd completely lost track." And that was that.

I crept upstairs and stood in the hallway between our two bedrooms, waiting for my eyes to adjust to the darkness. Lorna's door was open, as always, and after a minute or so I could make her out clearly—under the covers, sleeping on her side. I whispered her name, and got no response. I tiptoed inside and stood by the bed, wondering whether I should wake her, whether I should simply slide in next to her. In the end I did neither, but went next door and brushed my teeth.

11

Sleep was slow in coming, sporadic when it arrived. I woke at one point to a surprising stillness, wondered briefly if I'd failed to emerge from a dream. There was no rain, no wind; it was three-thirty in the morning. I got up and walked to the window, raised it, and felt nothing more than a cool, docile breeze. The storm had passed. The sky was not absolutely clear, but stars twinkled here and there. Still, I imagined, many tons of rain-saturated cliff could come plunging down onto the Roosevelt Highway hours after the rain had stopped. Back in bed, I fell asleep with a vengeance.

I didn't stir until eight o'clock, by which time Lorna was gone. With trepidation I put on my pants and went downstairs. Was there a note? No. The sun was out. The day was cool, but hardly wintry. The beach was covered with debris, fifty or sixty feet beyond the normal tideline.

The telephone worked. Had this after all *not* been Hudnut's Great Storm? If there had been power or telephone interruptions they'd been minor and brief in Malibu, hardly consistent with Hudnut's recollections of failed communications between East Coast and West.

I called to request a taxi for 9:30. I asked the dispatcher if there'd been any trouble on the Roosevelt Highway. Not a bit, he replied. There were roads closed all over town, but the Roosevelt, as far as he knew, was in excellent condition.

— —

My taxi took me to the Buick dealership in Santa Monica. As a small child, barely able to discern one automobile from another, I had been unaccountably fascinated by Buicks. Now, with no *Consumer Reports* to turn to, with no reliable Japanese alternative available, it seemed a case of as well Buick as another. I chose a dark green Special Convertible Coupé, like Lorna's a two-seater, otherwise not terribly similar. It was huge, with great, wide running boards and a long, down-sloped rear. "You won't be lacking for power with this baby," the salesman assured me. "Got the standard Buick V-eight, with a hundred and seven horses. You do a lot of traveling? She's got the double rear deck lids, one for your rumble seat, then the lower one for your spare and a small grip or two. Your big bags go right behind the driver's seat. Plenty of room."

How much for all this? I peeled eleven hundred-dollar bills and one fifty from my bankroll and handed them to the salesman, a pleasant young man in a fedora, who had doubtless never made so easy a commission.

With the top up on a cool, gray morning—all the better to immerse oneself in new-car sensations—I found my way cautiously over hill and dale toward Burbank. I needed neither map nor directions, but often wished I were behind the wheel of a bulldozer. There were trees down everywhere, vehicles overturned, streets flooded where storm drains had clogged.

I took Santa Monica Boulevard to Highland, followed Highland through the hills to Barham Boulevard, which ran into Olive virtually at Warners' doorstep. The Buick at first seemed huge and unwieldy; it

probably weighed twice as much as my Toyota, and without power steering it was like cornering in a medium-sized truck. But by the time I reached Burbank I'd come to feel at ease with my car.

Bill Wadsworth awaited me outside the second-class commissary, as hale and chipper as before. He had great news for me: Bernie Wiseman, the "fourth or fifth most important man on the lot," had looked at my western treatment this morning and been impressed.

"He loved it, Gabriel. Went absolutely crazy for it. He wanted to know when you could come in for a chat and I said hell, I'm having lunch with him at noon. So if it's all right with you, old pal, we can go straight from here to Bernie's office."

Was it all right with me? Seventy hours removed from 1994, I was falling in love with the woman of my dreams and I was about to be hired as a screenwriter at Warner Brothers. "I think I could make room for that on my schedule," I said.

"You're a kidder," Wadsworth said. There had been no change in his tone nor his expression, but the remark itself implied some dissatisfaction with my response. That surprised me, because I thought my tone had been identical to his. Perhaps I was being oversensitive here. Perhaps this had something to do with the fact that the man across the table from me was doing me a tremendous favor and I had designs on his girlfriend. Before I could say anything at all, Wadsworth resumed. "Was the storm pretty bad out there?"

"Very bad. Very loud. I was afraid the waves might come all the way up to the house. How was it in your part of town?"

"Hollywood? Windy as hell. Damn fools trying to drive in winds like that, with the rain coming down, can't see a thing." He shook his head. "I understand there's another one on the way."

"Another one?"

"Another storm in the Pacific. They say it might be worse than what we've just had."

"Good Lord, no," I said.

"But what in hell do they know?" Wadsworth gestured toward the ceiling. "Doesn't look particularly ominous to me."

Bernie Wiseman, a well-dressed man of about forty who ranked not too far below Warners' chief of production, Hal B. Wallis, told me that while he had certain reservations about my work, and while he usually wished to see more from a writer than just the few treatments Wadsworth had shown him, he was going to go out on a limb and offer me employment as a contract writer at Warners. He offered a salary that seemed quite reasonable to me, but Wadsworth gave me a little kick in the ankle that I interpreted to mean *ask for more*, so I hemmed and hawed a bit, and ended up getting an extra twenty dollars a week, a figure that Wadsworth seemed to find appropriate.

"All right, then." Wiseman reached across his broad desk to shake my hand. We could barely make contact. "When can you start?"

"How about tomorrow?"

"Tomorrow it is."

Wadsworth walked me to my car, looked it over. "So, you're a convertible man."

"Guess I am."

"Not me. I prefer a roof over my head. I won't get in that little thing of Lorna's unless I have to." He gave my back a healthy slap. "Well, congratulations, old pal. You're on board. You're officially a screenwriter."

"I can't thank you enough."

He made powerful eye contact. "Gabriel, now that this is all taken care of, is there anything you want to tell me?"

I felt myself flinch, struggled to maintain my gaze. "What sort of thing would I want to tell you, Bill?"

"Anything about your past." I exhaled. Wadsworth said, "You're pretty much of a mystery man. You don't seem to have existed at Princeton. There's no mention of you in any of the yearbooks."

"I daresay that's true of quite a few of us anonymous types."

He slapped my back again. "You don't really strike me as the anonymous type."

—◆—

During the drive back to Malibu the sun made periodic appearances through the clouds. The weather was definitely getting better by the hour. I cruised the radio dial in search of information; what I got was an awful lot of big band music and a fair amount of theater.

I sat down with the *Times* at about four-thirty. Hermann Göring had given the world warning that the Luftwaffe was prepared to "protect tens of millions of Germans on our borders." Goering's speech had been widely interpreted as aggressive and expansionist. Look out, Austria and Czechoslovakia. My namesake Gabriele D'Annunzio, the amoralist/fascist soldier/poet, had died at age seventy-five in Italy.

The next thing I knew Lorna was urging me awake. "Gabriel! For God's sake, why didn't you come by the set and tell me you got the job? I had to find out from Bill."

"It didn't seem like the right thing to do."

"Why not?"

"I feel pretty evil where Bill's concerned. It's hard not to see myself as a hypocrite when I look at you . . ."

"We haven't done anything."

"It's my fondest hope that at some point we will."

She sat next to me on the couch. "You're so . . . sweet, Gabriel. You're so unlike him. You can be mature, and graceful, and endearing. You have to understand, Bill has no hold on me. We're all adults."

"But obviously he's helping me because I'm your friend, or your family's friend . . ."

"And because you're schoolmates."

"No. I don't think he even believes I went to Princeton."

"God!" Lorna snorted. "He's such a snob! I get so fed up with him. He's a complacent, narrow-minded snob."

"All I know," I said, "is that he seems to be a very nice guy, he got me in to see Wiseman, and thanks to him I have a job."

"You *mustn't* feel guilty, Gabriel. Just wait till you see Bill after he's had a few drinks, and I'm sure you won't have to wait too long for that. He's weak and he's mean."

I couldn't resist asking, "What did you see in him?"

"I'm not altogether sure."

—◗◖—

At twenty past six Lorna suggested driving into Santa Monica for hamburgers. The wind was picking up again, the surf was noticeably heavier. I said, "Why don't we just get something and cook here?"

"Fine. Except by the time we drive into Santa Monica, get the food, and drive back here I will have starved to death."

"What if we go west instead?"

"There's nothing there."

"Nothing?"

"There's a little town, Calabasas. There are some farms. If you head up the coast about an hour you come to Oxnard and Ventura."

"What if we go up one of the canyon roads? Wouldn't we find a market?"

"Gabriel, what's the point? There's nothing closer than Santa Monica."

I insisted that we take my car, and I drove with extreme caution on the various stretches of Roosevelt Highway where cliffs hovered above the roadway. The wind now seemed to be gusting to thirty or forty miles an hour; periodically my headlights picked up good-sized rocks that must recently have tumbled from above.

I insisted as well that we stop at the big Ralph's Market at Third and Wilshire (open till eight!) for some supplies. Chicken and sirloin steak were both on sale at twenty-nine cents a pound. If the storm were about to resume in earnest we might be marooned for several days, but in all probability we'd have no power. I bought us two chickens, plus six cans of tuna (fourteen cents per seven-ounce can) and six grapefruits (seventeen cents for the half dozen), some fresh lettuce and tomato, and a quart of olive oil for the outrageous sum of $1.05.

Dinner was filling and forgettable. Rain began to sprinkle as our hamburgers arrived. I hurried us up. Parked at most fifty feet from the restaurant door, we were good and wet when we got in the car. The rain had become a torrent by the time we reached the Roosevelt Highway, a deluge when we passed Sunset. From there to Malibu and the Colony ours was the only car on the road, in either direction. We listened to weather reports on the radio: power outages were being reported all over town; areas already flooded were preparing for a new tempest; schools would be closed, businesses shut. "You're not going to work tomorrow," I said to Lorna.

"What about you? What if you don't show up on your first day? That's not going to look very good."

"No one's going to show up. The studio's going to be closed."

"You can't be sure, Gabriel."

"Yes I can."

She laughed. "You've been here four days and you can predict the weather."

"It doesn't take much predicting. This isn't going to stop for a while."

Lorna's SS was in the garage. I pulled up directly by the front door; it was as if we had to pass under eight feet of Iguaçu Falls to get from the car to the house. Inside, it was pitch black. Lorna fumbled for the light switch in the alcove; I heard its solid click; darkness maintained. "Try the phone," I said.

"If I can find it." I heard her pick up the receiver and tap the cradle several times in rapid succession. "Nothing," she said.

There were candles, one flashlight, a pair of extra batteries. We read and talked until Lorna went up to bed at nine-thirty. I dozed off, woke up, dozed off, woke up to extraordinarily loud storm sounds: wind whistling supernally, gargantuan waves crashing a few feet from the house, trees breaking from the force of the wind.

I knew, of course, that the house was safe. I had every reason to suspect Lorna was not. At some point in the dead of night I seized the flashlight, slipped into the garage, opened the hood of the SS, and removed its distributor cap. She would not steal away this morning; if the cliff were going to fall, it would have to do so in her absence.

I was stretched out on the couch when she descended at five, in her nightgown, looking beautiful and sleepy. The storm raged unabated. She said, "Hi. Why aren't you in bed?"

"Fell asleep here," I replied.

She padded to the phone, picked it up, put it down. "Not working," she said. She stopped by the couch, leaned down, and kissed my forehead. "Go to bed, Gabriel."

"What about you?"

"Going back to bed."

Had we collaborated, Lorna and I, in beating the Reaper?

— • —

We had no electricity, no telephone, and by midday no running water. She was still not convinced that Warners would actually shut down just because much of Southern California had been washed away, she feared that the two of us would turn out to be lone truants. We had tuna sandwiches. We had the car radio. All major stations had remained on the air and were broadcasting nonstop weather updates. This was now officially the heaviest storm in a quarter century. Los Angeles was isolated by air, by road, by rail. At least thirty people had been killed in the storm, most of them drowned. Rain would continue for at least another twenty-four hours, but its intensity would lessen gradually, as would the wind's. All this was received and digested by a vast and drenched community sitting, much as ourselves, in automobiles, because there was power almost nowhere and there would not be a transistor for another decade or so.

What was there to do? Saturated with storm news in the early afternoon, we read. After an hour of reading, we ventured out on the porch in rain gear and watched the surf pound the beach. This morning's high tide had stopped some thirty feet short of the house, and Lorna wondered whether the next one might sweep it away. "If the people on the radio are right," I said wisely, "we don't have anything to worry about."

At three o'clock, during a slight lull in the storm, I thought I heard a knock at the front door. Who would be out in this weather? Perhaps a neighbor in distress. Lorna was upstairs; I called her name and went to the door, arriving just as it opened and a very tall, extremely wet man stepped inside. "I'm Charles Hudnut," he said. "Who are you?"

In the two anxious minutes before Lorna joined us, I attempted to identify myself, to assure Charles Hudnut that Lorna was upstairs and in good health, to establish that I was simply a friend staying over for a few days, and to figure out who he was and how he'd gotten here. Charles, meanwhile, having gradually divested himself of his saturated outer clothing, revealed an eerie resemblance to Jasper Hudnut, or to what Jasper might have looked like thirty years before I met him—all of which was especially odd because Charles (if I had this figured right) was Jasper's uncle.

Lorna arrived at last, descending the staircase bearing a candle, as if she'd stepped out of a nineteenth-century novel. She said, "Charles— how in God's name did you get here?"

"It's a long story," he said, "which I'll be happy to tell you. But I must say I'm delighted to see you're all right." There ensued another anxious moment during which the three of us stood in the alcove waiting for someone to take charge. Lorna said, "I keep wanting to offer you a cup of hot tea, but I'm afraid I wouldn't be able to make you one."

"I'd take some brandy," Charles said. That we could do. Charles went upstairs to change his clothes. I said, "Is this all right? I'm not getting you into trouble?"

"Of course not. I think we've made it quite clear we're not lovers. For that matter, if we *were* lovers I don't think it would make a bit of difference to Charles, or anyone else in my family, as long as we didn't make a spectacle of ourselves."

Charles returned, now wearing white tennis gear under a heavy red-and-white checked jacket. He sipped brandy from a snifter and began the tale of his adventure. "Your mother," he said to Lorna, and then to me, "My sister," and then to Lorna, "got through to us yesterday before the lines went down in Glendale. Evidently on the East Coast they've heard we're experiencing Armageddon, and I suppose that's not too far from the truth. She said she'd been trying to reach you since Sunday, with no luck. I called Warners this morning, but of course they're all shut down."

Lorna gave me a quick look of acknowledgment. Charles said, "So I talked it over with Sally, and we decided I should come out here and see if you were all right. I left Glendale at nine o'clock sharp. Normally it takes no more than an hour to get here. I've made it in forty minutes, in the Packard. I can't tell you the number of detours I took. Every place there's a bridge, it seems, you have to take the long way around, and there've been floods everywhere. Huge accidents. I was in Hollywood when I heard on the radio that the Roosevelt Highway was closed in Santa Monica. So I took Ventura Boulevard west. Then I heard there'd been floods in Santa Monica Canyon and Topanga Canyon, so I went all the way to Calabasas. The Highway Patrol had Malibu Canyon Road closed, but I convinced them to let me through. There were a couple of big slides, but I managed to get nearly all the way to the highway before I had to leave the car and walk."

"Good lord, Charles," Lorna said, "how far did you have to walk?"

"Not particularly far. Three miles, at most. But I'll tell you, I certainly was relieved to get that first glimpse of the Colony—to see it was all still here. The first person I saw past the gatehouse was Frank Capra—"

"The director?" I interrupted.

"He's about five houses up from here. He said there are at least sixty people marooned in the Colony. Evidently some of them were pretty concerned during the night."

"I had no idea," Lorna said.

"Capra said they prevailed upon Wally Beautrow from the Malibu Patrol to get through to Santa Monica—"

"We were there last night," Lorna said. "The road was fine."

"You're lucky, then," Charles resumed. "Wally evidently had to drive his vehicle over some fifteen-foot slides. Apparently at about seven-thirty this morning there was a huge landslide right onto the highway, and some poor sons of guns got buried under it. Nobody knows whether they were crushed or suffocated, but either way it's a pretty horrible way to go."

And if not for my intervention, it was the way Lorna would have gone. I recall thinking at the time how odd it was that she'd never know I'd saved her life.

— —

Charles spent the night, of course. He was a fine fellow, if a bit dour, a structural engineer with a thriving business in the burgeoning San Fernando Valley. He was forty-three, the third of four siblings—younger than Jasper's father (Edgar) and Lorna's mother (Joanna), older than brother Wilfred.

I had to reprise the story of my arrival here, which seemed far flimsier now than during its euphoric creation. And Charles had to have a look at the boat I'd brought for Edgar. Of course he was full of questions about it, which forced me into abject defense mode. I knew virtually nothing about the boat—only that I'd been asked to transport it. Charles made me promise to find out what I could about it; he was a sailor of sorts, and very interested in plastics.

— —

Thursday dawned drizzly and windy. I shared the front seat of my Buick with Charles for a postsunrise hour, listening to the radio, learning that the storm's worst was probably finished, but that flooding was still a threat, that outlying areas might be without electricity and telephone service for days to come. In 1938 there were few areas more outlying than Malibu.

Charles urged Lorna and me to trek with him back to his Packard; he and Sally could put us both up in Glendale. I urged Lorna to go. In return for hospitality already extended, I said, the least I could do was stay here and mind the house until all had reverted to normal. At nine o'clock, they set off.

That afternoon, walking on the beach in a cool, breezy mist, I encountered a young woman with a large dog, the two of them admiring the spectacular surf. We chatted briefly; she seemed familiar. That evening, enjoying a can of tuna by candlelight, I realized who she was: Madeleine Carroll, who'd starred in Hitchcock's *The 39 Steps*.

Friday afternoon the highway was cleared. Early Saturday morning I took the Buick out and reconnoitered. Everything near the canyon roads had been demolished by floods; otherwise, damage between Malibu and Santa Monica was minor. The Gold Coast, the stretch of Roosevelt Highway in Santa Monica inhabited by the likes of Cary Grant, Mae West, Darryl Zanuck, Samuel Goldwyn, and Marion Davies, was unscathed.

I bought a copy of the local paper, the *Outlook*, and found in the classifieds a tidy little ground-floor studio apartment just off Olympic Boulevard. The neighborhood was seedy but benign, the rent thirty dollars a month. The landlady told me she'd just replaced all the kitchen appliances. They didn't look terribly new to me, but no matter: the apartment wasn't for my use. While it might have been sensible, even prudent, to separate myself from the Hudnut house, and

while I had been no stranger to self-denial at earlier stages of my life, I was not about to move away from Lorna.

Late Saturday night I stuffed the machine, swathed in blankets, into the Buick; it would only fit with the top down, so we had a chilly ride into Santa Monica. I hauled it into the apartment, double-locked the front door, and returned to the Colony with the top up and the heat on.

Sunday the sun shone on Malibu. In the early afternoon I heard a car outside, looked out the window, and saw Lorna emerging from Charles's huge Packard.

She did not notice the machine's absence. I asked her if, under the circumstances, it would be a good idea for me to move out. Of course not, she said emphatically.

Monday morning we drove together to our jobs at Warner Brothers.

PART II

DUTCH
TAKES A
RIGHT
TURN

12

"It seems to me," Bill Wadsworth was saying, "that there's a useful lesson in this for the rest of Europe. God knows I don't condone loss of life in any form, but what happened over the weekend has got to be sobering to the Communists everywhere. It's got to make them think twice, don't you think?"

What had happened over the weekend was the bombing of Barcelona by Francisco Franco's insurgents. Preliminary estimates were that at least a thousand people had been killed. The great Southern California storm, by last count, had killed eighty-five. Wadsworth and I were en route to the second-class commissary at noon on a sunny March 7.

While eager to talk about the war, he didn't recall the Condor Legion's bombing of Guernica, and seemed generally not to be a terribly keen observer of the passing parade. But he had his opinions. "I mean, Gabriel, there's no denying the Communists were a dominating force in the Republican government. A man like Franco, who I believe is a true democrat as well as a patriot, isn't about to start a revolution unless he believes his country's in very real danger."

I believe *constrained* is the word that best describes my condition in this conversation. In that I knew how everything would come out, in that I had a passing knowledge of the next fifty-some years of Spanish history, I was prepared to argue on a much higher level, but of course I couldn't. It was rather like participating in some genteel martial arts exhibition with both arms tied behind my back, plus a pulled hamstring. I imagined this would not be my only—or my most frustrating—experience of the phenomenon. "Bill," I said, "let me understand something. Do you believe that all of Europe is in danger of falling to Communism?"

"I certainly do. Before Mussolini the Communists were very strong in Italy. They're an important force in France, as well as Greece. All across the Balkans, for that matter. Eastern Europe I think is safe for now because Hitler and Stalin came to terms."

We entered the commissary and installed ourselves at the back of a longish line. Lorna would be joining us in fifteen or twenty minutes. I said, "But if Franco's going to win, if Mussolini's going to stay in power, if the Germans and the Russians are going to glare at each other across Poland and the Baltic states, where do the Communists pose a threat?"

"Greece," Wadsworth replied. "Yugoslavia, Bulgaria, Albania, Rumania, the whole region."

"And do you think, if all those countries were to turn Communist, that would truly have an effect on the rest of the world?"

"I do, Gabriel. I believe Communism is a cancer. I think it's got to be eliminated wherever it takes hold."

"And you think the deaths of a thousand civilians in Barcelona are justified because of that?" It was not I who had spoken. The question—much more direct and dramatic than anything I had in mind—came from behind us, from a voice whose cadence and tone were eerily familiar, whose pitch was a little wrong, as if it had been electronically altered.

Ronald Reagan was about Wadsworth's height, a couple of inches taller than I. He wore a contemporary brown suit, double-breasted, and thick-lensed glasses with brown frames. "I don't mean to butt in," he said, "but this is a subject that sets me off."

Wadsworth made a barely audible noise, what I interpreted to be a derisive snort. "Your question's really very disingenuous, you know. There's no point quantifying something like this. I mean, a *thousand civilians*, as if the Republicans hadn't committed atrocities of their own . . ."

"The Loyalists," Reagan interjected.

"What difference does it make what we call them? The point is, Franco's trying to put as quick an end as possible to what's been a very messy war. Better to have a few hundred innocent people die today than a few thousand spread over the next several years, wouldn't you say?"

"There'd have been no deaths at all if Franco hadn't started the war." Reagan had appeared momentarily intimidated by Wadsworth's extended sneer, but was bouncing right back. "There'd have been no deaths at all if the Fascists had given democracy a chance to work."

"Oh, *really*," Wadsworth said, his voice exuding contempt. "What do you know about this? The point is that democracy *wasn't* working, *hadn't* worked. Have you been to Spain?"

"No, I haven't. Have you?"

"I have, as a matter of fact. More to the point, a good friend of mine from college lived there for five years before the war. Did business there, in Madrid, traveled all over the country. He says it's a land of peasants. Delightful people, with no desire whatsoever to run their own government. For centuries these people have been pushed around by one tyrant or another. They need order. They need authority."

"Well," Reagan said just as Wadsworth and I picked up our trays at the head of the line, "I don't see what bombing civilians has to do with order. Seems to me that's more along the lines of disorder."

I ordered the chicken fricassee. While Wadsworth's attention was on his lunch-to-be, I turned to Reagan. "I couldn't agree with you more. And I thought you put it very well."

"Well, thanks," he grinned. "Say, by the way, I'm Dutch Reagan." He pronounced it "Reegan."

I put my tray down and offered my hand. "Gabriel Prince. Pleasure to meet you, Dutch. This is Bill Wadsworth." Wadsworth was forced into a perfunctory handshake.

"The spaghetti here is the cat's pajamas," Reagan said. "Hey, you fellows mind if I join you?"

Wadsworth had already taken a step toward our table. He whispered to me, "Get rid of him, for God's sake."

By the time a mountain of fat strands of pasta drenched in scarlet meat sauce had been deposited on Reagan's plate, Wadsworth was well out of earshot. "If you don't mind sitting with a couple of writers," I said.

Dutch Reagan did appear fond of the sound of his own voice. Ten minutes after we'd all sat down (with me in the middle) Wadsworth and I were both done with our food while Reagan had barely scraped the top off his Vesuvius. He told us how frustrating it was to eat with his fellow actors day after day; after acting and talking about acting all morning on the set, they would proceed to talk about acting all through lunch, as if the outside world didn't exist. And there was so much happening in the outside world! He believed, he said, that the writers were probably the smartest group, certainly the best educated group, on the lot. He himself, unlike many of his fellow actors, had a college degree. He assumed we did as well. "Princeton," Wadsworth uttered his first word since we'd sat down. "Me too," I said.

"So you fellows are old friends," he said. "That's swell."

"Actually, we didn't know each other there," I said.

Reagan beamed. "Well, that's even better, isn't it? Obviously you were meant to be pals. You missed each other at college for one reason or another, but now destiny's caught up with you here at Warners." He took a huge forkful of pasta, strands of it dangling from his mouth. "Princeton," he resumed. "Hobey Baker. Woodrow Wilson. What a great tradition. It must give you goose bumps just to stroll around the place, surrounded by all that history."

"Dear Lord, save me," Wadsworth murmured. Our seating arrangement was such that Reagan might not have heard him.

It seemed an opportune moment to resume our political discussion. "With all deference to your friend the businessman, Bill, I think there's an aspect of the Spanish situation that you're both ignoring. You talk about Spain as if it's homogeneous, as if it's composed of a few million peasants wandering around in search of leadership, when in fact it's a very diverse country, with several ethnically distinct regions. If he wins the war I don't think Franco really has to worry about Communists—"

"Gabriel, for God's sake, are you denying that the Communists are the heart of the Republican side?"

I was surprised by the anger in Wadsworth's voice. But of course he was in most uncomfortable territory—starting to realize that I knew quite a bit more about Spain than he, not wishing to be humiliated in front of the starry-eyed idiot who'd barged into our company.

"Of course he is." Reagan spoke before I could formulate a response. "Why are you so damned obsessed with the Communists?"

"Because they're a goddamn *cancer*," Wadsworth said to Reagan, acknowledging his presence for the first time since we'd sat down. "Because they're a threat to our way of life! It's a wonder to me you wide-eyed idealists can't see that."

"Hold it!" I said. "Gentlemen, let's not give ourselves indigestion over this. Bill, I'm certainly aware that there's a strong Communist presence on the Republican side. But I'm trying to point out that the war in Spain isn't a Communist-versus-capitalist struggle—"

"Exactly," Reagan cut in when I'd made the briefest of pauses. "It's a fascism-versus-democracy struggle."

I had intended to conclude my previous argument, to suggest that the war was between one side that wished to create a monolithic Spain, something that had previously existed only in myth and could never truly exist otherwise, and another side that wished to struggle toward some sort of modern, egalitarian society that would recognize all of Spain's diversity. Before I could speak, two things happened. The first was my recognition that Reagan had already—simplistically, obtusely, effectively—taken the words out of my mouth. The second was that Wadsworth shifted in his chair and waved.

It was Lorna coming through the door. She saw him, saw *us*, and waved in response. I cannot better describe my emotions at that moment than to say that seeing her thrilled me. I had expected her to walk into the commissary at about this time, so there was hardly an element of surprise. I did not expect that her presence would improve the social situation, so there was no element of expediency. I was simply thrilled to watch her take her place at the end of the line—now much shorter than it had been fifteen minutes earlier—and spot us, and wave. It was not even my role to stand up and join her. That went to Wadsworth, who said, "Pardon me, Gabriel," and got to his feet without so much as a glance at the B-movie contract player who'd been annoying him.

Reagan sat with his back to the entrance. A small, pleasant smile played on his lips. "Have I gotten under his skin or something?"

"I guess you have."

"I seem to do that." The smile broadened.

I was staring at Lorna. With Wadsworth at her side, she'd already taken a tray and reached the ordering stage. I saw her in profile. She was in costume, in another low-cut gown, one visible high cheekbone accentuated by makeup. Looking at her, I was exhilarated, filled with joy, with anticipation. As Wadsworth towered over her, chatting, she looked intermittently in my direction, and I must have made some sort of response.

"I've met her," Reagan said. "What's her name again?"

I redirected my gaze. "Lorna Fairchild." I could have left it at that, but I felt oddly obliged to continue. "I'm a friend of her family's."

Lorna sat down. She had chosen the fricassee as well. She sat next to Wadsworth, nearly facing me. "So," she said to me, "you found your friend of the friend of the truckdriver." She turned to Reagan. "Hello, Dutch. Nice to see you."

"Nice to see you, Lorna," Reagan replied. He turned to me. "What's this about the friend of the truckdriver?"

"Nothing," I said, experiencing a little chill, a vague fear that my web of artifice might be in some danger. "I rode out here from New Jersey with a truckdriver named Ralph who had a friend who knew you."

"No kidding? Knew me from where? I've never even been in New Jersey."

"Ralph works out of Chicago, actually. He's from a town south of there . . ."

"Not Dixon? That's my hometown."

"Doesn't ring a bell."

"Well, what was his friend's name? You've got me on the edge of my seat."

Certainly the phantasmic Ralph would have mentioned his pal's name somewhere along our journey of three thousand miles plus. I noted that Wadsworth seemed to be eyeing me very carefully at this juncture. "Bush, I believe," speaking the first name that popped into my head. "Dan Bush, perhaps, or Dave Bush?"

Reagan shook his head. "No, I don't believe I knew any Bushes in Dixon. The only Bush who comes to my mind was Joe Bush, who used to pitch in the American League."

"Bullet Joe Bush," I said. It was not for nothing, evidently, that I had spent several childhood summers immersed in baseball lore.

Reagan's eyes illuminated. "Are you a fan, Gabriel?"

I saw myself dancing away from peril. "When I was a boy. Not so much anymore." I did in fact still have an affection for the New York Mets, who unfortunately were not to see the light of day for another twenty-four years. "I love the game, though."

"Say, they've got a couple of pretty good teams here, you know, the Stars and the Angels. Interested in a game some Saturday afternoon?"

"Why not?" I said.

"Did you know, I used to broadcast the Cubs games in Iowa," Reagan said, delighted to have found a subject on which he was clearly the local expert. "They're training right now on Catalina Island. I know all the fellows—Billy Herman, Stan Hack, Gabby Hartnett. . . ."

"Big Bill Lee," I said, another name I'd quite inadvertently memorized in 1964 or so.

"See," Reagan grinned, "you still know what's going on. Let's take the boat out there some morning, what do you say?"

I looked at Wadsworth. "I'm not sure I can get away."

Wadsworth—who evidently knew as much about baseball as I did about the Princeton faculty circa 1927—spoke to Reagan. "The Cubs are located in Chicago, aren't they? How in God's name were you broadcasting their games in Iowa?"

Reagan, having been given carte blanche, launched into a dissertation on the re-creation of baseball games, the technology and the cultural significance thereof. I watched Lorna consume her chicken; watched the little bit of cleavage above her gown. She looked up at me as Reagan was imitating for Wadsworth's dubious benefit the recorded sound of bat meeting ball. Her eyes met mine, and all was well in my world.

— —

"I don't want you to get a swelled head," Bernie Wiseman said, "but I showed your treatment to Hal, and he was crazy about it." He referred to my western, *Four O'Clock*. Hal, I could be fairly sure, was Hal Wallis, who answered to no one but Jack Warner. I had spent most of my working hours the past two weeks on the actual script of *Four O'Clock*, had submitted my first draft yesterday to Wiseman, who would be the line producer for the picture.

"I'm flattered," I replied. Wiseman was behind a huge oaken desk whose broad surface was decidedly uncluttered; there was a heavy, brown, modernistic swiveling lamp, a large ceramic ashtray to accommodate the succession of Chesterfields Wiseman sucked down, a telephone, and there was one script. The other dominant feature of his office—more than twice the size of Wadsworth's—was a zebra skin on the wall to my rear. I wondered whether Wiseman had shot the zebra or it had just wandered into his office and died.

"Don't be flattered, Gabriel. Nobody's flattering you. A very important man with excellent taste and a record for making big, successful pictures likes your idea. That's not flattery, that's a compliment. You're a Princeton man, I'm sure you understand the difference." Wiseman looked to be in his early forties. He was short and lean with strikingly sharp features—a long, pointed nose and strong, angular chin. His black hair was cut short and he made no effort to cover a monkish bald spot. He wore reading glasses and an impeccable gray suit.

"I'm complimented, then." This was the first time we'd sat down together since he hired me. I must admit that my reservations about borrowing from works not yet created had eroded as I worked on the script. While I had by no means kidded myself into thinking *Four O'Clock* was my original idea, I don't believe there was a single line of dialogue that wasn't my creation. I had made other significant changes in storyline and characterization and, if anything, I believe that my plot and pacing were tighter and more effective.

"You know what this means?" Wiseman said, lighting a Chesterfield some two minutes after he'd extinguished its predecessor. "This means we're talking about an A picture, Gabriel. It's not very often someone walks on this lot and writes an A picture for us, right off the bat. Do you understand that?"

"I do, Mr. Wiseman."

"Please. I'm not that much older than you. Call me Bernie. What I'm getting at here, Gabriel, I think you're a talented man. I don't want to hand this script over to some hack for a rewrite. You're a talented man, but you're new at this game, and maybe sometimes you're thinking a little more about art and what have you than putting people in theaters. You understand what I'm talking about?"

"I'm not sure."

"For instance, what is this cutting? The wife's at the train station, the outlaw's waiting for the train, the sheriff's back in town, you've got what, in maybe three minutes of film you've got maybe twenty, twenty-five cuts. You can't do that. You make people seasick. They'll be puking in their popcorn."

Wiseman would probably live to see the French New Wave, either be dead or a very old man by the time MTV arrived. It was just as well. "I thought it helped build the tension," I said. "But it's not important to me. If you want fewer cuts, I'll make fewer cuts."

"And what about these damn shots of the clock? It's like every two minutes you've got a shot of the clock. Gabriel, look, the audience may be stupid, but they can tell time. Most of them. You establish the goddamn train's coming at four o'clock, you tell them a few times at the start of the picture, then once in a while you show the fucking clock, not every five seconds."

He was probably right about the cuts. A movie with that many in 1938 would thrill cineasts around the world, but wouldn't play in Peoria, or in Burbank. The clock, however, was a very different matter. "No," I said. "The clock's essential."

Wiseman looked at me as if he'd just discovered me smothering his cat. "How many pictures have you made?"

"None."

"How many have I made?"

"Quite a few, I'm sure."

"Thirty-two. Who's going to know what's *essential?* Some college boy that just dropped into the business, or somebody that's produced thirty-two pictures?"

"In most cases I would go with the latter," I said, "but this time—with all due respect, Bernie—you're wrong."

"I'm *wrong?*" Wiseman leaned back in his chair and grinned at me. Was it a grin of appreciation for my candor, or was it the sort of grin a baboon shows an insubordinate underling before biting him to death? The chair returned to earth and Wiseman said in quite a normal voice, "Tell me why I'm wrong."

As usual, my best evidence was inadmissable. I couldn't mention the test audiences in 1952 who'd hated the version without the clock, nor the Academy Award for the version with the clock. "Because the clock is a constant frame of reference. The closer it gets to four o'clock, the more often we see the clock. It's not just that we see the clock, but that we hear the clock ticking. At the start of the picture, when the marshal finds out what's in store, it's as if he's got all the time in the world. When it gets to be three, then three-thirty, then quarter to four, and it becomes clearer and clearer that no one's going to help him, that he's going to face four dangerous men on his own, then that clock becomes his enemy. It's ticking away what's left of his life."

Wiseman nodded slowly; there was nothing simian about this little smile. "You put it well. I'm not saying I agree with you, necessarily, but you put it well. I can see what you're saying."

"So the clock stays?"

"Maybe it stays. What does it cost to photograph a clock? If I'm right, if it doesn't work, we take it out."

"Good," I said. "That's a relief."

Still nodding, studying me, he said, "Have you thought at all about casting? I mean, it's not like your opinion makes any difference, but I'd be interested who you see in the two starring roles."

"The marshal, I'm not sure . . ."

"I talked to Flynn about it. He likes the part."

"Errol Flynn? He's Australian, isn't he? Playing a marshal in the Old West with that accent?"

Wiseman shrugged. "Who knows he's Australian? Who cares?"

I shrugged in return. "For the wife, I did have someone in mind. She's not a star, but I think she'd be perfect. She looks right, sounds right, and even though it's the second biggest role in the picture, it's not that big a part. . . ."

"Stop with the song and dance, Gabriel."

"Lorna Fairchild," I said.

His face was blank for a moment. "Ah . . . pretty little B-picture girl? Kind of aristocratic? *Love on a Shoestring?*"

"That's the one."

His look became sly. "Gabriel, tell me. Is this the girl you're shacked up with?"

Shacked up with? "Why do you say that?"

Still sly. "I have it on good authority you're living in sin with one of our actresses."

"Not at all," I said. "I'm living in her family's house. Look, Bernie, it's embarrassing even to talk about this with you. I mean, Lorna introduced me to Bill Wadsworth, Bill introduced me to you. I assumed you knew about Lorna and Bill. I don't want anyone to have the wrong impression . . ."

Wiseman's expression now metamorphosed from sly to defensive. "Hey, everybody gossips. Everybody thinks this or that. I don't keep tabs on everybody at Warners, for Christ's sake." Finally, from defensive to avuncular. "Just the same, Gabriel, if I were you, I'd watch my step."

13

It was Thursday evening, the seventeenth of March. I had spent a few
moments this afternoon on the set of *Crime School*, watching
Humphrey Bogart work with the Dead End Kids in a movie I'd never
heard of back in my original time frame. Bogart, who of course had
been the gangster idolized by the kids in the original *Dead End*, was a
good guy, a reform school reformer, in this one. He did not appear to
be enjoying himself. I introduced myself during a break. Bogart said,
"Nice to meet you, Gabriel." I told him I thought he was the best

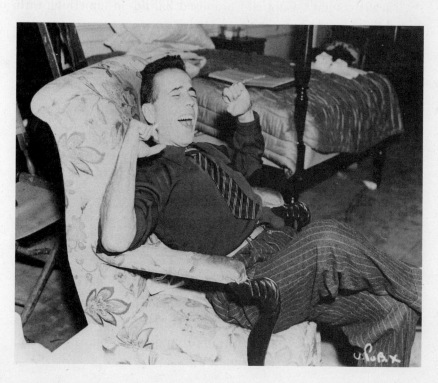

actor on the lot. He said, "Hey, then write something decent for me, would you?" I will not belabor the strangeness of being in the company of Leo Gorcey and Huntz Hall, electronic companions of my childhood, but I spent a good five minutes trying to decipher the identity of another actor before I realized that it was Doc from *Gunsmoke*, Milburn Stone, twenty years before his time.

Standing with Lorna in the kitchen, I felt a small wave of sadness, of frustration, at being unable to tell her that I'd met, that I'd had the briefest of conversations, with one of my idols. I was removing the skin from a gigantic chicken I'd bought at a farm up the road in Calabasas; Lorna was washing the breakfast dishes. For the third time since my arrival, Bill Wadsworth was coming to dinner.

I said, "What would you say to a trip to Santa Catalina?" I'd be going one way or the other; as much as I craved being with her, I was uncomfortably ambivalent awaiting her reaction.

"Sounds wonderful. When?"

"This weekend."

"I really couldn't, Gabriel. I promised Bill I'd do something with him. I think he's been feeling neglected."

"We could all go," I said. "Dutch Reagan's invited us to come along with him. The Cubs are having their spring training there."

"The Cubs are the baseball team Dutch used to talk about on the radio?"

"Exactly."

She shut off the water and turned to face me. "Gabriel, I don't know how to feel about this. It's a little complicated, wouldn't you say? I mean, Bill's been very much the gentleman, but I know he's jealous that I spend so much time with you, and you must know that Bill and I . . ."

"Have been lovers."

She looked away for a moment, then met my eyes again. "I'd feel a little uneasy," she said.

"It had crossed my mind," I said, "that if we invited Bill he wouldn't want to come. I don't think Dutch is one of his favorite people."

"I'm not sure he's one of mine, either. Dutch is a very sweet guy, but sort of boring and . . . unsophisticated. And Bill, as far as I can tell, despises him. Thinks he's a Communist."

What a curious moment it was, what a crossroads, what a choice for me to make. "I enjoy Dutch's company," I tried to choose my words very carefully. "And it's supposed to be a beautiful weekend. I'd like to go. If you'd rather not be with Dutch, it certainly wouldn't hurt my feelings if you didn't come."

She was silent for a long moment. "You're probably right. If we invite Bill he'll just say no."

"That would be my guess."

"But what if he doesn't? What if he thinks it's a great idea? He'll be expecting to spend the night with me. Wouldn't you care about that?"

"Of course I would. But I'm not a teenager, Lorna. I realize there's been something between the two of you, and it's not simply going to disappear . . ."

Did I detect tears forming in her eyes? She turned away from me, back toward the sink. This was turning out to be awfully difficult. I traversed the five feet of kitchen floor that separated us; I wiped chicken residue from my hands and let them rest on her shoulders. As I searched for a system, a sentence, a word, she spoke.

"Gabriel, I don't know what to make of you. Do you care about me?"

"Very much."

"And it doesn't bother you that I'd be in bed with another man while you were just down the hall?"

"Of course it bothers me." What was I to say next? That I couldn't afford to offend too quickly or too deeply the one man capable of sabotaging my house of cards? That I saw the weekend in Catalina as a vital, strategic time to spend with the man who was the reason for my being here? That I'd already begun hatching the plan that would turn the 1980s upside down and gratify Jasper Hudnut? I said, "But I can wait for you."

She turned to face me; she looked into my eyes. "I've never known anyone like you."

I kissed her lips. "Everything's fine," I said. "Everything's going to work out. It's just a matter of time."

I had made a chicken stir-fry, with rice and fresh peppers, tomatoes, and onions. It would have been perfect with some water chestnuts, but short of driving to Chinatown there was nowhere to find them.

Lorna had put together another tasty salad, thanks in part to the olive oil I'd found at the Ralph's in Santa Monica.

Wadsworth had put away two Scotch and sodas before dinner, was now midway through his second glass of California chablis. I had not yet discovered a reliable wine shop. He said, "Gabriel, I've got to hand it to you. I'm sure I'm repeating myself, but you're one hell of a cook."

"You're very kind, Bill."

"You do love chicken, though, don't you? Beggars shouldn't be choosers, I know, but tell me why it's always chicken."

"It's versatile," I said, "and it's healthy."

"Well, sure, but so's beef. I'm the last person to tell you how to cook, but substitute beef in this concoction of yours, you'd have yourself a more vigorous dish. More protein."

"I think it's fine the way it is," Lorna said. "When was the last time you saw the inside of a kitchen, Bill?"

"Hey, I'm not claiming I can cook, and Gabriel's obviously got the gift for it. I just think it's a little odd that he's so stuck on chicken."

"Actually," I said, "there's not that much protein difference between beef and chicken. And chicken's much better for your heart."

"Oh, please," Wadsworth said with a smirk, "sounds like you've been paying too much attention to Gayelord Hauser."

"Beef's very fatty, Bill. The fat causes a gradual clogging of your arteries. Does you in."

"Nonsense. My grandmother, my father's mother, has eaten beef I'd imagine every day since she was two, more or less. She's eighty-seven now and she's healthy as a horse."

Lorna said, "What about your grandfather?" I'd been about to ask the same question.

"Well, that's different," Wadsworth said.

"He died of a heart attack thirty years ago, didn't he, Bill?"

"That was because he worked himself to death, not because he ate beef, for God's sakes."

Wadsworth hardly spoke for the rest of the meal, and when he did it was to me, as if Lorna had betrayed him. After dinner Lorna poured him a snifter of cognac and he smoked one of his Cuban cigars. Each morning following one of Wadsworth's dinner visits the dining room was nearly intolerable; the cigar smoke seemed to cling to the walls. Lorna cleared the table and Wadsworth and I discussed my progress on *Four O'Clock*. After a time, Lorna returned and sat down next to him, across from me. She said, "Bill, Dutch Reagan's invited us all to join him on a trip to Catalina this weekend."

"Dutch Reagan? Why would we want to do anything with Dutch Reagan?"

"Gabriel's rather fond of him, I think."

Wadsworth gave me a quizzical look. "I do like him," I said.

He snorted, and thrust an inch of cigar ash into its ashtray. "His nickname's just a bit off the mark, you know. He should be Deutsch, not Dutch."

Lorna said, "Why should he be Deutsch? He's Irish, isn't he?"

"Because the Germans are always so cocky, so damned sure of themselves. They don't know a bloody thing, but they're full of facts and figures, just like our boy Deutsch."

Lorna resumed. "As far as I'm concerned, it's Catalina and not Dutch Reagan that's the important part. I've never been."

"Well, I have," Wadsworth said. "My dad used to charter a boat and take us all fishing, then we'd have dinner on Catalina and spend the night. It wasn't all that spectacular back then, and I daresay it's gone completely to hell now that the tourists have found it, not to mention the baseball teams."

After a brief silence Lorna said, "Well, I'd like to go."

Wadsworth swirled his cognac and sniffed it, sucked on his cigar, and propelled a great cloud of smoke toward the ceiling. Was he about to give us his blessing? "You, too, Gabriel? Another easterner drawn inexorably to the mountainous island wilderness? A writer of travel books who can't resist the call of a new resort, somewhat seedy though it may be? A baseball fan, like our pal Deutsch, eager to see the Chicago club in its western digs?"

"I couldn't have put it better."

Wadsworth took a huge swallow of cognac. "Well, far be it from me to be a killjoy . . ."

I had shifted my gaze to Lorna, whose own was fixed expectantly on Wadsworth. He continued, "So, why don't we make it a foursome? A double date." Lorna closed her eyes and turned her head so I could not see her expression; Wadsworth, I believe, was oblivious.

14

Our boat was scheduled to leave San Pedro at eight o'clock Saturday morning. The plan was for the three of us to drive there in Wadsworth's spacious Studebaker, but Wadsworth overslept. He was to have picked us up at six-thirty; when he hadn't appeared by six-forty, Lorna said, "Let's go without him."

"Give him another couple of minutes."

"Why?"

"He'll be pretty upset if we go without him, won't he?"

"So what, Gabriel? It's his responsibility to be on time. We're not going to miss the boat because Bill's in a stupor."

"Call him, then."

We stood in the little nook by the front door, two bags packed and ready to go. Lorna was four feet away from the telephone. She picked up the receiver and said, "Why am I doing this?"

"Because Bill's a decent guy."

"Old school tie," she said, and she dialed. We waited. Lorna said, "Seven rings . . . eight. Maybe he's on his way here. Nine rings. No, wait . . ." She covered the mouthpiece. "He's up. I woke him. Why don't we just go now, on our own? He can take a later boat if he wants."

"Just ask him, for God's sake."

"Bill?" Lorna spoke sweetly into the phone. "You're supposed to be here, dear." She listened. "No, it's too late now. We'll see you there." She hung up. "He must have had a few after he got home. He sounded terrible. Maybe he'll just go back to sleep."

Lorna drove us in her car. Thank God there wasn't much traffic. We zoomed along the coast, through Santa Monica, then inland to Lincoln Boulevard, to Sepulveda through El Segundo and Torrance. The poststorm cleanup had been remarkable: a few bridges were still out, but for the most part everything was up and running.

We made it to the ferry terminal at seven-thirty. Dutch Reagan was there ahead of us, looking like a bit player in a yachting movie: white pants, white sneakers, white shirt, blue blazer, captain's hat. He didn't acknowledge us until we were a few feet from him. I realized he wasn't wearing his glasses, that his vision must have been pretty awful without them, that not wearing them bespoke a fair degree of vanity. Dutch greeted me as if I were an old friend he hadn't seen in years, kissed Lorna on the cheek, asked, "Say, where's old Bill?"

"Overslept," Lorna said. "Maybe he'll make it, maybe he won't."

He did. We saw the Studebaker churn into the parking lot well after we'd boarded, just before the gangplank was pulled up. "Oh, my God," Lorna said. "Why did I call him? Why didn't I just let him sleep it off?" The cool look she gave me suggested that she wasn't the one to blame.

Wadsworth scrambled aboard, unshaven, unkempt, unticketed. The sun was brilliant; what little fog there had been was burned away. It was going to be a beautiful day. Lorna made her way to the purser's window and led Wadsworth to us. He lugged an oversized leather grip. "God," he said, "I hope it's not rough seas. I get ill at the first roll."

The Pacific, this little bit of it between San Pedro and Catalina, was as gentle as a duck pond. Still Wadsworth, the veteran sailor, got fairly green. "I never *enjoyed* the damn trips with my dad," he told Lorna. After a short night's sleep, I was content to laze in a deck chair on the bow, but Dutch was full of energy. He treated us to an hour of Catalina lore and history: "Did you know there was a *gold rush* on Catalina? Most people don't know that. Of course, it wasn't as big as the one up north. Fourteen years later. 1863. People came from all over. The problem was, it was so expensive to mine the gold, it really wasn't worth it. So it just fizzled out. Now, on the other hand, the sea otter trade, that was something else. Did you know sea otter pelts were the most desirable fur in the world in the early nineteenth century? No question about it. The Chinese, the Russians, they had to have sea otter fur. Of course that was what did in the Catalina Indians. Very friendly, very civilized, got along fine with the Spanish. Everything was fine until the Russian trappers showed up in 1806, oh-seven or so, just about wiped out the otters *and* the Indians. . . ."

When Dutch wandered away to toss doughnut chunks to the gang of gulls trailing the boat, Wadsworth wearily muttered, "If there are any Russian trappers left, do you suppose they'd be interested in a gabby contract player?"

We came ashore at Avalon, Catalina's main center of population and attraction, which possessed at once the stunning natural beauty of a Greek island and the primitive commercial vulgarity of the New Jersey shore towns I'd visited as a child. Dutch pointed to the Casino, a huge, dazzling white circular building on the point across the bay from us—large enough so that we'd been able to see it from several miles away—and said, "Mr. Wrigley built that in twenty-nine. It won some big architectural award in 1930. Mr. Wrigley owns most of the island."

Lorna said, "The chewing gum Mr. Wrigley? *Spearmint?*"

"One and the same," Dutch said. "He owns the Cubs, too. That's why they train here."

"God," Wadsworth said, "it's sure changed since I was a boy. I must say I like that Casino, though. What do they do there? It isn't legal to play roulette and that sort of thing, is it?"

Reagan laughed. "Gosh, no. Mr. Wrigley's kind of straitlaced anyway. He won't sell booze in the Casino, not even beer. There's a great

ballroom in there, and a movie theater. When they built the Radio City Music Hall in New York, they sent engineers out here to study the acoustics in that theater."

"Please," Wadsworth said. "Do you expect me to believe the Rockefellers couldn't find good acoustics closer to home?"

"It's a fact, Bill," Reagan said. "I don't know much about acoustics, but I know that's a true story."

"And I'm sure no one's ever accused you of being gullible?"

"Sure they have, but just the same I know that's a true story. I heard that story from one of Kay Kyser's trombone players. I didn't believe it myself. So do you know who I asked?"

"Whom," Wadsworth said.

Dutch ignored the correction. "I asked Mr. Wrigley himself. Just walked up to him at an Angels game last September. I said, "Sir, is it true the engineers from Radio City modeled their acoustics after the Casino's, in Avalon? He said, 'You bet it is, Dutch.' He remembered me from spring training two years ago, when I was still broadcasting the Cubs games. He's really a pretty swell guy."

Wadsworth said, "I'll think more fondly of him now when I have to scrape gum off my shoe."

Dutch had stayed at the Catherine Hotel during his previous visits. It was fairly large and stately, with an expansive view of the harbor. Rooms were a little steep at fifteen dollars for a double and ten for a single. As we approached the desk, Dutch had asked me if I wanted "to double up." He was a bit short on cash, he said, and could use the ten dollars he'd save. I didn't know what my chances were of some time alone with Lorna, but I figured it was worth holding out for. So I declined. I told Dutch I was a light sleeper and required a private room.

Our negotiations turned out to have been academic: the Catherine had exactly two rooms left, both doubles. Should we try elsewhere? A simple question, an awfully complex moment.On the surface were Reagan's finances and my sleeping habits; submerged were issues of pleasure, deception, friendship, danger, and trust, to name a few. If I insisted on a single, of course, there was always the possibility that Wadsworth, hung over and in desperate need of a bath and a shave, would groan and announce he wasn't carrying his goddamn suitcase another step, and I'd end up alone in a different hotel.

"Let's just stay here," I said. "Swell," Dutch professed, with a broad smile. "That's a relief," Wadsworth said. And Lorna avoided eye contact with me. I made a point of reminding the desk man, so all could hear, that if another room became available anywhere in the hotel, I wanted it.

Dutch wasn't treated exactly like a conquering hero at the Cubs training facility, but several of the players recognized him, and the manager, Charlie Grimm (who was familiar to me because he would, very briefly, manage the Cubs again in my childhood and his dotage) greeted him effusively. Grimm, not too many years removed from his own playing career, was now in early middle age and letting himself go. He kept pounding Reagan on the back and saying things like, "So ya made it big, Dutch! You're a movie star! You're a big shot now!" Dutch introduced me and Lorna (Wadsworth was back at the hotel, sleeping off his funk), and Grimm, despite Dutch's protestations, was convinced that he and the beautiful starlet were an item. For her part, Lorna seemed baffled although not necessarily displeased by the presence of this chunky man in the flannel uniform, the blue cap, and the black shoes with little spikes on their soles.

While I suppose our surroundings would have fit within the broadest definition of "ballpark," it was by no means a stadium—just a beautiful baseball diamond, exceedingly green, without walls. The stands, with simple bench seating, ran several rows deep from third base to home plate, from home plate to first base. Lorna and I sat in the front row alongside the first baseline as Dutch in his sailor suit and his glasses chatted with this player or that, played catch briefly with Stan Hack. The practice of stitching names on the backs of uniforms wouldn't come into being for decades, so this was truly a case of needing a scorecard to tell the players. There were none, so I could only guess that the guys playing pepper were Billy Herman, Bill Jurges, and Augie Galan. Surely I recognized the young Phil Cavarretta, and Gabby Hartnett was unmistakable. Pregame, I wandered about the grounds for half an hour, shooting everything in sight with my glorious new Leica.

The White Sox, in from their training camp on the mainland, took the field for infield practice at noon, by which time there were perhaps fifty or sixty people in the stands. Compared to the Cubs the White Sox were a ragtag crew, devoid of stars except for the shortstop, Luke Appling, and one aging pitcher, Ted Lyons. Lorna, who had never seen a baseball game, was impressed by the sheer speed of everything she

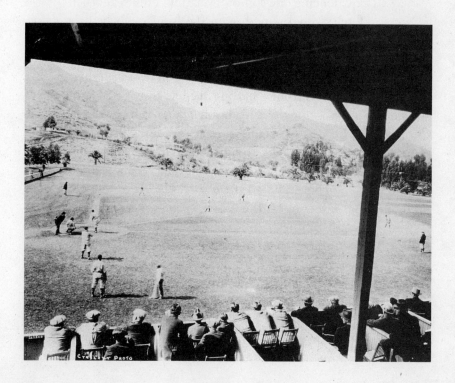

saw. We were so close to the field that we could hear the *whoosh* of every pitch, appreciate the acceleration of a hard-hit ground ball as it bore down on an infielder.

The game itself swept me back to my childhood, to my eleventh and twelfth years, when in July and August I would with a small group of friends take the train into New York, descend at 125th Street, and take the subway to the Polo Grounds, where the Mets would regularly be overmatched by some established National League team. I would by the time of our first visit already have watched untold games on television, in black and white, and I would upon emerging from the dark labyrinth that separated the street from the stands be narcotized, mesmerized by the dazzling green of the playing field, the smells and the sounds of the game.

Here of course there was the additional, occult element. Much as I had been stunned the first time I stood outside the first-class commissary and saw in vital color scores of faces I'd known in two-dimensional shades of gray, I now watched in close-up action a cast of athletes previously familiar to me from black and white *still* photographs. Lorna was experiencing one sort of revelation, I quite another.

Not so Dutch, who'd joined us in the front row when the game began. There was nothing novel or mystical about baseball to Dutch. He loved the game, clearly, and he knew it fairly well, but there was an immutable superficiality, a speciousness, to his observations and his analysis. He knew everyone's batting average from last season, knew every name on this spring's roster, but he didn't seem to care about all the marvelous little things going on—the way outfielders shifted a few paces in or back, left or right, from batter to batter, the curious wide-open stance of a White Sox rookie, the fact that the home plate umpire seemed to have a broad strike zone when the White Sox were up, a much narrower one for the Cubs.

When Lorna had questions, and she had quite a few, most of a fairly basic nature, Dutch would at first wait impatiently for me to explain (Why is he trotting off to first base? Because the pitcher has thrown him four bad pitches. Why is he out? Because even though he hit the ball quite far, someone on the other team caught it.) and then add his own tutorial. After a few instances of this routine I remained silent and left the explanations to Dutch. I imagined that in different circumstances I might have considered Dutch's behavior annoying, at

the very least. But Lorna didn't seem to mind. Dutch's instructions were long-winded but pleasant, simplistic but genial, delivered with good humor and a certain Middle American style.

The game flew by. Batters tended to put the first or second pitch into play. The catcher threw the ball to the pitcher, who stared in for the sign and threw the ball to the catcher. There were no long caucuses on the mound. Batters didn't call time and step away from the plate to recite their mantras.

Hatless, meanwhile, I was getting baked. At the end of the sixth inning, with the Cubs ahead 10–2, Lorna said, "Gabriel, my God, you're red as a beet."

"She's right," Dutch said."Why don't I get you a cap from the Cubs dugout?"

That sounded like a good idea, but Lorna had a better one. She said, "Actually, I wouldn't mind getting out of the heat myself." And then she whispered to me, "Maybe we could go back to your room for a few minutes. I think we should talk."

Dutch said, "I'd kind of like to see the rest of the game, if that's all right with you folks."

"That would be fine," I said.

Lorna tapped gently on the door to her and Wadsworth's room. There was no response. She knocked a bit more firmly and waited a few seconds. "Either he's sound asleep or he's out," she said.

"Why don't we peek in and find out which?"

"I don't even have a key. I suppose I could go down to the desk and get one. . . ."

"No. Don't bother," I said.

My room—Dutch's and my room—was next door. It was comfortable and well appointed: hardwood floor with small area rugs, two double beds with brass frames and thick, soft pillows, a writing desk with stationery and envelopes provided, an excellent view of the harbor, a sturdy radio on the night table between the two beds ("Scott—the Stradivarius of Radio"), a bathroom with all the amenities.

Lorna sat cross-legged on Dutch's bed. I stood in front of mine. "You really got burned today," she said. "Don't you feel it?"

"I'm fine. A little hot. What do we need to talk about?"

"What we're doing here. I have no intention of spending the night with Bill. Why don't you and I catch the last boat back to the mainland? We can come back here some other time."

"I'd rather not, Lorna. I was hoping to talk to Dutch about something, an idea I had for a picture. And I don't think we should just leave Bill in the lurch."

"Why do you care so much about Bill? He doesn't even believe you *went* to Princeton, for God's sake."

"He's been decent to me. He did me a big favor."

"The *hell* with Bill," she said. She uncrossed her legs and sprawled out on the bed.

After a moment I thought I detected a sob. "Lorna?" I said. I got to my feet. Profuse tears ran down her cheeks. I sat beside her. "Lorna, look, I'm so sorry. . . ."

She opened her eyes. "What about *my* feelings, Gabriel?"

Full of remorse and ardor I searched for words, found nothing but instinct, leaned down and kissed her lips. It was our first contact of any significance since Wadsworth's call had forestalled our incipient passion nearly three weeks earlier, and Lorna responded as if she had been waiting all that time for me to reinitiate the process. Whatever qualms I had were promptly stifled in a frenzy of caressing and unbuttoning.

We were half naked when Lorna suddenly sat upright. "What if Bill's next door?" Just as her three-dimensional self had outshone her photograph, she was that much more stunning without clothes than with them.

"We're not worrying about Bill," I said.

She bounced on the bed, and the springs complained loudly. "God, this won't do," she said.

I got up and switched on the radio. Lorna bounded off Dutch's bed and bounced onto mine, which was only slightly quieter. Watching her, in her silk underwear, I could hardly have been more excited. The radio took half a minute to warm up, whereupon some sort of Latin music filled the room—a rumba, perhaps? A merengue? "Make it louder," Lorna said.

We lost track of the time. In retrospect, that is all I can say for sure. I recall estimating as we walked into the room that we had a good thirty minutes. Probably, more, actually. There were three innings remaining when we left the game, and unless Dutch ran back to the hotel it would take him as long to get here as it did us. If anything, he'd stay and socialize a while with the Cubs. So we may have had forty minutes, fifty, an hour. The Catherine had provided us with no clock, only the radio, the Stradivarius of radios, and it is quite possible there was a station break, a time check, at the hour or the half hour, but I was not aware of it. Nor do I have any recollection of the music after that initial rumba. On the other hand I could—if this were a different sort of exercise—give you a detailed account of all the things Lorna and I did that caused us to be so oblivious of time. There were awkward moments at first. . . . No, in fact there were no awkward moments. There were tentative moments at first, but then everything fell into a marvelous rhythm I would imagine to be most uncommon in first couplings. Since my arrival we had spent hundreds of hours in each other's company, coming to know each other in every sense but this. Perhaps it was that intimacy that made us such natural lovers, or perhaps we were simply made for each other.

In any case, after an indeterminate time had elapsed we were in a position no traditional missionary would ever have endorsed, when suddenly I felt Lorna's limbs tense. I looked up and I saw her in the process of covering her head with a pillow; I looked to my right and I saw Dutch Reagan standing open-mouthed (much as myself) in the doorway.

"Oh, good Lord," Dutch shouted over the music. "I'm sorry. I did knock."

15

I found him downstairs in the bar, accompanied by some sort of exotic drink in a tall glass. It was still only midafternoon and there wasn't much of a crowd. I perched on the next stool. "What've you got there?" I asked him.

"Not sure," Dutch replied. "I saw somebody else drinking one of these and I asked the bartender if he could make me one with no liquor in it. It's got some fruit juices, and something fizzy. I'm not much for the booze, you know."

I knew that Reagan's father was a problem drinker, that his mother was an evangelical Christian who strongly disapproved of liquor, and that Reagan rarely if ever drank alcohol. I said, "Listen, Dutch . . ."

"That was embarrassing as hell, Gabriel. I can't tell you how sorry I am." His glasses off, he was making a kind of fraudulent eye contact. He seemed to be looking at my forehead.

"I'm the one who should be apologizing. There's no way you could have anticipated."

"Well, *that's* certainly true," he said with a hint of a laugh. "I never would have guessed that *you* and Lorna . . ." He shrugged and took a sip of his drink. "I'll tell you, the more time I spend out here, the more of an education I get. I wonder, do you get used to it?"

"I wouldn't know. I'm new here myself. But from what I hear, half the people on the lot assume Lorna and I are having an affair."

Now Dutch laughed out loud. "It's pretty funny, then. I never would've suspected you were, but then I guess all those people on the lot are right, aren't they?"

"It's not what you think," I said, searching for a way to describe how it was. The direct approach seemed called for. "I'm in love with her, Dutch."

He smiled. "Good for you, then." He took another sip. "Look, Gabriel, I'm no one to talk. I mean, please don't think I'm passing judgment on you. I was brought up to believe you didn't go all the way with a girl till you were married. Out here, my gosh, it's a whole different . . . I don't know what."

"Set of values?"

"It's almost like they fall into your bed. I don't pretend to be a Casanova, but you take a girl out, you go to dinner—I mean, even one of these things arranged by the studio—and the next thing you know you're spending the night at her place."

"I wouldn't know," I said.

"Then the next day you see her on the set, it's business as usual, like last night never happened."

"Not such a bad life, is it, Dutch?"

He laughed, perhaps a bit embarrassed. "I guess not, but it's a little hard getting used to. One of the girls I've been seeing is married, for crying out loud, doesn't live with her husband, they're separated, he lives hundreds of miles away, but what I'm trying to say, marriage is supposed to be a holy sacrament. It bothers me that I can't restrain myself. I think, what does God make of all this? Isn't he looking down on me and shaking his head?"

"Don't you suppose," I said, "God's not all that officious? That he doesn't care too much about the little offenses?"

Dutch's expression gave me a bit of a frisson. It was that half smile, that endearing expression he would make in later life when someone, for instance, would ask him a tough question at a press conference and he'd spend a few seconds gathering his thoughts. He said, "I don't think I know what you mean."

"God shouldn't care if her marriage is only on paper. If they're separated, then God shouldn't have any quarrel with you."

He gave this thorough consideration. "Do you believe that?"

"Yes."

"Good. I'm glad you feel that way. But what about you?" Dutch asked.

"What about me?"

"What about all of you: Bill and Lorna and you? How does God feel about that?"

"I'd hope God would understand that we're trying to work things out."

He was silent for several seconds. "All of you? All of you are trying to work things out?"

The question struck me as vapid, meaningless. Was I missing something? I must say that in my life before that conversation, contemplations of God's inclinations had been extremely rare, and Reagan's acceptance of my views on spiritual matters had perhaps left me giddy and overconfident. I said, "Yes, we're all trying to work things out."

Dutch took a walk into town; I returned upstairs. As I had expected, Lorna was gone when I entered my room. I stood by the common wall for a good while, listening for voices, then went to the hallway and knocked on the door. There was no answer, indicating that Lorna was asleep (which I considered unlikely), was ignoring me (which I preferred not to believe), or had gone out. She had reacted—after the initial shock—to Dutch's intrusion rather stoically, but I thought I had detected considerable displeasure in her manner. Its extent I hadn't been able to judge, in my rush to get dressed, to make myself presentable, to get downstairs.

Should I now go search for her? Most probably she was trying to find, or had found, Wadsworth. My emotions, my instinct, urged me to do something assertive, to show Lorna what she meant to me. My common sense told me to stand back and wait.

— —

I peeked into several nearby eating and drinking places, making my way gradually to the Pleasure Pier, a little bit of Atlantic City out here in the Pacific. Given Lorna's sense of whimsy, she might as well be found here as anyplace else.

Poking my head into a succession of hot dog joints, beer parlors, and pinball emporiums, I became aware that there was someone following the same path as I. Or perhaps he was simply following me. I kept seeing him out of the corner of my eye: a slim young man, in his mid- to late twenties, on the short side, very odd looking. The more I saw of him, the stranger he looked. His hair was blond, verging on platinum, and cut very short, in a fashion that would be popular in 1957 and 1994, but certainly wasn't now. He wore baggy tweed trousers, a black leather jacket, and white sneakers. None of these items was anachronistic in itself, but taken together they formed a bizarre picture.

I came to the end of the pier: nowhere to go from here except swimming. To my surprise, he caught my eye. He said, "*Vous parlez français?*"

Did I speak French? Was he simply a tourist in need of directions? That I doubted. I shook my head. "Ah," he spoke in French-accented English, "but you see, you understand my question, so maybe you do speak French, a little?"

"Maybe a little," I acknowledged.

Now he was within three feet of me. "Well, it's no difference. As you can hear, my English is excellent. Don't you think?"

"Quite good," I said.

"My name is Jean-Baptiste," he said. He offered his right hand; it was bony and cool. "I don't believe in modesty. What is the point? I believe in *franchise*. How do you say it in English?"

"Frankness."

"Ah, see, your French is very good. But tell me, please, where is a good place here to go for a drink?"

"I'm afraid I don't know. I've only been here a few hours."

"*Alors—vous êtes touriste aussi.*" The little blond man was beaming. "Maybe we can find a place together?"

"I don't think so."

"I mean, just a place to have a drink."

"I really don't think so. I'm looking for some other people."

"Of course," he said. "The beautiful girl. She's an actress, I think."

I was beginning to feel queasy. I said, "Who are you?"

"Come with me for a drink." He grinned. "I can tell you all about myself. I'll buy the drinks. Everything is so cheap here, but it's hard to change your money."

"I'm not interested in a drink." I became aware that I had been backtracking toward the shore; we were now perhaps fifteen feet away from pier's end. "How do you know who I'm with?"

The little blond man shrugged. "Look, maybe I am too aggressive. I am adjusting to a different culture. Maybe I offend you with my attitude. If so, please forgive me. Now I'll have a drink by myself, you can go and find your beautiful friend."

"How do you know who I'm with?" I repeated.

"Is it the right thing to say 'who,' in this case? Isn't it correct to say 'whom?' "

"Correct, yes, but a little stilted in conversation."

"*Stilted?* I'm sorry, doesn't it mean walking on platforms, to make you very high? Excuse me—very tall?"

We had somehow spun slowly around, so now he was closer to the shore. "This is extremely foolish," I said. "If you're not going to answer my question, I don't see any reason to continue."

"As you wish," he said, with a bow of sorts. "Possibly I'll see you later. *C'est une petite île, n'est-ce pas?*" And he flounced away.

I remained nearly motionless for what must have been several minutes, standing close to the end of the pier amidst intermittent pedestrians and plenty of noisy gulls. I felt as one does after a sudden, vituperative encounter with a stranger—angry and confused, adrenaline running amuck. Who was this man, why was he following me, how did he know so much? Indeed, how much *more* did he know?

After a great deal of deduction, having reached no conclusion that made any sense, I began walking back toward the Catherine. For the moment at least I had lost interest in finding Lorna; I was sunburned and exhausted, and yearned to sleep.

— —

Dutch woke me at seven-thirty. My face felt like a toaster oven. I'd slept three hours, Lorna and Wadsworth were downstairs waiting for us, and the dining room was about to close. As I washed and dressed, Dutch filled me in on the afternoon I'd missed: he'd found Gabby Hartnett and Augie Galan of the Cubs and had "a few drinks." At six they'd run into Lorna and Wadsworth on the Pleasure Pier. Dutch had managed to take Lorna aside at one point and apologize for his intrusion; Lorna had told him to forget it. Wadsworth, perhaps feeling gentlemanly after his own nap, had bought the ballplayers a drink. Wadsworth himself had had quite a few drinks.

"So he's drunk?" I said.

"I wouldn't say he's exactly drunk." I realized Dutch had changed outfits: he still wore the blue blazer from his sailor suit, but now it was augmented by gray trousers and a blue shirt. "Maybe he's a little tipsy."

Wadsworth and Lorna had already been seated by the time Dutch and I walked in. It was a smallish room, with fifteen tables at the most, and at this hour, given Americans' predilection for early dinners, only five or six were occupied. Wadsworth raised his glass, which contained a blondish liquid I presumed to be Scotch. "Good evening to the actor

162

and the lobster," he greeted us, then turned to no one in particular and added, "I'm sure you're wondering which is which." My eyes were on Lorna, who appeared happy neither to see me nor to be with Wadsworth.

"You've had your day in the sun, Gabriel," he continued. "But I wonder why you're so much pinker than Lorna and Deutsch."

"He didn't wear a hat, Bill," Lorna said. "Now why don't you shut up and concentrate on the menu?"

"I was referring to his politics, darling," Wadsworth said. "Although in point of fact, I think our friend Deutsch may be the pinker one. My error, in that case." He saluted Reagan with his glass.

"I wish you wouldn't make fun of my name, Bill," Reagan said, smiling pleasantly. "It's Dutch."

"The hell it is. Are you trying to tell me Reagan's a Dutch name?"

"Of course not. It's an Irish name. But my nickname is Dutch, not Deutsch."

The waiter chose this moment to arrive. Not at all bad timing, I thought. I ordered the sea bass, having been assured that it was fresh and that it would be grilled. Lorna chose the tuna, Wadsworth the albacore steak, and Reagan a porterhouse steak, medium-well. Wadsworth asked if anyone would object to the Nierstein Riesling. I have never been terribly fond of German wines, but I was not about to make waves. Wadsworth then spoke directly to Dutch: "It's a good year, 1933. Fine year for Rieslings."

"All right with me," Dutch replied. "I won't be having much, anyway."

"I don't know," Wadsworth said. "Anybody iconoclastic enough to order a steak medium-well in a dining room a hundred feet from the ocean deserves to have plenty of white wine."

"Just the same," Dutch said, "I'm not much of a drinker."

There was an interlude of more civil conversation. Lorna spoke about her discoveries in town. Our salads arrived, and moments later came the wine. The waiter selected Wadsworth for the tasting ritual, and Wadsworth, who by my estimation could hardly have told a Riesling from a glass of goat urine at this point, pronounced it acceptable. To my surprise, I found it delicious.

Dutch then announced that he'd like to make a toast, and for some reason it struck me as altogether a bad notion. Dutch held his water glass high and said, "I'd like to drink to the three of you, in hopes that our companionship will endure, and in hopes that I can learn a few things from your unique friendship."

Dutch and Lorna and I clinked glasses. Wadsworth said, "What the hell are you talking about?"

Slightly taken aback, smiling nevertheless, Dutch said, "I'm glad that we're friends."

"No. I'm asking you what the hell do you mean by our 'unique friendship'?" In my enduring sleepiness, the significance of those words was just sinking in to me. I tried to catch Reagan's eye; he was sitting just to my left, his attention fixed on Wadsworth, who sat across from him.

Lorna touched Wadsworth's arm. "Please, Bill. You're raising your voice." Did she have any idea what Dutch had meant?

"I *know* I'm raising my voice. I want to find out what this idiot's talking about."

Dutch seemed in a state approximating shock. I could imagine the questions he was asking himself: Had he completely misinterpreted what I'd said earlier, or was Wadsworth simply furious because he didn't want anyone to know about our "unique" relationship? Either way, Dutch was probably beginning to suspect he'd overstepped his bounds.

It appeared incumbent upon me to minimize the damage. I kicked Dutch's leg. Specifically, with the toe of my left shoe I kicked the calf of his right leg, and he was sharp enough not to react abruptly, but to turn rather slowly in my direction. Nearly simultaneous to the kick, I began talking, having at first very little idea what I was going to say. "This reminds me," I said, and I must have spoken very forcefully because I realized that all eyes were now on me, making it all the more important that I discover a conclusion for the first words I'd spoken (excluding a brief exchange with the waiter) at the dinner table. Suddenly my mind seized upon a picture of myself and Hudnut at the little café down the street from the Musée National des Techniques, as if Hudnut had sensed my moment of need and telepathized the image back across the years.

"This reminds me," I recommenced, "of something I heard about Arturo Toscanini."

"What the hell could this have to do with Toscanini?" Wadsworth growled.

Dutch, who had made his ill-fated toast with water, now gulped down his Riesling and refilled his glass. I resumed: "I heard that Toscanini had been in jail. In Italy, as a young man."

"That's ridiculous," Wadsworth said. "And I don't see what it has to do with Reagan's toast."

"For murder," I said.

"Patently absurd," Wadsworth snarled. "I happen to know the man's from one of the finest families in Italy. My old man had dinner with him at the Princeton Club, for God's sake."

Lorna said, "Why don't you let Gabriel finish, Bill?"

And he did. I made the story last through the interval between salads and entrées, made it last (with plenty of interruption by Wadsworth and subsequent digressions) through the entrées, the arrival of a second bottle of Riesling, all the way to the waiter's arrival for dessert orders—by which time I had hardly touched my dinner. (Just as well, because the bass was miserably overcooked, and the accompanying vegetables had clearly spent quite some time as canned goods.) I knew enough about Toscanini—and Wadsworth, just as important, turned out to know virtually nothing about him— to make the story marginally credible, so Lorna kept saying things like, "This isn't *really* true, is it, Gabriel?" and Wadsworth seemed gradually and progressively drawn in, if not to the point of believing then at least to a modest interest in the outcome. When I finally had Toscanini say, in a rather elegant Italian accent, "Well, I suppose I must be a bad conductor," Lorna exploded in laughter as—half a second later—did Dutch, and even Wadsworth couldn't resist a smile.

Whether it was my story or his drunkenness that distracted him, Wadsworth did not again raise the subject of Dutch's toast; nor, as you might imagine, did anyone else. We had consumed two bottles of wine. I had finished one glass and half of another; Lorna had not even got through her first; Wadsworth had probably downed a bottle and a quarter. This left a relatively prodigious amount to Dutch, who did not normally drink at all.

After dinner, when Wadsworth and Lorna were visiting their respective toilets, Dutch told me that he'd found the wine very tasty and had enjoyed my story quite a lot, but there was something about it he hadn't understood. "Toscanini's a great conductor, one of the best in the world, right?"

"Right."

"Well then, why at the end does he say, 'I guess I'm just a bad conductor?'"

"It's a play on words, Dutch. The electric chair couldn't kill him because he didn't conduct electricity, so he was a bad conductor."

"Ah," Dutch said, "I get it." And he chuckled appreciatively. "So then obviously it's not a true story."

"No. It's a fantasy. It's made up."

He slapped my back. "You're a clever fellow, Gabriel. I've got to hand you that."

16

"Who's for a midnight swim?" Wadsworth was already unbuttoning his shirt. We were on the beach between the Pleasure Pier and the ferry terminal; it was well past ten o'clock and the night was still fairly pleasant, but enough of a breeze had developed so that—in my light jacket and cotton trousers—I'd begun to feel a chill.

"For God's sake, Bill," Lorna said, "it's getting cool, and you've had too much to drink."

"Nonsense." He handed her his jacket and his shirt. He did not exactly have a bodybuilder's physique, nor did he yet have the flabby torso of a big drinker going to seed. "What do you say, Gabriel?"

"Not for me, Bill."

"Jesus! Where's your sense of adventure?" As he leaned to unlace his shoes he nearly keeled over. Reagan reached out to steady him. "How about it, then, Deutsch? You and me and the great Pacific?"

"I don't think so," Dutch said, shaking his head.

Wadsworth was having a great deal of trouble getting out of his trousers. "*Please*, Bill," Lorna said.

He continued to address Reagan. "Used to be a lifeguard or some such, didn't you?"

"I did."

"Where was that, Deutsch?" Wadsworth now had extricated one leg. His buttoned boxer shorts came nearly to his knees.

"Back in Illinois, Bill."

"Plenty of surf there, I'd guess. Bet you had a hell of a time pulling kids out of the undertow." He leaned against Lorna, pulled his other leg out of the pants.

"I did, actually. There was an undertow, and I saved a few lives, if I do say so."

"I'll bet you did, Deutsch." Wadsworth winked at me, kissed Lorna on the lips, and went bounding into the bay. When the water was knee deep he dived, and disappeared.

"Gabriel," Lorna said, "I don't like this at all. Why didn't we stop him?"

"How could we have stopped him?"

"I don't know. Hit him or something."

"Is he a good swimmer?" Reagan asked.

"Very good," Lorna said. "He grew up here. The odd thing is, in normal circumstances, when it's a beautiful day and everyone's in the water, he won't go near it. But when he's drunk and there's a challenge involved . . . well, you can see for yourself."

I said, "Did you actually expect me to *hit* him?" And Lorna ignored me.

"Then he should be all right," Reagan said. "The wind's picking up but there's still not much surf."

The three of us stood at water's edge, listening to the waves splash lazily on the hard sand. There was no sign of Wadsworth. Dutch said, "Lorna, what I said at dinner, look, I don't normally find myself in such embarrassing—"

Lorna interrupted him. "Please forget about it."

"Twice in one day, I mean," Dutch resumed. "You must think I'm some kind of clumsy—"

"I said, please *forget* about it, Dutch." Lorna looked out to sea.

There was a fairly long silence. I put my arm around Lorna's waist, and she moved away. Dutch spoke to me, under his breath. "Did I misunderstand you this afternoon, Gabriel? I had the impression that the three of you—"

"You misunderstood me, Dutch."

Dutch said, "So he doesn't know about you two?"

"He *didn't* know," said Lorna, who had evidently not been out of earshot. This was getting worse and worse.

"Oh my gosh," Dutch said. "Then I did let the cat out of the bag?"

"I'm not sure," Lorna said. The breeze rustled her hair and her skirt, and I wished we could be alone.

All three of us heard a sound. To my ears it could have been, *Hey!* It seemed to come from offshore. Dutch said, "Was that Bill? What did that sound like to you?"

"Like *hey*," Lorna said.

"It sounded like *help!* to me," Reagan said, and he began untying his shoes.

"Dutch, it was definitely not *help*," I said.

"The way this looks to me," Reagan said, tossing aside a second shoe, "is that your friend Bill has just figured out what's going on between you two. Either he's out there trying to drown himself or he's out there too drunk to get back in."

"You're not that sober yourself," I said.

Reagan handed me his pants, stripped off his jacket, fumbled a bit with the buttons of his shirt. "I'm fine," he said.

The voice, perhaps a bit fainter now, called out again, and this time I could not say for sure that it wasn't someone calling for help. As Reagan handed me his shirt, Lorna said, "I just wish I could *see* him out there. How far could he have swum?" Dutch stumbled a bit as he turned toward the water. "It sounded to me like he's out there about sixty or eighty feet, straight ahead, I'd say."

"How can you possibly judge that?" It was hard to tell whether the edge in Lorna's voice represented distress or exasperation. I said, "I thought the voice came from way over there." I pointed left and seaward. Lorna seized Reagan's arm. "Dutch, for God's sake, you're still wearing your glasses." He removed them and handed them to me. Lorna, who had not so much as looked in my direction during the past several minutes, still held Reagan by the forearm. "Let's be sensible, please, Dutch. Bill's a strong swimmer, so he's probably all right. In the event that he's not, we don't have the slightest idea where he is . . ."

"Straight ahead, sixty feet out," Reagan reiterated.

"I don't think so," I said.

". . . and you've had quite bit to drink, too. So why don't you just get dressed and stay here?"

There was the voice again, fainter, less distinct, definitely off to the left. Reagan used his left arm to remove Lorna's hand from his right. "That's a man who needs help," he said, and he bounded off into the bay, swimming straight ahead.

His stroke was strong and athletic, and within a couple of minutes he'd vanished into the night. I took a tentative step toward Lorna, who stood with her arms crossed against the wind. I said, "I don't know what to make of all this."

She would not look at me. "Don't talk to me, please, Gabriel."

"Should I have hit Dutch, too? Should I have knocked them both cold?" I regretted the words the moment I'd spoken them.

"You shouldn't have brought us all here in the first place. I don't know why I listened to you. I don't know why I didn't trust my better judgment."

"You're right," I said. "It was foolish on my part to assume . . ."

"To assume *what*, Gabriel?" She turned to face me and I thought I saw tears on her cheeks. I moved to embrace her, but as I stepped forward she retreated.

"To assume that we could all be friends."

"All be friends? How can you expect to be Bill's friend when you're stealing his girl? How can you expect Bill to be Dutch's friend when he has nothing but contempt for him? And God knows, I didn't want you to be *my* friend, I wanted you to be my lover."

Was there to be no salvation? There was no questioning the validity of Lorna's every word. There could be no argument on my part, no excuse, no bluff, no bold front, and finally no explanation. I had had reasons for all of this, perfectly good reasons, but it was impossible even to hint at them. I was just beginning to absorb her choice of the past tense when I saw her eyes widen and, not a second later, heard a voice from behind me. "Boy, that felt great! Nothing like a swim to sober you up."

Wadsworth was shivering, a bit blue in the lips, breathless, otherwise none the worse for wear. He picked up his shirt and shook the sand off it, looked around while sliding his right arm into its sleeve. "Say, where's Deutsch?"

"Out there, rescuing you." Lorna's tone had if anything turned a bit colder.

"Are you kidding?" Wadsworth fumbled with his shirt buttons. "What made him think I needed rescuing?"

I said, "We thought we heard your voice."

"You did. I was about thirty feet over that way"—he caught his breath and pointed to the left—"and about thirty feet out. I could see the three of you over here. The water felt terrific. I kept shouting, 'Hey!'"

"That's what we thought," Lorna said. "Dutch thought you were calling for help."

Wadsworth stopped buttoning, stood motionless for two seconds, a large man, soaking wet, in underpants and a half-buttoned shirt on a dark beach. "Why didn't I see him on my way in?"

"Because he swam straight out," Lorna said. "He figured you were sixty to eighty feet straight out, calling for help."

"God, the man's a total idiot," Wadsworth said.

"Just the same," Lorna said, "he's out there trying to save your life."

Wadsworth trotted to water's edge and peered out, as if searching for Asia. He took several steps into the bay. "I don't see him," he said.

"We couldn't see you," Lorna reminded him.

Wadsworth removed his shirt, rolled it into a ball, flung it in our direction. "All right then, I'll go find him."

Lorna said, "No, Bill, for Christ's sake. Stay here. This is getting crazier by the minute."

"Look," Wadsworth shouted, "I'm fine. I can swim forever. I'm going to go out and find that halfwit, and bring him back." To complicate things further, the surf had gained a little edge in the last few minutes; Wadsworth waded through waves breaking against his thighs, and plunged in.

"I don't believe this is happening," Lorna said, as much to the wind as to me.

What was I to do? To stand worthlessly on the beach next to the woman I loved, groping for words that didn't exist? "I'll find the police," I said, and I set out for the hotel, alternately sprinting and stumbling through the sand.

I was back at water's edge twenty minutes later with a disgruntled deputy named Seligman. By this time, according to Lorna, Wadsworth had twice returned to shore empty-handed, discovered Reagan had not emerged independently from the sea, and resumed his search. By now, the breeze had become a modest wind, and waves were actually breaking against the shore. Seligman, who let us know that he'd been half an hour from the end of his shift and his week, since he had Sunday off, was at first skeptical that anyone was in danger, then increasingly irritable with us when it became apparent that our friend might really be lost at sea. Seligman was a short, squat man of about thirty-five, dressed in khaki from head to foot. "Let me understand this once and for all," he said to me. "This Wentworth takes off his clothes and goes running into the water, ten o'clock at night when the water's getting rough, and no one stops him."

"The water wasn't getting rough," I said.

Lorna said, "We *tried* to stop him, for God's sake. He's drunk, and he's headstrong."

"He's drunk," Seligman said, "but he's spent the last half an hour swimming out there in the surf, looking for the other member of your party, Mr. Reagan?"

"That's right," I said.

"He's an excellent swimmer," Lorna said.

"Mr. Reagan is an excellent swimmer?"

"No," Lorna said, "Mr. Wadsworth."

"But Mr. Reagan was a lifeguard back in Illinois," I said, "so he's probably an excellent swimmer, too."

Seligman said, "Had Mr. Reagan been drinking?"

"He wasn't drunk," Lorna said.

"Not as much as Mr. Wadsworth," I said.

Seligman said, "So you have a drunk man swimming out there in rough surf, looking for a sober man who used to be a lifeguard?"

"Not altogether sober," I said.

"Has Mr. Reagan been known to play a practical joke?"

Lorna said, "We don't know him that well."

I said, "No one's playing a joke here." Looking off to the left, I could suddenly make out a form in the water, no more than fifteen feet away. I saw hands, then a head, and for a period, for perhaps eight or ten seconds, I truly believed it was Dutch. But when the man emerged from the water he was unmistakably broad and blond. He shouted over the wind, "Is he here? Did he make it back in?"

"Which one is this?" Seligman said.

Wadsworth was clearly a case of hypothermia. Lorna swathed him in his own and Reagan's clothes, but he couldn't stop shivering, nor muttering that he'd covered every square foot of bay at least twice. After a couple of minutes ashore, he fell to his knees and was unable to get up again. His face had the cast of a man who'd endured either great physical exhaustion or considerable dissipation. Seligman said, "Let's get this man warmed up."

I took one arm, Seligman the other, and we dragged him up the beach. Alongside, Lorna carried two pairs of shoes and Reagan's glasses. Wadsworth's voice was so weary I could barely hear him: "Gabriel, you know the pathetic bastard better than I do. Is this a big joke?"

"I don't know, Bill. I don't think so."

"Because if it isn't, if he just went out there and sank like a stone, then he must have been as lousy a lifeguard as he was an actor."

— —

Wadsworth insisted on spending the night in his hotel room; Lorna accompanied him there. I passed the night with Seligman and, it seemed eventually, every public servant and volunteer on Catalina, fruitlessly searching the sea and the beaches for the young actor who'd risked his life for a friend he thought was in trouble. When I got back to the Catherine in the early hours of daylight, I was astonished to find that Lorna and Wadsworth had already taken the first boat back to San Pedro. Had anyone left a message for me?

Yes, the desk man replied, and handed me a small envelope. My heart sank when I saw cramped, European handwriting, decidedly not Lorna's. I read:

Gabriel:

Was looking for you and your lovely frend in all the clubs and bistros of Avalon! Not exactly Paris, is it? We must meet soon and discuss our common interest. I think you know what it is! Will be looking for you today, or shall I come see you in Malibou? À tout à l'heure . . .

Votre ami,

J-B

What was I to make of this? Not much in the mood for games, I trudged up to my room and crawled into bed.

At noon I was awakened by a bellhop. Seligman, looking like death warmed over, waited for me in the lobby. He told me a body had been found at the outer edge of Lover's Cove, just south of Avalon. Had we not searched there? We had, but the body was concealed by a thick cloak of kelp, and had not become visible until daylight. The description matched Reagan, Seligman told me grimly, the body was "fresh," and no one else had been reported missing during the night.

He drove me out there. Although I'd already made up my mind that this had to be Dutch, the sight of him in death still shocked me. He was somewhat devoid of color, but otherwise cosmetically perfect. Wobbly, in a cold sweat, I listened to Seligman's reconstruction: Reagan had swum well past his target distance of sixty feet; he had swum several hundred feet straight out, parallel to the long pier and then past it. He had at that point evidently become disoriented and swum around the outcropping called Cabrillo Mole, then taken a hard right and found himself in turbulent seas that were forcing him away from the only land he could see. "He must've been a pretty fair swimmer," Seligman said. "If he hadn't taken that right turn, he'd have been just fine."

Catalina's ambulance arrived and took Dutch away. Seligman drove me back into town. In front of the Catherine, he said, "What the hell gets into the minds of people like you? Why do you want to take chances like that, go against nature?"

In my fatigue, tangled in a web of emotions I could not begin to describe to you, I thought for a moment that this squat little man somehow knew me better than he possibly could. I said, "What do you mean when you say 'people like you?'"

He thought for a moment, then he gave me a sour little smile. "Big shots. Fast livers. Hollywood people."

"All I can tell you is that the man who died was trying to save someone's life. I don't see how you can fault him for that."

Seligman's expression didn't change. "Seems to me he'd have been better off if he'd stayed on the beach. You'd all have been better off if you'd just stayed home."

Those sentiments I had already heard from Lorna. I thanked the deputy for his time and effort, and I excused myself to go pack my bag.

17

I have never been quite sure whether I believe there is a God, but as I rode the ferry back to San Pedro I was convinced there must be, and that He has a fine sense of irony. Jasper Hudnut had insisted to me that his intention was never for me to kill Ronald Reagan, but I suspected that had I been of such a mind he would not have objected. In any case, I had made it quite explicit that it was something I could not do. And if my primary focus soon after arriving in 1938 had switched from Reagan to Lorna Fairchild, I had never lost sight of my mission. I had even developed something of a plan. The details were still a little muddy, but the essence of the plan was perfectly clear. The beauty of it was that I could continue to work at Warners, continue to seek a future with Lorna, while sending Reagan down a path so divergent from the original that he could not possibly arrive at the same destination.

But in attempting to construct the first, vital leg of that path, I had somehow managed to blow up the entire roadway: In mid-March of 1938, Ronald Reagan was dead. He would not act in *Kings Row* or *Bedtime for Bonzo*. He would not become president of the Screen Actors Guild. He would not marry Jane Wyman, divorce her, and marry Nancy Davis. He would not be transformed from Dutch Reegan to Ronald Ragan. He would not become cozy with corporate America by hosting *General Electric Theater*. He would not be urged by a coterie of rich, conservative friends to run for the governorship of California. I hardly need to tell you the rest of what he would not do.

So it was that I had unwittingly performed my errand to perfection. The man I'd known for a couple of weeks—the man who doubtless considered me a friend, the ingenuous B-movie actor from the Midwest, my fellow baseball fan, my shallow but compassionate ally in political conversations—was dead. And I, by falling anomalously into his life from a distance of fifty-six years, had killed him. What did I feel? Remorse, certainly, and a good deal of the sort of guilt that sets in after something shocking and final has just occurred. What—there on the beach—could I have done differently? What specific action of mine would have caused Dutch not to die?

What a perplexity! The visceral emotions were run-of-the-mill, irrelevant to my backward turn in time. But then there was the overview: the knowledge that while (compared to Wadsworth) I'd had a small, passive role in Dutch's drowning, it would never have occurred had I not crashed this temporal party. And finally there was my redemption, which was a curious hybrid of the relief one feels waking from a gruesome dream—realizing its occurrences did not extend beyond one's unconscious—and the rationalization every sane political assassin must make: I have sinned in killing, but in killing I have made the world a much better place. If Hudnut was right, if all (or most, or even a great deal of) the obscene venality of the 1980s could be attributed to Ronald Reagan's presidency, then I had performed an immeasurable service for the world.

But I had quotidian concerns as well. Lorna had left me without a good-bye, without a word. The news of Dutch's death could hardly improve my standing with her. I imagined, I prayed, that if I were humbly contrite, if I gracefully accepted every recrimination Lorna might fling my way, if I proposed (now that it made no difference) telling Wadsworth about us, she would take me back.

So was I musing, sitting quite alone in a deck chair on the stern of the ferry's upper deck, half an hour out of Avalon, when I heard an unpleasantly familiar voice. "Gabriel, what a surprise to find you here! And why are you not traveling with your lovely girl?"

The little platinum-topped Frenchman, Jean-Baptiste, had evidently just climbed the steep metal staircase some fifteen feet to my rear; now he stood in front of me. On a cool, gray afternoon he wore yesterday's outfit: leather, tweed, canvas. When I made no reply, he said, "I left a note for you. Did you read it?"

"I'd appreciate it if you'd leave me alone," I said. "I'm not in a very sociable mood."

He squatted by my chair. "Don't tell me. The one who drowned—he was one of your friends?" Had the news spread so quickly? The

Frenchman continued, "And here you are, it must be very painful, being so *hâlé*. How do you say it in English, when you are all red from the sun?"

"Sunburned," I said. "But look—what's the point of this? Obviously you're following me. You know who I'm with, you knew I was on this boat. What do you want from me?"

Jean-Baptiste performed an exaggerated French shrug. "Shall we come to the point so quickly? We have quite a long ride still to San Pedro."

"Yes. Let's come to the point."

"All right, then. You have something that belongs to me. Give it back to me, and I stop bothering you. Don't give it back to me, and I will get it back eventually, after a great amount of trouble for you."

There seemed little doubt as to the nature of the object in question. Everything else was an utter mystery. Who *was* this froggy punk and how in God's name had he found me? In my state of sleeplessness and dolor I was perhaps not reasoning in top form, but neither was I about to panic. I said, "Please identify this thing that belongs to you."

Jean-Baptiste issued a quick and nasty laugh. "So we make sure it's the right one, Gabriel? All right. It is a model A-4 Tempocruiser. It has a bad control panel, so sometimes you don't go exactly where you intend. Shall I describe it some more?"

My heartbeat had easily doubled its pace in the last two minutes. It was a strange and difficult game I found myself in; was it more important to digest (*a bad control panel*, indeed!) or to feint and parry. Could I possibly do all at once? "How did you find me?"

"Your friend in Malibu, 1994. First name Jasper, and I find the second name difficult to pronounce."

"Jasper told you I was here?" How could that be, when Hudnut had thought he was sending me to 1941? Unless the control panel malfunctioned consistently in the same manner, how could Jean-Baptiste have known where to find me?

"Maybe we apply some pressure," Jean-Baptiste said with a malign smile.

My brain, limping to begin with, was now hamstrung by a score of different questions. I tried to choose the best. "You've just come here from 1994?"

"*Évidemment.*"

"How did you get here?"

"The same way as you."

"Then why do you need my machine?"

"*Your* machine?"

"The machine that brought me here. Why do you need it if you have another one?"

"Because it's my machine."

"What are you going to do if I give it back to you? You can't transport it on your other machine."

Jean-Baptiste made a sound of exasperation. "What do you care, Gabriel? You have stolen property. It belongs to me, so you should give it back. It's the just thing to do, no?"

"No," I said. "There's a lot about this I don't understand, and before we go any further I want to know what's happening."

He shrugged again. "I suppose it does no harm to tell you this much. There are two of us. We were on two machines—the A-4 that you stole, and a B-2. The B-2 has places for two people, but with two people it has a limited range. To go back where we started, we need both machines. Now you understand?"

"Where did you start from?"

Jean-Baptiste got to his feet. He was nasty, he was animated, but he was hardly an intimidating figure. "I'm not going to tell you that. I don't have to tell you that."

"Tell me this, then. Jasper believed that someone had left the machine for him to find. Is there any truth to that?"

"For him to *find*?" Apparently Jean-Baptiste thought this an extremely amusing notion; he was seized by half a minute of giggles before catching his breath. "He *found* the machine at that museum. It was in the museum because of a little error of my friend, who was trying to impress some girl, who called the National Police. We left the machines in separate caves. Why am I telling you this? Because it makes me so angry to think about it. Because Hans is such an idiot. He *tells* the girl he is from the twenty-second century, precisely the sort of thing we agreed we don't boast about. But the girl is stupider than Hans. Does she believe him? Of course not. So he takes her to the cave to prove to her. All this for what? Maybe one, how do you say it, one blow job. Now he's satisfied, he doesn't think any more about it. The girl goes to the police because she doesn't know what it is, this thing in

the cave, but she decides Hans is a thief. She thinks there is a . . .
récompense. What is the English word?"

"A reward."

"Exactly. But of course there is no reward. The National Police
don't know what this thing is. They call the *Bureau de je-ne-sais-quoi*,
and some idiot comes and takes my A-4 to the fucking Museum of
Technicalities. What a trail we have to follow! By the time we get there,
your friend, the old man, Udnut, has paid some money to someone,
and no one even has his proper address." Jean-Baptiste flung both
arms outward, clapped his hands when gravity brought them down.
"So, let me tell you, Gabriel, this has not been easy. I don't wish to be
here any longer than necessary. I'm sure you will cooperate."

Had this encounter occurred two days earlier, when everything
about 1938 was wonderful, I might have given up the machine with
minimal resistance. Now I was not so sure. If it turned out I'd earned
Lorna's undying enmity, 1938 might just be intolerable. I said, "What
were you doing there in the first place?"

"At the museum?"

"In 1994."

Jean-Baptiste had commenced pacing in front of my chair as if
engaged in a dance with neither prescribed nor rhythmic steps. "It
should make no difference to you what we were doing. We are scientists. We are engaged in terribly important research that you could
never understand."

"About what? Let me try to understand."

"Impossible."

"Forgive me," I said, "but you don't strike me as the sort of person
who'd be doing terribly important research. You don't have that look."

He stopped pacing and glared at me. "What do *you* know about it?
A hundred and twenty years have gone by, more or less. You know
absolutely *nothing* about my time."

"I'd be eager to hear about it."

Jean-Baptiste was not listening to me. He was looking behind me,
in the direction of the staircase. Presently he waved and shouted, "Ay-
oh!" I rose from my chair and turned to see a large man walking rather
unsteadily in our direction. He appeared to possess the same incongruous sense of fashion as Jean-Baptiste, wearing a double-breasted
tweed jacket above denim overalls and hunting boots, which upon

closer inspection turned out to be made of a glossy plastic. He too was in his late twenties, perhaps six and a half feet tall, with dark hair several millimeters long. Perhaps Jean-Baptiste was not intimidating, but his friend could have passed for a middle linebacker.

"Shall I introduce you?" Jean-Baptiste said. "This is Hans."

Hans gave me a look that was more sullen than hostile. He did not offer his hand. I said, "Very nice to meet you," and Hans nodded grimly.

Jean-Baptiste said, "Hans is not happy to be on this boat, am I correct, Hans?"

The large man spoke for the first time. "Yah. I was puking all the way to this fucking island. Today I am puking just a little."

"Hans is not happy to be here at all. Is it true, Hans?"

"I want to get the hell out of this fucking time. Fast."

Spoken like a solid scientist, I thought. Jean-Baptiste said, "Tell Gabriel what you'll do to him if he doesn't give us back the A-4."

Hans fixed his eyes on me, giving me a malevolent stare only slightly tempered by seasickness. "I'm going to break your fucking neck."

Jean-Baptiste put his arm around my waist. "What do you think then, Gabriel? You tell us where it is?"

"It's in a safe place."

He tightened his grip. "I'm sure it is. But tell me where."

"Look," I said. "What if I promise to give it to you tomorrow? Let me go about my business today. I'll tell you this—it's in an apartment in Santa Monica. We can meet anywhere you like, anytime you like."

Jean-Baptiste chatted with Hans in a language I couldn't quite decipher; it was neither French nor German, although it resembled both, and I thought I heard an English word here and there. Was it a hybrid dialect, a rejuvenated Alsatian, or some tongue developed to be spoken in a united Europe in the year 2114, more or less? After several minutes Jean-Baptiste said to me, "Our decision, ordinarily, is no. We don't trust you. But you've just lost a friend. So we give you the rest of the day. But tomorrow morning, eight o'clock, we meet you in Malibu. If you take my A-4 and go somewhere, we always will find you."

"And I break your neck," Hans said. He moved toward me and extended his long arms. At first I thought he was going to place his very large hands on my shoulders, which would have been unsteady-ing enough. But instead he clasped his fingers behind my neck, with his thumbs meeting under my jaw. He raised me a good six inches off the ground, then untwined his fingers and dropped me to the deck.

I spent the remainder of the journey in uneasy solitude.

18

Wadsworth's Studebaker was still in the ferry terminal parking lot; Lorna's car was gone. I spotted Dutch's Nash convertible a row down from the Studebaker, wondered briefly whether I could start it without the keys. Dutch certainly wouldn't be needing it. But the thought of fiddling with a primitive ignition while my new acquaintances, the Futureboys, lurked somewhere nearby wasn't enticing. Though a taxi to Malibu would cost a small fortune, I reminded myself that at 1938 prices I could afford a taxi to Constantinople. I picked up an *Examiner* at the terminal, got into the first cab I saw.

I spent the first ten minutes of the ride looking out the rear window. Nobody was following us. I found the story a couple of minutes later. It was on page seven, headlined ACTOR DROWNS OFF CATALINA. One column, four paragraphs. The body of Ronald Reagan, twenty-seven, had been found on a beach on Santa Catalina Island. Reagan, who had appeared in several Warner Brothers pictures, had drowned in stormy seas. A Catalina police spokesman (not Seligman) was quoted to the effect that the actor had probably overestimated his swimming ability. That was that. I imagined that in later editions, or in tomorrow's morning papers, at least one well-known actor and one Warners executive would speak to the dead actor's talent and promise. Perhaps an industrious reporter would track down Dutch's parents and extract a poignant quote or two. But Reagan wasn't important enough to merit a follow-up, and no newspaper would send someone to Catalina to look into the circumstances of his death.

I ripped page seven out of the paper, folded it, and slipped it into the breast pocket of my jacket. Perhaps I would create a scrapbook to commemorate the success of my mission. Or, perhaps I would simply show Lorna the story and then throw it out.

— —

It was dusk when I reached the Hudnut house, none of whose rooms were illuminated. I let myself in and switched on the light in the entryway, feeling as I did a comforting sense of having returned home. It did not last terribly long. There was a note by the telephone:

Dear Gabriel:

I'm writing this at noon. Bill is very sick. Probably pneumonia. I've taken him to the hospital. Don't know when I'll be back. I've thought a lot about the events of this weekend and I am pretty disgusted with things. With myself, with you. For all I know Dutch swam ashore somewhere and is in fine fettle. But even if that were the case I don't think I would want to see you again. If you're reading this tonight (Sunday), I should be back sometime between nine and midnight, and I'd appreciate it if you're gone when I return. I am afraid I feel very strongly about that.

L.

I had expected something like this, but I was shocked by the note's coldness, by its finality. Still, I thought I understood her state of mind. While she could hardly be blaming me for Dutch's drowning, for Wadsworth's asinine behavior and Dutch's overreaction, it was I who had urged her to make the trip, I who had failed to find us a trysting place somewhere other than in the Catherine. And when Dutch walked into the room, it was I who had been involved with her in an act that Dutch Reagan might never even have dreamed about. Even if the rest of the evening had proven entirely ordinary, I expect that Lorna would not have been very pleased with me.

There was a bit of Thursday night's stir-fry in the refrigerator. I heated it up and opened a bottle of Carling's Black Label. The stir-fry was still good, especially so because I'd eaten absolutely nothing since my several bites of miserable sea bass the night before. I washed my dishes and changed my clothes. The night had become cool, so I chose a tweed jacket and trousers and repaired to the living room, where the combination of a comfortable sofa, sleep deprivation, and the current issue of *Variety* rendered me unconscious in a matter of minutes.

I dreamed of Dutch. He and I and Wadsworth and Marie-Laure

were driving down the Oregon coast in 1994, or thereabouts. Dutch was rambling on about Oregon, giving me a history course that might have been complete nonsense. I was much more concerned about what was transpiring in the backseat between Marie-Laure and Wadsworth, who were embracing fervently and noisily. I made sporadic attempts to speak to Marie-Laure, who ignored me, and I made occasional noises of acknowledgment to Dutch, who appeared oblivious to the activity in the backseat and unaware that my attention might be divided, in the manner of someone terribly obsessed with his own voice. The highway, meanwhile, became progressively serpentine, and I seemed to be losing the the ability to steer, or perhaps I was losing interest in steering. It was fortunate there was no one coming in the opposite direction, because I was all over the road, no one within the car paying the slightest attention—not even when we left the road, flew over a cliff, and descended with the velocity of a morsel of eiderdown toward the rough seas below. There was no moment of impact. One instant we were in the air, the next we were underwater. "Can everyone get out?" I asked, and discovered that Wadsworth and Marie-Laure were no longer around. Nor, in the truest sense, was Dutch. The man in the passenger seat had metamorphosed into the elderly, presidential Ronald Reagan. "I'll be all right," he said, with the crinkly smile that had unaccountably communicated warm, grandfatherly wisdom to a nation sitting in front of its television set.

"Gabriel!" Lorna was standing over me, and she wasn't happy.

Nor was I ascending gracefully from slumber. I said, "What time is it?"

"It's eleven. I thought I made it very clear that I didn't want you here when I got back."

Despite her own state, whose elements by my estimation included exhaustion, anger, grief, and disgust, I found her immensely attractive. She wore pleated and cuffed khaki pants, a beige cottony blouse, and white sneakers, probably the outfit she'd chosen for the ferry this morning. Everything was wrinkled and there was some sort of greasy food stain on the blouse, just above her left breast. I said, "How's Bill?"

"He'll be all right. He's very sick, but he'll be all right. Not like your friend Dutch."

"You saw?"

"Of course I did. I got Dutch's parents' number from information and I called them. They hadn't heard. They thought he was still out there, with the damn baseball players. It was absolutely horrible. I feel very stupid and decadent."

"No," I said, waking up, sitting up. "Not you. Why should you?"

"Don't *you*?"

"I don't feel good about what happened. I have to take the blame for a lot of it. It's amazing how a foolish, embarrassing situation can turn into a disaster. But it's not your fault, Lorna. You were a voice of reason. And it was very brave of you to call his parents."

"How can you say those things so blithely, Gabriel?" Tears began to flow. "A man is dead! A perfectly innocent, decent man who was just starting his career. I don't think he would have gone down in history as a great actor, but the point is that he's dead because of *us*." She wept in earnest, and began pacing the floor, as if standing still were intensely painful.

"Not because of you," I said. I got to my feet, a bit dizzy from sunburn and fatigue, waited for my head to clear, moved to intercept her as she paced toward the sofa.

"Don't touch me!" She drew back as if I were contaminated.

"I love you," I said.

"No you don't!" She beat both fists against her thighs. "How *could* you? How could you want me to spend the night with Bill if you loved me?"

"I *didn't* want you to . . ." I caught myself. I said, "It was wrong. It was stupid. There was a reason, that had nothing to do with us or with Bill, that I can't possibly explain to you—"

"No!" Her voice was just short of a scream. "I can't tolerate that nonsense from you anymore, Gabriel. If you can't explain things to me, then why should we be seeing each other? It doesn't make any sense!"

In the best of circumstances, in an atmosphere completely absent of strife and tension, how do you suppose someone would react if you told her you'd dropped in on her life from fifty-six years in the future? Even if you could present impressive pieces of evidence, don't you imagine the process of convincing her would be a long, painstakingly empirical one? I was in no position this evening to—for instance— give Lorna the next several days' prices of selected stocks, courtesy of the laptop that had been sitting virtually untouched in the garage.

I said, "Lorna, please, for God's sake, give me another chance. I don't think it's asking too much. From now on, everything's in the open. We'll tell Bill about us, when he's feeling better—"

She interrupted me. "No! I don't trust you, Gabriel. There's something very strange about you. I don't know what it is, and I'm not sure I want to find out." She paused for a moment, still pacing. "And every time I see you I'm going to think of poor Dutch, lying dead on the beach in Avalon because of whatever was going on in *our* lives, not his."

I could think of nothing more to say, so I sat down again, leaned back on the sofa, and tried to gather my wits. Lorna continued to pace and, intermittently, to sob. After several minutes I said, "What are you going to do?"

"As soon as you get out of here, I'm going to bed."

"I mean in the longer term."

"It's none of your business."

There was quite a long silence. I said, "Lorna, I love you very much. You can't possibly know—"

"Shut up, Gabriel. You don't. You're a self-involved, egotistical pig like everybody else out here, and the faster you're out of my life the better I'll feel."

"How can you say that after Saturday afternoon? After what we did in my room? That was so . . . transcendent, Lorna. I don't think I've ever experienced anything like that—"

"*Transcendent?* Dutch walking in on us, as if we were a couple of animals rutting in the zoo?"

"If you knew . . ." I thought seriously about telling her how I'd saved her life, about retrieving the laptop from the garage as incontrovertible evidence of my identity. I imagined her skepticism. I imagined myself waiting, probably for weeks or months, for her anger to subside. I imagined myself without a way out of here, having turned the machine over to the Futureboys. Alternatively, I imagined myself darting around Southern California, one step ahead of Hans, waiting for Lorna to decide she might take me back. I said, "Would it be all right if I spent the night? In my own room, of course."

"No," she said, her back to me.

"Come on, Lorna. I'll pack up my stuff and take it with me to work in the morning."

"No. You can come back for your things tomorrow. I don't want you here tonight. You can find a room in one of the motor courts on Sunset." She stalked off into the kitchen.

I followed. She stood by the refrigerator, hesitant, as if in search of some foodstuff that might solve all her problems. "Well," I said, "good-bye, then."

She barely looked at me. "Good-bye," she said, her voice cool and flat.

I felt as if I were being pulled in several directions at once by forces I could not entirely identify. I felt considerable anger at Lorna's intractability, frustration at the constraints that prevented me from fully pleading my cause, and, ultimately, something bordering on despair. When I said, "I hope I'll see you again," she did not reply, and I took my leave.

—◦—

Of course there was no need for me to stop at "one of the motor courts on Sunset." I had an apartment in Santa Monica. Or rather, my machine had an apartment in Santa Monica. Or rather, Jean-Baptiste's machine. I realized a hundred yards out of the Colony that I'd left behind the laptop. Would it make any difference? Would I need it in 1994? I couldn't begin to deal with the questions, and so kept moving.

I had the nagging sense that a big gray sedan was following me, but then virtually every other car on the road was a big gray sedan. I pulled over several blocks from my destination, perceived nothing behind me, pulled out again. I arrived at a few minutes after ten, discovered everything exactly as I had left it. I had one piece of mail, advising me of the grand opening of a dry cleaning shop around the corner.

As I sat on the floor next to the machine (for lack of any furniture) under the light of one dim overhead fixture, I had my first clear thoughts of a hectic and disturbing day. I realized first that my dilemma wasn't necessarily as dire as it seemed. The machine provided me with at least two alternative courses of action. The first— the one that struck me first—was immensely attractive. I could set it to take me back three days, or four, or five—in any case, to a point before the disastrous weekend journey. Dutch would be alive. I would politely decline his invitation to Catalina, suggest that we do something together later on, propose to Lorna that she not spend the weekend with Wadsworth, that she go away somewhere with me instead, and let the chips fall where they might.

There were flaws, of course. Wadsworth would certainly feel angry and betrayed, do his utmost to find out about me, discredit me. Jean-Baptiste and Hans would show up on schedule, not on Catalina, to be sure, but elsewhere, and demand their machine. Why should I not simply hand it over? With the machine gone, presumably returned to the twenty-second century, the only evidence of my alien nature would be gone as well, so what could Wadsworth conclude? That I was a mystery man, a man without a past. So what?

On the other hand, Wadsworth might engender enough doubt and suspicion to get me fired. I was here for a purpose, and if Warners canned me, my access to Ronald Reagan would be far more difficult.

Then too, there was the matter of the control panel. Had Jean-Baptiste been blowing smoke? Hudnut had succeeded in sending me back exactly a day, but then he'd been off by two or three years on my trip here. What would happen if my attempt to retrogress several days landed me several weeks, or months, or years in the past? What if two successive trips backward caused me to have a headache like Hudnut's, or a worse one? What if I found myself in 1937, for instance, knowing no one, immobilized by pain?

Now came the second alternative: I could return to 1994, to my point of origin. I could confer with Hudnut, tell him what I'd achieved in my brief visit to 1938. Here I found myself stumbling into a hall of mirrors: in a sense Hudnut would already know my achievements, because they'd be faits accomplis. We knew from my original retrogressive visit to Santa Anita that history could be changed, and that the changes didn't somehow undo themselves when one returned to one's starting point. Thus were I to return now to 1994, *Lorna would never have died in the Great Storm, Ronald Reagan would always have drowned off Catalina.*

But would Hudnut know *me?* Would he have vivid memories of our time together, or would I have slipped out of his consciousness altogether when I went backwards in time? Thinking about that one made my brain throb.

Muddled, sunburned, thoroughly exhausted, I decided that a night's sleep, even on the cold hardwood floor, was what I needed. In the morning, when Lorna was at Warners, I could haul the machine back to Malibu, so I would arrive in the Hudnut garage no matter which direction I chose. I was in the process of rolling my jacket into a pillow when I heard a light tapping at the front door, and my adrenaline ran amuck. Could it be?

The voice was discreet, the accent unmistakable. "Gabriel? Why do I think you're not going to meet us tomorrow morning?" A pause. "Gabriel? You have to let us in, okay? Or do you wish that we make some trouble for you?"

Trying to remain calm, trying to be silent, I put my jacket back on, checked for my wallet, ascended the machine. Outside the door, Jean-Baptiste's voice was rising and now I detected Hans's basso snarling as well. Which way was I to turn? I set the controls with unsteady fingers, held my breath, and pressed the "go" button.

PART III

An Inexact Science

(Where Are You, Eric Blair?)

19

It did not particularly surprise me that going forward took no longer than going backward. The surprise, as before, was that the process was so extraordinarily quick. Three seconds, five seconds, certainly no more than that. I had time for one thought: had I elected to go back a few days, and had I succeeded in setting the controls to do just that, I would have arrived in this very studio apartment leased to me, with virtually no possibility of unwanted company.

The first thought I had upon arrival, as the familiar and very welcome giddiness began to set in, was that I had been lucky. It was night; it was quite dark; I was alone; I was no longer indoors.

I was sitting on the machine about three feet away from a small blue monolith. A gas pump. I got to my feet. The building in which Jean-Baptiste's machine spent its brief tenancy had been supplanted by a Chevron station. Regular unleaded was going for 121.9, premium for 135.9. The station was closed, its lights extinguished for the most part. One underpowered fixture high on a stanchion provided enough illumination for me to get my bearings; a security light inside the station's office enabled me to discover that it was just past five in the morning.

Did I have a headache? No. I shook my head violently from side to side. Not a trace of a headache. I felt awfully good, ready for just about anything. I grabbed the machine by the seat and dragged it into a narrow alley between the station's rest rooms and a wooden fence topped with barbed wire. The machine weighed seventy or eighty pounds and had been hell to hoist into the back of the Buick, no fun to drag into its ground-floor apartment. Now I might as well have been pulling a baby carriage.

What next? There was a pay phone not thirty feet from me. I suspected Hudnut wouldn't appreciate a call at 5 A.M., even from such a distinguished and unexpected visitor. My own house was no more than two miles away. But the machine would hardly fit into my Toyota, or in the trunk of any 1994 taxi I'd ever seen. Where could I find a pickup truck at this hour? I could rent one at the airport. I could get to LAX in twenty minutes. Would Hertz or Avis be open? Probably. Then it would take another twenty minutes to rent the truck. . . . Stop right there. I had no credit cards, no current driver's license.

But I had plenty of cash—enough to take me halfway around the world in 1938, enough to buy a cheap pickup in 1994. When would the used car lots be opening? Eight-thirty? Nine o'clock? Unless it were Sunday, in which case they might not be opening at all. In that case, certainly, I could call Hudnut and make different arrangements. But if the machine had done its job properly, taken me back to my point of origin, it wouldn't be Sunday. I had left early of a midweek morning.

Now some fifteen minutes into this new sequence, standing huddled in the alleyway, I realized that something was at least slightly amiss. Despite my tweed jacket, despite my post-travel high, I was decidedly chilled. My sunburn was probably a contributing factor, but wasn't it overly cool for a May morning in Southern California? I began walking briskly around the gas station's grounds. Within a few minutes I had broken into a jog. I trotted to the corner, trotted back, trotted to the corner again. In predawn light I could make out a cluster of newspaper machines one block west. What better to do while awaiting business hours than get a head start on the new 1994?

There were six machines: a real estate giveaway sheet, an *L.A. Express*, a *USA Today*, a *Los Angeles Times*, a *Santa Monica Outlook*, an old *Herald-Examiner* box that no one had bothered to repaint, but that was obviously being used for something else because the *Herald* had ceased to exist several years earlier. Other than the giveaway, the only box with anything in it was the *Times*'s. I found two quarters in my right pants pocket—some lucky numismatist would soon come across a couple of mint Standing Liberties—and was surprised when the box popped open after I'd inserted the first. Evidently this was my lucky day.

I jogged back to the Chevron station, checked on the well-being of my machine, and positioned myself under the tall light stanchion, where I might be able to read text in addition to headlines. I had no difficulty making out the banner head on the front page: ANGRY HIN-

DUS SEEK REVENGE. And underneath it a photograph of Indira Gandhi whose caption I strained to read: "The Indian prime minister assassinated by Sikh members of her security guard."

This was curious indeed. My first thought, of course, was that my actions in 1938 had somehow had a much greater effect on history than I'd imagined. I couldn't remember exactly when Indira Gandhi had been killed the first time around, but it was sometime in the mid-eighties. Had I granted her an extra decade of life?

My focus moved to the top of the page, and I came abruptly to my senses. Today, the *Times* informed me, was Thursday, November 1, 1984.

I tried to gather my wits. This state of elation had worked wonders for me a couple of weeks ago, providing a web of charming artifice in which I captured Lorna. How would it serve me on a cool, dark morning a decade away from my intended destination? Probably, I reasoned, in my haste to get away before Hans broke down the door and broke my neck, I had mis-set the date. So now I put aside the newspaper, took my seat on the machine, set the controls painstakingly, held my breath, and pressed the "go" button.

I did not go. Instead, a tiny but very bright light to the left of the "go" button—one I had not been aware of before, one Hudnut had not brought to my attention—began blinking. It did so for about a minute, then shut off. Perhaps it was telling me I could not reactivate the machine so soon. Perhaps I could wait an hour, a day, or a week, and arrive successfully in 1994. More likely, I feared, I had set the controls perfectly the first time, and Jean-Baptiste had been telling the truth. The control panel was out of whack, the machine was convinced it *had* transported me to May 1994, the blinking light signifying that it couldn't take me where I already was.

Were this the case, it would mean I could go forward no further: the machine could take me only to my point of origin, and it believed I was there.

What then? If I tried to return to 1938 there was no guarantee I could make it, and even if I did I'd have the Futureboys to contend with. Here in 1984 I could still find Hudnut, who wouldn't know me from Adam, but I suspected that it wouldn't be too difficult to convince him of our connection. I had overwhelming evidence.

━ ━

The station manager, a tall man of obvious subcontinental origin, arrived at a few minutes before six to open the place up. He appeared a bit bemused by my presence, but not at all put out. I told him I'd been dropped here, along with my experimental boat, by a friend bound south, and would be heading north as soon as I could rent a truck. Embroidered in cursive on his Chevron uniform was his name: V. Singh. I did not inquire as to his feelings regarding the Gandhi assassination. He did ask me whether I would feel more secure with my boat indoors. So it was that the machine sat next to a lift occupied by an old Pontiac undergoing minor surgery, while I sat in the office with this morning's *Times*.

The front page was dominated by news from India, but there was a three-column headline at the bottom that caught my eye: BUSH SAVAGES MONDALE, DEMOS, IN 11TH-HOUR STRATEGY SWITCH.

It was Thursday, the first of November, which meant we were five days from the election that in my 1984 had given Ronald Reagan his second term. We were five days from the election and it didn't even rate the middle of page one, suggesting that the presidential race was not a great provider of suspense, not to mention interest. I read:

> NEW YORK—In a campaign speech tonight, George Bush asked a half-empty arena whether America needs "four more years of the same aimless, spineless leadership provided by Jimmy Carter." Mr. Bush cited the Carter administration's reluctance to take action against the Soviet Union's invasion of Afghanistan as an example of "inexcusable inaction bordering on the amoral."
>
> The speech, at Madison Square Garden, marked an apparent radical change in policy on the part of the Bush campaign, which has been criticized in the press and by Republican leaders for its lack of aggressiveness. A Gallup Poll of likely voters released this morning showed Vice President Walter Mondale, the Democratic candidate, leading Mr. Bush by a margin of 54% to 38%, with 8% undecided.
>
> Mr. Bush, whose campaign has been additionally hampered by numerous blunders, both by staff and by the candidate himself, drew laughter and applause from a partisan audience when he said, "Maybe I'm not the smoothest guy in this election, but at least I've got a track record. I haven't spent the last eight years being somebody else's caddy."
>
> In Chicago, where he attended a fund-raising dinner, Mr. Mondale

said, "I think my record speaks for itself. I think George Bush is a desperate man, and desperate men tend to say desperate things."

In Los Angeles, Democratic vice-presidential candidate Howell Heflin characterized Mr. Bush's remarks as "completely irresponsible and uncalled for. How can you use words like 'inexcusable' and 'amoral' when you're referring to an administration that's virtually eliminated nuclear weapons from this world."

The Alabama senator pointed as well to normalized relations with Cuba and acknowledged U.S. influence in Central American stability as achievements of the Carter administration.

Mr. Carter, with his wife, Rosalynn, and Education Secretary Jerry Brown, is in Moscow, serving as co-chairman with Soviet Premier Konstantin Chernenko of the First Worldwide Disarmament Conference.

The story proceeded for another several paragraphs, returning to the Bush speech, citing a few other targets of George Bush's wrath, such as the intimacy of the Carter administration with Daniel Ortega's Sandinistas. Bush promised that if he were elected president he would do his utmost to restore true, non-Marxist democracy to Nicaragua.

In my own strange state, this combination of great fatigue and expanding elation, I wondered briefly whether someone, somehow, had engineered a practical joke of epochal proportions, sending me back and forth through time just so I might come across the very joke issue of the *Los Angeles Times* I was holding. But evidently it was all true: by bringing together Ronald Reagan and Bill Wadsworth on a darkened beach in March 1938, I had turned history—or at least the global politics of 1984—on its ear.

I paged through the rest of the paper. An infant girl, named Baby Fae, had been the beneficiary of transplanted baboon heart. She was doing fine. I feared she would not last long. The usual complement of crimes and accidents had occurred around Southern California, the United States, the world. An electronics chain that would go out of business in a matter of years was well enough today to take out a full-page ad; among other things, it offered a primitive telephone answering machine for $89.99. On the next page, a state-of-the-art IBM computer, with 512 kilobytes of memory and a twenty-megabyte hard disk, was on sale for $5,795, monitor extra. For $5,795 I could have bought two Buick convertibles in 1938, had enough left over to buy my laptop in 1994.

"Something is amusing?" This was V. Singh speaking. Evidently I had laughed out loud.

"The world can be confusing," I said, and he nodded in pleasant agreement.

— —

Shortly after eight I ventured ten blocks down Olympic Boulevard and bought a 1979 Datsun pickup for $950. The salesman, a man of sixty-five or so, asked me where I'd found my suit. "I haven't seen one tailored like that since I was a kid," he said.

V. Singh helped me load the machine onto the truckbed, and reluctantly accepted my twenty-dollar gratuity. Feeling giddy, disoriented, but highly confident, I cut over to the Santa Monica Freeway—most of whose fearsome rush-hour traffic was headed in the opposite direction—and took it to the Pacific Coast Highway.

At quarter past ten, the last few wisps of morning fog were in the air, but the temperature was already well into the sixties. The Malibu Colony was now flanked by a shopping center and a gas station. I made a discreet U-turn and pulled up by the pay phone in the Unocal station adjacent to the highway. One Mercury dime enabled me to make a call; I dialed Hudnut's 1994 number, and an unfamiliar male voice answered on the second ring. I said, "Hello, I'm trying to locate Jasper Hudnut."

"May I ask who's calling?"

"My name is Gabriel Prince. I'm an old friend. May I ask who you are?"

"This is Charles Hudnut."

"Charles? I think I met you, many years ago. In Malibu, at the house. . . ."

There was a short silence. "You're probably confusing me with my father. He's also Charles Hudnut. I'm usually called Charlie, actually."

"Of course," I said. "And how is your father?"

"He's doing fine," Charlie replied. "Still in Glendale, he and Mom are still in the same house. He's eighty-six. You'd never know it."

I resisted a strong urge to ask Charlie about Lorna. She would be nearly seventy now; if I saw her again, I wanted it to be in 1938. I said, "Well, that's good to hear. And what about Jasper?"

"May I ask how you know him?"

How did I know Hudnut? Neither the truth nor my previous ruse would be of much use here. "He was my teacher."

"At Cal Poly?"

"No, actually. Is he still there?"

"I'm still trying to place you," Charlie said.

Had cousin Jasper given strict instructions to grill all ostensible old friends, or was Charlie just a pain in the neck?

"Oregon State," I said, although the chronology was all wrong.

"I've got to tell you," Charlie said, "the last thing I'd ever want to do would be look up someone who'd taught me physics thirty years ago."

"I'm sure you can imagine that Jasper wasn't an everyday teacher."

"I'm sure," Charlie said. "But obviously you haven't kept up with him."

"Obviously. I've been out of the country, for quite a long while. Completely out of touch."

"You must have been. He's kept a pretty high profile. I'd have assumed any old student of his would know where to find him."

"Well, not this one."

There was a disarmingly long pause, as if Charlie were making up his mind once and for all whether I were truly an old friend or actually a Sikh assassin. Finally he said, "He's at Cal Tech."

"In Pasadena?"

"Right. Would you like the number?"

I'd thought he'd never ask.

20

I took Malibu Canyon Road up to the Ventura Freeway and headed east to the Foothill. I could have turned off the Ventura in Burbank and been about two minutes from the Warners studios, but there was nothing there for me now. Instead I continued east, through Glendale, past the Rose Bowl, into Pasadena. I'd left the Unocal station outside the Colony at ten-thirty, arrived in Pasadena at quarter past eleven. On a weekday morning in 1994 the same trip would have taken me ninety minutes, minimum.

My temptation was to drive straight to Cal Tech and find Hudnut directly, but that would mean leaving a battered pickup truck with a time machine in its bed parked amidst thousands of scientists. Instead I found a street-level room at a Ramada Inn on Colorado Boulevard two miles from the campus. Somewhat less energetic now than I'd been six hours earlier, I dragged the machine into my room. I was delighted to discover a full complement of toiletries on my bathroom sink.

I called the number Charlie had given me, and a lilting female voice answered, "Physics Department." I was told Professor Hudnut was in class, class was out at noon, and he might pick up messages on his way to lunch. I gave my name and number, added that it was a matter of urgency. I took a long shower, indulging myself in an abundance of Ramada shampoo. I lay down, then, on a bed as wide as a football field, and the next thing I knew it was two o'clock. Could I have slept through Hudnut's call? The front desk disabused me of that notion: there had been no calls to my room.

I dialed the Physics Department again, was told by a different voice that Doctor Hudnut always picked up his messages at five, after his last class; I left my name and number again, said this time that it was extremely urgent.

When had I eaten last? The stir-fry last night, before that the ghastly sea bass on Catalina thirty-five hours ago: two meals in forty-six years. I ordered a turkey club sandwich and a bottle of Heineken from room service. The sandwich was delivered promptly, was marginally edible. I considered going out to buy some underwear and a shirt, but fell asleep again.

The telephone was ringing. It was dusk, and for the briefest of moments I hadn't the slightest idea where I was. I caught sight of the machine—hovering over the foot of the bed like a flightless bird designed by Marcel Duchamp—switched on the light, rose immediately to a state of full awareness, picked up the phone, and heard a familiar voice.

"Gabriel Prince? Do I know you, and what the hell is so urgent?"

As much as I had rehearsed for this moment, the words did not exactly flow. "Well, in a sense you do know me—"

He interrupted, "This kind of thing is very frustrating, when someone's name is familiar to you, but you have no idea what the connection is."

What was he talking about? Was there some peculiarity to time travel, some retroactive mind-jolt powerful enough to have imposed me on Hudnut's memory ten years before he was to meet me? "Look," I said, "you'll have to excuse me. I'm kind of groggy. I just woke up. I don't believe you know me, but I know you, if that makes any sense."

"Not to me, it doesn't."

"If we could meet, Dr. Hudnut, I have something pretty extraordinary to show you."

"You'll have to do better than that, Mr. Prince."

My mind searched for its ace in the hole, and at this instant a little post-travel acuity seemed to cut in. "Look, I know that you found a time machine in Oregon thirty years ago. I have one here with me now, and I want to talk to you about it."

There was a very short silence. "That shouldn't be any problem. You're at the Ramada, room one two seven? I can be there in fifteen minutes."

— • —

He didn't look terribly different. He was ten years younger, of course, and much more robust, as if he were taking better care of himself. I would never have taken him for an academic, with his rumpled blue jeans and gray suede jacket, his graying hair long and unruly. He shook my hand at the door, seemed to absorb as much as he needed to know about me in about two seconds, then shifted his attention to the machine by the bed. With an "Excuse me" he breezed into the room.

"Good God," he said, having already seated himself on the machine, "it could almost be the same one. I've got such a clear picture of mine. Hah! Mine, indeed."

"I wouldn't be surprised if it is the same one." I'd sat down on the edge of the bed.

"Before we go any further, I want to know one thing." He'd switched his attention back to me. "Did I tell you about finding that machine, or did someone else?"

"You did."

"When?"

"1994."

Hudnut let out a great snort of a laugh. "God! This is terrific! Let me guess, now. From the looks of you, from that excellent suit, I'd say you either came from the best damn thrift shop in town or from about 1940."

"Close enough. 1938."

"Boy! I love this stuff! Well, I suppose you know that. I suppose you know all sorts of things about me. We could be good pals ten years from now, or for all I know we could just have met at some twelve-step loony program. Recovering time-machine nuts! Which is it, Prince?"

"You call me Gabriel."

"Fine. I'll call you Gabriel."

"No, I mean in 1994 you call me Gabriel."

"All right, Gabriel it is. Get on with it."

"We met in Paris. At a museum. The Musée des Techniques."

"Of course. One of my favorite places."

"The machine, *this* machine was there. You acquired it, in your own words. Evidently you bought it. I'm not sure how legitimately. You were convinced that somehow it had been left for you to find, because the odds against one person finding two time machines in his lifetime were unimaginable."

"Yes. Obviously. Fantastic. This is marvelous."

"You proceeded to recruit me for what you called an errand. Something you wanted very much to do yourself, but you felt you were too old . . ."

"Send you back before the war to take care of Hitler, but evidently you've failed. But you've escaped with your life and now you've come here . . . except why wouldn't you have returned all the way to ninety-four?"

"No," I said. "This is where you might have a little trouble accepting what I'm going to tell you. You sent me back to change things, and evidently I've done an awfully good job. From what I've learned since I've been here, Jimmy Carter was reelected four years ago—"

"Yes, of course. Three hundred and some electoral votes. Not exactly a landslide, but a decisive victory, especially when you consider the Iran business."

"All right. In the original 1980, in the one *I* lived through, Carter was pretty thoroughly trounced by someone who went on to be president for eight years, who represented the very right wing of the Republican Party, and who you felt was one of the most . . . damaging figures of the twentieth century."

"Who? Not Goldwater, certainly. Of course not. Someone you took care of back in thirty-eight, so I probably never even heard of the guy."

"Probably not. He was an actor. Not a very good one. Went on to be governor of California. His name was Ronald Reagan."

Hudnut looked at the ceiling. "Wait a minute. The name's familiar." He looked at me. "How do you spell it?" I spelled it. "*Reegan*," Hudnut shouted. "Are you kidding me? The guy who drowned off Catalina? Lorna was there! Some pathetic guy from the Midwest. Lorna was all messed up about this."

He looked at me for acknowledgment, and I nodded, whereupon Hudnut took a huge breath, let it out slowly. "It was a long time ago and the details are a little fuzzy, but Lorna was in the process of breaking up with her Ivy League jerk—Wadsworth was his name—and this poor bastard drowned. *He* became president of the United States? How is it possible?"

How could one explain it, concisely? "It developed."

Here was the Hudnut stare again, that unnervingly intense gaze. "You're saying I sent you back to kill him?"

"No. It just turned out that way. I had no intention for him to die. I had a very clever plan, actually, but things got complicated because I fell in love with Lorna. . . ."

"Yes. Easy to see."

"There was a good deal of irony involved, really, because you'd told me that Lorna died in a big storm, when her car was crushed. I happened to show up a few days before then, and I saved her life. Did that intentionally. And then quite unintentionally I got Reagan killed, and now here are we are in this Shangri-La of a 1984."

Hudnut's expression had changed, softened. "We've got an awful lot to talk about," he said.

— —

After a stop at the Gap, where Hudnut insisted on paying for black Levi's and a corduroy jacket, we headed up Del Mar Boulevard toward Altadena, where I was to have dinner with him and his wife. Our vehicle was the Porsche—the very automobile I had driven to Santa Anita in the spring of 1994. His wife was the one person, he said, who knew about his discovery of the time machine in 1952. That given, she had been neither astonished nor incredulous when Hudnut told her (on the telephone) about me. He was amused when I told him that in our previous acquaintance he had never been married.

I had already given him a précis of the first Reagan administration, spilling over into the second, much of it a reprise of our conversation at the café the afternoon we met. While much of Reagan's presidency had seemed an exercise in surrealist satire as it occurred—if one could stand back and gain a little perspective—to Hudnut it now appeared to be pure burlesque. When I told him his own favorite Reagan anecdote, in which the president addresses Liberian dictator Samuel K. Doe as "Chairman Moe," Hudnut burst into sustained laughter.

It struck me that the situation of the moment was all the more bizarre because Hudnut had no context. He had not witnessed the evolution of Ronald Reagan from B-movie actor to television personality to respected spokesman for American values to governor of California to charismatic leader of the Right. Hudnut was dealing with nothing more than the preposterous notion of a second-rate actor, "some pathetic guy from the Midwest," becoming the most powerful man on the planet.

Under control now, Hudnut said, "There's something very sad about this."

"You don't have to tell me that."

"No, I mean particularly what you've just told me. On one hand it's a story about an important man who's in way above his head making a mistake that reveals his ignorance, his incompetence. On the other hand, it's a story about the president of the United States giving legitimacy to a really sleazy dictator. . . . I mean, do you *know* about this guy Doe?"

I did not. Virtually all of modern Liberian history was *terra incognita* to me. Hudnut told me that Doe, an army sergeant, had with a number of colleagues broken into Monrovia's presidential palace, wiped out all the presidential guard, and shot the president himself, only after gouging out one eye and disemboweling him. Doe then promoted himself to general and took the helm, whereupon Liberia maintained its stature as one of Africa's most corrupt and squalid states.

"This was right at the start of Carter's second term," Hudnut said. "Carter wouldn't touch the guy, which showed a lot of guts, because Liberia had so much 'strategic importance,' sitting next to the Ivory Coast, the Russians' big conquest. I don't know how much that accomplished as far as Liberia was concerned, but it sure as hell sent a message to Brezhnev. Carter was saying, 'Look, I don't want to play this game anymore. I don't think we *need* to play this game anymore."

"And the Russians didn't jump right in?"

"They didn't. So all the Cold Warriors here, which meant practically everybody in the Republican Party, and about eighty percent of the newspaper columnists, and about sixty percent of the Democratic party, and a hundred percent of the military, said either the Russians were biding their time, *or* Liberia just wasn't important enough, *or* the Russians were saving their money for something even more insidious."

"When in fact," I said, "it wasn't that the Russians were saving their money, it was that they didn't have any money left."

"Right!" Hudnut slapped my leg for emphasis. "So obviously that happened in your place, too."

"Yes. All of a sudden. 1989. It turned out the whole Iron Curtain had been hanging by a thread. But it didn't work out particularly well. The conservatives and the military took credit for spending the Communists to death, which also meant we had a national debt of a few trillion dollars, which the conservatives try to blame on the Democrats, and most of the Soviet Union and Eastern Europe pretty much went to hell."

"Incredible," Hudnut said. "As if every single worst move was chosen." He paused. "Germany reunited?"

"Yes. Fairly painlessly."

"Any repercussions?"

"Not really, by the time I left. Neo-Nazis setting fire to Turks' houses, but not on a major scale, so far."

"You say that the Soviet Union went to hell. What about all the nuclear weapons?"

"Well," I said, "none had been detonated, and none had fallen into the wrong hands, at least that anybody knew about, but there was all sorts of potential for nastiness, because just about all the individual republics declared their independence, and there wasn't a lot that Russia could do, so the bombs and warheads stopped belonging to the USSR and started belonging to Ukraine, or Kyrgyzstan. Along with a lot of plutonium and God knows what else."

"Good grief," Hudnut shuddered. "What a mess." He patted my shoulder. "We're a hell of a lot better off here, Gabriel. If I were you, I'd stay here."

Was he joking? "Forgive my ignorance, Jasper, but wouldn't 1994 now just be a continuation of *this*? I mean, since Reagan died in thirty-eight, won't things just proceed from here? Won't the ninety-four I experienced be obliterated forever?"

"Possibly. It would be nice to think so."

"*Possibly?* Look—what little I understand about this stuff is based on what you told me in 1994. Am I missing something?"

He laughed, and swung the Porsche through a corner with such force I felt I had to hang on to the door. "I can't possibly know what I told you ten years from now, can I?"

"No, I don't suppose you can."

21

From the outside, the house struck quite a contrast to the one I knew so well in Malibu. It was three stories, but by no means huge. A stone chimney, open porch, and ivied sides put one in mind of a New England college town, but one's mind was shuttled back to California by glass doors and a young Japanese maple. Mrs. Hudnut was in the kitchen. She was forty, give or take a year or two, of medium stature, and quite good-looking, with shoulder-length brown hair and green eyes.

"Gabriel Prince," Hudnut said, "this is my wife, Annabel."

Annabel! Of course. I offered my hand. She offered a firm grip and said, "Where did you get that sunburn?"

"At a baseball game. It's a long story."

"Yes, of course. Jasper's told me about your machine. But I keep thinking I know your name. How could that be?"

"I have no idea," I said, "but I know yours."

"How could you possibly know mine?"

I looked at Hudnut, as if for approval, and he shrugged. "Jasper told me about you, very briefly, several weeks ago, in 1994."

"This is all very disorienting, isn't it?" Annabel said. "What did he tell you about me?"

"It's another long story," I said. "I mean, what he told me was three or four sentences. It's the context that's a long story."

"Some strange person becomes president," Annabel said. "Some bad movie actor. I know that much."

"Yes. When the movie actor was governor of California, he—or some functionary of his—had you fired. You were teaching math at Cal Poly in San Luis Obispo. Jasper was a physics professor. There was some sort of distant connection to the math building bombing in Madison. Jasper quit in protest."

Hudnut said, "I haven't told him anything about you. I promise."

Annabel's eyes had widened considerably. "This is extraordinary. I mean, it's not what happened, but it's what could very easily have happened. So what became of us?"

"You didn't stay together," I said. "I believe you married an engineer at NASA and went to live in Florida."

On short notice, Annabel had prepared salmon Florentine that was moist and delicious, the spinach done just right, not overly salted. I remarked that I'd seldom had salmon this good, that two occasions came to mind—once with my erstwhile employer at an expensive restaurant in Seattle, and once at an even more expensive restaurant in Paris. Annabel accepted my compliment graciously, and Hudnut told her this was no ordinary diner commending her salmon, but a professional critic, whereupon Annabel asked where she might find my books, and I was stumped for the moment. It was in October of my original 1984 that I had initially been contacted by Harvey Wells Greenglass. Not until March 1985 had I gone to research the first edition of the Paris *Entrée*. In fact, at this point only my first book, the unfortunately titled *Ottomania: A Guide to Unexpected Treasures in Turkey and Bulgaria*, had been published.

"I must say," Annabel said, "that there's an awful lot about this time travel business that confuses me. For instance, I don't suppose Gabriel's books are just going to materialize."

"Exactly," Hudnut said. "Not unless he writes them."

"That's an easy one," Annabel resumed, "but this one's much harder, I'd say. Unless he's a very elaborate liar, Gabriel's just changed history. By going back in time and—quite accidentally, of course—knocking off this strange man who would have turned out to be very important, he's changed *our* lives. What perplexes me is . . . Gabriel, how long ago, in your personal time frame, did the Actor drown?"

I calculated. "About forty hours ago."

"What perplexes me," Annabel continued, turning now to Hudnut, "is that evidently up until forty hours ago I was married to some NASA engineer and you were doing God knows what. Then the Actor drowns, and *wham!* everything changes. Does that mean that the last eleven years you and I have spent together are a sort of illusion? That we didn't really experience everything we recall doing in that period, that in fact a week ago I was playing golf in Orlando and you were chatting up some waitress in Tampico? But now that Gabriel's taken care of what's-his-name our memories have been instantaneously supplied with everything that conforms to the nature of the world minus the Actor?"

Hudnut gazed at Annabel with what appeared to be great admiration. "Of course not, darling. Think of Einstein."

"Exactly how shall I think of Einstein, sweetheart?"

"The elasticity of time. First, it is quite possible that Gabriel *is* responsible for our marriage, that if he hadn't gone back to 1938 you *would* be in Orlando and I *would* be in Tampico. But that doesn't mean we haven't lived those eleven years. We have proof. We have photographs. We have newspaper articles."

Annabel said, "Einstein or not, I can't say I'm terribly sure how all this works."

I spoke to Hudnut. "One of the first things you told me was that time travel is seamless. The image I have is of some kind of viscous liquid—miraculously fast viscous liquid—immediately moving to fill all the cracks the time traveler has created."

He nodded and smiled. "It's a very nice image."

"But does it work? Does it apply?"

"I don't think so," Hudnut said. "And again, Gabriel, I'm afraid I can't be responsible for what I've already told you. It's possible that ten years from now I'll know a great deal more than I do now, but then I wonder if 'ten years from now' is really an accurate description of your 1994. But I'd be happy to tell how I *think* this all works."

"By all means," I said.

"Please," said Annabel.

"All right." Hudnut got to his feet and left the dining room. He returned inside of ten seconds, holding an African throw rug he'd retrieved from the living room. He extended the rug to its full length and said, "Gabriel, describe this, as fully as you can."

"It's about four feet long, maybe two feet wide. It's a sort of linear quilt, with parallel strips of fabric running lengthwise. They're about an inch and a half wide, so there are thirty of them, more or less, in about ten different colors . . ."

"Good enough," Hudnut said. "*Linear quilt.* I like the phrase. The important part here is the parallel strips. Imagine that there were an infinite number of them, that they might occasionally overlap, that the rug's width ran infinitely, and the rug's length also ran infinitely."

"Yes," Annabel said. "Of course!"

Still basking in Hudnut's admiration of my phrase, I hadn't reached the yes, of course! stage. I held my hands apart, palms upraised, indicating mystification.

"*Timelines*, Gabriel," Hudnut said. "An infinite number of timelines running parallel to infinite length. In the one you left, the Actor was still president, will always have been president, and Annabel and I went our separate ways. In this one, he was never president, and we've been married for eleven years."

I digested. I considered. I said, "So every time I use the machine, every time *anyone* uses the machine, he jumps from one timeline to the next?"

"From one to the next, or from one to another." Hudnut dropped the rug and reclaimed his seat at the table.

"So I started in one timeline, where Reagan had been president. I jumped to another, where Reagan died . . . forty-two years before he'd become president, so in that one obviously he'd never be president. But then I jumped to a third timeline, and it just happens that in this one Reagan isn't president either."

"That's how it works," Hudnut said.

"It makes sense," Annabel said.

"I'm not sure it does," I said. "In my first timeline, I'm not there in 1938, so Reagan doesn't drown. In my second timeline, I'm there and he drowns. In my third timeline, I'm not there, so why should he drown?"

Hudnut said, "There's an infinite number of possible reasons for him to drown. Maybe your timeline's the exception. Maybe he drowns in all the rest."

Again I considered. "No," I said. "Logic tells me no. True, I've only been here a few hours, but everything seems awfully similar to the 1984 I remember. Music on the radio. The baby who got a baboon heart. Everything that's *different* can be ascribed to the absence of Ronald Reagan, and he's dead because of me."

"Don't forget, Gabriel, that the lines aren't discrete. They can overlap, so it's quite possible your last timeline has bled into this one."

"I don't really think it's a question of *bleeding*. I think there's a linear connection between the 1938 I was just in and the 1984 I'm in right now. If we need proof we can call Warner Brothers in the morning. Or you could talk to Lorna. For God's sake, don't let her know I'm here."

Hudnut and Annabel exchanged glances. He said, "I'm afraid that wouldn't be possible."

My heart fluttered a bit. In my mind's eye, of course, Lorna remained twenty-three years old. "She's died, then? It's not that unexpected, is it? She would have been close to seventy."

"No," Hudnut said, "I'm afraid she died a long time ago, in this timeline."

I had intimations of nausea, not liking the sound of this. "When?"

"December, thirty-eight," Hudnut said. "Two weeks before Christmas. The night of the premiere of her big movie. I couldn't bear to tell you back at the motel, because you were obviously so proud you'd saved her life. But of course in *that* timeline you did save her life. And in this one she simply died several months later."

I was speechless. The timeline business, while it made some objective sense, seemed in this instance a case of science rather obtusely contradicting common sense. And I couldn't escape the suspicion that I'd rescued Lorna from the frying pan only somehow to have hurled her into the fire. Filled with dread, I was formulating my next question when Annabel exclaimed, "That's it! Jasper, that's it!"

"That's what, darling?"

"Lorna's movie—*that's* where I've seen Gabriel's name!"

The Hudnuts had a 16-millimeter print of *Four O'Clock*, and the sort of small, roll-up screen that was so common in the prevideo home movie era. There were degrees of inquiry as to the advisability of my watching the film. I assured both my hosts that I would be just fine. In reality, I was scared to death.

Watching *Four O'Clock* was a succession of revelations, a carnival haunted house for my psyche, a peculiar corollary to the cliché of the playwright standing anxiously in the back of the theater as his work is performed. Only Errol Flynn got star billing. Lorna's name was bigger than those that followed, including Ann Sheridan, evidently in the Katy Jurado role, and Wayne Morris prefiguring Lloyd Bridges. The one moment that left me gasping for breath was:

SCREENPLAY BY
William Wadsworth & Gabriel Prince

So they'd taken my treatment and the bits and pieces I'd left on my desk, and when I didn't return after a few days they'd turned the project over to my pal, to the man who'd recommended me for the position, Bill Wadsworth. Why was my name even on the screen? Was Bernie Wiseman a man of great integrity, or had Lorna fought for me? The director was Michael Curtiz—a nice touch, not unsurprising—and the producer Bernard Wiseman.

Credits over, Errol Flynn and Lorna Fairchild hurried down the church steps on their wedding day, surrounded by well-wishing extras. Not twenty seconds into the picture there was a closeup of Lorna, and here my heart came close to stopping. Curtiz knew a star when he saw one. Lorna glowed. Flynn dazzled. They embraced. Right here, in the very next shot, Wadsworth had some grizzled cowpoke rush in to inform the marshal that his old nemesis had been released from prison and was on his way back to even the score. That wasn't the way I'd planned it. Flynn entered his office. Shot of the clock. Here was Lorna again, reminding Flynn that she's a Quaker, a woman of peace, telling him he's no longer marshal and the proper thing is to leave town with her, as planned. Lorna was terrific. Flynn was all right, would have been much more credible with better dialogue.

Shots of the clock were few and far between. I spoke to Hudnut: "Was this a hit?"

"I don't think so—couldn't say for sure. All I knew was that my cousin was due to be in a big movie, and then she was dead. I never even saw it until I got this print—from Lorna's parents about thirty years ago."

Twenty minutes later, one more shot of the clock. The movie had become static, no buildup of tension. Flynn couldn't carry it and Lorna wasn't onscreen enough. As time passed, as the climactic gun battle approached, my dichotomy grew deeper: when Lorna wasn't on the screen, the movie was a travesty; when she was on the screen I couldn't take my eyes off her, but I was possessed by a profound sadness watching the performance of a woman I'd slept with not three days earlier, a woman I'd just discovered had been dead for forty-six years.

The battle arrived: Lorna picked off the villain who was about to shoot Flynn in the back. In the process of doing so, she took a step backward, as if propelled by the pistol's recoil. I wondered whether this was something Curtiz had ordered her to do, or whether it was her own touch. An immense lump had formed in my throat.

When I could speak again I asked Hudnut, "Do you know, was there a western maybe fifteen or sixteen years later than this, very similar plot, with Gary Cooper?"

"If there was, I missed it."

So with Warners' collusion, I had deprived the world—or at least two timelines—of a masterpiece. As Hudnut rewound the film I sat nearly catatonic on a plush love seat, filled with thoughts of anger and betrayal and loss. The most logical target for my anger was Wadsworth, who had butchered my project, who had goaded Dutch Reagan to his death. But the betrayal, I feared, was all mine. In attempting to flee back to 1994, I was easily as responsible for Lorna's death as Wadsworth was for Reagan's.

Annabel ended an uncomfortable silence. "It's something of an antique, it's kind of quaint, but I'd say it's not bad at all. You've got nothing to be ashamed of, Gabriel."

"I didn't write it," I said. "I'd only given them a treatment and worked on a few scenes. And I stole the idea from a great western that was made in the early fifties. So I suppose I've got quite a lot to be ashamed of."

"We do what we have to do," Hudnut said.

Annabel said, "Well, Lorna was wonderful." She paused; when no one responded, she resumed. "I'm sorry. It must be very tough for you to see her, under the circumstances." I could do no more than nod agreement. She said, "There's one thing I find very puzzling, about your time travel. Do you mind if I ask?"

I welcomed a change of subject. "Please do."

"After the Actor drowned, when Lorna was so angry at you, didn't you have the option of using your machine to go back just a few days, and giving yourself the opportunity to remedy what had gone wrong?"

"I did have. I wasn't very confident about setting the controls, but I suppose that pertained to going in either direction. As you can see, I ended up ten years off here."

"Then why didn't you just go back? And why couldn't you just go back now?"

Hudnut said, "One question at a time, Annabel, for God's sake."

"No," I said, "I'm afraid my problems apply to either question, and I guess now's as good a time as any to deal with them."

The projector's holding reel came to a flapping halt, and Hudnut sat down next to Annabel. I said, "I guess I wanted to ask your permission—that is, I wanted to ask permission from the 1994 version of you—because I couldn't have done a much better job of what you wanted me to do. And if I were to return to 1938 *now*, unless my timing were more accurate than this machine seems capable of, I'd undo everything I'd done. I mean—let's imagine I came down on March thirteen, exactly a week before the night I left to come here. Everything would be fine between me and Lorna, but Reagan would be alive—"

"In that timeline," Hudnut said.

"Yes, all right, in that timeline. But so far, everything I did in the timeline I just left seems to have affected this timeline as well."

"It's the quantum bleed," Hudnut said, "and there won't be any consistency to it. For one thing, you'll probably be going to an altogether new timeline, and I'll bet whatever you do there won't affect things here one bit."

"Wait a minute," I said. "If I go to a *new* timeline, then what are the chances Lorna will even recognize me?"

"What if she doesn't? You can just start afresh."

This didn't strike me as such a bad idea, but then I had a disturbing thought. "What if I go to a new timeline and Lorna's already *dead?*"

"She's not scheduled to die until November."

"But that was only because I kept her from dying in March. Oh, hell—this is much too complicated for me."

"No, it's not, Gabriel. It's quite simple, really. It all boils down to a matter of probabilities. We're missing a few of the figures so we can't calculate the probabilities very accurately. But I'd stake my reputation on two things: if we can get you back to the middle of March 1938 Lorna will *not* be dead; and bringing your actor back from the dead won't make a damn bit of difference here."

"So I have your blessing."

"You do."

Annabel spoke to me, "You said 'problems,' in the plural."

"Yes," I said. "There is one other matter. I'm afraid the owners of the time machine have shown up in 1938."

"You're kidding!" Hudnut said. "Wait a minute—there's more than one?"

"Two. And they have another machine—they call it the B-2—that can accommodate two people."

Hudnut was as energized as I'd ever seen him, virtually lurching off the couch he shared with Annabel. "This is amazing! Where are they from? I mean, *when* are they from? Have you seen the other machine? Did you ask them if they'd left the machine for me to find?"

"Our relationship has been a little antagonistic, but I've figured out they're probably from early in the twenty-second century. They're fairly strange. They claim to be important scientists, but they strike me more as a couple of punks. I'd guess they stole the machines and came here—came to 1994—on a kind of joyride. The machine, *our* machine, ended up at the Musée des Techniques because of something really stupid they did, and they laughed at the idea it had been left for you. They say their other machine, the two-seater, is low on fuel, and they need both machines to get back where they came from."

"Good Lord," Hudnut said. "This is amazing. Absolutely incredible. How did they *find* you?"

"They did some detective work in 1994, found you, and they said you told them where to find me. I'm skeptical about that, because you don't strike me as the sort of person who'd give up information too easily, and besides, you thought you were sending me to 1941."

"Right. Right." Hudnut had made fists of both hands and was revolving them at chest level. "More likely some kind of tracking device. God, *think* of that—a temporal tracking device! I'll tell you, I'd like to talk to these boys." Now he used his fists to pound his knees. "Tomorrow, Gabriel, we'll take a look at that thing. Hell, how advanced can technology be if it's just more than a hundred years down the road? Maybe I can figure out what's wrong with the controls, maybe I can neutralize that tracker."

Across the living room, a telephone issued its jangling, pre-electronic ring. I was startled, Hudnut apparently oblivious. Annabel rose from the couch and moved gracefully across the room. After a moment she said, "Jasper, it's for you. It's Charlie, calling from Malibu."

Hudnut strode to the phone, and Annabel returned to keep me company. It was a frustrating situation because ultimately I found both conversations fascinating. Annabel said to me, almost under her breath, "Charlie's Jasper's first cousin, his uncle Charles's son."

"Yes, actually I spoke on the telephone this afternoon with Charlie, and I met Charles a few weeks ago, after the storm."

Annabel nodded, as if I were telling her about something that had occurred on the next block. Hudnut, meanwhile, in surprisingly gruff tones, was saying, "Yes, I know. He's here. He's all right. Yes, old friend of mine."

Annabel, her voice still hushed, said, "Charlie's really screwed up his life. His fourth wife just left him. He can't hold a job for more than a year or two. He's living in Malibu because he couldn't afford to keep his apartment."

Hudnut said, "Describe them, please."

I said, "He seemed very loyal, on the telephone. He wouldn't give me Jasper's number until I jumped through a few hoops."

Annabel nodded. "That's just officiousness. If you'd offered him some money he'd probably have given you a key to this house, except Jasper would never trust him with a key."

Hudnut said something I missed, and then, "How the hell did they get in, Charlie?"

Annabel's tone grew even lower, "It's extraordinary that a father like Charles could have a son like Charlie. Not that Charlie's entirely disreputable, but Charles is absolutely typical of the Hudnuts, all gentleness and tolerance."

Hudnut said, "So *did* you call the cops, for Christ's sake?"

Annabel said, "Jasper's got the tolerance, most of the time."

Hudnut said, "Yes, I think you did the right thing." A brief pause. "Sure, then we'll deal with it when the time comes. All right, Charlie. Good night." And he hung up. He came back in our direction, shaking his head, looking at the floor; he stopped by the projector. "Charlie's had a busy day. First some guy calls him trying to find me—"

"That would be me," I said.

"Right. Then he gets a visit from—in his own words—two weirdos. Doesn't know how they got past the guardhouse. A couple of foreigners, one short, one tall, looking for Jasper Hudnut and for someone named Gabriel—which he thinks may have been the name of the guy who called earlier."

"God," I said, "I'm sorry about all this. I figured I'd left them behind."

"Of course you did. There's no way you could have known about the tracker. Don't worry about it."

"How did it end, then? Did Charlie call the police?"

"No, and a good thing. I don't think the police would do anybody any good. No, Charlie did the same thing with them he did with you. He gave them my phone number at school."

At eleven o'clock Annabel went up to bed. I accompanied Hudnut to the kitchen, where he began picking up plates and silverware and pots and pans scattered about the counter, rinsing them, and placing them in the dishwasher. I told him that in 1994 he was the sort of man who would fastidiously use the same dish over and over, cleaning it individually after each use. "Doesn't surprise me," he said. "I'm sure that's the way I was before I was married. We make compromises in domestic life."

I decided then to pose the question that had been on the tip of my tongue since the movie. "Jasper, do you suppose you sent me back to 1938 on purpose?"

"How do you mean?"

"I mean, I wonder if the control panel didn't malfunction. If you didn't intend to send me to 1941 at all, if you wanted me to arrive in 1938 and save Lorna's life."

He continued stuffing the dishwasher. "Why wouldn't I have told you?"

"If you were afraid I'd be put off . . . you know, here we are with a time machine, with an opportunity to redress all the great crimes and injustices of history, and this guy wants me to save his cousin's life."

He nodded. "Right. I see what you mean."

There was a long silence. Finally I said, "So?"

He turned to face me. "Well, it's an intriguing question, isn't it?"

22

I had every reason to expect a good night's sleep. I was exhausted and the bed in the Hudnut guest room was wide and cozy. Hudnut had offered me hope that I might rejoin and regain Lorna, and assured me that while the Futureboys had been able to track their Tempocruiser through time, they wouldn't be able to locate it at the Pasadena Ramada Inn. But looming between me and blissful unconsciousness was this timeline business.

The theory was exquisite: an infinite number of lines running mostly parallel, occasionally crossing. Somewhere Ronald Reagan was president, somewhere else he was dead, somewhere else yet again, God only knew, he was selling carpets in Dubuque. But unless there were lots of us zipping around in time machines, changing things willy-nilly, wasn't it likely Reagan was president just about everywhere? He was dead in the timeline I'd just left because I'd appeared there and tripped him up. But I was new to *this* timeline and he was dead here, too.

Just as Reagan would logically be president almost everywhere, Lorna would almost everywhere have been killed when the cliff fell on her. But here she'd lived an additional nine months. Why? Because I'd been there to save her from the avalanche. So *I'd been here*, in this timeline. My name was in *Four O'Clock*'s opening credits. But of course I'd never been in this timeline before, at least not in 1938. So what was the explanation? Quantum bleed, Hudnut said. If I understood him correctly, my influence must have oozed from one timeline to another.

Good and well. Using "quantum bleed" as a wild card, Hudnut could explain away any inconsistency. But wasn't it far more logical to posit that there was a simple continuity at the heart of all this? I had traveled back to 1938, where my presence had caused Lorna to live and Reagan to die. Nowhere at all would Dutch have become president, because he'd drowned off Santa Catalina Island in March 1938. He was dead everywhere.

If I was right, then, and timelines had as much basis in reality as the tooth fairy, I had to pay serious attention to the consequences. Any travel at all, of course, would be contingent on Hudnut's repairing the control panel. But if he did, and if I did return to 1938 mid-March, pre-Catalina, predeath, wouldn't everything revert? Wouldn't it mean Reagan back into the White House, Carter back into private life, early demise of the Cold War down the drain, Chairman Moe redux, no Cal Tech for Hudnut, Annabel back to Orlando? Of course it would.

Must I not then return to 1938 *post-Catalina?* Wile my way back into Lorna's heart. I'd done it once. Reagan would stay dead, the Hudnuts' marriage intact. But what if Lorna would have none of me? What if my best efforts couldn't budge her? Not only wouldn't I have her, I might not be able to keep her alive.

Two o'clock in the morning, three, three-thirty. I ran down the possibilities, the permutations. What if I could manage to drag Wadsworth out to Catalina *without* Lorna, get him and Dutch drunk, reenact the beach scene? She couldn't fault me for that. What if we weren't to call Wadsworth Saturday morning, leave him sleeping, go to Catalina with Dutch, get him drunk, urge him to swim? The scenarios grew progressively macabre, and ridiculous.

Around four o'clock I reached the obvious conclusion, the inevitable one. *I'd had a perfectly good plan in the first place.* That was the important thing. I had a perfectly good way to divert Reagan irrevocably from his course. He'd never become president. I could return to mid-March 1938 without guilt. This marvelous 1984 would still come to be, and Lorna would live.

By 9 A.M., when I descended to the kitchen, both Hudnuts had headed off to academia. On the kitchen table were a set of keys and a note to the effect that the car in the garage was at my disposal, that Hudnut would be free at one o'clock and would meet me at the Ramada unless I chose otherwise.

In a Volvo sedan of recent vintage, I drove there immediately after breakfast. I checked on the machine, which was intact and precisely where I'd left it. At the front desk, I reported that I'd be spending at least one more night, and inquired where I might find the closest bookstore. After much consideration, the clerk told me she was pretty sure there was one in a mall several blocks up Colorado Boulevard.

There it was: a branch of one of the major chains. Alas, they probably wouldn't have *Ottomania*, but surely they could order it and send it to Annabel. As I'd suspected, it was not on their shelves. But to my consternation, the young woman at the counter could find no record of *Ottomania*, nor of author Gabriel Prince, in her various catalogues.

I drove back to the Ramada. During my absence, the room had been made immaculate and sprayed with something probably intended to synthesize a generic floral aroma, but gone dreadfully wrong. I managed to open the window.

I knew by heart the *Entrée* number in Seattle, recognized the voice of the woman who answered the telephone. Proceeding with great caution, I asked her whether there was a Paris *Entrée* in the works. There was. Did she happen to know, was the author to be one Gabriel Prince? It was not.

What had begun as an uncomplicated shopping trip had turned into metaphysical detective work, and put me into something of a cold sweat. I called Princeton University and asked for the Alumni Office. I wondered if they could give me the current address of Gabriel Prince, class of 1974. They were terribly sorry, but there was no one by that name in the class of 1974. Ah, I responded, feeling queasier by the second, perhaps I have the wrong year; could you check '73 and '75? No luck, nor was there in '72 or '76. It appeared I did not exist.

That wasn't quite right. I existed quite palpably, sitting on a well-made bed in the Ramada Inn with a Tempocruiser A-4 five feet away from me. But it seemed that—other than this visitor, this interloper, this temporary occupant—there *had been* no Gabriel Prince in these parts. Perhaps, I told myself, this was the answer to a physics problem: could two complex entities made up of precisely the same atoms exist concurrently? Little though I knew about physics, the answer to that one had to be "no." And perhaps as soon as I cleared out of here, the Gabriel Prince who was supposed to be here would snap right back into place.

Hudnut arrived at precisely 1:15, armed with a tool kit and a small acetylene torch. I told him something had just happened that caused me great concern; he told me, in effect, to shut up and be patient. He told me there'd been a message for him at Cal Tech from someone who "sounded foreign" and left a number in Santa Monica. He had not called back.

He examined the control panel, tapped it a few times with his index finger, a few more times with a screwdriver. He then ran the thin-bladed screwdriver horizontally across the plastic side of the panel, revealing a tiny fissure that ran its length. Using an uncanny combination of gentleness and force, he pried away at the panel until it popped open. With great care he removed the top; he called me over.

"Look at this," he said. "Three-dimensional circuit board. Tell me something—in 1994, what kind of RAM do home computers have?"

"Four megabytes is common, I guess. But people have sixteen, thirty-two, sixty-four."

He chuckled. "You'd be hard-pressed to find more than half a Meg today. So you know the progress made in one decade. It's hard to imagine the steps they've taken in—what are we talking about here? Twelve decades, thirteen?—until you see something like this. . . ." He pointed with the screwdriver at the little rectangular solid, perhaps four inches long, one high, two deep. "There's probably a chip in there with the equivalent of, who knows, five or six gigabytes of RAM. Something incredibly powerful. And look at this. . . ." In front of the circuit board was a ridge about half an inch wide with what appeared to be a complex of little gears and spheres. "What do you make of it?"

"It looks mechanical," I said.

"Exactly. Tiny ball bearings in there. When you touch the controls, that's what activates them. With all the technology they must have, why in God's name would they have a mechanical component controlling this thing?"

"There's a good chance it was made in France," I said.

Hudnut chuckled again. "Yes. That could explain it. The only other thing I can think of—and I suppose they're not mutually exclusive—is that they were aiming for the utilitarian. Something easy to get at, easy to repair. Unfortunately, also something that attracts dust." His large right hand descended again into the tool kit and removed a small aerosol can. "Tuner cleaner," he said. He sprayed a generous amount. "I wouldn't be surprised if that's at least a temporary fix for the accuracy problems. If it is, it doesn't say much for the scientific abilities of your pals from the twenty-second century."

"Thieves, I'd guess, not scientists."

"But talented thieves, necessarily. Think about it—if these things were like Ferraris in the year two-thousand-something, which is to say readily available but very expensive, we'd see joyriders all over the place. Chaucer would have written 'The Time Traveler's Tale.' I'll bet there aren't many of these machines and they're top secret. So your Futureboys had to break through some pretty impressive security."

"They're glorified hackers, then," I said.

"Don't know the word," Hudnut muttered.

"Computer hackers. Sort of amoral idiots savants who eavesdrop on the power structure and figure out ways to get everything for free."

"Sounds about right," Hudnut said. He snapped the cover back onto the control panel, fiddled briefly with the dials. He pointed to the night table and said, "What time is it?"

I read the bright green numerals of the clock radio. "It's one thirty-five." Hudnut was sitting on the machine. Had he been there a moment ago?

"Good. Now, in my shirt pocket there should be a piece of paper." There was. "Read it to me," Hudnut said.

The handwriting was mine. I read aloud, "The time as I write this is one thirty-eight."

"There you go," he said. "I guess it works."

"I don't remember writing this," I replied.

"Of course you don't. How could you? In effect, you haven't written it yet."

I had, for a change, been a bystander to time travel. "My God, it really *is* seamless, isn't it?"

"And I'd say this thing works. I set it to take me back three minutes, it took me back three minutes." His face broke into a broad grin. "Let me tell you, Gabriel—I remember this rush. God, I feel good! No wonder your Futureboys want their machine back."

"What about the tracker?" I said.

"Ah, yes." He descended from the machine. "If it's in here," he pointed to the control panel, "we can't do a damn thing about it. But if it's somewhere here"—he moved to the rear of the machine and began tapping with his screwdriver—"if it's separate, then we can rip it right out."

With Hudnut deep into surgery, I said, "Jasper, I don't want to disturb you, but I did a little calling around this morning, and I've come to the conclusion that I don't exist."

He did not look up. "What are you talking about, you don't exist?"

"There's no record of me here, in 1984. I haven't written any books. I didn't go to college. I daresay if I called my aunts, the women who raised me, they'd never have heard of me."

His attention remained fixed on the machine. "And this surprises you?"

"Of course it does."

"Despite everything I told you about timelines?"

There didn't seem a thorough correlation between what he'd told me and my own predicament. I was about to point that out when the telephone rang, and I jumped half a foot. Other than Hudnut, who would be calling me here? It was a female voice that said, "Hello, could you possibly call Professor Hudnut to the phone?" I could have sworn the voice belonged to Annabel, but surely she would have addressed me by name. I turned to Hudnut and said, "It's for you."

He gave me a shrug, took the receiver, sat on the bed; I watched as his expression made the journey from neutral to concerned to anxious. Meanwhile, I could glean little from his half of the conversation until he said, "Can you tell me how they found the house?" and I realized with sinking heart what was happening. If there was anyone in this odd little circle who deserved no retribution from Jean-Baptiste and Hans it was Annabel, who had been next door to Disney World when Hudnut made off with the Tempocruiser.

Hudnut said, "Are they listening in?" And then, "Do they know that Gabriel's with me?" And then, "Do you have the feeling you're in danger?" After that he did not speak for, I would estimate, a minute and a half, and when he resumed speaking it was clearly to a different party. "Yes," he said, "I know where it is." And, "Well, I think that's something we could negotiate." And, "No, of course I don't want money. As a fellow scientist I'd just like to find out a thing or two about you and your friend." Next he listened for quite a while, another ninety seconds, after which he replaced the receiver.

He looked at me with a half-smile. "They're not complete idiots. The theory is that they got our number from Information. Our address, of course, isn't listed. So they went to the public library and looked in the reverse directory. Voilà."

The solution to that puzzle hadn't been uppermost in my mind. "Is Annabel all right, for God's sake?"

"On the other hand," he maintained the half-smile, "they're not exactly geniuses. If you were in their shoes, wouldn't you have listened in? We've got three phones at the house."

"Please, Jasper—how is she?"

"She's fine. She told me they *don't* know we're here together. Then she told me in Pig Latin, a language evidently not known to French hackers of the twenty-second century, that the one guy is extremely big, but sick as a dog, so she doesn't *think* her life is in danger, although she wouldn't swear to it. That's when the French guy grabbed the phone."

"Jean-Baptiste."

"Jean-Baptiste wants me over there in half an hour or he'll assassinate Annabel. His words." Hudnut had already made his way back to the machine's hindquarters.

"Let's go, then."

"It's a ten-minute drive this time of day, and I think I'm on to something with the tracker."

"Good God, Jasper, she hasn't done anything to deserve—"

"If I haven't figured this out in ten minutes, I'll go."

"Then *I'll* go. That'll satisfy them. I can take your Volvo or my truck. You'll have to give me directions, though."

"You're staying right here," Hudnut said. "Annabel's perfectly capable of taking care of herself."

23

Half an hour later, at about the time Hudnut should have been entering his front door, I was westbound on the Ventura Freeway, the machine in the bed of my Datsun, swathed in a queen-size Ramada sheet, my tweed suit next to me in the Gap plastic bag.

I was not happy with the situation. I had suggested to Hudnut that he was acting under the influence of post-time-travel euphoria; he had replied that he was acting under the influence of pure reason. He wanted to find out as much as he could about the Futureboys. Were I present, especially accompanied by the Tempocruiser, they would not talk. On his own, he was convinced, he would soon have Jean-Baptiste reciting his autobiography. I, Hudnut further posited, wanted nothing more than to return to 1938. Now that we had the control panel repaired (perhaps temporarily) and we had discovered and removed the tracking device (almost certainly), there was nothing stopping me from doing that—unless, of course, I were to hand the machine back to the Futureboys.

And what would those Futureboys do when it became clear that once again their A-4 had eluded them? That, Hudnut assured me, was not even worth worrying about.

I worried nevertheless. I worried that the guard at the Malibu Colony would not let me in, but he did. I worried that Charlie Hudnut would sabotage the plan somehow. He met me at the front door and seemed pleasant enough; he was another large man, not quite as tall as his cousin. He wore khakis, a white shirt, and a club tie, as if intent on establishing himself as a noneccentric. He opened the garage door electronically from within, and I pulled the Datsun inside. He helped me remove the machine and station it on the floor almost exactly where it had sat in 1994 and 1938. He said, "I'm having a hell of a time figuring out what this thing is."

"I'm just in charge of moving it," I replied.

Charlie looked the machine over carefully. "Could be a boat, kind of like a jet-ski, but it's pretty lopsided. How would it stay afloat?"

"Couldn't begin to tell you," I said.

The house was almost identical to its 1994 configuration—just the odd bit of furniture different. I asked Charlie if he'd mind my looking at the photographs in the dining room. "I didn't realize you'd been here before," he said.

"Fairly often," I replied.

All the pictures taken between 1984 and 1994 were of course absent. Where the adult Jasper Hudnut had been spottily represented on the wall I'd originally seen, he and Annabel aged gracefully on this one. There were two new photographs of Lorna: one in her *Four O'Clock* costume, and an eight-by-ten that took my breath away. In a party dress, holding a champagne flute, she stood flanked by two well-dressed men, one of whom was certainly Charlie's father, Charles. The other man, too, looked familiar.

Charlie said, "Need any help?"

I pointed to the picture in question. "Is that Howard Hawks, the director?"

"Could be. I know he was around when I was a kid. The funny thing is, I took that picture. I was about twelve and I had one of those little Brownies. You'd think I'd remember who was in it."

The next part of the plan was the go-ahead call, to come either from Hudnut or Annabel, probably Annabel. I'd arrived in Malibu at quarter to three, and during two hours of uneasy conversation my gaze had often fixed upon the cordless phone on the coffee table between us, willing it to ring, wondering if its batteries were charged. Charlie and I had discussed my writing career, my connections with Jasper (hastily amended), and then Charlie's various business ventures, his children, his infant grandchildren. From time to time he would give me a serious look, a sort of tepid version of his cousin's intense look, and finally he said, "I keep thinking I know you from someplace."

"Well," I said, not even trying for good subterfuge, "could be any number of places. I've known Jasper since I was an undergraduate."

"No," Charlie said, "the thing is that I have an image of you just as you are, so I imagine this would have had to be recent."

It was at that moment the cordless telephone chirped. Charlie answered it and began to chat, then stopped in midsentence as if halted, whereupon he looked at me and said, "Yes, he's right here."

It was Annabel. At this moment, she told me, Jasper and the Futureboys were en route to the Ramada Inn. Upon their departure five minutes earlier, she had called the police and advised them to be waiting at the Ramada. Her husband, the well-known Cal Tech professor, would be accompanied by two men who had held them captive at their house. Annabel said she doubted the charges would stick, because neither Jean-Baptiste nor Hans carried a weapon, but it would certainly throw them off the trail for a while. "So," she said, "Jasper advises you to get the hell out of here."

I had gradually wandered out of the living room, into the kitchen and pockets of interference, onto the deck, into the clear, out of earshot from Charlie. "But did they talk? Did Jean-Baptiste tell you anything?"

"All sorts of things. Jasper had him eating out of his hand."

"Like what? Where did they get the machines?"

"They stole them. Jean-Baptiste didn't put it that way, of course. He said they 'liberated' them. According to him the government in the year 2111 is a huge, sluggish bureaucracy—"

"Which government? France?"

"No . . . everywhere, really. I mean, it's pretty complicated, and I'm not sure I caught all the nuances, and there were times he wasn't terribly clear. But there seems to be this International Trade Network that's in charge of everything. There are still national governments and territory disputes and some pretty awful wars, but everything seems to pale next to this ITN, which has five commissioners who are supposed to represent the world with some kind of geographic equality, but it's always America, Europe, Japan, and China that have one commissioner for sure, so there's one left for the rest of the world—"

"What about the machines, Annabel?"

"Yes, well, according to Jean-Baptiste, the ITN churns a tremendous amount of money into research and development, which he finds offensive because the products they develop aren't used for the good of society. They've evidently adopted a worldwide currency, which has kept inflation pretty low, but he estimates that a 2111 dollar has about a tenth the buying power of a 1984 dollar. He somehow tapped into this ITN central computer and he found out they'd spent three trillion dollars on the time travel project—"

"So about three hundred billion 1984 dollars?"

"Right. There had been rumors for twenty or thirty years that the project was in the works, but no information was ever released. Jean-Baptiste claims he's a higher-up in some sort of revolutionary organization, and they figured out where the machines were stored. He guesses—he's pretty sure—that these Tempocruisers are first-generation machines, that they're obsolete, because it only took him a few months to get through the security."

"Why did they come here, to this century? Why did Jean-Baptiste and Hans choose 1994?"

"Jean-Baptiste claims to be very high-minded. He said he'd learned in school that the origins of the ITN were in the late twentieth century, and he wanted to come here and throw a monkey wrench in the works if he could. But he said that Hans—whom he had to bring along because he represented some other faction of the revolutionaries— that Hans just wanted to have a good time. Evidently they were aiming for 1990, but the machine put them down in 1994. He said you can't trust the controls."

"What about the other machine, Annabel? Did they talk about that? Jean-Baptiste claimed to me that it doesn't have enough fuel left to take them home."

"Yes—Jasper kept asking about the fuel, but Jean-Baptiste wouldn't talk about it, maybe because he doesn't know what it is. But he was adamant that they need the other machine to get back, and the ostensible reason they need to get back is that Hans keeps getting sick. Apparently there are all sorts of diseases that have been wiped out by 2111, that his immune system can't deal with—"

"But Jean-Baptiste's can?"

"So it seems. Hans looked horrible today. He had a fever and he was all blotchy. I wondered if he had chicken pox, and Jean-Baptiste said, 'No, he never eats chicken.' The only contribution Hans made, other than sitting there trying to look menacing, was to catalogue his diseases. They've been in this century nearly a year, I think, and he's had measles and the mumps, and whooping cough, and a bad case of the flu. Jean-Baptiste is obviously very impatient with him, but at the same time he's very protective. Anyway, Jean-Baptiste seems to think they can sneak back to 2111, hide the machines, and see a doctor for some sort of miracle drug. Then he wants to come back."

I had a flicker of sympathy for Jean-Baptiste, slightly more than that for Hans. I wished to contribute to no one's ill health, but given a choice between saving Lorna's life and curtailing Hans's spate of childhood diseases, my mind was clear. I said, "I wish I could have been there."

"Just as well you weren't."

"Tell me something. Do you believe most of what Jean-Baptiste told you? Do you believe he's really a revolutionary?"

"I'm sure he's telling the truth about his society. I'd imagine he's probably aggrandizing his own station, but he does seem to be an intelligent young man, interested in a lot of things. He's always very concerned about his English."

"Tell me one more thing, Annabel. Am I doing the right thing, taking the machine? Am I being completely selfish?"

"Of course not, Gabriel. You've been given an opportunity to do something wonderful. Do it, for God's sake."

I thanked Annabel. I told her I wished I could have spent more time with her, and that I wished that she and Jasper would not be bothered further by the Futureboys. To be sure, I did not know whether Hudnut had successfully removed the tracking device, or that the machine would even work lacking its excised component.

In the living room, Charlie napped. I placed the phone in its cradle and treaded softly toward the garage entry. Within, I changed from my 1984 garments back to my 1938 tweed suit. With great care I set the controls for Thursday, March 17, 6 P.M. exactly. Having no idea what to expect, I pressed the "go" button.

PART IV

À La Recherche Du Temps Perdu

24

The light-headedness was there, but not the sense of well-being. In the dark, I stepped a bit warily off the machine and gave my head a tentative shake. Indeed, it felt as if something were slightly loose; I had what might be simply described as a mild headache, as well as a serious case of anxiety. Gradually my eyes adjusted to the darkness, and I recognized the familiar surroundings of the garage, so I hadn't come down in 1920 or 1820. Should I switch on the overhead bulb? No need; as I turned I saw a crack of dim light at the base of the door that led within. I let myself in, walked through the living room where I'd left Charlie dozing moments earlier, and headed for the kitchen, whence came the light.

Her back to me, Lorna stood at the sink, washing dishes. On the counter three feet away from her was the chicken I had been preparing the night Wadsworth came to dinner. The machine had taken me exactly where I'd ordered it. I felt my eyes fill with tears. How shall I describe my second discovery of Lorna? I perceived before me the woman I loved, the woman I had lost and feared I would never see again, the woman who forty-one hours ago had told me to get out of her life, the woman who several minutes ago had been dead for forty-six years. I attributed an exponential increase in the throbbing of my head to the sudden rush of emotions I'd never had before.

I wanted to seize her, to envelop her, to possess her, but of course I could not, because as far as she was concerned we hadn't yet even become lovers. Instead I took a small liberty, moving closer, linking my arms lightly around her waist, and kissing the back of her head. She said, "That's funny—I could have sworn you were there cutting up the chicken, and then all of sudden you were behind me."

Now I tried to speak, but could not. She turned, still within my grasp, to face me. "Gabriel, are you crying?"

I nodded, utterly unable to seize a facile explanation. Lorna said, "And how did you get that sunburn? Your forehead's peeling! It wasn't like that a minute ago."

I forced my vocal cords to work; the result was high-pitched and constricted. "Allergies. All of a sudden."

"To what?"

"Don't know. Happens once in a while." I took the dish towel from her left hand and blew my nose in it, cleared my throat.

Looking very concerned, Lorna said, "I hope it clears up as fast as it hits you."

"Nothing to worry about." My voice had dropped an octave and a half, but still sounded as if I'd narrowly avoided strangulation.

"Well, look," she said. "About the weekend, I just don't see . . ."

"I don't either. Let's not worry about it." She was still inside my arms. I stroked her back, wondering if there were a way to divert the enthusiastically circulating blood from my groin to my temples.

"I'm talking about Catalina."

While not putting a dent in my arousal, the word accelerated the pain in my head. "Me too," I said. "Let's not go."

"Gabriel, a minute ago you were so excited about the Cubs and Dutch Reagan and everything. . . ."

"Let's just stay here. We don't need to go anyplace. We've got each other."

"That's sweet, Gabriel." She pulled away from enough to shut the water off. "But what about Bill? He's expecting to spend the weekend with me."

The rate of throbbing seemed to have doubled in the last minute. "We'll tell him."

"Tell him what?"

"Tell him you've got a new fellow."

She returned to my arms, ran her fingers down my moist cheeks and my pink neck. "God, you're so adorable. You're so unpredictable." She kissed my lips and pulled away. It was as torrid as a kiss so brief could be.

I said, "Don't you ever have one of those moments where everything comes into focus?"

"Sure I do."

"I had one. A particularly vivid one."

She kissed me again. "What did you see when everything was in focus?"

"You and me. No Dutch. No Catalina. Especially no Bill."

Now I kissed her, and we lingered. My fingers began exploring the small of her back.

She said, "Shall I call him and tell him not to come tonight?"

"That would be a good idea." I held her extremely close. My head felt as if it were in a drill press. I stroked the curve of her buttocks, not terribly conscious of the liberties I was taking. She did not move away. She began kissing my neck.

She said, "How are your allergies?"

"I'm not sure," I said. "I don't care."

"Let's go upstairs," she said.

It was as if every nerve in my body had been supercharged, so my second first coupling with Lorna was just as pleasurable as its predecessor. But much shorter—because after ten minutes, or twelve, or fifteen, or however long that perfervid embrace lasted, I could barely move.

She knelt over me, glistening and beautiful. "Are you all right, Gabriel?"

"Headache," I murmured.

"A migraine? Do you get migraines? Or is it connected to the allergy?"

"I don't know. This is something new." I couldn't think terribly clearly, but it seemed to me that Hudnut's speculation regarding the cause of his catastrophic 1952 headache had included the possibility that he simply hadn't waited long enough before using the machine again. In my case, only thirty-seven hours had separated two forty-six-year trips.

"Can I do something? I've got aspirin in the bathroom."

"Sure." As she sprang over me, droplets of her sweat fell on my chest. She padded off across the hardwood floor; I tried to sit up. It was not easy. I made it to my feet and began inching toward the door like a huge, naked mutant sloth. Lorna emerged from the bathroom, a wood nymph bearing medication. "What are you doing, Gabriel?"

"Trying to make it across the hall." She handed me the little white pills and I got them in my mouth.

"Why?"

"Don't want to be in your bed when Bill gets here." She handed me the little glass of water and I swallowed the aspirin.

"My God . . . I didn't call him, did I?" She had her arm around my waist now, as if I needed support. Perhaps, it occurred to me, I did.

"Tell him gently," I said. I had a plan of action, and the man still posed a threat.

Dinner remained uncooked. Upon Wadsworth's arrival he and Lorna visited me in my bedroom. The aspirin had been ineffectual, a drop in the bucket. I lay completely immobile, transfixed by pain. "Bad luck," Wadsworth said, hovering over me, a man who had been deprived of a good meal. "You look like a damned lobster, to boot."

"Could be worse," I whispered, eliminating pronouns to minimize pain and conserve energy.

"I'm going to take Bill out for a sandwich," Lorna said, and she added a half-smile that I interpreted as meaning "and some pertinent conversation." I would have nodded in response, but I feared that doing so might kill me. "Will you be all right for an hour?"

"Fine," I said. "Call Dutch, please. Tell him sorry about Catalina."

It was such a wondrous, painful paradox, being at once imbued with love for life and fearing oneself at the brink of death. I discovered that if I lay absolutely motionless the pain was no worse than, say, oral surgery without novocaine. Lorna was gone much longer than an hour, and I presumed that she was having a long and difficult discussion with Wadsworth. When I could sustain a train of thought for more than three seconds I concentrated on the gift I'd been given— the renascence of the woman I loved and the man I'd killed—and my resolution to make the most of it: to keep Lorna alive, to steer Dutch toward stardom and an indelible identification with the Left. Periodically I dozed, having had one night's sleep in the last four days, but my unconscious—stubbornly unaware that anything was wrong with its environment—broadcast movement signals to limbs and digits willy-nilly, and as a result every attempt at sleep lasted no more than a few seconds and ended in acute pain.

Lorna returned at nine or ten or midnight—I have no idea when, really. I heard her car pull up, heard a brief, unintelligible exchange, heard Wadsworth's car drive off, heard her close the front door (not slam it, mercifully), heard her climb the stairs. She entered my room on kitten's feet and stood by the doorway in the darkness. I said, "I'm awake," and she approached the bed.

"How are you doing?"

"About the same."

She leaned to kiss me, and touched my peeling forehead. "No fever."

"No," I said. "How did it go?"

"With Bill? I told him it was over, told him we had very strong feelings for each other, you and I. He didn't take it very well. Do you want to hear about it now?"

"No. Later, please."

"Should I call a doctor, Gabriel? Should I take you to the emergency room at Santa Monica Hospital?"

"No. This will pass, I'm sure. You call Dutch?"

"I did. He was sorry to hear we couldn't join him. He wished you a speedy recovery."

I felt a strong, irrational sense of relief at evidence of Reagan's vitality, followed by a particularly vicious explosion of pain, as if terrorists had set off a little wad of plastique in the frontal lobe. "Thanks," I said.

"Is there anything I can do?" Her voice was low and gentle, as soothing as anything imaginable under the circumstances.

"Nothing. I love you very much." While this was the third, the fourth time in the last few days I had told her I loved her, I realized that in this new version of reality it was the first time either of us had spoken those words to the other.

"You're so sweet to me, so wonderful to me, Gabriel. I love you too, you know." She kissed me again. "I don't want to upset you now, but I should tell you this. Bill's very angry at you. I told him it wasn't your fault, it was my decision. He said some nasty, stupid things about you. I hope he'll think better of it."

"Me too," I said.

I urged her to get some sleep so she wouldn't be a wreck in the morning, and eventually she did move across the hall, but not before she'd left me with a bottle of Bayer and a tall glass of water. I feared at various junctures in an excruciatingly long night that I would at some point have to seek pharmaceutical comfort—something much more powerful than aspirin—because the pain proceeded incessant, and it was certainly not the sort of thing one becomes used to. I continued in my pattern of a minute's sleep followed by several minutes' splitting stupor, followed by another minute's sleep, until that period before dawn when the birds begin singing. I became gradually aware that I must be improving because I did not find this cheeping chorale unpleasant at all. My head still felt as if it had been used in an infernal game of table tennis, but clearly the game was over. I sat up and drank the water Lorna had left me. My head twinged, but did not reverberate.

I slept until ten, awoke free of pain and ravenous, went downstairs for a snack, and found a note on the kitchen table.

> Dear Gabriel:
>
> I could not bear to wake you when I left this morning. You were angelically pink, and you were sleeping as soundly as a person can. I hope the headache has left you for good. I've already called to say you won't be in to-day. I will try to talk some more with Bill at lunch. There is no point in his having hard feelings because he and I were going nowhere.
>
> You and I are going somewhere, everywhere. I cannot tell you how much I love you. One night with you away from my bed is enough!
>
> L.

Last night's abandoned chicken was on a plate in the refrigerator, uncovered. I spent ten minutes slicing it up and another ten stir-frying it as I had in the first version of last night. I ate just a bit of it, wrapped the rest in tinfoil, went back upstairs, and slept until one.

Wadsworth called me. It was just past two, and I had been about to do some shopping. He seemed not to be in bad spirits; he inquired as to my headache, and wondered if I would be returning to work tomorrow. I said I surely would. He said, "Gabriel, when Lorna told me about you and her last night, I was angry."

I searched for a reply; before I found one, he had resumed. "When I got home, I was furious. I was thinking you two had really stabbed me in the back. I'm not deaf, and I'm not stupid, so of course I'd heard the rumors on the lot about the two of you, but you know, I'd really believed you were just friends."

There was another pause, and I had enough time to say, "I feel very bad about that, Bill."

"No," he said. "Let me finish. I got some sleep. I thought about things. I came to the conclusion that I was angry principally because I had disbelieved those rumors, so now I felt foolish. Then I said to myself, what's the point of that? Where's the satisfaction in that? I mean, Lorna's damned right when she says nothing was happening with us. Our affair was stagnant, she told me last night, and it's true. It's always going to hurt when someone tells you it's over, especially someone as lovely as Lorna. But you've got to be able to realize that it's just your pride that's been wounded."

The last few sentences sounded as if they'd been read from a script. Had he finished? "Yes," I said, "that's important."

"Just pride, nothing more," he said. "It was inevitable we'd end it soon, one way or the other."

"I've certainly been through it," I said.

"Listen," he said. "It may be over between me and Lorna, and perhaps it's a good thing, but I want you to know I still care about her, Gabriel. There are things about you that worry me. I said as much to her last night. You're a good fellow at heart, I'd say, but a lot of the time I don't know what to make of you."

Was I supposed to reply? After two seconds of silence I said, "Well, a lot of the time I don't, either."

"Know what to make of me?"

"No," I said. "Of me."

"I don't know what you mean by that," Wadsworth said.

"Nothing, Bill. I'm sorry I said it. I feel very ill at ease having this chat. But believe me, I appreciate your speaking to me this way. I know you care about Lorna, and I'm sorry things have worked out the way—"

He broke in, "Got to go now, Gabriel. Got to get back to work." And the line went dead.

—▪—

Saturday morning Lorna and I did not jump in her car and race down to San Pedro. We stayed in bed until noon, then drove into Santa Monica for lunch. Saturday night, we sat on our own beach and watched the ocean; when a healthy breeze came up, we retired inside. While I did not know the exact whereabouts of Bill Wadsworth, I could assume he was not out swimming. And Dutch Reagan, I felt sure, was carousing on dry land with Charlie Grimm and a few of his players, recalling good times.

25

Monday morning I paid a brief, cordial, strained visit to Wadsworth's office. We talked about our respective projects, my headache, his weekend. His face seemed puffier than usual, his eyes redder rimmed. At noon I met Reagan in the commissary. Over his customary plate of spaghetti he raved about Catalina, told me I'd missed a terrific excursion, a couple of fine ballgames, a chance to meet the Cubs stars. He spoke enthusiastically about their chances for the coming season. I could not disagree.

"Charlie Grimm remembered me," Dutch said. "It just thrilled the heck out of me. A couple of years ago, when I was there for spring training, it was as if I was a few rungs below those fellows—just a radio announcer from Iowa hanging around the camp. Now we're on kind of an even footing. Maybe they even look up to me a little bit. Charlie told me he and his wife went to a double feature last year, the programmer was *Love Is on the Air*, and he turned to his wife and said, 'Hey, I know that guy.'"

"Bet you felt great," I said.

"Boy, did I." Dutch was beaming. "But you know, Gabriel, there's always that moment when I think, it's one thing to be up there on the screen in these little pictures where half the audience may be out getting popcorn, or to have a part that lasts about thirty seconds in an A picture—but when am I going to get my break? I think I've got the talent to be a leading man. Maybe I'm no Cagney or Flynn . . ."

"But you could be a young Dick Powell," I suggested, although I knew there was not a chance in hell that Reagan could ever be in Powell's league.

"Well, I can't sing," Dutch said. "But I know what you mean—Powell's at home with comedy and drama, he's got that . . ."

"Amiability?"

"Right. That easy-going style, good looks but not pretty."

"Dutch," I said, "there's a project I've been thinking about. I haven't talked about it with anyone here, but I think you could be perfect for it."

"I'm all ears."

"You've got to be back on the set in just a bit, don't you?"

He glanced at his watch. "Six minutes."

"Why don't we get together later this week?"

"Sounds great to me," Dutch said. He gave me the broad Reagan smile. "Gabriel, I really think destiny's got something in store for you and me."

— • —

Friday night, Dutch came to dinner. He was impressed by the Hudnut house. He lived in a cozy apartment near the Hollywood Bowl and this, he told us, was his first visit to Malibu Beach. Lorna gave him a tour while I put the finishing touches on a paella, all of whose ingredients I had been able to find, fresh and cheap, along with a couple of bottles of Marqués de Riscal red, in Santa Monica. I have always had a weakness for wines from the Rioja region, but this 1935 *reserva* was nothing short of excellent. Dutch was impressed by the paella: it was a dish, it was a *word*, entirely new to him. "Gabriel, this is so good, this is just about the most delicious thing I've ever had. I didn't even know you cooked!"

"He's amazing," Lorna said.

"But how do you learn to do something like this? Where do they teach you how to cook something like this?"

I tried to put myself in the position of someone accustomed to a regimen of lamb chops, mashed potatoes, steak, baked potatoes, string beans, someone whose notion of exotica was spaghetti with meatballs. The colors alone on a plate of paella would be a wonderment. "In Spain," I said.

"I didn't know you'd been there," Dutch said.

"A few times."

"Before the war, obviously?"

"Yes." Before the war, several decades after the war, who was going to quibble? I said, "Dutch, try the wine."

"I don't drink. Don't like the taste of it."

"Try this," Lorna said. "It's delicious."

Dutch had a tentative sip, and smiled. "That's not bad." He sipped again. "Not bad at all. But tell me—to a particular place in Spain, or all over?"

I moved carefully through a few familiar anecdotes, editing scenes for chronological considerations as necessary, although truth to tell I didn't have much to worry about. Neither Dutch nor Lorna had ever set foot in Spain, and while Dutch had evidently paid close attention to the war, he knew next to nothing about the country.

We had flan and coffee. Dutch said, "I can't take the suspense any longer, Gabriel. Tell me about this project."

I took a deep breath. "No one's done a picture, a decent one anyway, about the war in Spain."

"It's a hot potato," Lorna said. "Everyone's afraid to take sides."

"Typical," Dutch said. "If they went out and talked to the American people, they'd find out everyone who gives a damn is backing the Republic. Especially after Franco bombed Barcelona."

"What if we came up with a picture that doesn't identify the sides, that technically could be construed as neutral, but that takes an obvious humanistic, antifascist point of view? Do you think the studio would make it?"

"Depends," Lorna said.

"I'd have to hear the story," Dutch concurred. "And say, do you think I could have another glass of that wine?"

"All right," I said. I filled Dutch's glass. "This is still a little sketchy, but I've got the basics down. There's an opening scene in a small town in Andalusia, southern Spain. This is fifteen years before the main action. Our hero, a boy of about fifteen, is walking into town. He's a strong, good-looking kid. On the outskirts of town there's a fight going on, a couple of bullies beating the hell out of a smaller boy who's trying to put up a fight, but it's hopeless. Our hero joins in and saves the day. The camera pays a lot of attention to one of the bullies, who's got a distinctive birthmark on his forehead.

"Now—at the smaller boy's house, we learn names. Our hero is Felipe. The little boy is Pablo. Pablo's sister Teresa is there, and we can see she takes a shine to Felipe. Pablo's mother tells Felipe that the older kids call Pablo a sissy and beat him up because he writes poetry

243

and plays the piano. Pablo looks embarrassed, but Felipe says, "Play something for me," and Pablo is thrilled. He sits down at the piano, rips through some tough, showy piece, and the scene fades out.

"Now we jump fifteen years into the future. We see Pablo's apartment in Madrid. It's an artist's place, attractively cluttered. There's a spinet piano, closeup of sheet music on it, by Pablo Torrealba. Books piled on the piano, and each of these is by Pablo Torrealba. Then we see Pablo: he's packing a suitcase, looking anxious. Outside there's sporadic gunfire. And the scene fades out."

Lorna said, "It's García Lorca, isn't it?"

She didn't miss a trick. "Not exactly."

"But the character is clearly based on García Lorca."

Dutch broke in before I could respond. "What are you talking about? Who's Garsy Alorka?"

"Federico García Lorca," Lorna said. "A Spanish poet who was killed by the Nationalists near the start of the war. Reading his poems in English makes me want to study Spanish, because I'm sure they're even more beautiful untranslated."

Dutch reached for the *reserva*, filled his glass again. "He was killed in battle?"

"No . . ." I began, simultaneous to Lorna, who said, "They killed him because he was a leftist and a homosexual."

Dutch made a face. "A *homosexual?*"

"That's just conjecture," I said.

Lorna said, "Gabriel, if you write a script about García Lorca no one's going to touch it. They'll be reluctant to make a picture that takes sides, and they're *never* going to make a picture about someone as well-known as García Lorca, especially because everyone knows his lovers were all men."

I said, "Dutch has never heard of him."

"So what?"

"Lorna, I doubt that anyone else at Warners just took Modern European Poetry at Smith. Think about it: do you really suppose any of those people—Bernie Wiseman, Hal Wallis, Jack Warner—do you think any of them would know García Lorca from a hole in the ground?"

Lorna said, "Someone will figure it out. They're not all idiots."

Dutch said, "This isn't the part you had planned for me, is it?"

"Look," I said, "this is ridiculous. It's *not* a movie about García

Lorca. The character bears a certain resemblance to him, yes. But there's no reason this poet has to be homosexual, no reason he has to be a Communist. Hell, we can give him a wife."

"All right," Lorna said, "don't worry about it for now. Tell us the rest."

Dutch said, "If you could clear one thing up, Gabriel—am I Felipe, or am I the other one?"

"You're Felipe, Dutch. Don't worry about it." I took a deep breath. "Pablo—and his wife—are on a bus headed back to his hometown. The bus stops at a roadblock, soldiers get on. Pablo doesn't have the proper papers. Soldiers escort him off the bus, bring him to their commander, and we see a man with the same birthmark as Pablo's childhood antagonist. He says, 'I know this man! This is Pablo Torrealba, an enemy of the people,' and he uses his pistol to whack Pablo in the face.

"Now there's a legend: TWO WEEKS LATER. The scene is a soccer game, professional or semiprofessional, because it's being played in a fair-sized stadium, with a few thousand people in the stands. The camera gradually fixes on one player in particular as he gets control of the ball, dribbles around a couple of defenders, breaks into the open, fakes a pass to a teammate, and kicks the ball past the goalie. The stadium erupts in cheering and the player is engulfed by his comrades. Now there's a shot of the scoreboard as its keeper puts up the numeral that makes the score Granada one, Málaga nothing. A gun sounds, indicating the game is over. As the player makes his way through crowds of ecstatic fans, one very pretty young woman—Teresa—is struggling to reach him. When she does, she shouts, 'Felipe, it's Pablo! He's been taken prisoner!'"

"I like this very much," Lorna said. "I like the way you make transitions. There's something very avant-garde about it."

"I think it's terrific," Dutch said. "But I'm not sure how I'd do as a soccer player."

"Just get shorts that fit, Dutch," Lorna suggested.

I resumed. "All right, big exposition scene now, at Pablo's mother's house, where it's made clear Felipe and Teresa are sweethearts, Felipe's a schoolteacher in town in addition to playing soccer for Granada. Pablo's mother—or make it Pablo's *wife*, now that we've got her—reveals that Pablo's being held in a makeshift military prison north of the city, that he's at the mercy of his childhood antagonist, whose name is Gonzalo Márquez, and there are implications of torture."

"No," Lorna said. "That's a giveaway."

"Why is it a giveaway? Are you saying the Loyalists wouldn't torture a fascist poet?"

"Maybe they would, but everyone in this country associates torture with the fascists."

"Does everyone, or just people on the side of the Loyalists?"

She stopped to think. "I suppose we could call Bill and ask him."

"How *is* Bill?" Dutch asked. "Say, how come he's not here? I always see the three of you together."

Lorna said, "We've broken it off, Dutch. Bill and I have stopped seeing each other."

"Sad to hear it," Dutch said, with a look of true concern.

"There's nothing to be sad about," Lorna said.

Dutch said, "So . . . you two . . ." He gestured toward Lorna and me.

Lorna said, "Yes. I'm sure it comes as no suprise. Evidently half the lot assumed we were having an affair."

"I had no idea," Dutch said. "But hey! This is great news for the two of you! I always figured you were better suited for each other. I know Bill's your friend, but he's kind of a sour apple."

"It's true," Lorna said. I saw no need to add my voice to the consensus. Lorna said, "Back to the story, please."

"Wait," Dutch said to me. "I wanted to say something about . . . all the political stuff. I wanted to say I think you're both right. It's clear as can be which side Pablo's on, but I think that's all right. If you keep to the letter of the law, if you don't name names, then everything's fine. This is shaping up to be a heck of a picture so far, and I think any Warners producer would have to have rocks in his head to turn it down for political reasons."

"Thank you," I said.

Lorna said, "That was very eloquent, Dutch." To my ears, there was not a trace of irony in her voice. It took me the better part of an hour, then, to run through the rest of the plot. Some scenes were far more detailed than what I shall set down here:

Felipe rides his motorcycle to the military prison, where a guard— who recognizes him a soccer star—brings him to Commandant Gonzalo Márquez's quarters. Márquez, too, recognizes Felipe, as the boy who humiliated him twenty years earlier. Felipe argues for Pablo's release. Márquez becomes increasing belligerent and insulting; when he disparages Teresa, it's more than Felipe can stand. He lunges at Márquez and knocks him down. Guards enter and subdue Felipe, whereupon Márquez beats him to within an inch of his life.

Felipe is tossed out of the prison into the pouring rain. The friendly guard helps him onto his motorcycle, and he makes it back home. He vows to Teresa and Señora Torrealba that he'll free Pablo if it's the last thing he does. His recuperation is agonizing. Fiery Teresa urges him forward when the pain seems insurmountable. After a month he's back on the soccer field. Scenes of his brilliant athleticism are intercut with scenes of Pablo's concurrent degradation at the hands of Márquez.

From there, the plot would be quite familiar to devotees of a certain action hero who specializes in a subgenre that might be called Revenge of the Invincible. Felipe and Teresa return to the prison by automobile. They face insurmountable odds, and indeed both appear on several occasions to be done for, but Teresa is clever and brave, Felipe impossibly strong and intuitive, both of them luckier than the man who broke the bank at Monte Carlo. They manage to leave the prison not just with Pablo, but with the evil Márquez as hostage. They eschew their car for Márquez's bigger, faster one—and so ensues the first epic car chase of cinema history.

Felipe's driving, Márquez in the passenger seat, Teresa in the back with a pistol trained on Márquez, Pablo in and out of consciousness next to her as they zoom through the Andalusian countryside, careen through villages, skid among shoppers in open-air markets—followed by a squadron of military vehicles—all the while the interplay within the car as tense as the chase itself.

"Boy!" Dutch exclaimed. "Boy oh boy! You're on to something big, Gabriel. The way you're building the tension, I'd say it makes the politics irrelevant. They'd have to be crazy to turn this down."

Lorna said, "The way your plot works . . . there's something so logical about it, and yet everything's *novel*, so it can't really be called a formula. It's almost as if you've invented an entirely *new* formula."

I opened the second bottle of Marqués de Riscal, and I told them the ending.

— —

We lay in bed just past two o'clock. Dutch had left at one. Lorna said, "It's awfully good, Gabriel, but it's so dangerous."

"I don't see why it's so dangerous."

"I've told you why."

"We can get around that, I'm sure."

She shifted from her back to her side, supported her head on her hand so she looked down at me. "I know you like Dutch, but don't you think it's kind of a tough part for him?"

"I think he can handle it."

"I know he's very natural, but he's not all that versatile. You might be getting him in over his head, don't you think?"

"I think he's made for the part."

26

Time passed. For the most part, life was awfully good. I would never have imagined I could enjoy a nine-to-five job, but working at Warners was a pleasure. I was doing something I loved. Certainly I had mixed feelings about the nature of my first project, but from now on everything would be original. I worked for Bernie Wiseman, a man I liked and respected. I saw Lorna most days at lunch. I had had anything from brief encounters to substantial conversations with Humphrey Bogart, Bette Davis, Errol Flynn, James Cagney, Edward G. Robinson, Olivia de Havilland, and a score of lesser lights. With my Leica, I was a frequent visitor to a variety of soundstages. If I had not done it already, I would soon pass Bill Wadsworth in the writers' hierarchy, and while he had at least made a pretense of turning the other cheek regarding Lorna, I suspected he would not be so gracious in the future.

That was the first of my worries, that Wadsworth would at some point become vindictive, and do something to undermine my growing stature at Warners. Then too, I thought often about the Futureboys. I'd left 1984 under the comforting impression that Jean-Baptiste and Hans might be spending some time behind bars. Not much time, probably, because as Annabel had pointed out they had no weapons. But I'd realized not too many days after returning here that the length of their incarceration was in a large sense irrelevant. Whether they were released on their own recognizance or held for a month in the county jail or sentenced to a year at San Quentin, they would head for the B-2 at the earliest opportunity, and begin looking for me.

If indeed Hudnut had succeeded in removing the tracking device, they would have to rely on trial and error. But what were their choices? Nineteen ninety-four, where they would quickly discover I didn't exist, and 1938. It could take them years to find me, but I could expect them any day; it was simply a question of when their machine would set them down.

And what do I do when they arrive? Hand over the machine with my best wishes, in hopes they're content to let bygones be bygones? What if Lorna then, despite my best efforts, proceeds to die on schedule, and I'm powerless to do anything about it?

There was never a day I didn't consider telling her about myself. Something about myself. The whole truth would have been preferable, but impossible. I could have told her that I had not really been Jasper's teacher, that I had not known her aunt and uncle. But surely, I reasoned, this would lead to questions for which I had no answers. The Edgar Hudnuts would not, I knew, be coming west this summer; Lorna communicated with them less than she did with her parents, with whom she exchanged letters once every five or six weeks. Although the telephone was already a familiar and popular instrument, long distance was something both exotic and expensive. And this extended family was clearly quite libertarian. I had at first been tempted to run and hide when the Charles Hudnuts and the Wilfred Hudnuts arrived for weekends—a practice whose frequency increased as summer approached and arrived. But if anyone objected to Lorna's cohabitation with Jasper's former English teacher, no one showed the slightest sign.

I have already introduced you to Charles, who visited the day of the landslide that did not bury Lorna. It was his branch with whom we spent the most time. As luck had it, our own weekends in Santa Barbara or Tijuana or points in between tended to come when the Wilfreds were in residence. All the adult Hudnuts were cordial and engaging, both uncles bearing considerable resemblance to the adult Jasper, both wives tall and good-looking, both families with four bright, blond children, all tall for their ages.

I had achieved a certain degree of popularity with all these Hudnuts because of a small addition I made to the house. Lorna and I spent virtually every weeknight at home; we talked and we read, often with the radio on in the background. It was a fairly high-quality radio, a substantial Crosley table model, and for several weeks I was anywhere from mildly interested to quite intrigued by the pretelevision mixture of comedy, mystery, and music that accompanied our evenings. But after a time the comedy became inane, the mystery banal, the music boring. No matter whose orchestra was coming to us live from which ballroom, there was a dreadful sameness to Swing. One Saturday we drove into Santa Monica and bought a phonograph. It was a Capehart, a console with AM and shortwave as well. We bought a huge quantity of 78 RPM records. One place or another, I found fifty or sixty albums of Bach, Mozart, and Vivaldi. Lorna was partial to Handel and Glenn Miller. I had listened to 78s before, and always assumed they sounded so terrible because they were old and their grooves had been ruined by Cretaceous needles. How disillusioning it was to play my first record—Vivaldi's *Concerto in C Major*—and discover that the surface noise was more prominent than any of the instruments.

But none of the Hudnuts had ever heard a compact disk, a cassette tape, even an LP. As far as they were concerned the Capehart was the epitome of aural sophistication. Edgar and Wilfred offered to chip in. Please, I demurred, in lieu of rent this is the least I could do.

But not all went smoothly. One Sunday evening in mid-June Lorna and I returned from some little expedition as Charles and family were preparing to drive back to the Valley. The oldest child, Charlie, whom I'd first met as a sour and uncooperative adult, was now a twelve-year-old nearly as tall as I. "I hope you don't mind," Charlie said in a voice without a hint of apology, "but I took a look at that boat in the garage. It's a keen-looking boat." I had decided to keep it here, and forfeited a month's rent in Santa Monica. The "boat" had been covered by a heavy canvas dropcloth for three months.

His father said, "I didn't even realize you had the thing here. I guess Charlie keeps better tabs on things than the rest of us. We were trying to figure out how it works. For that matter, we were trying to figure out what it's made of."

"Plastic," I said.

"Thought so," said Charlie. "What does it run on?"

Why was I so woefully unprepared for a moment that should have seemed inevitable? "Gasoline," I said off the top of my head.

"That's what we figured at first," said Charles, "but there doesn't seem to be a gas tank. At least there's no place to pour it in."

"No, it needs an outboard."

"That's what I guessed, but Dad says there's no place to attach one."

"Boy," I said, warding off panic, "you Hudnuts are fast on the draw. It needs a special adapter for the motor."

"But," Charlie said, "if it's built to take an outboard, why would you need a special adapter?"

"I'm not really sure about this," I said, "but I think the original design called for a small inboard two-stroke engine. That didn't work out too well, so they went to the outboard."

Charlie seemed caught somewhere between reluctant respect for his elders and profound skepticism. His father said, "I don't guess you've got the adapter? We could rent an outboard. We were all thinking how great it would be to try the boat out, with Edgar's permission, of course."

I laughed as heartily as possible. "Don't have the adapter, and I'm not qualified to run the thing, believe me. . . ."

"I'll bet Uncle Edgar could tell us," Charlie said.

"He doesn't even know it's here," I said. "It's supposed to be a surprise."

"But if they're not even coming out here this summer, then why . . ." Charlie began.

Charles put a large hand on the boy's shoulder. "Remember your manners, Charlie. I'm sure Mr. Prince will let us try the boat when the time is right." And he ushered his son toward the car.

Could I count on Charles's compassion indefinitely? Should I find a new apartment for the machine? If I removed it at this point, wouldn't my action cause further suspicion?

—·—

I settled in to my job. At Warners in 1938, no matter if one had written an A picture right off the bat, one did not transcend the studio system. *Four O'Clock* made its way up the ladder: Bernie Wiseman told me he loved my second draft, but returned it to me with a three-page, single-spaced list of suggestions for changes, none of which involved shots of the apparently sacrosanct clock. I made changes, handed in my work, and waited. In the meantime, I was given other chores, screenplays in various stage of development that "needed work" of one sort or another.

Lorna, meanwhile, had small parts in *White Banners* (with Fay Bainter, Claude Rains, and Jackie Cooper) and *Four's a Crowd* (with Errol Flynn, Rosalind Russell, and Olivia de Havilland.) She was the ingenue in a B picture called *Girl with the Golden Eyes*. She had a tiny part in a bad Dick Powell comedy called *Cowboy from Brooklyn*, in which Dutch was seventh-billed. It was his first role of any signifi-cance in an A picture, and Lorna reported that once he got the hang of his character, Dutch was better than she'd expected—that unlike a lot of good-looking beginners he didn't seem compelled to "act"; he was self-assured enough to be himself for the camera.

Dutch starred in a B picture called *Girls on Probation*. He played a lawyer who defended Jane Bryan and fell in love with her. It was an

inane bit of melodramatic garbage, the sort of "programmer" Warners turned out with efficient regularity, and Dutch endured it. One of the girls on probation was Susan Hayward, who was twenty years old and stunning. Dutch's first big break came while *Girls on Probation* was still shooting, when he was cast in *Brother Rat*. This was one of the movies I'd watched with Hudnut; it was an A picture, a comedy in which Dutch and Wayne Morris and Eddie Albert played cadets at the Virginia Military Institute; Dutch was third-billed, and he wasn't bad at all. I dropped in on the set now and then, and watched the dailies when it was convenient and I felt inconspicuous. What I found was a rather striking lesson in perspective. Viewing the small screen in 1994, with Hudnut making derisory noises throughout the movie, I'd had no reason to alter my idée fixe of Reagan as a hack, someone with minimal talent at best. Here, in three dimensions or in vivid black-and-white in the screening room, I saw something more. He might never give Dick Powell a run for his money, but Dutch had a flair, an easiness, a presence. It was enough for me.

Hardly a day went by that Dutch didn't corral me somewhere—on the set, in the commissary, on the telephone—and inquire as to my progress on our project. I didn't have a title for it. Lorna referred to it as "Lorca." Dutch called it "Felipe," or the "bust-the-fascists picture." I had an outline, a few pages of first draft, and not much more. I was sufficiently occupied by busy work during the week and by our excursions over the weekends so that I rarely had an hour to myself. What's more, everything I'd written up to this point had been done with a certain facility. I was getting very good at script doctoring—taking other people's work and polishing it, finding it increasingly easy to mimic other writers' styles and rhythms. And *Four O'Clock*, although its style and rhythm were very much my own, had not required a great deal of contemplation regarding characterization and plot.

— —

I had arrived in Malibu after the Great Storm and it had seemed truly foreign territory, waterlogged and deserted. By this time, by early July, virtually everything swept away or destroyed by the floods had been put back together or replaced. But the reconstructed Malibu was still quite alien to me.

Where I had come from, Malibu in July had a population of tens of thousands. In the odd, daydreaming moment now, returning from Burbank, say, on a hot summer evening, I might come around a bend in the road expecting to find cars parked alongside the beach, clusters of tacky little fast-food places and convenience stores across the street, coveys of tattooed in-line skaters on the sidewalk—and discover instead a continuation of this rather narrow, beautiful, and quite deserted seaside highway. Each time this occurred I encountered the same paradox: while I was infinitely happy to be in *this* Malibu, this unspoiled, undeveloped one, I felt what might be described as more than a mild sense of loss at the inaccessibility of the other one.

27

Once a week, at least, Bernie Wiseman called me into his office for a chat. The routine hardly varied. Wiseman would sit and smoke Chesterfields, ask me about myself, ask me how I'd like to see *Four O'Clock* cast, remind me that my opinion was probably worthless, ask me how things were going in general, tell me about movies he'd produced in the past, tell me what a future I had in this business, give me little bits of wisdom. I enjoyed our conversations. I liked Wiseman, and I felt he liked me.

On this June morning I handed him the treatment I'd just finished for the Spanish Civil War picture. Perhaps in deference to Dutch, I'd given it the working title *Felipe.* Wiseman accepted my twenty typewritten pages and assured me he'd read them at his earliest convenience. But for now, he wanted me to know that Jack Warner had read my second draft of *Four O'Clock* and "loved the hell out of it. Except he says, 'What is it with this kid and the clocks?'" I began to speak, but Wiseman held up his right hand. "You know what I said to him? I said, 'J.L., I love the clocks. I think this kid's got great ideas, he wants the clocks, I think the clocks should stay.' You know what he says to me? He says, 'What the hell. What does it cost to photograph a clock?' I'm not lying to you, Gabriel."

"Wonderful," I said, "so what's—"

"What it boils down to is J.L. thinks—and I have to say I agree with him—this is gonna be a very big picture for Errol Flynn. I know you don't see Flynn as a cowboy."

Of course I had already seen Flynn as this very cowboy—in point of fact a U.S. marshal—in Hudnut's living room. While the notion was a travesty, I could certainly write better dialogue than Wadsworth's. I said, "I wouldn't imagine I'd have much of a say in this."

"It's true, you wouldn't. But I respect your judgment. You think it's nuts to cast Flynn as the sheriff?"

"Bernie, all I really care about is the marshal's wife."

Wiseman grinned at me across the great expanse of his desk. "See, sometimes I think you're the mystery guy, sometimes I think I know you backwards and forwards. Did I sit here a few months ago and ask if this was the girl you were shacked up with? Did you tell me no, she's Wadsworth's sweetheart?"

"Things change," I said.

"So you're gonna come in here and risk your ass for some little girl you don't care about?"

"The important thing is, Bernie, does she have a chance?"

"I wouldn't get my hopes up," Wiseman said.

Was it possible Lorna could *not* get the part she'd once won with little assistance from me? "But there's a chance?"

"She's got a chance," Wiseman said, his smile lacking its frequent tinge of malignancy. "What's against her, it's a hell of a jump from nowhere to female lead in an A picture. What's for her, I watched a few minutes of what she's done, and she's got the look. I mean she looks like she could play the part, and she looks like a little push here, a little push there, she could be a star."

"Sounds like a pretty strong endorsement."

He shook his head. "It's a *possibility*, Gabriel. Look, I don't like to rock the boat. You want to write a nice part for your girlfriend, you shouldn't write a big picture. There's five, six actresses on this lot that are household names would scratch each other's eyes out for that part. How are they gonna feel when it goes to some little girl no one's ever heard of?"

"Everybody's got to start somewhere," I said.

"Usually not this close to the top, though." Wiseman stubbed out his cigarette. "Hey, speaking of bad blood, what *is* the story with you and Wadsworth? Is it just that you stole his girl, or is there something more to it?"

"I thought we were getting along pretty well," I said.

Wiseman chuckled. "That's not what I hear."

"Bernie, you know the way people gossip . . ."

"I'm talking about what I hear directly from the horse's mouth."

"Wadsworth talks to you about *me?*"

"Not normally. Couple of weeks ago, Estelle and I went to a party in Beverly Hills. Some rich lawyer. His wife and Estelle go way back. It was a mixed crowd. Some Hollywood people—Eddie Robinson was there, Paul Muni—but mainly a lot of lawyers, doctors, people with money falling out of their pants. I'm at the buffet around nine o'clock when somebody taps me on the shoulder. I turn around and there's Wadsworth—this big, blond guy at a party where everybody's a Jew. Turns out he's there because the girl *he's* with knows the lady of the house too. And it turns out I'm the only person at the party he knows—so for the next, I don't know, hour and a half, two hours, he puts away maybe ten glasses of champagne and he bends my ear till I'm worried it's permanently out of shape. He's complaining, mainly, about everything and everybody at Warners except me, and I figure if he was talking to somebody else, he'd be complaining about me, too. But the nastiest shit was reserved for you, Gabriel."

"And what was that?"

"First he starts out with the old school tie. It seems you tried to impress him and Lorna with the fact you went to Princeton. But did you go to Princeton? He went through all these yearbooks, didn't find you anyplace. Wrote to some professor you mentioned, the guy wrote back and said he never heard of you—"

"Wait a minute, Bernie—"

"Listen, I don't give a damn about any of this. He's drunk, he's jealous, he's bitter, you tell me. He said you gave him some treatments to read when you first came to town. Said you took advantage of him, but that wasn't the main thing. He said when he first read your stuff he thought it was impressive, very versatile, very modern. But now when he looks at it, when he thinks about it, he says it's almost like you're taking a little bit from this style, a little bit from that, each of these scripts is so different from the others. It bothers him."

After a moment I said, "It's sad."

Wiseman shrugged. "That was my conclusion. It must be tough for a guy, he loses a girl to somebody, he knows deep down he doesn't have half this guy's talent. It would eat away at him."

There was a moment's silence. Bernie Wiseman was an important man at Warners and it appeared I could be confident of his support in the event Wadsworth chose to engage in more overt character assassination. Still, even though I'd considered it pretty much a matter of time, it concerned me that Wadsworth had gone so far as to write to someone at Princeton, presumably my ersatz thesis adviser. "Bernie," I said, "I want you to know: no matter what Wadsworth may tell you, I did go to Princeton."

"Gabriel, tell me you went to Oxford, Cambridge, Heidelberg, I'll take your word for it."

— —

The Wadsworth business bothered me. It was a frustrating situation, to say the least. I did not like Wadsworth, nor did I loathe him. He had, after all, been supportive of my work, he had helped me get my job, and in return I had slept with the woman he hoped to marry. On the other hand, he was the sort of person I had spent my life despising and avoiding. He was a snob and a bigot, a narrow-minded elitist cretin. He was capable of cruelty bordering on murder. He had thoughtlessly goaded Dutch Reagan into a fatally irrational act. On the other hand, he had made a concerted effort to save Dutch's life immediately afterward.

Wadsworth had, in another drunken moment, said dangerous things about me to my boss. My boss, this time, had taken them with a grain of salt. What would come next? What was the worst Wadsworth could do? I didn't imagine Bernie Wiseman or Jack Warner, or anyone in between, would fire a talented writer because he'd fibbed about college. What was the best I could do? Keep my distance and hope that eventually Wadsworth would find something more constructive to occupy his time.

— —

I found myself spending studio time on *Felipe*, working on it at home, some nights waiting until Lorna was sound asleep, then slipping out of bed and creeping downstairs, seizing the laptop from its garage hiding place, tapping away in virtual silence. I grew fond of the story, of the characters. Writing had always been easy for me, and this sort of writing—this minimal scene setting accompanying blocks of snappy dialogue—was a breeze. How odd, I realized at three o'clock one summer morning, that I had had to travel back fifty-six years in time to discover my calling.

— —

I began seeing more of Dutch. His social life focused primarily on sports. He loved baseball, but he was almost as happy at a track meet, a bowling alley, a skating rink, and perhaps happiest of all on the golf course. He traveled often with his claque of ex-fraternity boys, cheery fellows from Drake University in Des Moines (Dutch had been a member of Tau Kappa Epsilon at Eureka College), who drank lots of beer and listened respectfully to Dutch's manifold holdings forth on whichever subject struck his fancy. In May and June I attended baseball games with Dutch and members of this crew. I turned down the golf invitations; it was a game I did not play, whose social implications did not appeal to me.

The fraternity boys spoke often of Dutch's parents, especially his mother, Nelle, of whom they were obviously very fond, and with whom they evidently spent a lot of time. Even as our friendship grew, Dutch did not invite me to meet his parents, and I was never altogether sure why. Was he afraid the Princeton screenwriter would look down on the working-class Midwesterners, or did he fear that good Christian Nelle would look askance at Lorna's and my sinful relationship?

Nevertheless, as our movie began to take form, our excursions became more intimate. It was Dutch and I, or occasionally Dutch and his starlet date and Lorna and I, who went to the Stars game or the Angels game on a weekend afternoon. Dutch spoke earnestly about Felipe's character, the importance of his being a soccer player, an athlete, the purity of sports. Dutch wondered if I had given my treatment to Bernie Wiseman, if Wiseman had given me a report, if there was anything he could do, personally, to impress upon Wiseman that he and the role were made for each other. I told Dutch he would be the first to hear Wiseman's reaction, and that I did not think Wiseman would appreciate any intervention on his part.

As the filming of *Brother Rat* progressed, so did another metamorphosis. While Dutch was still "seeing" a very pretty B actress and dating numerous others, often at Warners' behest, he began spending a fair amount of time with his costar, the temporarily blond Jane Wyman. He assured me that he and Jane were "just friends," that he found her "stimulating," and loved to talk to her.

One evening in July he called me at about nine-thirty, wondering if he could come over. It was late, he knew. He had to be on the set at six the following morning, but he'd just had a troubling conversation with Jane and needed to talk. I covered the mouthpiece and asked

Lorna, who had to be on her own set at six, whether it was all right if Dutch paid a visit. She shrugged, said, "Why not?"

Dutch was in some kind of high gear I'd never seen before. He noticed the Capehart, gaped at its magnificence, tried to tune in WHO, his old station in Des Moines, but managed to get no farther east than Denver and Oklahoma City. He sat for a moment, then stood up, paced about, sat again. "I hardly know this girl, I guess," he said when finally stationary, "but normally we get along very well. We don't disagree about things. I think I'm a pretty decent, level-headed fellow. Don't you, Gabriel?" I nodded. "You, Lorna?" She nodded. Dutch sat. Lorna said, "What did you argue *about*?"

"Of course," Dutch said. "I haven't even told you that. Well, that's why I'm here. If we'd fought about, you know, something that didn't concern you . . ."

Lorna said, "It's Gabriel's picture, isn't it?"

"She says I'm obsessed." Dutch leaned back in his chair until I feared it would tip over. "Maybe I am, but she doesn't seem to realize the kind of opportunity this would be for me. I tell her you wrote the part specifically for me, and her attitude is, what the heck, Ronnie, just do what the studio tells you and in a year or two the big parts will come." The chair came back forward and struck the floor noisily. "Well, that's not entirely the point, is it?"

I said, "I wouldn't say so."

"It strikes me that this is one of those times in your life when everything comes together. It's not just the part. It's that, I don't know, that somehow it seems we were ordained to meet, that you'd write this picture with me in mind, that the picture isn't just some silly bit of nonsense, of entertainment. It's the kind of thing that makes people *think*. If it's well done, first it thrills them, then maybe it moves them to action." He looked at me—or should I say his look implored me—for confirmation.

"I couldn't agree with you more," I said. "I spend too much of my time writing to do my job, to make money. It's important to me to create something that serves a purpose, that fulfills a commitment."

Dutch rose from his chair, stood above the couch I shared with Lorna. "Gabriel, if you knew how much this meant to me. How much, in my heart of hearts . . ."

Lorna said, "What exactly is it about all this that has Jane so upset? It's not the politics, is it?"

Dutch thought. "No." He thought some more. "In a way, I suppose. We *don't* disagree politically, or at least I don't think we do. But she feels that I'm letting my politics get in the way of my career. I tell her this is a time when politics and career are pretty much inseparable. To her it's just another part. Maybe it's a great part, but there'll be other great parts. Not like this one, I tell her. I tell her that it would be like a knife in my heart to see some other actor get this part. . . ."

I said, "You don't have to worry about that, Dutch."

He sat down. "But I don't want to throw a monkey wrench into your career, Gabriel. I mean, if Wiseman loves the idea and wants you to write the picture . . ."

"He can't make me write it."

Lorna said, "You've got to watch your step, Gabriel. You gave him a treatment. You're under contract. As far as Warners is concerned, it's their property. What if he just assigns it to someone else to write?"

"There are laws against that kind of thing."

"Are you sure?"

"I'd sue them in a minute if they did that."

Lorna gave me a pained look. "You and Bette Davis."

Dutch said, "She didn't sue Warners, Warners sued *her*."

"The point is," Lorna said, "that she rocked the boat. She fought the studio. She tried to get what she felt was rightfully hers, and they brought out all their lawyers. That's exactly what would happen to Gabriel."

"Wait a minute," I said. "Bette Davis just walked away, so she breached her contract—"

"Which I feel she had every right to do," Lorna said. "RKO wanted her for *Mary, Queen of Scots* and Jack Warner wouldn't let her go. He kept casting her in junk like *Satan Met a Lady*. So she decided to take a long vacation."

"Good for her," Dutch said.

"Hey, I'm agreeing with you," I said. "If I'd been in her position I'd have done exactly the same thing. What I'm saying is, she breached her contract, which gave Warners the chance to sue her—"

"And she didn't work for a year," Lorna said.

"But she made her *point*, for God's sake. Jack Warner bought *Jezebel* for her, she won every award in the book, and now she's as big a star as there is, which is exactly what she set out to be. She fought the system, and she won."

"But Gabriel, she was an established star. She'd already won an Academy Award. You're a writer who hasn't had a single script produced."

"But I wouldn't be breaching my contract. If they take my story and give it to someone else to write, they're stealing from *me*, and I'd be suing *them*."

"Wonderful. So you sue them and *you're* out of work for a year, or two years? Is it worth it?"

Of course I didn't believe it would ever get that far. I believed I had Bernie Wiseman in the palm of my hand, that he wouldn't risk losing me over one project. I said, "Sure, it's worth it."

"God!" Dutch said. "That's the kind of thing I love to hear!"

I was brushing my teeth when Lorna said, "I wonder if Jane isn't right?"

I replied through a mouth full of Squibb. "About what?"

"I wonder if Dutch wouldn't be better off staying at the studio's pace."

"Why? This part's perfect for him."

"He's not a very good actor, Gabriel. I'm sure you've recognized that. I wonder if you're pushing him a little too hard, too soon."

"Lorna, for God's sake, I wrote the part for him. He can't miss."

"He's so ingenuous, though. He obviously admires you. You're older, you're sophisticated, you went to Princeton. You're what he'd like to be, I'd guess. I just hope you're not taking advantage of that, not manipulating him."

I spat and rinsed. "Look, he's a competent actor, I wrote the part to suit him, everything's going to be fine."

—■—

Bernie Wiseman was contrite. "I should have gotten to it sooner, but do you have any idea what comes across this desk every day?" He made a sweeping gesture with his right hand. "Scripts, treatments, outlines, novels, novels-in-progress? Jesus, all this crap they send me?" He paused now, reached for another Chesterfield, lit it, and sucked in the smoke as if it were life-giving. "Any idea, Gabriel?"

"A lot," I said. "Mountains of material."

"Exactly. Mountain *ranges*." The right hand again swept across the desktop, which was shined to a high gloss and utterly devoid of scripts or scripts in the making. Now he leaned toward me for effect, his forearms splayed flat on the beautiful desk. "Why do I do this? Why do I wade through all the junk? Because I wait for something like this. I'm not in it just for the money, Gabriel. I think I've got a little bit of taste. And I think we've got a picture here everybody—Jack Warner, the critics, the people in Peoria—is gonna be crazy about."

" 'This' would be my Spanish Civil War story?"

"What else, Gabriel?"

I felt a great wave of relief, of affection for Wiseman, this sage judge of material. "That's wonderful news," I said. "You can't know how happy I am to hear that."

"There are problems, of course."

My wave was interrupted. "What kinds of problems?"

"Nothing major. Nothing we can't take care of."

"What? Tell me."

"The main thing, you should know, you should be aware, that nobody's going to make a picture at this time that's so biased toward one side in the war."

"How do you mean?"

"Well, this guy Torry-whatsis. He's a poet, he's a musician. The kids he grew up with are bullies. That's like a code, it's like, what, an *allegory.*"

"But that's the story, Bernie. How do we take care of it?"

"We change him a little bit. The *story*, as I see it, is about one friend who risks his life to save another friend. So what the hell difference does it make if Torry-whatsis is a poet or an engineer? You see what I'm talking about?"

"I think I do. What if I refuse to change it?"

"Nobody makes the picture."

"Nobody at Warners."

Wiseman leaned back in his chair, smoke exuding in two great plumes from his nostrils. "I know what you're thinking, Gabriel. You've got a one-year contract. You wait till it's up, you go and you shop this thing around the other studios. Take my word for it, kid. Don't waste your time. Don't screw up your career. Nobody's gonna make this picture as is. Nobody."

I had an inspiration. "I'll tell you what, Bernie. I'll make a concession to you if you'll make a commitment to me."

"I'm listening."

"I'll make Pablo anything you want him to be: a math teacher, a lawyer. You promise me you'll bend over backwards to cast someone as Felipe."

"Who? Some other Princeton boy? Does Lorna Fairchild have a brother?"

"Someone on the lot. A Warners contract actor."

"Who, for Christ's sake?"

"Ronald Reagan."

Wiseman looked at the ceiling for a moment, then back at me. "Do I have the right guy? Tall, good-looking, used to be a radio announcer in Kansas or someplace? He's in that military school picture with Wayne Morris, *Brother Rat?*"

"That's the one."

He guffawed. "Are you kidding me?"

265

———

I broke the news to Dutch, told him that Wiseman loved the Felipe story, told him that Lorna's warnings had proved accurate, that certain changes would have to be made to Pablo's character. Dutch had mixed feelings: too bad we couldn't make it clearer which side we were on, but not so bad at all if Pablo were further differentiated from the real-life homosexual poet. I saved the worst news for last, and at that I watered it down a bit. I didn't tell Dutch Wiseman had simply laughed in my face when I suggested him for the part of Felipe; I concocted a lengthy, gentle explanation whose gist was that while Dutch (in Wiseman's imagined estimation) was an actor with great potential, he was too much of an unknown for such an important role.

Dutch took the news well—took it like a man, I might say. He asked me who Wiseman saw in the part, and I told him I didn't know, that Wiseman's and my conversation had pretty much stopped right there. At that point I said that as far as I was concerned Wiseman's preference was irrelevant, because I'd conceived the picture with Dutch as Felipe. Of course the truth went a bit further: I'd conceived the picture *because* of Dutch.

"Under the circumstances," I told him, "I'm not sure I even want to start writing it."

"You're a pal, Gabriel," Dutch said, his voice breaking just a bit. "You're a real pal."

As we spoke, I had of course nearly completed my first draft.

28

There was a telephone call from Charles Hudnut on a Monday morning in early August. Charles was polite, cautious, apologetic for having called me at the studio. When he told me he'd thought it better to call me at work, I felt a twinge of anxiety. He then said, "I don't want you to have the impression that I suspected you of anything. I don't want you to think I was *investigating* you." Then of course I knew my anxiety had been justified. I said nothing. Charles continued after a moment's pause, having graciously given me an opportunity to step in if I wished. "I happened to be talking to my brother Edgar. I'm in charge of the finances for the house, and Edgar had overpaid—"

At that point I did choose to interrupt. "That's something that's been bothering me, Charles. I mean, it's one thing for Lorna to live there rent free, but quite another for me, and I could certainly afford to pay my share. Lorna always assures me you wouldn't consider it, but I'd be happy to."

"Very thoughtful of you." Charles's voice was as even and emotionless as before. "It's certainly something we should consider, something Wilfred and Edgar and I could talk about, along with the women. But that's not why I called. Edgar had overpaid, had *been* overpaying, actually, and I called to point this out. I would have written, but I knew they were going to Europe for a month, and I was afraid the letter wouldn't have got there in time. In the course of the conversation I happened to mention how happy Lorna seemed with her new friend, and I happened to describe you as Jasper's teacher, whereupon Edgar told me he had no idea that Lorna was seeing one of Jasper's teachers. In fact, he said the notion seemed quite odd to him. I told him your name. I did not mention the boat, of course, because you'd told me it was meant as a surprise. He did not know your name. Now, at that point he called out to Jasper, who was in the next room, evidently. Jasper arrived presently, and I could hear their conversation quite clearly. Jasper said he had never had an English teacher named Mr. Prince at Lawrenceville or anyplace else."

There was another pause, a longer one, as Charles gave me a chance to respond. Again, having nothing to say, and in a state approaching shock, I did not. Charles resumed. "So, I suppose my first question would be: Are you using an assumed name?"

"No, I'm not," I said. "And I feel I should explain things to you, as much as I can."

"That would be called for, I think," Charles replied.

My mind was spinning. I did not enjoy lying. I had thought myself, as I have explained earlier, incapable of lying, and I had discovered myself to be quite adept at it under certain circumstances. This was evidently not one of those. Once again I faced the paradox of having to explicate without revealing, the difficult task of telling the truth while withholding the part of the truth—the heart of the truth—that would brand me as an abject liar or a lunatic. I said, "The day I met Lorna she made certain assumptions about me. For my part, I could feel myself already falling in love with her. I'd just arrived in California, my past was uninteresting, so I decided to take Lorna's assumptions and elaborate a bit. It's not something I feel good about. I've been tempted many times to explain all this to her, but it embarrasses me. I'm afraid it would do more harm than good."

Now Charles was silent for a few seconds, as if choosing among a laundry list of secondary questions. "But it seems you did know certain things about our family . . ."

"Yes sir, I did. I knew the house was yours. The boat truly was intended to go there, as a surprise. I'm afraid I can't tell you any more than that about the boat's origin. I didn't know Lorna would be there, didn't expect to find her there, and when I did I was swept off my feet."

Now there was quite a long silence before Charles said, "Why wasn't the boat simply shipped to Edgar in Connecticut? They're right on the water there, too."

"I wish I could tell you that. I was told to bring it here. I was given certain information about your family, about Edgar's family, that is. Other than that I was walking into a blind situation. I can assure you that until I met Lorna, I had no intention of becoming involved with your family."

Five seconds went by, then ten. I felt sweat trickling down my sides. Charles finally spoke. "I'm trying very hard to believe you, Gabriel. You've struck me as a decent person, and Lorna clearly has nothing but the highest regard for you. But there are aspects of this that don't make a great deal of sense. I think I'd find the story more credible if you could tell me anything at all about the origin of the boat."

I replied immediately. "I'm afraid I can't do that, Charles. All I can tell you in good conscience is that it was first shown to me in Europe—"

"Good God. Not in Germany, I hope."

"No, sir. I can assure you this isn't a Nazi boat. It was shown to me in a free, nonfascist state."

"By whom?"

"Someone of impeccable reputation. A scientist. An American, someone known to your family. Someone Edgar knows quite well."

Another silence. "Well," Charles said eventually, "I wish I saw a clear path on this. My instinct is to trust you, Gabriel, although I must say much of the information I have points in the opposite direction. Do you mind if I discuss this with Wilfred?"

"I don't think it's really my decision to make."

"The thought that keeps going through my mind is that you might be some kind of sociopath. Of course if you were, it's the last thing you'd admit, almost by definition, isn't it?"

"I suppose it is." I wondered what it would be like to play poker with Charles.

"One thing I've got to insist upon," he said. And I braced myself. "One of these weekends we've got to try out that boat. I swear I'm not going to have any peace with Charlie until we do. Will you make an effort to locate that adapter?"

"If it's available, I'll get it," I said. I was in the process of hanging up when I thought I heard Charles's voice. I replaced the receiver to my ear. "I'm sorry, did you say something?"

"Yes. There was something I forgot to ask you. Do you have a friend who drives a gray Chevrolet sedan? Probably about three or four years old? The car, that is."

"Not that I can think of."

"I ask because it was parked out front last weekend. Sally approached the man sitting inside and he drove away. I asked at the gatehouse and the guard said he'd let the man in because he had an appointment with Miss Fairchild's friend. I assumed that to be you. It seems odd he would have driven away, doesn't it?"

"Very odd. I promise you, Charles, I don't know anyone who drives an old Chevrolet, and I certainly didn't have any appointments last weekend."

"Strange," Charles said.

━ ━

Perhaps it was the day of Charles's call, perhaps a day later, Wiseman asked Lorna to test for a part in *Four O'Clock*. I was with her when the call came and she virtually asphyxiated me in her glee after she'd hung up the phone. She asked me if I supposed she was up for the lead, and I pointed out that there were essentially only two female roles in the movie: the marshal's wife, and the marshal's old girlfriend who's now living with his deputy. Since the latter role called for a considerably older woman, I told Lorna, she would definitely be testing for the female lead.

She wasn't told, of course, which scene she'd be reading, but I happened to have my own copy of the latest version of the script, which gave Lorna three evenings to familiarize herself with the part. Not that she needed it, I suspected. She was perfect for the part. It was too small for Olivia de Havilland. Claire Trevor and Ann Sheridan, who would also be tested, were already acting in A pictures, and each would be adequate, but Lorna would be perfect.

She read the scene in which the wife tries to dissuade the marshal from staying and facing the bad guys, after it's become pretty clear he feels he has no moral choice but to fight. Wiseman let me watch all the tests with him—because I'd written the script, he said. Trevor was good, Sheridan overacted a bit; Jane Bryan was appealing, clearly too young; two of the Lane sisters were interchangeably mediocre. Lorna nailed it.

"She's pretty good," Wiseman said as the lights came up in the screening room.

"Come on, Bernie. Tell me she wasn't the best of the bunch, by far."

"Maybe not by far, but yeah, she was the best."

"So does she get it?"

"She gets my vote. My recommendation. Then we wait and see what J.L. says."

I found her on the set of *Girl with the Golden Eyes* and gave her the news. She pushed me toward the soundstage's front door, then out onto the thoroughfare, let out a scream of celebration, and gave me a hug easily the match of the one that had nearly killed me the day she learned she'd be testing. Still squeezing me, she said, "Gabriel, this is so wonderful! It's such a dream! And it's all because of you."

"I didn't do the test," I demurred.

"But we both know they wouldn't even be considering me for this if you hadn't written it."

"Maybe. What we both should keep in mind is that you don't have the part yet."

"Mr. Warner's not going to overrule one of his producers, is he? Especially not Bernie Wiseman."

"I'm sure it's happened in the past."

Lorna insisted on a celebration. We returned to Jack's, on the Venice Pier, where we'd eaten the evening of the day we met. The food was no better this time, but the night was seductive—languidly warm, with a fresh ocean breeze—and Lorna was somehow even more beautiful than usual. When the waiter came to offer us the dessert menu we made eye contact that amounted to a sort of sexual telepathy. We paid the check and hastened back to Malibu, to our bed, where we made love with a ferocity that shut out everything but ourselves, much as we had that dread afternoon on Catalina, when we failed to hear Dutch's knock. Lying next to Lorna near ten o'clock, both of us soaking wet, I recalled with a bit of a chill that—as far as she was concerned—our tryst at the Catherine had never happened.

I sat up in bed, propelled by a wavelet of anxiety. Lorna, on her back, arms spread back against the headboard, said, "How can you move?"

"I have to tell you something."

"How can you talk?"

"Have you talked to Charles in the last week or so?"

"Uncle Charles? Not since we saw them here whenever it was, weekend before last. Is something wrong? Did we forget to water something?"

271

"No," I said. A little pond of our sweat had accumulated around her navel. "Charles spoke to his brother, to Edgar . . ."

"Are they coming out here after all? I'd love to see them, especially Jasper."

"No, not as far as I know. Lorna, Charles mentioned me to Edgar, and Edgar told him he'd never heard of me."

"Why would he do that?" Lorna's voice was quiet and languorous, evincing no concern.

"Because it's true. I lied to you the day we met. I wasn't Jasper's teacher at Lawrenceville or anywhere else. I've never met Edgar or Grace."

She rolled onto her side, facing me. "Then why did you come here?"

"Because of the machine. The *boat*. I was supposed to deliver it here."

Now she supported her head with her right hand. Her voice was more animated. "Why did you think you had to lie to me? That seems so unlike you."

"It's complicated."

"I'm not in a hurry."

"I can't explain it to you."

"Because it's something you don't want to tell me?" Her voice suggested nothing worse than curiosity. "Or because it's something you don't understand?"

"A little of both."

"Something you're ashamed of?"

"I'm ashamed I had to lie to you. I'm not ashamed about the reason."

She ran her left index finger from my Adam's apple to the middle of my breastbone. "You're not a criminal, are you, Gabriel? Not some notorious con man who's just been released from Leavenworth and been hired by the Japanese to deliver a mysterious armament to the West Coast?"

"Charles asked me if I'd been dealing with the Nazis."

"Charles can be very odd."

"Odd he may be, but all things considered he treated me pretty well. He caught me in a lie, after all."

"What about me?" There seemed a subtle change in her tone. "Why are you telling me this, Gabriel? Because you were afraid Charles would talk to me?"

"I don't think so. Well, that may be part of it. But I've wanted to tell you these things nearly from the start. I couldn't figure out how to go about it."

"All you had to do was tell me."

"I wish I could tell you everything. Can you wait?"

"What do you think?"

"I think that if I were in your position I'd be fairly curious, fairly impatient."

She eased beside me, kissed my lips. "Gabriel, for God's sake, since you showed up on my doorstep five months ago, everything's been wonderful. Sometimes I wake up in the middle of the night and I see you next to me, and I touch you to make sure you're real, that you're not a fantasy, or an angel. It's almost as if you popped out of the sky, and you saved me from Bill, and you seem to know what I want, in every way. And now I'm on the verge of getting this marvelous part because of you, in a picture you wrote, that's probably going to be Warners' biggest hit of 1939." She kissed me again, and embraced me, her breasts flush against my chest, the two of us fitting together in perfect, moist symmetry. "Gabriel," she said in my ear, "I trust you, I *love* you. Whatever you have to tell me, I can wait."

I could not have heard sweeter words.

— • —

"I've got to admire the kid's balls," Bernie Wiseman told me. The balls in question belonged to Ronald Reagan, who had struck up a conversation while Wiseman was visiting the *Brother Rat* set. "At first—I've got to tell you the truth—I didn't know what the hell he was talking about. I mean, I barely know who the son of a bitch is, and he's talking to me about actors' rights or some bullshit, telling me how in Europe the actor actually has some kind of say in every stage of the production. Is that true?"

It was a hot August afternoon and we were speaking on the telephone. In my office, a large fan created plenty of noise but not much breeze. I said, "I don't know, Bernie. But Dutch Reagan tends to be up on these things."

"Does he? Well, I told him I don't know what the hell goes on in Europe, but that's the best example I ever heard of inmates running the asylum. Unless they have a more sensible class of actor in Europe. But you know what, Gabriel, I saw that French picture with von Stroheim a few months ago. Did you see it?"

"I did." In my other life I had seen it at least a dozen times.

"Not bad. Good story, well told, except it drives me crazy to read the goddamn titles. But see, if that director, the guy is the son of the painter, what's his name, Renoir—if he's gotta put up with von Stroheim, can you imagine? I mean, tell von Stroheim to make a movie of Mary Had a Little Lamb, he'll come back two years later with a three-hour picture, tell you to stuff it up your ass if you want to cut it. The point is, Renoir makes this picture without any advice from von Stroheim. Am I right?"

"I'd have to think so," I said. "But what about Reagan? What did he want?"

"Your fucking Spanish War picture is what he wants. You didn't put him up to this, did you? You've got more sense than that."

"I didn't put him up to anything, Bernie. I told you I wanted him for the part. I still do. But I know better than to sic him on you."

"Good. Call him off, Gabriel. For his own sake."

29

It had been quite a mild summer by Southern California standards, the temperature rarely exceeding the low eighties, but in mid-August the Santa Ana winds blew in off the desert and the days became miserably hot. Air-conditioning existed, but it was primitive and costly, and nowhere to be found in the writers' quarters at Warners. Bernie Wiseman didn't object to my leaving early, even taking a day off when the weather got miserable.

Dutch called me Thursday evening, the eleventh, to say that the entire cast of *Brother Rat* had been given Friday off in anticipation of the hottest day of the year. Predictions were for a high somewhere between ninety-five and a hundred. Dutch wondered if I'd like to join him in a jaunt down to Del Mar, the new and very fashionable racetrack a hundred miles down the coast. "I'm not a big bettor," Dutch declared, "but I love to see them run. And there's a match race tomorrow—Seabiscuit against some horse from Argentina."

Indeed, in Friday morning's paper it was all over the sports section: a twenty-five-thousand-dollar matchup with Ligaroti, the South American upstart, who would be carrying 114 pounds to Seabiscuit's 130. Still, although there was to be no official pari-mutuel action on the match race, Seabiscuit was estimated by reliable sources to be a three-to-one favorite. As much as I appreciated a second opportunity to see the great American horse, I would be paying more attention to the races I could bet on. Despite the occasional extravagancy, my cash reserves were still healthy. But if *Felipe* were to be made without Warners' help, I'd be needing plenty of money.

I picked Dutch up in front of the Montecito Apartments at ten and we set out for Del Mar. The temperature was already in the high eighties, but with the top down in my Buick the heat was tolerable. At Dutch's insistence we stopped for lunch at a hamburger joint he knew in San Clemente, where the fare turned out to be edible, at least, and generous. In his fashion, Dutch was bursting with information concerning every aspect of our day on the town. He engaged in a lengthy essay on the nobility of rooting for the underdog, from which I inferred he'd be pulling for Ligaroti today. Not at all, Dutch protested: Seabiscuit would be giving the Argentine horse a sixteen-pound handicap, and certainly that made Seabiscuit the underdog.

While Dutch's logic seemed more than a little flawed I did not argue the point, and we sped down the coast road, so mercifully free of traffic this blazing Saturday noon, so clear of habitation. It was not as if we were traveling through the Outback. The towns were already there—Oceanside, Carlsbad, Encinitas—but they were tiny, quaint, and nothing filled the gaps between them, no malls, no industrial complexes, no sprawling housing developments, no looming Interstate 5. More than once, as we motored around a bend and caught sight anew of the startlingly blue Pacific, I felt that sort of chill reserved for the sudden appreciation of a transitory beauty, and I found myself caught in that confusion that plagued me more and more. There was first the lament, that this little strip on the edge of North America was doomed to the squalor and vulgarity I would know in my time. Then there was the recognition that (if I so chose) *this* was now my time, and I would never have to see a Taco Bell again.

Having exhausted the topic of Seabiscuit, Dutch moved on to the track itself, to Del Mar, which was just over a year old. Did I know that Bing Crosby was responsible for the place? I did, as a matter of fact, but there was no stopping Dutch. "He's got a great big place, beautiful place, I hear. I've never been there, of course, but it's a few miles inland from here, in Rancho Santa Fe. Anyway, when Crosby found out they were putting a fairgrounds in at Del Mar, he jumped right in. They say he was in on the planning, the layout, everything. He loves racing, of course. Breeds horses and everything. So he's president of the Del Mar Turf Club. You know who else is on the board? Oliver Hardy, for one. And Pat O'Brien. Have you met Pat around Warners? No? I'll introduce you. Heck of a nice guy. I did a couple of pictures with him earlier this year. Well, you know, he was the star. *Cowboy from Brooklyn*, kind of a silly comedy, but a lot of fun. I had a nice little part in that. And we just wrapped up *Boy Meets Girl*. That one was a real scream. Jimmy Cagney, of course. Anyway, Pat's on the board. And on any given day you might see half of Hollywood at Del Mar. I came down with some of the fellows last month and we saw, let's see, Jolson, and Mickey Rooney, Jimmy Durante. And you know who else? J. Edgar Hoover, director of the FBI. Right there at the two-dollar window—a regular guy like you and me."

I had, incidentally, seen a rough cut of *Boy Meets Girl*. It was a Broadway farce Warners had tried to transform into a screwball comedy. Dutch, playing to type, had one long scene as a radio announcer. The movie was noisy and enervating, not a bit funny.

Del Mar was a gem of a place, tiny compared to Santa Anita, but packed for the match race; I would read in tomorrow's paper that the attendance was slightly in excess of twenty thousand, minuscule by the standards of the big tracks. But they couldn't offer this view—the Pacific and a long, sparkling white beach clearly visible past the oval track, the bell tower straight out of *Vertigo*.

We arrived barely in time for the first race. It was cooler here than it would now be in Hollywood or San Clemente, perhaps in the mid-eighties. I bought us clubhouse tickets; Dutch reached for his wallet, didn't protest greatly when I told him it was on me. I hastened to the betting area, having carefully laid out my day's plan, joined the shortest line at the ten-dollar windows with two minutes until post time. "That's for ten-dollar bets, Gabriel," Dutch chided.

"I know."

Every once in a while Dutch did some small thing eerie enough to make my head spin. At this moment he gave me a look, a sort of questioning, bordering-on-ironic smile, that I knew from press conferences, from campaign debates. When someone said something that Ronald Reagan wasn't prepared for, that wasn't on his flash cards, this was the face he made. It was neither an unfriendly nor a threatening expression, but it managed to imply a sort of superiority, perhaps bordering on omniscience, when in fact it represented almost the opposite. At this moment, Dutch was clearly taken by surprise. On our long ride from Hollywood I'd given him no indication I was any different from him: a guy here to enjoy the scenery, the pomp, the celebrities, the match race, and maybe place a few two-dollar bets.

Our eyes remained locked for quite a while, perhaps fifteen seconds, before Dutch said, "You can lose a lot of money fast at that window, Gabriel."

"Don't worry about me," I said.

Dutch was still beside me when I placed my bet: Redrock Canyon to win, twice. "Twenty dollars on a five-to-one shot? My dad would call that a sucker bet."

"Not when the horse wins," I said.

And of course my horses won. Redrock won by a head, and paid $13.40; I put my winnings on Crafty Fox's nose and he won by four lengths, putting $420 in my pocket. Fella cruised to victory and paid $19.80; then Lady Jaqueline waltzed home ahead of the favorite in the fourth. Dutch calculated my winnings: $2,064. He was awestruck. With two thousand dollars you could buy a new Cadillac. You could make a down payment on a house in a good neighborhood.

The match race was terrific—a Hollywood mini-script all on its own. The great Seabiscuit and the Argentine interloper ran neck and neck wire to wire, bumping frequently, jockeys whipping, red-faced Dutch yelling his lungs raw for the American horse, who ended up winning by a nose. I bet $500 on Bartlett to win the sixth race, and solemnly promised Dutch I'd quit if my horse lost. He did not. I sandbagged the seventh race, losing a small bet, showing my fallibility. Convinced my run was over, Dutch pleaded with me to leave. Just one more bet, I pledged.

It was $500 on a forty-to-one shot named Payne. Dutch was appalled: "Gabriel, for God's sake, he's the longest shot in the field. You might as well be flushing your money down the toilet!"

"If I lose," I replied, "I'm still twenty-five hundred ahead. If I win, maybe we can make our movie without the Warner brothers."

Payne started badly, seemed out of it in the stretch, and Dutch flashed me a look of condolence, whereupon my horse took off as if electrified, passing three rivals, winning by a neck, stunning the heat-stroked crowd, and paying $69.60.

"How much did you win?" Dutch's voice was a croak.

"Not quite seventeen thousand. Twenty for the day."

"Twenty *thousand!* Good God, Gabriel—how many years' salary is that?"

I said, "Think of it as a down payment on *Felipe.*" If I needed to, how long would it take me to turn twenty thousand into two hundred thousand on the stock market? A month? Two?

Bound now for the cashier's window, then for the parking lot, we would miss a ninth race to be won by a horse named Voting Hour, with Supreme Court finishing third. Would that the place horse had been called Judge Bork, or James Watt, or Just Say No. Alas, serendipity did not extend quite that far.

In the odd moment at work, much more often while lying awake next to Lorna during those supernally quiet morning hours, I had anticipated the first new sighting of Jean-Baptiste, wondered where he would pop up, guessed it would be in Malibu, or at Warners, two places he knew to find me, two places where his presence would be aggressively inconvenient. I had never imagined he would be standing by the cashier's window at Del Mar. I would not, in fact, have recognized him. He appeared older, perhaps simply because his hair, while still short and spiky, was no longer platinum, but a mundane dark brown. His clothing verged on the ordinary: baggy cotton trousers, plain blue shirt, and despite this extremely hot day a light gray jacket. I would not have recognized him had he not spoken to me. He said, "You've had a good day, yes?"

And I glanced at this run-of-the-mill runt, not altogether sure he was speaking to me, while some part of my brain was processing the accent. I nodded. All I could think of to say was, "How have you been?"

He shrugged. "Not so good. Are you going to introduce me to your friend?"

Dutch stood next to me, in a state of interrupted animation. We'd been discussing how much it would cost to make *Felipe*. There were two people ahead of us in line. Jean-Baptiste had been watching us, observing us, spying on us. How long had he been spying on me? Where was Hans? I felt a sort of social imperative, that it would be impolite not to introduce these two acquaintances of mine, and I felt a subtle but dread trepidation, that something horrible would be in store were I to make the link between two very different districts of my existence. I said, "Jean-Baptiste, this is Dutch Reagan." I pronounced the name the old-fashioned way.

Dutch extended his hand and said, "Pleased to meet you."

His eye still on me, Jean-Baptiste shook Dutch's hand. In French, he said, *"This is the guy who was dead on the island, is it not?"* I spoke to Dutch. "Jean-Baptiste is French."

Dutch grinned. "I've just seen that French picture, *Grand Illusion*. Thought it was terrific."

Jean-Baptiste continued to speak French to me. *"You know each horse that's going to win. How do you do it? You have the information stored somewhere?"*

I said to Dutch, "I don't think Jean-Baptiste is a very big fan of the pictures."

"Ah, too bad. Too bad." Dutch remained hearty, not yet aware he was in the presence of someone very strange.

"What do you know about me?" Jean-Baptiste said in English. "You don't know about my education. You know nothing about how I have spent my life. In fact, I have seen many films you could not possibly see, so you are the stupid one."

"I beg your pardon," I said. "I was making an assumption, since you hadn't responded to Dutch . . ."

"*Grand Illusion?*" Jean-Baptiste turned now to Dutch. "Yes, of course I've seen it. Renoir. Gabin. The German with the monocle. Excellent film, if you like that old style *statique*." He turned to me. "How do you say it in English, *statique?*"

"Same word," I said. "Static."

"Static?" Dutch said. "Like on the radio?"

"The radio?" Jean-Baptiste said. "Why is he talking about the radio?"

"Don't worry about it," I said, as it became my turn at the window. I handed my five hundred-dollar tickets to the cashier, a chubby man with a green visor and a sweat-soaked shirt. He let out a little whistle and did some math with a pencil. "Seventeen thousand four hundred?"

"That sounds right," I said.

"How d'you want this? Thousands?"

"No—better give me hundreds." The chubby man began counting out hundred-dollar bills. It would be a while before he got to a hundred and seventy-four. Dutch asked Jean-Baptiste if he and I had gone to school together, and Jean-Baptiste made a snorting noise. He spoke to me again in French. *"You're going to give me how much of that money?"*

"None," I said. "I could lend you some, if you need it."

He laughed angrily. *"And when do I get my machine?"*

"We can talk about that."

"You give me a lot of trouble, you have to pay for it."

"This is not the right time to talk, Jean-Baptiste."

"Then give me five thousand dollars."

"No."

"Look, I just came here. I have nothing, no place to stay, and I can make your life very difficult."

The chubby man handed me a lofty stack of bills, and I thanked him. I said to Dutch, "Excuse us for a minute, please." I led Jean-Baptiste to a corner fifteen feet away. The horses for the ninth race were being called to the post. He said, "Your friend looks familiar to me. Why do I know his face?"

"You were right. He was on the island."

Jean-Baptiste mulled. I wished simultaneously to be party to his train of thought and to put an end to it. "You came back to a point before he died, you made sure he stays alive."

"Exactly."

He paused again. "But I know him from some other place."

"He's an actor. You've seen his films."

"No, I don't think so," he said.

It was time to change the subject. "Look," I said, "you know as well as I do that you can't tell anyone about me. No one would believe you, unless you showed them your machine, and then they'd surely take it away from you."

He gave me a cunning smile. "You don't wish to defy me, please, Gabriel. I am not always so polite as this."

I peeled five hundreds off my stack and handed them to him. "You can live like a king with this money." He examined the bills one by one. I said, "What do you mean, you just got here? Obviously you've already got a car. And where is Hans?"

"You killed him," Jean-Baptiste said without much expression. Sweat was rolling down his cheeks, dripping on the collar of his cotton jacket.

"Exactly how did I kill him?"

"I told you we could not go back where we came from without the machine you stole . . ."

"You made it to 1984 all right."

He glared at me. "Yes, it's only forty-six years. We need to go almost two *hundred* years. The B-2 cannot make it with two people."

"So what happened to Hans?"

"Your friend Udnut tricks us. The police take us. Hans is sick again. He has the one where you're shitting all the time . . ."

"Diarrhea? Cholera?"

"I don't know. It's one we don't have. It's extinct. He has a big fever, sick all the time, he has *délire* . . ."

"And he *died?*" Jean-Baptiste shrugged in response to my question. I said, "Did he die, or didn't he?"

"Probably," he said. Now in a swift series of his movements he removed his jacket, and shook it as if it were covered with lice. His shirt was dark with sweat.

"What do you mean, *probably?*"

"I mean that I don't know for sure. I have to go looking for you. Udnut takes the little *traqueur* out of the A-4, I don't know where you are. I go to 1994, you are not there. I come here, I find you. A long time has passed. Hans is probably dead."

"And you don't want to go back to 1984 and find out?"

Jean-Baptiste was becoming visibly confused. All the anger he'd been storing for me was being upstaged by my indignation at his abandonment of his friend. He said, "Look, I have to make some choices. If you come back with me to 1984, if Hans is alive, I take care of him . . ."

"I'm not going anywhere with you."

"Then I have just one machine, so Hans must die, because you stole my other one."

"This is ridiculous," I said. "Take the money and leave me alone."

Jean-Baptiste gave me an icy look. "I don't think you want to treat me like this."

"If you want to have a straighforward conversation with me, if you want to be honest, we can talk about the machine. Not now. You can call me at work." I wrote Warners' number on the back cover of my program, ripped it off, and handed it to him.

He folded the page and stuffed it into his jacket pocket. "I don't know why you think you are in charge here," he said.

30

How could I explain Jean-Baptiste? I told Dutch he was an acquaintance from my pre-Warners days, a brilliant technician who was a little out of his mind. There turned out to be no need for further elaboration: Dutch was more than content to talk about our fabulous day at the track, about the seed money we'd earned for *Felipe*. We stopped for dinner at the poshest place within view of Highway 101, a French restaurant in Laguna Beach, where the food proved close to inedible, but Dutch was pleased. I dropped him at the Montecito in Hollywood, and got back to Malibu around nine.

Lorna was waiting for me, sitting on the porch swing in the evening heat with her *Four O'Clock* script. She wore shorts and a simple cotton top; she was barefoot. This is one of those irrationally indelible moments for me: I can see her with absolute clarity, see her expression as I walked out onto the porch and she looked up from the script. She smiled, happy to see me. I had become a part of her life, an important part, I daresay. And she, of course, *was* my life.

She got to her feet and we embraced. She said, "How did it go? Did you win a million dollars?"

"Not quite." I reached into my right pants pocket and retrieved my wad of hundred-dollar bills, stuck it in her left hand. She raised her hand to eye level, whereupon her eyes widened spectacularly and she stood back to have a good look at the loot. "My God, Gabriel, you've done it again! How much is there?"

"Almost twenty thousand."

"I don't believe it! What are you going to do with all this money?"

"I thought I might have a go at producing a movie."

A bit of apprehension crept into her expression. "Are you serious?"

"If Bernie Wiseman's right, if Warners won't cast Dutch as Felipe, if no studio will make the picture the way it's written, why shouldn't I make it myself?"

Lorna stood two feet from me, holding the cash, digesting all this astonishing information. "First of all, you're going to need a lot more than twenty thousand dollars."

"I can get it, in time."

She handed me the money, and I tossed it onto the glider. "Gabriel, have you given some thought to this? I mean, have you really thought about it?"

"I have."

"Basic things . . . where are you going to get them? Things we take for granted. Where are you going to find a soundstage? Do you intend to build one? Do you think someone would rent you one?"

"Why not?"

This gave her pause. Surely it was something she'd never given any thought. Certainly I hadn't. "Well, Warners wouldn't. Maybe one of the little studios, the fly-by-night places . . ."

"Tec Art rents to all sorts of people. They're just down the block from the old Warners lot. I think I'd want to do most of it on location, anyway. And there are always plenty of people looking for work, Lorna. I'd work with a union crew, wouldn't offend anyone."

"Wouldn't offend anyone?" Her smile accused me of naïveté, at least.

"It's not as if I'd be horning in on anybody's territory. I mean, I wouldn't be starting a studio, I'd just be making a movie. One movie."

"What about your friend Bernie Wiseman? One minute you're his hottest property, the next you're off making your own pictures. Don't you think he'd take offense?"

The thought had occurred to me. "What if he did? What could he do?"

"He could share his concern with Jack Warner, for one thing. Let's say you got your picture made, Gabriel, through some series of miracles, and let's say it turns out to be the masterpiece it could be. So there you are with a finished movie, prints struck, ready to go to the theaters, but for some reason you can't find anyone who's interested in distributing it. Because Jack's put the word out—touch this movie and you'll never deal with Warners again."

I was more than ever impressed by her knowledge, her concern. For someone so young, someone who had been here such a short time, she was awfully wise—wiser without question than her colleague Dutch Reagan. She was also, I suspected, much more cautious than the situation warranted. In a strange way I did consider Bernie Wiseman my friend, and as such why could I not assure him this would be nothing more than a leave of absence, a little movie with a tiny budget? Why would he not give my project his blessing?

I do not recall the exact evolution of our conversation, but soon enough we stopped talking about the prospects of my making a movie and eventually we stopped talking about anything at all, but became entangled on the porch swing and—in deference to the heat—reached a tacit agreement not to go upstairs, and found a way to conjoin rather successfully right there. No one could see us, to be sure, but I wondered several times whether on this hot, still night our voices—Lorna's in particular—might not carry to the next house in one direction or the other. I wondered whether someone might think Lorna was being tortured.

In any case, the authorities did not arrive, and after a time we sat, spent but still intertwined on the glider's soft cushions, fluctuating ever so slightly in the windless night. The ocean too seemed close to exhaustion, sending feeble, nearly inaudible waves our way. Lorna said, "Guess who came to see me today."

"I couldn't. Give me a hint."

"I'll give you a big hint. Bill Wadsworth. Unannounced."

I didn't like the sound of this. "Sober?"

"Not altogether. He knocked on the door—it was around noon—and he said hello to me and asked if you were here. I told him you and Dutch were off at the races. It was hard to tell whether he was disappointed or relieved. My guess is, he was intending to talk to you, glad he didn't have to, sort of amused you were enjoying the Sport of Kings with Dutch, who as you know he thinks is a complete idiot. I invited him in, made him a drink, a weak one, and he decided to tell me what he'd come over to tell you."

"Which was?"

"That you're a fraud."

This was of course not unexpected, and unless Lorna had suddenly become awfully adept at masking her emotions, it had not hit her terribly hard. "How am I a fraud?"

"Bill says you didn't go to Princeton. He says he's been communicating with the alumni office and they swear there's no record of you—not in the class of twenty-seven or anywhere around it. Also he checked at Lawrenceville, and you were never on the faculty there, but of course we knew that."

"What's the point?" I said. "What's he trying to achieve?"

"He said, if you were lying about these things, where you went to school and where you'd worked, who was to say that everything about you wasn't false? Who was to say that you really wrote these things, that maybe they weren't plagiarized?"

"Plagiarized from where?"

"I asked him that, too. He didn't seem to have thought it through."

We shared a moment of silence. I said, "What do you think about all this?"

Lorna ran a finger from my moist kneecap to the moist point of my ankle. "I think Bill is very disturbed because you've supplanted him in my life and you're leaving him behind at Warners. You're much more talented than he is, and he doesn't want to believe it."

"I'm glad that's what you think," I said, and that was as far as the conversation went. A couple of hours after dinner I recalled that my roll of cash was still sitting on the glider. I retrieved it, took it upstairs, stuffed it into the drawer of the bedside table, intending soon to put it in the bank.

—◆—

I had chosen not to mention Jean-Baptiste to Lorna. What did I know about *his* second visit to 1938? I stopped by the gatehouse Saturday evening, while Lorna was taking a bath. I described Jean-Baptiste to Horace, the guard: short, dark-haired, speaks with a foreign accent. Could this have been the man Mrs. Hudnut saw in the old Chevrolet? Horace, sixtyish and not awfully sharp, mulled. Could be, he decided. He only vaguely remembered this visitor. Short, yes, and dark-haired. Did he have a foreign accent, though? Possibly.

What could I do with the machine? Surely Jean-Baptiste would look for it first at its former apartment in Santa Monica. Next he'd come to Malibu. I hadn't the time to find a new apartment. I called Bernie Wiseman at home, got him just as he and Estelle were preparing to go out. I had an odd favor to ask. If he had a bit of extra space in his garage, I wondered if I could store—possibly for a few months—a little experimental boat that had arrived prematurely. It was to be a surprise. . . .

So it was that early Sunday morning I managed to fit the A-4 into my Buick, with the top down by necessity. I covered it with a couple of blankets, tucked them firmly under the seat, and—having ascertained that no one was following me—drove the machine to the fringes of Beverly Hills. "Jesus," Wiseman said, "isn't this something? It's a boat, huh? Well, it'll be safe here."

——

I suppose that from the time the notion of *Felipe* became firm in my mind, I had never considered anyone but myself as its director. This is not to say I was bound and determined to direct it. Had Wiseman agreed to cast Dutch Reagan as Felipe, I would gladly have suffered any hack Warners chose for the project, while of course hoping that someone competent was assigned. But once it became clear I was going to have to do the movie on my own, I never imagined handing it over to someone else, in part because it never occurred to me that someone with talent might be interested.

But of course I had not taken into account Uncle Charles's birthday. It was perhaps a week after Del Mar that Lorna told me we'd been invited to Charles's annual party, to occur August 27. This seemed slightly odd to me because such a distinct line had been drawn between our respective social lives, and more than slightly foreboding because Charles and I hadn't spoken since our telephone conversation three weeks earlier. It also struck me that it might be awkward for us even to be around during the party—which was by custom to be held in Malibu—that some of Charles's and Sally's guests might be more straitlaced than their hosts.

Haltingly, I fear, I pointed all this out to Lorna, who sat at the breakfast table, the remains of an orange on a plate in front of her. She wore her white terry cloth robe, belted loosely at the waist, revealing much of her upper torso. She assured me that I had nothing to worry about. "And," she said rather offhandedly, "I thought you might be interested in meeting Howard Hawks."

Why would Howard Hawks, one of the four or five great American film directors, be attending a birthday party for Charles Hudnut, San

Fernando Valley structural engineer? Because, it turned out, Charles and Hawks had been childhood chums, then gone off to Exeter together, then been fraternity brothers at Cornell. Why had Lorna never mentioned this before—for instance, when we had seen *Bringing Up Baby* shortly after my arrival, and I had professed my belief that it was the best comedy ever made? Why had she not casually turned to me and said, "Well, Howard Hawks and my Uncle Charles are like two peas in a pod?"

Her breasts peeking from within the robe, Lorna reminded me that my raving had largely concerned Grant and Hepburn, their chemistry and their timing. And, she said, to her way of thinking the worst sin of all was to be a name dropper. I kissed the top of her head.

— —

Hawks was tall and slim and gray. To this informal party on a warm night in late August he wore a checked suit, a beige wool shirt with a silk tie, and brown loafers that looked as if they had been shined by God. He had arrived late, at about nine o'clock, after the party had been in progress a couple of hours. He was not a celebrity here; the thirty or so people in attendance either knew him as a friend of Charles's or did not not know him at all. For someone like Hawks, I imagined, attending an extra-industry party must come as a relief. All the more reason for me to stay in the background for a while.

During a series of casual but earnest conversations with other guests, I kept my eye on Hawks, I never got too far away from Lorna. On this clear, beautiful night most of the party's activity occurred on the porch and on the beach just beyond it. Several guests had changed into bathing suits and romped into the ocean. Charlie Hudnut, the evening's official photographer, used his Brownie until the last vestiges of sun disappeared, then appropriated my Leica and its expensive flash attachment.

Somehow we all converged at around ten o'clock; Charles introduced us, and Hawks's eyes locked on Lorna's. "Yes, of course, Charles's beautiful niece. You're still at Warners?"

"I am. And so is Gabriel."

Hawks glanced at me. "Actor?"

"No," Lorna said, "he's a writer. He wrote the picture I'm about to do. God, maybe I shouldn't say that. It's not official yet."

Hawks said, "What picture is that?"

"It's a western, called *Four O'Clock*."

Hawks's head did a little snap, and he paid attention to me for the first time. "The thing about the marshal? Villains waiting for the train? All the shots of the clock?" I nodded. He resumed, "Hal Wallis showed me that script. It moved all right. I liked the way your characters worked with each other. Liked that Quaker wife. But why the hell have you got the marshal going around asking for help?"

"He can't take on the whole gang by himself. He's done a good job for the town, he figures they'll be by his side when he needs them."

Hawks shook his head. "I've never made a western, but it seems to me a man in that situation has to think: either I can do the job on my own, or I've got to get the hell out of the way."

I was in the midst of constructing a rebuttal when Charlie appeared from nowhere and said, "Everybody hold it right there." He pointed my camera at us and in an instant I was completely deprived of sight by a pre-nuclear flash explosion.

"Good God," Hawks said. "Charles should do something about that kid. Spoiling him rotten."

While I debated whether to suggest the existence of moral gray areas to a man whose films denied them, Lorna said, "Why did Wallis show Gabriel's script to you?"

"I'm not sure. Maybe if I'd been more positive he'd have asked me to direct it. Maybe it was just a little professional business. Maybe he wanted to show me the kind of talent you've got in Burbank these days."

It seemed an excellent time to change the subject. I said, "I thought *Bringing Up Baby* was a masterpiece." It was the first movie Lorna and I had seen together. Lorna had laughed till she cried. I—who had seen the movie innumerable times before, but always on television—had quite often simply cried, as I am sure Heinrich Schliemann would have had he been transported back to some critical juncture of the Trojan War.

"Thanks," Hawks said. "I wish a few million other people had felt the same way."

"Isn't it bizarre," Lorna said, "that such a funny movie, with such a wonderful cast, with Grant and Hepburn, would do so badly at the box office."

"It didn't do *that* badly," Hawks said.

"Ahead of its time," I said.

"You think so? Don't you think slapstick is kind of timeless? If anything, I might've thought that picture would have done better a few years ago."

"No. Well, yes, slapstick *is* timeless, but there's something much more sophisticated about *Bringing Up Baby*. I mean, in part it's because of the actors, because they're so good, and in part it's because of the very notion of a leopard, of *two* leopards, wandering around Connecticut. Right there, you're getting close to the heart of cognitive dissonance—"

"Of what?" Hawks said.

I had become awfully good at avoiding such temporal faux pas by being constantly, vigilantly self-conscious. Now here I was, wishing to impress an idol, wishing to find a way to imply, at least, what only I knew about the future's esteem for his movie but could not say. "Nothing," I said. "I got carried away."

"No, say it again."

Lorna was nodding at me, unconsciously imploring. I said, "Cognitive dissonance. It's not actually my idea. I heard it somewhere."

"Cognitive *dissonance*," Hawks repeated. "I like that. That's precisely what humor's about, what comedy's about, isn't it? Do you write comedy, Mr. . . ?"

"Prince. Gabriel Prince. No, I haven't. I'd love to someday, but . . ."

Lorna said, "Gabriel's working on a script now that's just wonderful. About the war in Spain."

"For Warners?" Hawks's question seemed more than idle.

"Possibly," I said. "But I doubt it. We've had some differences, some major problems."

"You work with Bernie Wiseman, don't you?"

"Yes."

"Well, he's a pretty straight shooter. But hell, tell me about it."

I gave him a three-minute synopsis, emphasizing the friendship between Felipe and Pablo, the nobility of Pablo, the heroic perseverance of Felipe, the tough sexiness of Teresa. From the start it was clear Hawks wasn't just listening politely. In my last minute, as I got into the really exciting stuff leading to resolution, he began rhythmically nodding like a musician carried away by the beat.

"It's good," he said. I waited. I could see my own sense of anticipation mirrored in Lorna's expression. Hawks said, "There's lots of potential. What do you see happening? What do you want me to do? Do you think Wiseman would feel better about your script if I were on the project?"

My pulse accelerated. "Are you saying you want to be on the project?"

"No. I'm simply asking you a question. You said you'd had major problems with Warners about the story. Do you think my being on the project would clear those problems up?"

"I don't think so."

"Can you tell me about the problems?"

My instinct told me at this moment that Howard Hawks did not want to hear about a casting dispute. Further, I had a sense that he and Dutch Reagan would hit it off just fine. So I said, "In my story, it's never stated which side is which. Wiseman feels that it's obvious Felipe and Pablo are Loyalists. He tells me it's not just a matter of Warners, but that no studio would risk taking a stand on such a politically sensitive issue."

Hawks's intense stare had been unremitting. Now he finally took his eyes off mine, looking straight ahead, thus an inch or two above my hairline. Now he locked on my eyes again. "And you're not willing to compromise?"

"I'd rather not. I don't think I have to."

Hawks's smile, or hint of a smile, took me by surprise. Was it supportive, conspiratorial, or did he just think I was a fool? "How do you get around it?"

"I think it's possible to make the movie outside the studios," I said. "You did it with *Scarface*."

"That was eight years ago," Hawks said.

"Have things changed that much?"

"Pictures have gotten more expensive to make."

"How expensive?"

He shrugged. "This one, if you kept the location shooting to a minimum, if you had a very economical director, you might be able to bring it in for three hundred thousand."

"I wouldn't want to do that. I think locations are important here. I wouldn't want to do it on someone's back lot."

"Four hundred thousand, then. But that's a rock-bottom figure. If you want a big star—and that's probably a good idea for an indy production—then you've got to add a little more. Someone like Gary Cooper, figure on another fifty thousand."

"I can raise that money," I said.

Hawks grinned and spoke to Lorna. "Is he independently rich, or is he just crazy?"

"I'm not sure," Lorna said. "He has a way of getting things done."

"The only thing I'm worried about is distribution," I said.

"If you make a good picture," Hawks said, "you can always find distribution."

There was a moment of silence. I said, "Do you think you might be interested?"

He removed his wallet from within his jacket and brought out a business card. "Here's where you can find me. Send me a treatment, or whatever you have. If you can get this organized really fast, we might have something. I've got to wait for Cary to finish *Gunga Din* before I can start my next picture. I doubt we could fit this one in, but it's possible, and of course there's always next year. A lot depends on the script, of course. I don't know how fast you work. Hell, I don't even know if I *like* your work. But if you can get the money, yes, I could be interested."

This was extraordinary. I was close to levitating, standing here speechless next to Howard Hawks. He said, "One more thing—have you got a title?"

"Not really."

"How about *Rescue? Mission Rescue?* No—*Operation Rescue.*"

It was a characteristic Hawks title: concise, significant; it conveyed the central issue of the plot, the military nature of the action. Of course it had a slightly different connotation where I'd come from, but only I would know that. "I like it," I said. "But with a colon between the two words." For my own peace of mind.

"A colon? *Operation* colon *Rescue?*"

"Right."

"That might work."

From within the house there came a sustained, high-pitched cry. Conversation on the porch stopped and Sally Hudnut, who had been in a group on the fringe of the beach, ran past us into the house. I had attributed the shriek to a drunken female guest, but evidently its source was Charlie. "I should see what this is about," Lorna said. Hawks said, "Well, I could use another drink." And we all headed inside.

Charlie was being comforted by his mother, who leaned against the wall by the interior entrance to the garage. That door was open, as was the exterior garage door. The garage light was on, providing a sort of film-noir backlighting to this odd scene. Between whimpers, Charlie managed to say, "I didn't do anything to him! Why did he have to *take* it?" After a period of several minutes Charlie's disarranged story became somewhat clear. He had entered the garage to change rolls, realized he had no film for my camera, decided to try the flash with his Brownie. He'd heard someone fiddling with the exterior door, stationed himself by the door, and, when it opened, taken a flash picture of the intruder. The intruder had in turn swung wildly and struck Charlie in the midsection—whence the sustained cry—and then spent several seconds wandering about the garage, muttering, before seizing the Brownie and my flash, and fleeing as Sally and guests arrived.

Could Charlie describe his attacker? A man. Not a tall man. Anything about him that stood out? Charlie could think of nothing. Guests shouted queries as if this were a parlor game. Charlie could recall no more, and finally Sally led her son through the crowd and up the stairs.

—•—

By the time the policeman arrived the party had thinned down considerably and the crime's only witness was in bed. Sally, Charles, Lorna, and I joined him in a stroll to the guardhouse. Horace wanted it known he'd been told to admit anyone claiming invitation to the party. Horace preferred to work with a guest list, but Mr. Hudnut hadn't wanted it that way.

Charles assured Horace that no one was blaming him; we just wanted some information. Could Horace remember anything about the latecomer? Sure he could: fairly young man, maybe thirty, dark hair, kind of a thin face, drove a black sedan, probably a Chevy, maybe a '32 or a '33. Horace looked at me as if a distant bell were ringing. I decided to beat him to it. "Could this have been the same man I asked you about two weeks ago? The man who said he had an appointment to see me?"

Horace thought long and hard. Sally spoke to me, "Are you talking about the man I saw parked outside the house?"

"Yes," I said. "Can you describe him?"

"Oh, gosh, I only saw him for a few seconds. I remember the car. It *was* a Chevrolet, at least four or five years old."

Horace said, "I don't have that clear a picture in my head of that man. I can say it could have been the same car. I can say it might have been the same man, but I couldn't swear to it."

Sally said, "He *was* about thirty. Or in his thirties. Dark hair, yes. I wouldn't necessarily describe his face as thin."

The policeman said, "Is this someone of your acquaintance, Mr. Prince?"

"I'm not sure," I said.

"Let me get this straight. Do you live here? And what is your connection to the family?"

"I live here . . ."

Sally said, "Mr. Prince is Miss Fairchild's fiancé."

The policeman hadn't taken his eye off me. "You say you're not *sure* whether it's someone you know?"

"I meant that the man who was here several weeks ago, since he'd used my name, might be someone I know."

"And do you have someone in mind?"

It was a tempting notion, giving Jean-Baptiste's name and description to the police. But how would I describe our relationship? How might Jean-Baptiste retaliate? Could he in fact do me any harm? Perhaps it was better not to find out. "No," I said, "I'm afraid I don't."

— —

Awake at three in the morning, I had a moment of panic. I turned over in bed and opened the night table drawer, reached in, and . . . yes, thank God, my roll of cash was there, thick as ever. I would take it to the bank soon.

31

I had two calls of note Monday morning. The first came virtually as I walked through the doorway. Jean-Baptiste said, "Did you enjoy the party, Gabriel?"

"Did you?" I replied. "It must be a great deal of fun, stealing children's cameras."

"I don't think you should talk to me about stealing."

"Fine," I said. "But why don't we cut out this mysterious nonsense. If you keep sneaking around places you shouldn't be, you're going to get caught. That won't do you any good. And believe me, the machine's not anyplace you're going to find it."

"Very good," Jean-Baptiste said. "You say you want to talk to me about the machine. I think that's a good idea. I have some free time this afternoon. There is a place just outside the studio gate called the Ideal Café. You know it?"

He had pronounced it in the French manner, *idéal*. I did not correct him. "Yes. What time?"

"Is three o'clock all right?"

The second call was from Bernie Wiseman, making it official: Lorna had the part of the marshal's wife in *Four O'Clock*. I met her in the commissary at noon and gave her the news. It had not exactly come out of the blue, and we were in a public place, so her reaction was much more restrained than when I'd told her she had the inside track. Still, our embrace in the food line lasted nearly a minute. Quite by accident I caught the eye of Bill Wadsworth, who sat solo at the counter some twenty feet away. That connection lasted half a second, after which he returned to his lunch and his newspaper.

Dutch joined us fifteen minutes later, and I told him about Saturday night's meeting with Howard Hawks. Very much in character,

Dutch rattled off the names of ten or eleven of Hawks's films, then questioned whether he was the right man to direct our war movie. I reminded Dutch that two of the titles he'd just mentioned (*The Dawn Patrol* and *The Road to Glory*) were war movies, and added that Hawks seemed capable of directing just about anything. Whereupon Dutch revealed that he hadn't actually *seen* any of those except *Bringing Up Baby, Ceiling Zero,* and, when he was at college, *Scarface.*

As we talked, as it began to sink in that one of Hollywood's most prominent directors had shown interest in our project, Dutch became visibly excited, then as anxious as I'd seen him since the night (that never happened) on the beach. "Gabriel, obviously I'm going to have to test for Hawks, right?"

"I'm sure you will."

"Give me some dialogue then, would you? Some really juicy stuff, so I can get the character down."

—•—

The Ideal Café was just outside the west gate of the studio, a five-minute walk from the writers' building. It catered to maintenance and janitorial workers, to deliverymen and employees of the Richfield station down the block. On a bright summer afternoon it was hot and stuffy, and mercifully underpopulated in the midafternoon. Jean-Baptiste was the sole occupant of a long table in the back, accompanied by a huge mug of beer. "Do you find it's true," he said, "that American beer from this time is far superior to American beer from your time?"

"I rarely drink beer."

"To me, American beer from your time is like medicine. It's like something you only drink because you must. How do you explain it? All these American people drinking medicine."

"I don't have a great deal of time," I said.

"Oh, excuse me." Jean-Baptiste made a French facial expression of mild derision. "You have a profession. Tell me, Gabriel—do you write for the cinema the same way you bet at the racetrack? Do you make use of the future? Do you have a computer somewhere with all the great scripts?"

"Shall we talk about the machine?"

"If you lend me that computer for a few weeks, maybe I don't mind staying here so much. Maybe it's not so bad to be a rich man in 1938.

I was thinking, you know, I could go to Paris and be an important man. Then I was thinking, maybe it's not such a good idea to be in Paris now, because in a short time we get a visit from the Germans."

"I'm not going to lend you the computer. But I'm going to give you back the machine."

Jean-Baptiste's eyebrows elevated spontaneously. "You are going to give me the machine when?"

"The end of the year. There's a possibility I may need it again in December. After that, it's yours."

He had a long drink of 1938 beer. "It's mine now. Always. I don't want to wait until the end of the year."

"Look," I said, "if you're concerned about Hans, what difference does it make when you get the machine? Set the controls for November first, 1984. You know he's alive. Or for May, 1994."

He snorted. "It's funny, you're telling me what to do. I told you already, the only way I can get Hans now is if we go there together. We need two machines. But you want to stay here. It's okay with me, Gabriel. You give me your computer, then I don't mind to stay here. Or you give me the machine tomorrow, this week, next week, I go away and leave you alone."

"If you don't care about Hans," I said, "what difference does it make which machine you have? If the B-2 has enough fuel to take you back alone, why do you need the A-4?"

"Maybe I don't want to go home," Jean-Baptiste said. "Maybe I cannot repair the mechanical parts like your friend Udnut."

"So the B-2 has a bad control panel too?"

He did not respond, nor did he take his eyes off me. After quite a while he said, "Tell me, Gabriel. You want to have the machine in December. Is this for your friend Dutch? You think maybe he'll die again?"

"No," I said. "I'm not worried about Dutch."

"You introduce me to him, Dutch Ree-gan. It's not the same man as Ray-gan? I was studying history in school, Gabriel. I was an excellent student. President of the United States, 1980 to 1988, Ronald Ray-gan. Then I visit 1984 to find you, I notice there is no Ray-gan. Just some days ago, I think—ah! Maybe by mistake Gabriel has caused to die Ray-gan, now he comes back to make sure he stays alive this time?"

I got to my feet. "Believe what you like," I said.

— ▪ —

I did not sleep a great deal the next fortnight. I wasn't sleeping that well to begin with, having visions of Jean-Baptiste around every corner. But now it became my routine to leave our bed at one or two, to descend to the garage and spend five or ten minutes digesting a sizable piece of the *Operation: Rescue* screenplay from the laptop, then to move to the dining room table, where I would transcribe it by typewriter. I rejected the much simpler version of this process—copying directly from laptop to typewriter—for fear that Lorna might wander downstairs and discover me with my tiny alien machine. But of course she never once even awakened. Or if she did, she had no memory of it. She told me over breakfast Friday morning—eleven days later—that I was looking awfully tired, whereupon I produced the script, 110 neatly typed pages.

I dropped the original off at Hawks's office on my way to work. I handed one of two carbons to Dutch at lunchtime. I slept much of the weekend.

Monday morning, Hawks called. There ensued an extraordinary five minutes or so, in which someone I greatly admired, someone I never in my wildest dreams expected to meet, someone who died when I was twenty-five, told me at some length how he'd read my screenplay and been riveted from start to finish. There was something about it, he said, that made him think we were destined to meet. It was *directly* up his alley.

He was so impressed by the script, he said, that he'd taken the liberty of calling Gary Cooper and telling him about it. Cooper would be busy for several months shooting *The Real Glory*, but had nothing lined up after that. This would allow Hawks to go ahead with *Only Angels Have Wings* for Columbia, which would give me time to raise money. Then, in the late spring or early summer of 1939, we could get to work.

I searched for my voice. I thanked Hawks for his kind words, told him I thought I could raise the money quickly, that my preference would be to make this picture first.

"Cooper's important," Hawks replied. "If we're not going to have a studio behind us, we need every weapon we can get. Cooper's not only perfect for the part, he's automatic box office."

"I don't see Cooper at all," I said. "Felipe's a young man, twenty-six or twenty-seven. Cooper's ten years too old."

"Gabriel," Hawks said, "don't give me a hard time. What the hell difference does it make how old Cooper is? For one thing, people don't care. For another, all we'd have to do is push the opening sequence back ten years, so it takes place in 1910 instead of 1920. Then Felipe and Pablo are *both* in their later thirties when the war starts."

It appeared I had to play my trump card right now. "I had someone in mind when I wrote the part."

I could hear Hawks sigh on the other end of the line. "Who'd you have in mind, Gabriel?"

"A contract player at Warners. You've probably never heard of him, but I think he'd be perfect. He's just finished his first A picture, third-billed. His name is Ronald Reagan."

"You're right," Hawks said. "I've never heard of him."

"Why don't you give him a look, Howard? You've got nothing to lose. He'd be happy to audition for you. Camera or no camera, however you'd like to do it."

Five seconds went by. "All right, look—I've got to go out to Palm Springs for a while. What's today, the twelfth? I'll be back in town in a week, on the nineteenth. We'll give your boy a test. Is that all right with you?"

"It's fine. It's great."

Another brief pause. "Gabriel, I'll tell you what—we could save ourselves a lot of effort here. If I do like this kid, why should we cause ourselves unnecessary trouble? This Reagan's a contract actor, you're a contract writer, why the hell shouldn't we just make the picture for Warners? I've done enough business with Jack Warner and Hal Wallis so I could set it up in no time."

"I told you at the party, Bernie Wiseman wants me to make changes that would ruin the story. I'm not going to do that."

"What if we went straight to Wallis?" Hawks said. "I get along pretty well with Hal."

"I don't know about that," I said.

— ∙ —

I did not mention Gary Cooper to Dutch. I told him only that Hawks had loved the script, and that he'd suggested doing it for Warners. I had perceived Dutch as being about as self-confident, as optimistic, as someone of middling talent in his profession could be. I was surprised by his anxiety.

We sat in the commissary, Dutch with an overdone hamburger because spaghetti wasn't on the menu today, I with a hot turkey sandwich that was not remotely warm. I'd just told him Hawks would arrange a test for him within a week. Dutch said, "What if he doesn't like me?"

"He will. I think the two of you have very similar chemistry. I think he's going to take one look at you and realize he's made a discovery."

Dutch grinned nervously. "I don't know that much about his pictures. I mean, I remember watching *Scarface* at college. I thought it was the greatest thing I'd ever seen. It's funny what you know, what you remember. *Ceiling Zero*, too. I thought Cagney was terrific in that, but both of those, you know, I think of Paul Muni in *Scarface*, of Cagney in *Ceiling Zero*, and I know Hawks directed them, but there's nothing about him, no particular touch, that comes to mind when I think of those pictures."

"Don't worry about it, Dutch. Now you know. Just tell him you really enjoyed a couple of his movies."

"*Bringing Up Baby* I didn't really get. The scene at the end, where the dinosaur skeleton falls down and all that, had me in stitches. But some of that other stuff in the middle of the picture, I didn't think it was so funny."

"Just don't mention that to him."

"He's proud of that one, I guess."

"I think he is."

"It wasn't that big a hit, though."

"True, it wasn't."

Dutch finally took a tentative bite of his hamburger, chewed a bit, swallowed, and said, "Gabriel, what if he doesn't like me?"

"He will, Dutch. I'm counting on it. And if he doesn't, we'll look for another director."

— ◆ —

Dutch came over Friday night. The Charles Hudnuts weren't coming this weekend, the Wilfreds weren't due until Saturday morning, so we invited Dutch for dinner and an evening of reading his lines. Knowing his passion for spaghetti, I made it *puttanesca*, figuring I might broaden his horizons a little, as well as giving him something exotic enough to put him in the mood for the Spanish Civil War. Dutch insisted on providing the wine, and surprised me by bringing a cute bottle of Verdicchio. I had fully expected one of those straw-covered jugs of Chianti.

He was obviously taken aback by this spaghetti that had no bits of ground cattle in its sauce, but he appeared to develop a taste for it, enough to request a second plate and devour it entirely. He hardly touched his wine.

We went through the script chronologically. We did the scene in which Felipe returns home from the soccer game; I played Felipe's mother, Lorna was Teresa. She was awfully good as Teresa, and I suppose to a great extent I had written the part with her visage and her voice in my mind. If everything worked out, if we waited until the spring of 1939 and did the movie for Warners, Lorna would be done with *Four O'Clock* and Teresa would be a logical next move for her.

Lorna said, "Dutch, you're trying too hard. You're overacting."

Dutch seemed surprised. "Overacting? Look, I've just learned that my best friend has been taken prisoner. I'm shocked and I'm worried about him. So I've got to show some emotion."

"Yes. But your strength—what makes you good onscreen—is your naturalness. You don't look as if you're acting. Just imagine how *you* would react if some close friend of yours were in trouble . . ."

"I'd be mad as hell, just the way I'm reading the scene." He looked at me for support.

"She's right, Dutch. You should be upset, but in control. You're angry, but you're cool. You're a man whose actions speak louder than his words."

We ran through the scene again, and now it appeared that Dutch was straining to be cool, acting like someone trying not to act. Lorna poured him a glass of Verdicchio and ordered him to drink it. Dutch had a sip and grimaced. "See," he said, "this is what wine usually tastes like to me."

I had bought two bottles of Château Guiraud 1929 Sauterne at a wine shop in Beverly Hills. I retrieved one from the kitchen and poured Dutch a glass. Very tentatively he tasted it. "Now, that's wonderful," he said.

We moved on to the big scene between Felipe and Márquez, Pablo's childhood antagonist who has grown up to be the enemy commandant. I played Márquez with a Spanish accent.

"I like that," Dutch said. "Maybe I should try that too, to get more into character."

I didn't imagine Dutch could begin to manage a Spanish accent, or any other kind, but that was academic. "No," I said. "It's a convention. The villain's identified by his accent. The hero never has an accent."

"Unless he's Errol Flynn," Lorna interjected.

"But I'm supposed to be Spanish, too."

"No, Dutch," Lorna said. "Just do it straight."

I dropped the accent. We did the scene twice more. Dutch drank another glass of Sauterne. On our third run-through something clicked. Whether it was alcohol or a growing familiarity with the material I could not say, but Dutch became himself. All of a sudden he was a younger, fiercer version of his presidential, his video persona, breezy and fearless, at one with a character who anticipates the punishment ahead but faces his evil adversary without so much as a flinch.

I wondered if Akim Tamiroff was available to play Márquez.

Lorna said, "Let's do the car sequence. I can read Pablo."

It was the movie's most important succession of scenes. Having returned to the enemy camp and through a series of clever and violent maneuvers both rescued Pablo and taken Márquez hostage, Felipe now must drive Márquez's car (with Márquez, bound, in the front seat, and Pablo, clinging to life, supported by Teresa in the backseat) out of the camp—through much enemy territory with several vehicles in pursuit, through a succession of towns where he must avoid innocent pedestrians, horse carts, flocks of sheep—until he finally reaches his own village, where the caravan comes to a halt and Felipe's townsmen help him annihilate the pursuers.

Properly executed, this sequence would carry the movie to triumph. It would also, I believed, be unprecedented in world cinema for its sheer, uninterrupted intensity. Much of that would be generated by the action, the extended, high-speed pursuit with plenty of near-misses. But the action, the second-unit stuff, would be intercut with scenes inside the car. For the sequence to work to perfection, the actor playing Felipe had to be good. He had to be tough and curt with Márquez, who keeps trying to talk him into pulling over and surrendering, gentle and encouraging with Pablo, who has been beaten within inches of his life, all the while appearing to drive like a humanistic maniac.

The first run-through, Dutch tended to exaggerate the different voices, yelling at me, whispering to Lorna. The second time he was better, far more realistic. The third, after his fifth glass of the Château Guiraud, he had it cold. Lorna clapped her hands and gave him a hug. Getting to his feet, Dutch nearly fell down. It was two o'clock in the morning, and we prevailed upon Dutch, who was drunk for the first time in his life (not counting the night he drowned), to sleep in my old bedroom.

—　—

Lorna woke him at seven, and Dutch dragged himself down to breakfast. Wilfred and family were due at nine, Lorna and I were off to Santa Barbara until Sunday night, so we wanted the house spotless and unoccupied within a couple of hours.

Not that any of us was exactly bright-eyed, but Dutch was a picture at the kitchen table—rumpled and unshaven, hung over in a mild, giddy sort of way, obviously still quite pleased with himself after last night's mastering of the material, but suffused with guilt because he had forgotten his promise to call Jane Wyman at some reasonable hour. It was too early to call her now, as like most people who have to start work at ungodly hours Monday through Friday, she valued her Saturday morning sleep.

Dutch struggled with his scrambled eggs. These were Lorna's alimentary contribution to our union, and I found them quite tasty in a primitive way. Dutch looked up through his thick glasses and said, "I wonder if there's romance in our future."

"Why wouldn't there be?" Lorna asked. "She seems like a wonderful girl, and you'd make a great couple."

"Well, for one thing, she's married."

I said, "But she's been separated from her husband for months, right? Doesn't he live in Louisiana?"

Dutch looked at me sideways. "Did I tell you that?"

"You must have."

Dutch returned his attention to Lorna. "I know I keep coming back to this, but she thinks I'm just asking for it by staying involved in this project. She's convinced it's the worst thing I could be doing."

Lorna said, "Well, most of the time I think it's the worst thing Gabriel could be doing. I don't think someone in his position has enough power to rock the boat. But he seems to lead a charmed life, so maybe it's going to work out fine for both of you. It certainly wouldn't hurt if Howard Hawks actually wants to direct."

Dutch's reply was not immediate. "It wouldn't hurt the picture. I'm not so sure it would be in my best interest."

I spoke despite a mouthful of eggs. "You and Hawks are made for each other."

Dutch said, "When I told Jane about Hawks, and, you know, I was all excited because Gabriel had just told me, she acted like it was some kind of nail in the coffin. She said, 'Ronnie, what in God's name is Howard Hawks gonna want with you?' And I guess that's the question I keep asking myself."

"It's a perfectly good question," Lorna said.

I spoke to Lorna. "He was *terrific* last night. Once he got the hang of it, once he got the rhythm, no one in Hollywood could have read those scenes better than Dutch did. Besides, I think I've got a little bit of influence here. Hawks has to know, if I ventured away from Warners to talk to him, I'll be willing to go somewhere else again."

Lorna met my gaze and nodded halfheartedly, from which I inferred that while she didn't altogether agree with what I'd just said, neither did she wish to reply. Dutch said, after a moment, "Jane says that Hawks never casts unknown actors in big parts. Actresses, yes; actors, no. We ran through all his pictures, and it's true. Muni, Cagney, Robinson, Cooper, Barrymore, Grant . . . it's like a Who's Who."

I had anticipated this. "There are two lead roles in this movie. If Hawks needs a big name, we'll get one to play Pablo."

Lorna said, "But Felipe's a much bigger part."

"The big name can go above the title, Dutch's below it. That would hardly set a precedent."

"Were you thinking of someone in particular?"

I cannot honestly say that I was. Montgomery Clift came to mind, but he was still in high school.

— • —

As was my custom, I got to my office at a few minutes before nine Monday morning. There was a message for me. In my six months at Warners all previous early-morning messages, perhaps five of them, had been from Bernie Wiseman. This one directed me to call Howard Hawks, immediately.

Immediately I did so, and Hawks himself answered his telephone. *Operation: Rescue*, he said, was a picture to be given all the time and effort it deserved, that we might get everything just right. He was now of two minds about the proper actor for Felipe. He still very much liked the notion of Cooper in the lead, yet he saw that the part should justly be played by someone younger. So, as we had agreed, he would give my boy Reagan a look. We would arrange for a test in the very near future, when it was convenient for everyone.

My end of the conversation consisted largely of grunts and verbal nods, with the occasional "thanks" and "that's very kind of you" thrown in. I had begun to suggest that we set the date and time of the test right now when Hawks said, "Oh, one more thing I should tell you. Were you about to say something?"

I deferred. He said, in a matter-of-fact voice, "I spoke to Wallis. Wanted to put a bee in his bonnet right away. He knew who you were, from the western, from *Four O'Clock*, but he didn't know anything about this script. Just as well. I guess Bernie Wiseman doesn't tell him about everything that crosses his desk. So I didn't even mention Wiseman's name. I told him you'd shown the script to me, independent of the studio, and that if everything worked out we'd prefer doing the picture for Warners, but that was subject to negotiation. I've done business with Wallis before, know how to handle him. So I just figured I'd warn you. Wallis'll probably be calling you, asking for a copy of the script, what have you."

I was feeling something distantly related to panic, which is to say that while I was quite calm, I had the curious sense that something had just been taken from me. I wondered whether it had been Hawks's intention to call Wallis all along, no matter what I'd said.

Hawks asked me whether all of this was "okay in my book," and I responded that I supposed it was. We set a tentative time for Dutch's test: Saturday morning, ten o'clock, subject, of course, to Dutch's approval. I was extremely tempted to ask Hawks how he'd have reacted if I'd said all of this was *not* okay in my book, but I couldn't bring myself to do it. I reasoned that while I might be losing some control, and while I might be alienating Bernie Wiseman, Dutch's prospects for playing Felipe could not look better, and that was what mattered. We said our good-byes, and I set the receiver down.

I was on an auspicious train of thought when—not three seconds later—the telephone rang, causing me to jump an inch out of my chair. Had Hawks forgotten to tell me something?

Quite the contrary. Bernie Wiseman wanted to ask me something.

"Gabriel? Listen, did I do something to offend you along the way, or are you just an ungrateful son of a bitch?"

While my answer to neither question would have been affirmative, it seemed difficult to avoid the implied accusation of the latter. Buying time, I said, "What exactly are you talking about, Bernie?"

"I just had a call from Hal Wallis, is what. I thought we had a nice arrangement, you and I. What is this with Howard fucking Hawks?"

"Complete accident. He went to school with Lorna's uncle, who had a birthday party, where I met Hawks. We were talking about *Four O'Clock*, which he'd read, and Lorna mentioned that I was working on something he might like—"

"That doesn't mean you have to hand it over to him, does it?"

"Bernie, two things. One, I didn't hand it to him. We simply talked about it, and he got very enthusiastic. Two, as much as I appreciate everything you've done for me, you and I seemed to be at a sort of impasse over this thing, so I don't really think I have an ethical problem showing it to Hawks, or anyone."

"Gabriel, two things. One, you handed Howard Hawks a finished script that I didn't fucking know existed. Two, the only point of contention between you and me was some half-assed contract actor you for some reason think should star in this picture. And if you think Hawks is gonna go for Ronald fucking Reagan, you are an insane son of a bitch."

This was not an argument I was winning. "Bernie, I have to admit I wrote the script because Hawks was interested—"

"Wait a minute—when was this birthday party, two months ago?"

"No. Just a couple of weeks."

"What are you, a miracle worker? You can write a script that Hawks goes nuts for in a couple of *weeks*?"

"Yes. But look, the point I'm trying to get to is that ultimately I don't see why all this should affect you. You're still the producer, right? What difference does it make who directs it?"

"Are you a complete schmuck, Gabriel? Did Hawks call *me* and rave about this script? No, he called Wallis. Wallis is my boss, and Wallis calls the shots. Wallis produces the picture."

"What if I insist on you?"

Wiseman made a noise between a laugh and a sigh. "Jesus, Gabriel, sometimes I think you're from some different planet."

32

I treated Dutch to lunch in the first-class commissary, where a recognizable face could be seen at virtually every table. He was dressed for his role in *Murder Plane*, a quickie programmer he'd just begun shooting. The cast of *Murder Plane* (which would very shortly be retitled *Secret Service of the Air*) contained two names of note: Eddie Foy, Jr., who would later play his own vaudevillian father in *The Seven Little Foys* and whose brother, Bryan Foy, ran Warners' B unit; and Ila Rhodes, who was nominally Dutch's girlfriend.

In his leather jacket and long, white scarf, with his hair virtually sculpted into a pompadour, Dutch looked as if he were ready to deliver the mail to some swank resort in Paraguay. I sat down across from him and said, "How's Saturday morning, ten o'clock?"

"For what?"

"Your test for Hawks."

Dutch beamed. "Well, I'd say it's swell. I don't have anything else in the works, but if I did I'd sure cancel it."

"Good. It's scheduled for somewhere on the lot. I'm not sure exactly where." Dutch had some sort of immense sausage on his plate, swathed in what might be mustard. I had selected the macaroni and cheese, which could best be described as hot and tasteless. I said, "How's everything going? How's Jane?"

Dutch's lips formed a forlorn smile. "She wasn't happy when I called her Saturday morning. I could have been more apologetic, I suppose, but I was so damn happy about what we did Friday night. Driving back to my place, it was as if all of a sudden I could see things so clearly. You know, what was I so *worried* about? Everything's going my way! After our picture, it's no more of this nonsense, no more serials, no more lousy B pictures."

"That's the spirit, Dutch. You can't lose with an attitude like that."

"I'll tell you, Gabriel, of all the girls I've met here, Jane is pretty special in a lot of ways. I get along with her so damn well. There are other girls who, you know . . ." He smiled and shrugged. "But Jane, I think we could go places. And I'm pretty sure she feels the same about me. There's just this one bone of contention, and I guess the only way around it is to prove her wrong."

Dutch's gaze rose well above my eyes; his expression underwent an odd metamorphosis. I turned my head and saw Bill Wadsworth homing in on our table. Wadsworth placed a hand on my left shoulder. "Don't get up," he said. "How are you doing, Dutch?"

"Just swell, Bill. How about you?"

"Fine," Wadsworth said. "Never been better." In fact, Wadsworth looked to have gained fifteen or twenty pounds over the last several months. His face was fleshier and more florid than usual; from the extent of his gut it appeared he would soon need a new wardrobe as well. "Gabriel, I wonder if we could have a little meeting this afternoon, say around three?"

"Of course, Bill. I'm just down the hall. All you have to do is knock on my door."

"Wanted to make sure you'd be in." Wadsworth gave Dutch a quick nod. "Nice seeing you. Enjoy your lunch." And with a brisk wave he was off.

— • —

He knocked promptly at three. I still hadn't done much in the way of furnishing my cubicle, so all I could offer him was a stiff-backed wooden chair that had probably been banging around this building twenty years before Warners took it over from First National. There was a glow about Wadsworth, not all of which could be attributed to the whiskey whose bouquet was conspicuous from across my desk. I said, "I don't imagine we're about to discuss script ideas."

"Of course not," he said. "I assume you've heard from various sources that I've been doing a little checking on you?"

"I have heard that."

"You seem to have established enough of a reputation here so that what I've discovered about you so far hasn't been sufficient to change people's minds about you."

"As well it shouldn't have, Bill. If I were you, I wouldn't put too much stock in what you've discovered so far."

Wadsworth's high-pitched chuckle served as very odd counterpoint to his messianic gleam. "You're not implying that you actually *did* go to Princeton, are you?"

I had no leg to stand on here, of course. I was in no position either to fudge or to explain how I actually had attended Wadsworth's beloved alma mater thirty-some years in the future, so I said, "That's really beside the point, isn't it, Bill?"

He chuckled again. "I hardly think so. Do you know that no one at all named Prince attended Princeton between 1922 and 1930? Do you know there was a Hector Gabriel Prince in the class of oh-five?" That would in fact have been my great-uncle Hector, but I could not say so. Wadsworth gave me the killer look of a prosecutor who's got his criminal dead to rights. "Let's see, Gabriel, if that were you, you'd be about fifty-five years old now."

The notion flitted through my mind that if I were forty-two passing for thirty-three, why might I not shoot for fifty-five? I said, "Bill, what's the point?"

"I had a long talk with the man you said was your thesis adviser, Professor Sidney. I asked him first if he'd ever had a student named Gabriel Prince. No. But what if you'd attended college under a different name? Had any of his students ever written a thesis on James's *Turn of the Screw*? No. I gave him your physical description. He couldn't think of anyone who might have been you. I called Lawrenceville, and of course they'd never heard of you, didn't have any English instructors who'd left the school in the last three years."

"Please, Bill . . ."

"You're a myth! Everything about you is false, bogus. When I heard that business about the friend with the truck, how all your manuscripts were missing along with your clothes . . . even then, I thought, what nonsense! I didn't know what you had in mind, but I knew you were spinning a tale."

"Fine," I said. "Let's say everything about my past is in question—"

"Not *in question*," he interrupted, "but a total, blatant, outrageous lie! Say it, for God's sake! Admit it!"

As yet, I was not in the least intimidated. If anything, I felt a progressing sense of pity for Wadsworth, whose intention clearly was to humiliate me out of Lorna's life and away from Warner Brothers, neither of which was about to happen. I repeated, "Let's say everything about my past is in question. You can believe what you want to believe. You can tell people whatever you like. You have to understand that it's not going to hurt me, Bill. If anything, it's going to hurt you. People are going to think you're petty and vindictive, Lorna especially. So why don't you just leave me alone, do your job, and I'll do mine."

"No." Wadsworth was glaring at me with a passion. I had no more defused him than he had intimidated me. "I had a chat with Charles Hudnut the other day. Didn't tell him anything about my Princeton inquiries. Just led him a little, and it seems he'd discovered you never taught at Lawrenceville. You told him you'd never actually met Jasper or Edgar. You told him that boat—or whatever it is—was given to you by someone in Europe to deliver here—"

I could imagine Charles, who seemed utterly without guile, without malice, utterly lacking the need most humans feel to gossip, responding to Wadsworth's questions and engaging in lively conversation out of a sense of scientific duty, or logical compulsion. But this was getting a little too close for comfort. How marvelously absurd it would be if a fat, pompous, alcoholic reactionary stumbled onto my machine and screwed everything up. "As it was," I interrupted. "By someone very close to the Hudnut family—"

"Whose name you're not at liberty to reveal," Wadsworth interrupted in turn.

"Unfortunately, I am sworn to secrecy. I'm sure honor is a concept you respect, Bill."

He gave me a sly, sideways look, as if he were on to my game and both of us knew it. "In *Europe*," he said. "Charles told me you assured him it wasn't a Nazi boat. I told him that wouldn't have been my suspicion."

"Bill, for God's sake, you're truly barking up the wrong tree now. That boat's been sitting in the garage ever since I got here, waiting for Edgar's family to come west. If it's some sort of diabolical device, do you suppose it would have been gathering dust for six and a half months?"

"Perhaps"—Wadsworth's look was intact—"it's waiting until you have enough money to use it."

"I'm sorry?"

"You've been accumulating money. I don't know how much you won at Santa Anita, when you impressed the hell out of Lorna. I don't know how often you've been to the track since then, but I have it on good authority that you won at least fifteen thousand dollars at Del Mar on August twelve."

Why would either Dutch or Lorna have told Wadsworth about Del Mar? I did not have to manufacture my indignation. "You've been having me *followed?*"

Wadsworth seemed to glow, to expand. "Perhaps I have."

"My God, that's pathetic."

"I don't think so. I'd say *ingenious*, perhaps. Or *sensible*. Or maybe *patriotic.*"

"Bill—we have a situation where a woman has chosen one man over another. That man has gone to the racetrack and had one extremely successful day. What does it say about the scorned man that he hires some sort of lowlife private detective?"

Wadsworth shook his head in negation and anger as he glared at me. "Listen, Prince, don't you try to belittle me. We both know there's something very fishy going on, and let me tell you I've been tempted more than once to call the police, or the FBI—"

"And tell them what, Bill? That you have suspicions about a

coworker who's done well at the track? You think he's lying about where he went to college?"

He leaned forward as if propelled, planted his elbows downward on my desk, stared at me with an almost palpable malevolence. "What about your little foreign friend? First at the racetrack, then at some sleazy joint down the street from here. According to my witness, you handed him quite a bit of money at Del Mar."

How oblivious had I been at Del Mar, piling up my winnings while Jean-Baptiste spied on me and Wadsworth's detective spied on Jean-Baptiste spying on me? And probably the first sighting of an old Chevrolet in Malibu—two months ago by now—hadn't involved Jean-Baptiste at all. I said, "Bill, I believe we could make a case against your man for trespassing. How's it going to look when he tells the judge he was working for you?"

Wadsworth pounded my desk. "*That's* a laugh. You're involved in God knows what kind of conspiracy, subversion, and you're going to call the cops on me?"

"Indeed I am."

"Tell me this," he said. "If that boat's waiting innocently for Edgar Hudnut, how come you've stashed it in Bernie Wiseman's garage? How's Bernie going to feel when he's got federal agents all over his property?"

Whenever Wadsworth mentioned the boat I suffered a nasty little shiver. But really, what chance was there that he could interest even a county sheriff in any of his nonsense? Still, the thought of some uniformed bumpkin rummaging around my boss's garage, poking his nightstick at the machine, perhaps carting it away for further inspection, made me exceedingly nervous. I said, "Bill, what can I do to mollify you? What can I do to assure you I'm not trying to overthrow the government?"

"Nothing. But I'm going to make you a very fair offer. I want you out of here. Out of Warners, out of Lorna's life. Just get the hell out, and I'll give you the benefit of the doubt. Whatever you're up to, just take it elsewhere."

"No," I said. "I'm sad it's come to this. I'm sad you've been reduced to such a miserable, vindictive boozehound."

He seemed surprised, if not exactly chastened. He slid his elbows back toward his chest, then got to his feet. He said, "I'm not going to let you get away with this," turned, and walked out the door. I was prepared for him to slam it, but he merely left it ajar.

33

It was something of a martial week. There was a huge American Legion convention in Los Angeles, and Legionnaires were everywhere. Tuesday morning, September 14, tens of thousands of them paraded through the city in ninety-three-degree heat. Tour buses took hundreds of them at a time to the studios, Warner Brothers included. Leaving work Monday evening I pulled the Buick, its top up, to the curb just outside the lot. Checking my papers to make sure I'd brought my copy of *Operation: Rescue,* I heard a voice say, "Excuse me?" and I looked up to see a group of paunchy, middle-aged Middle Americans, three men in Legion caps and string ties, three women in flowery frocks, all of them suggestive of overfed Grant Wood models. Their spokesperson, a fleshy woman of about fifty-five, said, "Are you anyone we should know?"

I could have told her yes, I am the man who wrote the movie that will make Ronald Reagan famous, make him a bigger star than he was supposed to be, will completely redirect his life, so he will not become a genial television host (and here of course I would necessarily have gone into a five-minute tangent about the imminent arrival and subsequent supremacy of television) in the fifties, will not marry Nancy Davis and espouse her family's rather extreme right-wing views, will not become governor of California nor, eventually, the man your children and grandchildren will elect president of the United States.

But I did not say any of that. I said, "Just a writer." The big woman asked if I knew James Cagney and Bette Davis. I replied that while I could claim neither as a good friend, I had met both—and yes, both were within those walls and would eventually emerge and drive by. She thanked me; they all did, and I drove off.

If there were memories of war in Los Angeles, there were portents

314

of it elsewhere, acts of it yet elsewhere. Neville Chamberlain had just
yo-yoed between Britain and Germany, journeying from London to
Berchtesgaden (where after describing Adolf Hitler as "very friendly"
he had insisted on the right of self-determination for the western
fringe of Czechoslovakia known as the Sudetenland), then returned
briefly to London and flown to Munich, where he'd caved in completely and agreed not to make so much as a peep if Germany were to
make the Sudetenland its own. Everyone—from Chamberlain's Tory
colleagues Anthony Eden and Winston Churchill to American political commentators to the Legionnaire on the street—was appalled.

In Spain the war was at a momentary stalemate. Franco's insurgents,
who now occupied most of the country, were catching their breath,
mobilizing for the last big push. The Republicans were holding their
breath, fortifying Barcelona as well as they could. On Friday, hours before
Dutch and Lorna and I did our reading in Malibu, 15 planes dropped
bombs on Barcelona, killing 31 people and wounding 112. Many of the
wounded were not expected to live. Most of the casualties had occurred
at a market where women stood in line to receive handouts of food. On
Monday, Fascist planes dropped bombs on the seaside resort town of Ali-
cante. Ten buildings were destroyed; the city was in disarray.

In Saigon, the Emperor Bo Dai responded to rumors of war in
Europe by assuring the French government of Annam's "profound
attachment and indefatigable devotion to the great protector nation."

In St. Louis, the Yankees lost a doubleheader to the Browns but
clinched their third consecutive pennant when the Red Sox were
rained out in Chicago. Dutch was in attendance when the Angels
swept a doubleheader from the Oakland Acorns to win the Pacific
Coast League pennant. His beloved Cubs, meanwhile, were three and
a half games behind the Pirates with thirteen to play. Dutch, true to
his nature, was optimistic.

On Wednesday, a monstrous hurricane cut a swath up the East
Coast, killing 450 people and leaving many thousands homeless.
Lorna got through to her parents early Thursday morning: the basement had been flooded; all of her schoolbooks and memorabilia,
stored there, were ruined, along with various other nonessentials; but
everyone was fine, and awaiting the restoration of electricity.

On adjacent pages of Friday's *Times* I discovered that Thomas
Wolfe, described as an "eastern writer" had died, aged thirty-seven, of

an "acute cerebral infection," and that "Smokers Find Camel's Cost-lier Tobaccos ARE SOOTHING TO THE NERVES."

What were my concerns this week? There was a certain dichotomy to my life. The woman I loved with a passion I'd never imagined myself capable of was soon to play a major role in a movie I'd written. A legendary director was soon to make another movie I'd written, and there was a very good chance he'd select as his star my friend Dutch Reagan. A blubbery, aristocratic drunk was about to turn me in to federal authorities on unspecified charges. An unpleasant and unstable Frenchman from the twenty-second century had something malignant in store for me, but I knew not what.

—▪ ▪—

Wednesday morning there was a note on my desk: MR. WISEMAN WANTS TO SEE YOU AT 10 O'CLOCK. I proceeded with trepidation.

To my surprise, he greeted me warmly, asked me to have a seat, and we assumed our customary positions at either side of the immense desk. Wiseman almost immediately lit a Chesterfield, sucked in the smoke, exhaled it, and fixed me with one of his intense gazes. "Gabriel," he said, "this is bad for me." He nodded at his cigarette. "I know it. I can tell. They advertise these things like they were medicine from heaven. But you can tell, you know. You cough, you're short of breath. Did you ever smoke?"

"When I was young. When I was a teenager, in college. Never really got hooked, I think."

"See, that's the thing. It's almost like you knew what was good for you. All your friends smoked, you smoked. Am I right?"

"Something like that."

"But then you said, hey, I don't wanna do this anymore. Maybe whatever pleasure I get from these things doesn't match up to the lousy way I feel when I get up in the morning. But you quit. And me, when I was fourteen and I smoked my first one in Bobby Cohen's basement and I got sick as a dog, I said right then, hey, what's the point to this? This shit makes you sick. But unlike you I didn't have the sense to trust my better judgment, to follow what my body was telling me. So here I am past forty, smoking two, three packs of these things every day." He took a huge drag as if to emphasize his lesson. "You have any idea what I'm telling you?"

It was a parable, I suspected, but one too abstruse for me, so I said, "Nicotine is addictive."

"Is it? You see, you're such a smart man. So knowledgeable, so talented. And yet everything should be telling you something now, but you're like me. You can't see the handwriting on the wall. Smart as you are, you can't see the obvious."

"You're going to have to explain it to me, Bernie."

He rolled slightly forward on his chair, so his midsection was directly against the desk. "Did I treat you well, Gabriel?"

"Extremely well, I would say. And I feel very guilty that things have worked out the way—"

He raised his right hand abruptly, telling me to shut up, which I did. "I'm not asking for apologies. Believe it or not, this is for your benefit, not mine. I don't think you have any idea *how* well I treated you. A kid from nowhere, no experience in the picture business, his first script, boom, it's an A picture for Errol Flynn. He wants his girlfriend to have the female lead, boom, she's got it." Only now did the hand descend, and the chair roll infinitesimally backward. "You're thinking, sure, but it was a good script, deserved to be an A picture. You're thinking, sure, but Lorna's a fine actress, she deserved that role." The chair rolled forward; Wiseman stubbed out his cigarette and leaned toward me across the desk, his eyes having become huge. "And you know what? You're right! Of course you're right! But sometimes, Gabriel, it takes quality to recognize quality. I don't like blowing my own horn, but there are producers on this lot that wouldn't have recognized the talent in *Four O'Clock*, would've had you cut it down to seventy minutes, put in some more action, put some second-unit hack on it. Do you believe me?"

"Of course I believe you. I appreciate that."

He sat up. "We had a deal, you and I, on the Spanish War picture, except for one thing, am I right? Your pal Reagan?"

"It wasn't all that simple. I hadn't even written the script—"

"You told me you would make pretty much any changes I wanted if I'd cast Ronald Reagan in the lead. Did I dream that?"

"No. It's true."

Now he edged ever more forward, becoming nearly serpentine against the fine, lustrous hardwood. "So you're a smart guy, you took the script to a big-shot director, he loves it. Did he tell you he was going to show it to Wallis?"

Hawks had certainly dropped Wallis's name, certainly hadn't said anything about showing him the script. "I'll just say that it took me by surprise."

"You think he's going to tell you anything else he decides to do? You think Hal fucking Wallis is going to pay any attention to what you want or what you think?"

"I guess I'll be finding out."

Wiseman sat up ever so slowly, rolled away from the desk. "Tell me what you want from this business, Gabriel. You want to make money? You want to be a great artist? What?"

What could I say? "There are certain things I'd like to achieve, Bernie. I don't know whether I can articulate them to your satisfaction."

"To my *satisfaction?* Is that a polite way of saying we're not on the same wavelength? We don't have the same education?"

"No. Not at all. Please don't think that. It's just difficult for me to explain my goals. I need to make an impact in a certain way. It's very important to me."

Now he leaned back in his chair, performing a great shrug of resignation. "I don't know what the hell you're talking about. You've got a winning combination, Gabriel. You know how to write. You've got a gift, an uncanny gift for somebody so new to the business, for what people want to watch. But if you can't even see the wall in front of your face, you sure as hell can't read the handwriting."

I felt a surge of emotion, of appreciation for a nice man who liked me, had helped me, and whom I had unwittingly betrayed. I said, "Bernie, I wish I could communicate to you how much I appreciate—"

He raised his hand to stop me. "Don't communicate. *Think.* And one more thing, Gabriel. That boat you've got in my garage? It has to go."

"Oh, Jesus," I said. "Don't tell me Bill Wadsworth—"

"Wadsworth? What does Wadsworth give a shit about your boat? Every time Estelle backs her car in the garage she's afraid she's gonna hit the damn thing. So why doesn't she go in front first? Because she has to come out front first."

"There isn't any other place you could put it?"

"Gabriel, look—rent some storage space. You can afford it."

— • —

The Los Angeles Times ran a daily column in its entertainment section, generally across the page from Hedda Hopper, that comprised an odd and occasionally fascinating mixture of picture business news and gossip. This was where, Thursday morning, we read the details of Lorna's incipient breakthrough. It was the column's lead item, and the subhead was:

CURTIZ, FLYNN WILL TEAM UP ON DIFFERENT WESTERN

The hot news from Warners has producer Bernard Wiseman setting aside the Technicolor western "Dodge City" in favor of another oat-burner, "Four O'Clock." Director Michael Curtiz and star Errol Flynn have both been pulled from "Dodge," which was to co-star beauties Olivia de Havilland and Ann Sheridan, to work on the different western. "Four O'Clock" will team Flynn with Warners ingenue Lorna Fairchild, so far seen only in programmers. "This is truly a different western," says producer Wiseman, "unlike anything the public has seen before." Production on "Four O'Clock" is scheduled to begin October 9. Wiseman adds that Curtiz, Flynn and company will shoot "Dodge" after "Four O'Clock" is completed.

"My God," Lorna said, at least a touch of distaste mixed with her wonderment, "that's *me* they're talking about. Does this mean I have to get a scrapbook?" It was the first time her name had appeared, to the best of her knowledge, in one of the daily newspapers.

That evening when I took out the garbage, I turned again to the second section of the *Times* and reread the item. I tore the column out of the paper, found scissors in the kitchen, pared off the rough edges, wondered what I was doing. It was not my custom to save such things, but there was something exciting about this one. It didn't simply observe Lorna's emergence, it linked her and me, it legitimized my presence in this place. I folded it neatly and tucked it into my wallet, with a thought to having it framed, but of course I forgot all about it.

— —

I asked Dutch if he wanted to join us Friday night for another session with the script. No, he said, he felt he was as ready as he'd ever be, that his best preparation would probably be a good night's sleep. Indeed, when we met him just inside the main gate at nine-thirty, he was clear-eyed and full of energy. The morning was sunny and windless, another hot day in the making. In her manner, Lorna wore white shorts, a light cotton blouse, and sandals; she looked magnificent. In his manner, Dutch wore white ducks, a light blazer, a blue-and-white striped tie. With his thick-lensed glasses he looked more like a doctoral candidate than someone about to test for the role of a Spanish soccer star/schoolteacher.

He gave Lorna a kiss on the cheek and shook my hand warmly. "I know that script better than anything I've ever learned in my life," Dutch said. "I'm convinced I can play that part better than any other actor in the world."

"And you're absolutely right," I said. "You can."

Dutch beamed. Lorna fingered his blazer and said, "Especially if Hawks sees Felipe as a fashion plate."

Dutch gave a little start. "Oh, God, did I screw it up? I couldn't imagine how I could dress for the part, and I knew that Hawks always looks great . . ."

"You're fine, Dutch," I said. "Tell him he's fine, Lorna, please."

"You look terrific," Lorna told Dutch. "Don't worry about it. I'd take the tie off, though." Dutch looked at me and I nodded. He undid his tie, folded it carefully, put it in the left side pocket of his blazer.

It was a five-minute walk across the lot to the test site, the soundstage where Dutch had shot *Girls on Probation*, the smallest on the lot, but still eerily cavernous with only the three of us around. We sat at the edge of the stage, our small talk becoming increasingly banal as the minutes slogged by. The Cubs and Pirates had both won doubleheaders yesterday, leaving the Cubs three and a half games out, now with only eleven to play. Although the mathematics were against them, Dutch still liked the Cubs' chances. "They've got the big three-game series with Pittsburgh coming up next week in Chicago. They're going to sweep that series, Gabriel, mark my words." I could not disagree.

Premier Negrín of Spain had announced that all remaining foreign volunteers—including the several hundred remnants of the Abraham Lincoln Brigade—would be repatriated in the next few months. Given the Republic's dire circumstances, Dutch saw this as an admission of defeat. I could not disagree.

I asked Dutch if he'd seen the story in the paper about a dog in Illinois who over a period of several weeks had brought his master fifty-two individual dollar bills. He had, he said; he'd never heard of the town, so it wasn't near his old stomping grounds, but he'd wondered why the master didn't simply follow the dog on its rounds one day, and thereby discover the whole stash.

"Because there *isn't* a stash," Lorna suggested. "If there were one, why wouldn't the dog bring a whole pile of bills, or at least two or three once in a while? The dog's only bringing one at a time because someone's giving him one at a time."

"I don't see that at all," Dutch replied. "Dogs do things by habit. The dog happens to bring its owner a dollar bill, the owner's pleased, so the dog brings another, then another, and so on."

"Dutch," Lorna said, "have you ever *had* a dog?"

"What difference does that make?"

"You don't seem to have a very clear idea of the way dogs function. Of course they do things by habit, but if a dog brings its master a dollar bill—or anything—and the master's pleased, then if there *is* a stash somewhere, the dog's going to go back and bring its master every last bit of that stash all at once."

Dutch gave this some thought. "What if there's something that prevents the dog from getting more than one bill at a time?"

"Like what?"

"Say there's a pile of bills under a porch, for instance, and it's all the dog can do to push its snout under there and get its teeth on one bill. It does that, it figures, well, here it is, this thing my master appreciates so much, I'm off to bring it to him."

"That's ridiculous," Lorna said.

"Why is it ridiculous?" Dutch asked in his perfectly affable tone. "It makes perfect sense." He answered his own question with such enthusiastic sincerity that when Lorna looked to me for support I was speechless, inasmuch as the young actor had just done a primitive but vivid impression of the old statesman. Lorna said, "Dutch, do you actually think the dog could repeat this process fifty-two times without ever *once* pulling out more than one bill? It's absolutely absurd."

Dutch shook his head vigorously and appeared ready for rebuttal when the huge front door of the soundstage creaked and Howard Hawks made his entrance, trailed by a detail of technicians.

Hawks greeted us with an efficient sort of cordiality; I introduced him to Dutch, who was about to speak his well-rehearsed paean when Hawks chose to introduce the crew to us: cameraman so-and-so, light man such-and-such, someone else who did something else. The three men shook hands all around, then went off to tend to their equipment, whereupon Dutch seized the moment. "Mr. Hawks, I just wanted to say how much I enjoy your work, and what an honor it is to have a chance to work for you."

"Thanks," Hawks said about as curtly as the word can be spoken. "What do you like about my work?"

Dutch had clearly not expected the question. I certainly hadn't, and immediately began formulating rescue strategy. Dutch neither blushed nor flinched, however; after a moment's hesitation he said, "I like the way you make pictures."

Hawks's long face hinted at a smile. Was it derisive or appreciative? He said, "What's your favorite?"

Dutch replied immediately, "Oh, *Scarface*, no question about that. Must've seen it three or four times."

But he wasn't quite off the hook. "How about the recent ones? You like any of them?"

"*Ceiling Zero* I thought was terrific. Thought you and Cagney worked together like champs." Dutch paused; Hawks was attentive, as if waiting for just one more. I could read Dutch's mind: by now he'd certainly done his homework, knew the names of Hawks's last few movies, but what if he mentioned something he hadn't seen and Hawks asked him about it? After a second Dutch said, "I was in stitches at the end of *Bringing Up Baby*, when the dinosaur skeleton fell down, and Hepburn was hanging on for dear life . . ."

"Sort of summed up the picture," Hawks said.

"Right, exactly."

"Well," Hawks said, "I'm glad you liked that one." Dutch stood poised and grinning, waiting to see if the exam had another section, and exhaled audibly when Hawks said, "So—what d'you say we get on with it?"

Dutch stood in the middle of the stage, bathed in light. Hawks spoke to me. "Normally I'd just have someone give him his cues, but since you know the script . . ." He nodded toward Lorna, who sat perhaps eight feet from us. "How about her? Does she know it?"

"Pretty well. I mean, not by heart."

"Good. Then let's do the scene after the soccer game, where

Felipe's just learned Pablo's been taken prisoner. She can read Teresa. You can read the mother—she's only got a few lines."

Lorna and I joined Dutch at center stage. We were good at this scene. The camera was stationary, pointed at Dutch, who suddenly looked up from his script and called out to Hawks, "I've got to wear these glasses to read the script." Hawks shrugged in reply. "I mean," Dutch said, "I wouldn't be wearing my glasses in the picture."

"Don't worry about it," Hawks said. "Now—no movement, please. Just read your lines, run through the scene."

We ran through it. It was perhaps not quite as smooth as our final performance in Malibu, but Dutch was good, avoiding histrionics, chewing no scenery, demonstrating cool, controlled fury. At scene's end Hawks yelled, "Cut!" and took a few steps toward us. "All right— this time, walk it through, from Felipe and Teresa's entrance into the house." We did so. As Dutch was no longer still, neither was the camera, but it seemed to me to be focused in Lorna's direction almost as much as in Dutch's.

We did six scenes in all, three of them twice over. We finished with the car scene, cast exactly as we'd done it in Malibu, with Lorna as both Pablo and Teresa and me as Márquez. That was one of the twice-overs, once shot head-on, with Dutch and me in adjacent chairs and Lorna behind us, once shot from a side view, with Dutch in the foreground. In both versions Dutch read his part close to perfection. It gave me chills. It was not exactly a matter of being onstage with Laurence Olivier; rather, it was a case of my having written these lines with a vision of Ronald Reagan speaking them for Howard Hawks, and of my now hearing him recite them precisely as they had been written, exactly as I had heard them spoken in my vision.

Everything proceeded with extraordinary smoothness. No lines were fluffed. Lorna, in her one scene as Pablo, was marvelous, in her five scenes as Teresa fantastic. While I was occasionally surprised by Hawks's proclamations of what we'd be shooting next, it did not dawn on me until later that Hawks had chosen every one of Teresa's major scenes.

We finished. The camera was switched off. Hawks was giving nothing away. "Good," he said. "Thanks a lot to all of you. Gabriel, do you want to step over here?"

I traversed the stage. "Script reads well," he said. "It's going to be a fine picture."

"Thanks. But how did the test go?"

"Reagan?" Hawks's eyebrows elevated, descended. "He's not bad. I had the feeling the material wasn't new to him. There's definitely something likable about him. I don't know whether he's tough enough for this part. I'll watch the film this afternoon. You never know how someone's going to look on the screen."

I knew how Dutch looked on the screen: if anything, twice as good as he looked in person. "Good," I said. "So I'll wait to hear from you?"

"Right. Tonight, tomorrow, maybe Monday, I'll give you a call." He shook my hand. "But I'll tell you something, Gabriel. That girlfriend of yours, Charles's niece, she's the one you want in this picture for sure."

As we walked back to our cars Dutch was high as a kite. He said he'd felt the way Stan Hack had once described being in the midst of a hitting streak: no matter who was pitching, no matter what pitch was thrown, Hack could see the ball approaching as if it were oversized and coming in slow motion. That was how Dutch had felt on stage, as if he *owned* Felipe's character, as if he could do no wrong.

In the parking area, Dutch asked me if Hawks had said anything about his performance. "He said he liked you," I replied. "He said he wanted to see how you look on film."

"What do you think?" Dutch said, having come down just a little. "Both of you."

I spoke first. "I thought you did the scenes just the way I wrote them, and since I wrote them with you in mind I can't pay you a higher compliment. I think the camera likes you, so if Hawks has any doubts they should be dispelled when he sees you onscreen."

Lorna said, "I thought you did a fine job, Dutch."

He was off to meet Jane for lunch, to tell her about his triumph, to try to convince her that this hadn't all been folly. He drove off first.

Lorna and I climbed into my Buick. She said, "Is that what Hawks actually said to you?"

"What do you mean?"

"Did he really say he liked Dutch?"

"His exact words were that Dutch was likable. Why do you ask?"

"I didn't have the impression he was paying much attention to Dutch. He seemed to be looking at me most of the time."

34

The house was ours that weekend. Hawks did not call Saturday night; Dutch did. He asked if I'd heard about the Cubs. I hadn't; they'd won that day after sweeping a doubleheader the day before, while the Pirates had split two games. I suspected this wasn't the motivation for the call. It didn't take long for Dutch to get to his conversation with Jane: she still felt he was being unrealistic, he was overreaching.

During the several weeks this romance had been brewing, I had spent no time with Jane, had not in fact been introduced to her. It seemed improbable this was Dutch's decision; he would likely have been eager to show her off to Lorna and me. So I presumed it was Jane who wished to stay separate from this other side of Dutch, as if she recognized me as something alien, someone who wasn't supposed to stumble about in the life of the man for whom she'd set her cap. Most probably she had assessed Ronnie's talent, found that although he was the man she loved, he was deluded if he saw himself in the same league as Gable or Grant or Cooper, and she didn't want him wasting his time chasing silly dreams, or she didn't relish the prospect of resuscitating him after the inevitable occurred.

Dutch was convinced that if he got the part Jane's reservations would disappear immediately. That seemed likely to me as well. I had to tell him Saturday night, though, that I hadn't heard from Hawks and wasn't sure what that meant, although Hawks had been indefinite about when he'd call. I reiterated that if Hawks didn't want him, we'd find another way to make the movie.

Early Sunday morning, while Lorna slept her usual impenetrable sleep, I set out for Beverly Hills. It was five weeks to the day—almost to the minute—since I'd dropped the machine off at the Wiseman residence.

At six-thirty there was almost no traffic on Roosevelt Highway, so I was more conscious than I might otherwise have been of the car that seemed perpetually to be two hundred yards behind me. Perhaps two miles from Santa Monica Boulevard, I pulled to the side of the road and stopped. My shadow did the same. At this distance I could tell little about the other car. I waited three or four minutes and pulled out again. My shadow let me go a few hundred yards before resuming the game. Half a mile from Santa Monica I pulled over again. This time he kept coming. Was it a dark sedan? It was. Was it a five- or six-year-old Chevrolet? It was, and it zoomed by me at fifty miles per hour, its driver's features obscured by a hat.

I made a U-turn and headed back toward Malibu. The notion of making an end run was appealing. I could get to Wiseman's house by way of Sunset, but what if the old Chevrolet were waiting for me on the return trip? If my shadow was Wadsworth's detective, no harm done. But if it was Jean-Baptiste, and I cruised into Malibu with the A-4 stuffed into my Buick, disaster.

Hawks did not call Sunday. Dutch and I had essentially the same telephone conversation Sunday evening, the one major difference being that this time Dutch suggested he might call Hawks and remind him how much he wanted the role. I dissuaded him.

Nor did Hawks call Monday. Hal Wallis did, however.

He was a stocky man with receding hair and a sharp nose; he was a little shorter and a little younger than I. His office was bigger and grander than Wiseman's, with plush carpeting, drapes thick enough to negate the sun's mightiest efforts, and a baby grand piano nestled in a far corner. It was not quite ten in the morning and he was treating me with a deference that both embarrassed and worried me. This was the man who had already produced *Little Caesar*, *Captain Blood*, and *Jezebel*; who would in due time produce *The Maltese Falcon*, *Casablanca*, *The Rose Tattoo*, and *True Grit*. He told me how fortunate the studio was to have me, how lucky I was to be at a forward-looking outfit like Warners, where a talented neophyte like myself could start working on A pictures straightaway. He reminded me that my first project, *Four O'Clock*, was about to go into production. He told me he knew that I was "engaged" to the rising star Lorna Fairchild, who was also a beneficiary of the studio's liberal policies toward gifted newcomers. *Four O'Clock* would surely catapult Lorna to a celebrity she richly deserved, and Wallis felt it was only just that the part of Teresa in *Operation: Rescue* should be her second starring role. This turned out to be the completion of Wallis's opening monologue, and he awaited my reaction.

"That would be very nice," I said. "It would please me, and I'm sure it would please Lorna."

"Good." Wallis studied me a bit. "I've worked with Howard in the past, you know. He's an excellent judge of talent."

"Yes."

"Howard feels that Miss Fairchild's relative lack of exposure wouldn't be a concern if we had Gary Cooper as Felipe."

Wallis had pronounced Felipe to rhyme with "sleepy." I said, "I know Mister Hawks wants Cooper, but I've told him I wrote the part for Ronald Reagan."

Wallis shook his head. "Howard and I have just had a long discussion. He spent several hours with Cooper yesterday, and Cooper wants to do the picture. If I were you, Gabriel, I'd be very happy about that."

"Yes," I said, "but I wrote the part for Ronald Reagan."

Wallis smiled. "I can assure you, we'll find a good part, lots of good parts for Ronald Reagan. He's a talented actor. But you've got to understand, Gabriel, that I can't say no to a Howard Hawks picture with Gary Cooper."

The time had come, evidently, to assert myself. "I don't believe it's your decision," I said.

The smile remained. "As I've just said, it was Howard's decision."

"I mean to say that it's my script. I've shown my script to Hawks, but it's no more his decision than it's yours or even Jack Warner's, because it's my script."

Wallis finally lost the battle with his facial muscles; with a twitch bordering on the spasmodic the smile perished. "Gabriel, you work for Warner Brothers. You are a contract writer. What you write belongs to us, and we make the decisions as to what to do with your work."

"That obviously doesn't extend to everything I write. I did not write this for Warners. I wrote it entirely on my own time, with other interests in mind—"

"But you brought it first to Bernie Wiseman."

"No. I showed Bernie a treatment. I asked him, in effect, whether he was interested in an idea, and he said he was. When it became clear to me that he and I differed on a crucial aspect of that idea, I withdrew the idea. I never showed the script to anyone at Warners. Maybe Hawks did, but I didn't."

A new smile appeared, this one spontaneous and evidently genuine. Did Wallis feel invincible, or was he simply enjoying the joust? "You can't win this, Gabriel. You make a terrific argument, but it comes down to our having the script, doesn't it? If we go ahead and make the picture, what are you going to do, sue us?"

"Precisely."

"What sort of chance do you imagine you'd have? What kind of lawyer could you afford? I don't want to seem cynical, but if this is a case of David and Goliath, David doesn't even have the slingshot. So Goliath is going to grind him into the dust."

I was not exactly David, however, nor would I be deprived of weapons. I had resources Wallis knew nothing about. I could hire lawyers just as good as Warners'. This line of thinking had been critical to my strategy since Lorna's and my conversation back in March, the night I first outlined the story for her and Dutch. Warners might have an edge on me if they were prepared to go into production right away: if they made the movie with Cooper and I sued and won a huge judgment, what good would it do me? But they weren't going to start for six months, minimum, which would give me plenty of time to prevent them from starting. On the other hand, if I did spend my nest egg on lawyers, I'd have to make that much more money. Could I find a scrupulous stockbroker? How much time would I have to devote to researching my files for a scheme that made huge amounts of money fast without being conspicuous?

Wallis resumed. "If I were you I'd seriously consider the alternatives. On one side you're flushing money down the toilet, maybe throwing away your career, on a battle you can't win. On the other, you're writing a picture for one of the standout directors in Hollywood, writing a picture for an excellent actor whose name is automatic box office, and to top it off you're writing a picture that's going to star your sweetheart."

I have to admit that I was beginning to consider the alternatives.

Sitting there across from Wallis, it occurred to me for the first time that I might have been stubborn, overly single-minded, even obsessive. Hadn't I already thrown Reagan sufficiently off track? Wasn't I well along the road to fulfilling my contract with Hudnut? Wouldn't it be relatively easy to explain this all to Dutch, to procure in the meantime some sort of guarantee from Wallis that I *could* write an A picture for Dutch?

I said, "There'd be no maybe about it—Lorna would be cast as Teresa?"

"You have my word."

I saw myself confronting Dutch, saw myself as the ultimate hypocrite, the definitive weasel. Irrational as it was, it was an image I couldn't avoid. "I don't know," I said.

Wallis pounced. "I had a long talk with J.L. about this, Gabriel. He loves the script. He wants to do this picture very much. He said, 'Isn't that the kid who wrote the western, too? This is not somebody we can let get away, Hal.' Those were his exact words. What kind of money are you making now, Gabriel?"

If what I'd read and heard was true, Jack Warner had never actually read a script in his life. I uttered to Wallis the infinitesimal figure probably already implanted in his memory. He said, "What if we added three hundred a week to that?"

The raise would more than double my salary. The money was unnecessary, irrelevant, but would establish me as one of the top writers at Warners, give me power, enhance my chances of writing a different picture for Dutch. I said, "Can I have a little time to think about things?"

Back in my office at eleven, my head spinning, I wondered what to do. That is to say, I wondered what to do with the rest of my day. The last thing I wanted to do was spend my usual lunchtime in the commissary with Dutch. I might be able to fudge a little, but I wouldn't be able to lie outright, and I didn't want Dutch's emotions affecting my decision. Nor would Lorna be there to help me, or distract me. She was at home, enjoying the first day of a week off before preliminary work on *Four O'Clock* was to begin. Nor could I bury myself in work. I'd finished my last bit of script doctoring the previous Friday, and I'd found no new assignment on my desk either before or after my meeting with Wallis.

I called the house in Malibu and felt a great wave of relief, of ardor, when Lorna answered. Did she have any plans for lunch, for the afternoon? None in particular. Good, then; I had just spent an hour with Hal Wallis and wanted to discuss it with her. Should we meet at my office, she asked, or elsewhere in Burbank? No—I was going to take the afternoon off and spend it at home with her.

"Can you do that, Gabriel?" she asked.

"I'm quite sure I can," I replied.

Was there someone I should call? Who was my boss now? Technically still Wiseman, really, and not Wallis, yet. I elected to call no one, and began gathering up my things. Where was the *Operation: Rescue* script? Had I brought it with me this morning? I was positive I had. Had I taken it to Wallis's office? I had not. Had I left it in the car? Possibly. It surely wasn't anywhere in my cubicle. It turned out not to be in the car, either. Had I in fact actually left it in the house? I could picture it sitting on the bedside table, could picture myself picking it up, my last act before leaving the bedroom this morning. But perhaps that was a memory of some other morning, of numerous other mornings. On another day I might have been more concerned, might have begun deducing, but this day I had other things on my mind.

It was a beautiful day, clear and warm, the heat wave done or dormant. I drove in light traffic with the Buick's top down, stopped in Santa Monica for the makings of a salade niçoise, concluded while driving north alongside the sparkling, placid Pacific that today was the day, that I could not adequately explain my dilemma to Lorna unless she understood its true dimensions.

She was barefoot and a little sweaty, having been weeding the flower garden on the east side of the house. She smelled like sun and ocean and like Lorna, best of all. I embraced her, I suppose, as if we'd been apart for months or years, because she said, "Boy, maybe we should do this every Monday." We ended up having the first part of our conversation not over salad but in bed.

I recounted the dialogue with Wallis as it had developed, and Lorna reacted pretty much as I had, except that while she was ideologically with me during the legal section, she kept shaking her head at my stubbornness, my gall. When I got to Wallis's offers—the part for her and the promotion for me—her eyes brightened and her body relaxed as if at the happy conclusion of a suspenseful movie. Then she said, "I don't need the part, Gabriel. You shouldn't worry about me in this. You've already done enough for me. And I don't think you should be too concerned about Dutch. I mean, he's your friend and you've made promises to him, but this is such an opportunity for you, and the alternative . . . God, it could be the end of you at Warners, and maybe him too."

"It isn't just that I've made promises," I said. "I've told him twenty times I'll turn down any arrangement that doesn't have him as Felipe. He's been staking a lot on this. He's run the risk of alienating someone very important to him—"

"You can't worry about that. That's Dutch's problem. You're not in charge of his life, for God's sake."

I loved her very much, and she'd told me exactly what I wanted to hear, but unfortunately I couldn't leave it at that. I cannot tell you how many times I'd anticipated this moment, played it out in my mind. I'd rehearsed a thousand different ways of telling Lorna my secret, but now that the time was here I found myself utterly without a plan, a script. I said, "In an odd sort of way, I am in charge of his life."

"He's not a child," Lorna said.

"That's not exactly what I mean." I sat up. "The things I've said I wish I could explain to you, Lorna . . . everything about the boat, everything Bill told you . . ."

Lorna sat up too, and embraced my neck. "You don't *have* to tell me, Gabriel. If you were in prison or something, or if your parents were spies—"

"No," I said. "It's nothing like that. Look, when Bill told you he had the alumni office search through the records for someone with my name—"

"You did something dishonorable, they kicked you out, and you changed your name."

"No. I did go to Princeton, but there's no way the alumni office or anybody else could have found a record of me, because I graduated in the class of 1974."

35

She did not recoil; she did let her arms slacken, and rested her hands on my shoulders. "That's preposterous, Gabriel. It's not possible. I don't need to tell you that."

"I can prove it," I said.

We got dressed. I led her to the garage. The machine was still visiting Beverly Hills, but my other artifact would be even more convincing. From a box against the wall, from between a couple of camphor-saturated winter blankets, I removed the computer. Its appearance alone would establish it as something from another time, or another world. An object as big as the time machine could pass as a ultramodern boat, but one as small and sleek as the notebook computer might exist only in the mind of some 1938 da Vinci, and even he (or she) certainly couldn't imagine its capabilities. "Have you ever seen anything like this, Lorna? Have you ever even imagined anything like this?"

"No, but that doesn't mean—"

"The boat that's been here, it's not actually a boat . . ."

"Where is it? What's become of it?"

"It's at Bernie Wiseman's. That's another story. I'll get to that. The boat isn't a boat, anyway. It's what brought me here. It's a time machine your cousin Jasper gave me in 1994."

"This makes no sense, Gabriel."

"I know. But it's real. It's actual."

"Why did Jasper . . . My God, 1994! Jasper would be an old man! Why did Jasper give you this time machine?"

"That's the part you're going to have a lot of trouble believing."

"I can't imagine having more trouble than I am right now."

Perhaps it would be easiest to do this by stages. Tucked into the inner pocket of the computer's carrying case, along with a selection of the photographs I'd taken since my arrival, were the pictures of Paris I'd brought along accidentally. I withdrew them and handed her the first one, which happened to be of the entrance to L'Hôtel, but taken from across the street.

"Why are you showing me this?" she asked.

"It's Jasper's hotel in Paris, but that's not what's important. Look at the cars."

She sucked in a breath. "They're tiny. They're so low, and sort of . . . streamlined."

"That's because they're from 1994," I said. More photographs, more cars, a billboard that had caught my eye, featuring a woman in a bathing suit that hardly covered any of her, a shot of a Latin Quarter restaurant full of diners wearing late-twentieth-century clothing. Lorna's eyes seemed to expand. Now I handed her the computer, and she caressed its smooth plastic surface. "What is it?"

"What do you think? What do you suppose?"

"It's too small to be a radio, too shallow, unless they've invented some new kind of tube." I pressed the release button and the laptop opened. "It's a typewriter," Lorna whispered. "It's a tiny typewriter. But there's no place to put the paper. There's no ribbon."

I'd been running it off the AC adapter every night I used it, so the battery was fully charged. I touched the power switch and the computer came to life, its screen flickering through the details of its AUTOEXEC.BAT. "My God, Gabriel," Lorna said, "it's *television*. It's a little typewriter with television!"

We moved into the kitchen. I put the laptop on the table. "It's a little typewriter with a brain," I said. "And with a memory. With an amazing memory." I showed her the racetrack files, showed her the stock market files.

"That's how I did so well at Santa Anita," I said. "That's how I won so much at Del Mar, with Dutch. Because I knew what was going to happen."

"It's not exactly playing fair, is it?"

"No, not at all. But I haven't taken advantage of this. If I'd simply wanted to make money, I could have gone to the track every day. I could have bought and sold stocks from the start and made millions of dollars. But that's not why I'm here. I needed some money to get started that first day at Santa Anita, and at Del Mar I was raising capital for our movie."

Lorna sat silent for an uncomfortably long time—forty seconds, a minute, or two, I cannot say. She could have been pursuing any number of trains of thought. It was my fervent hope that one of them was not the relatively simple deduction that just as I had access to financial happenings between that era and this, so did I to the cinema. I did not want to complicate things at this juncture. I did not want her having second thoughts about *Four O'Clock*. Finally, she spoke. "Why did you need money to make *Operation: Rescue?* Everything had worked so well with Bernie Wiseman and *Four O'Clock*. Why couldn't you just have followed the same routine?"

I could have obfuscated. I wouldn't have been lying if I'd reiterated concerns stated previously: the script going through the usual channels at Warners would have been diluted, sanitized, trivialized, emasculated. But what was the point? Lorna had given me the opportunity to go directly to the heart of the matter. I said, "Jasper gave me the time machine so I could do something to keep Ronald Reagan from becoming president."

She burst into laughter at my tension-breaking joke. I said, "No, I'm serious."

She examined me, doubtless perceived that I *was* serious, and said, "President of what?"

How could I make this more credible? "Roosevelt's reelected in 1940, and again in '44, with Harry Truman, the senator from Missouri, as his vice president. Roosevelt dies in office in 1945, Truman takes over, gets reelected, just barely, in '48. Dwight Eisenhower, a Republican who was a big hero in the war—the war that's just about to happen now—is elected in 1952, and again in '56, with a really creepy guy named Richard Nixon as his vice president. Nixon runs against a young democrat named John Kennedy in 1960, and Kennedy wins. Kennedy is assassinated in '63, and his vice president, Lyndon Johnson, takes over. He's reelected in '64, and then there's a very stupid war in a country in Southeast Asia that doesn't exist now, and America's in shambles, and in 1968 the creepy guy, Nixon, is elected, and things really start to go downhill, despite which he's reelected in 1972, but there's a big scandal and he has to resign in '74. His vice president, who's a complete idiot, takes over, and loses in '76 to a Democrat from Georgia, a strange man who gets in a lot of trouble that's much too complicated to explain. And when he runs in 1980 he's annihilated by the former governor of California, the former president of the Screen Actors Guild, Ronald Reagan." I pronounced "Reagan" in the revisionist manner, as I had the first time I'd spoken it to Lorna nearly seven months earlier.

She said, "Dutch?"

"Dutch," I replied.

Again Lorna was silent, not for so long this time. "It just seems so . . . absurd. I mean, the idea that a Hollywood actor could become president. And it's not as if it's someone like Fredric March, or Spencer Tracy—someone you could *imagine* being president."

"Believe me, the perspective forty or fifty years from now is quite different, but it's no less absurd."

"But Gabriel," she said after a short while, "your politics and his— well, I guess his are sort of simplistic—but you and he seem to have pretty much the same ideology."

"He changes," I said.

"What does he do that's so terrible? From the way you described all those other people just now, it's hard to imagine he could be much worse."

"In some ways he isn't. Nixon's a much more evil man. So's Johnson. They're both cynical and calculating and power mad, and they do awful things, but they also do good things. They achieve things. But Reagan . . . Your cousin Jasper, when he's seventy, believes that Reagan is one of the most evil men, one of the most destructive men, of the twentieth century. Because he becomes president at a critical time, when the world is going through tremendous changes, and he really doesn't do *anything*. He just lets his rich, sinister friends run the country, and the country goes to hell."

"Then he's voted out after one term?"

"No. He wins big in 1984."

"Why? How can a man ruin the country and still be popular?"

How could I explain? To someone who'd never seen television, how could I explain its power? How could I explain the paradox of Ronald Reagan—surely one of the least erudite, probably among the least articulate men ever to occupy the White House—coming to be known as the Great Communicator? I said, "Because the country hadn't figured out it was being ruined."

I made the salade niçoise. I had a tremendous appetite. I said, "Do you believe me?"

"Well, in a sense I don't at all. It's completely insane. I keep thinking that maybe you're some kind of brilliant maniac who really believes his delusion. But then I have to look at the evidence. That typewriter, I guess it's pretty unlikely there's a genius somewhere turning out things like that."

"Not for a very long time," I said.

"I keep bouncing back and forth, Gabriel. There's so much I want to ask you, but then I don't think I want to know the answers."

"No, I don't think you want to know."

Lorna stabbed a chunk of tuna and nibbled on it. Her plate lay almost undisturbed. "This is delicious," she said, "but I'm afraid I'm not very hungry." She paused for a few seconds. "I suppose there must be a war in Europe?"

"There is."

"Oh, God. Is it as bad as the last one?"

"Not as bad in some ways, much worse in others."

"I shouldn't ask any more, should I?"

"You shouldn't."

"I keep thinking of things," she said. "If this is all true, I'm something like forty or fifty years older than you."

"Not really. In a meaningless way."

"Does Jasper *make* the time machine? Does he invent it? Is he that smart?"

"No, he finds it. He actually finds two of them. One in Oregon when he's a young man, one in Paris just before I meet him. He's convinced that some people from the future—I mean probably from a couple of hundred years in the future—left the machines for him to find them. So there must be a reason they did it, and Jasper's convinced it's so we can keep Reagan from becoming president."

"That sounds pretty fantastic to me," Lorna said. "But I guess you believe him, because you're here."

"Well, it gets kind of complicated at that point. I'm not sure I ever believed that part of it, but there have been developments since I left that have pretty much disproved Jasper's theory. I can explain that to you later. I think it would be a little confusing right now."

"I can't imagine things being too much more confusing than they are right now," Lorna said. There ensued quite a long silence, during which I finished my portion of the salad and took several bites from Lorna's plate as she stared in the general direction of the kitchen door. She said, "Gabriel, are you planning to stay here or go back there?"

"I'm staying," I said. "I love you very much. I couldn't possibly leave."

"It's going to be very strange, being aware that you know everything that's going to happen. I can see that it could make me very uneasy."

"Not everything," I said. "Not by any means. I know the general flow of history. I'm in a position to know who's going to win the fifth race at Santa Anita. After 1945 I won't even know that. Our life together is something entirely new. We can have children, we can go live somewhere else. We can have a life independent of everything that's happened, or that's going to happen."

Lorna said, "Can you do anything about the awful things?"

"Which things?"

"You said in some ways the war that's coming up will be worse than the Great War. Since you know what's going to happen, can you do anything? Can you make changes?"

"Probably not. I can try, I suppose. But in some cases, if I tried to warn people I don't think anybody would believe me, and in some cases I'm afraid even if people did believe me they wouldn't do anything."

There was an extraordinarily long silence. I considered getting up and doing the dishes. I considered embracing Lorna and telling her everything would be all right despite my being a person from fifty-six years in the future. Eventually I put my right hand over her left and said, "Do you want me to stay?"

"I think so," she said. "I can't imagine being without you. It's just that all of a sudden you're not the same person you used to be."

"I am, though. Really. Very much the same."

Her eyes met mine, then returned to the door. Her hand clasped mine, then went limp. These transitions occurred three or four times over. Then Lorna said, "If you're staying, what would keep you from writing another script for Dutch? I don't see why you shouldn't take Wallis's offer."

— —

We talked through the afternoon. Tacit ground rules were established. I did not tell Lorna and she did not ask me about anything that did not directly concern one of us. At some length I related my encounter with Jasper in Paris, which led to a description of my former career, and then it was back to Jasper and his discovery of the first time machine in the Oregon woods. I told her quite honestly that I knew very little about her family, that Jasper had shown me photographs of various relatives but I did not know what would become of them, except for her cousin Charlie. I did know, of course, that the house would still be Hudnut property in 1994, and this pleased Lorna a great deal. I also knew that when Jasper and I occupied this house seven months earlier (in my very particular time frame), Lorna had been dead over fifty-five years. That was something I had chosen not to tell her. But as things turned out, I did.

She asked if at some point I could demonstrate the time machine for her. I said I would prefer not to: that its fuel supply appeared to be finite and that there was the headache problem. I described Jasper's disastrous headache, and it was Lorna who then made the connection to mine, whereupon I felt obligated to tell her about my attempted return to 1994, and I realized I had ripped the lid off a new can of worms.

Why had I left? "Because something terrible happened here."

"What, Gabriel?"

"Something I'd rather not tell you."

"But if I understand this right, you're talking about a time we were together—something we experienced together that you remember but I can't. You have to tell me."

The logic was tenuous but the emotion was compelling. I resisted a few minutes longer, but finally I confessed that Dutch had died. How, she wanted to know. "He drowned. Bill got drunk and went for a swim. He was gone quite a while. Dutch heard his voice and thought he was calling for help, swam out to rescue him, got caught in a strong tide, and that was that."

I had not mentioned Catalina. Lorna said, "So then all you would have had to do—if I understand this right—was get in your machine and go back to some point before Dutch had died, and he would have been alive again?"

"Yes."

"But instead you took the machine to 1994?"

"I tried."

"Why? Because Dutch was dead and you wanted to see what the world would be like if he hadn't lived?"

She was getting remarkably good at this. "No, actually I had a much more ordinary reason. There were—"

"*Wait*, Gabriel. What happened when you tried to go forward?"

"I ended up in 1984. The control panel—"

"And what *was* the world like?"

"Much better. Indescribably better, really. It was exactly the sort of world Jasper was hoping for. I mean, I was there for a little more than a day, but everything seemed wonderful. It's difficult . . . since you haven't seen the original 1984, to try to explain the differences."

"Then why did you come back?"

"For you."

Tears rolled down her cheeks and she leaned across the kitchen table to embrace me. I appreciated the contact, and it was my fervent hope that the inquiry would proceed no further. She said, "But wasn't there more at stake than just me and you? When you returned here, didn't you undo everything you'd done? Dutch is alive now, so won't he just become president again?"

"Jasper didn't think so. I did this with his blessing."

"But Gabriel . . . God, this all makes my head spin. Shouldn't it simply be reciprocal? You come here, you change things, you make a better world. You return here, to a point before you changed things, the world reverts to what it was."

"Yes, but Jasper—the Jasper I met in 1984—has a theory about timelines running parallel to each other, sometimes blending into each other . . . it pretty much mystifies me, to tell you the truth. But the gist of it is that each time you use the machine you skip into a different timeline, so by coming back to save you—"

"To *save* me?"

Ah, Doctor Freud. Had I slipped in my state of mental clutter, in my effort to explain so much so fast? Or had I slipped to stop Lorna from further speculation on the relative worth of one love affair versus utopia? I said, "I came back here to keep you from dying."

She drew in a deep, audible breath, as if she had been punched in some vulnerable spot. "Can you do that? Do you know when I'm going to die?"

"I've already done it once. You were supposed to be buried in the landslide on Roosevelt Highway during the big storm. Remember, I wouldn't let you go to work. . . ."

"Good Lord," she said. "Good Lord."

"In 1984, Jasper had a print of a movie called *Four O'Clock*. It was from my idea, but I'd left, I'd disappeared, in the middle of March . . ."

"When you took the machine to 1984, after Dutch drowned?"

"Exactly. So apparently Bernie Wiseman handed the project over to Bill, who wrote a really awful script. But you were wonderful. And you died the night of the premiere."

"How?"

"A traffic accident. That's all I know. Sometime in December." Lorna's expression was uncommonly grim. Bloodless. I got to my feet and stood behind her chair, began massaging her shoulders and her neck. I said, "You're already on a different path, a different schedule. Whatever led to the accident in that version of 1938 isn't going to happen this time."

"But Gabriel . . ." Her voice was soft and thin. "You've just told me that I've already died twice in 1938. Maybe I'm not *meant* to live."

"Nonsense," I said. "There was a freak accident, one of those anomalies of probability. And then the next time it was because I left. Bill wrote a lousy picture, I disappeared. Who knows what was involved. But it's not going to happen this time."

— —

When the phone rang at a few minutes past five I knew it was Dutch. Lorna and I made the trek from kitchen to phone nook together. In somewhat better spirits now, she answered, chatted for a minute, said, "Yes, he's here," and handed me both pieces of the telephone.

"I missed you at lunch," Dutch said.

"Sorry about that. I took the afternoon off."

"You feel all right? Not coming down with something, I hope."

"No, I'm fine. Had the opportunity to leave, so I took it."

My explanation had been elliptical at best, and Dutch did not respond for several seconds, as if waiting for elaboration. Eventually he said, "Still no word from Hawks?"

"No." It would have been easy enough to say no more, but obviously this was something I'd have to deal with sooner or later. I resumed before my heart had beaten twice. "Not directly, anyway. But Hal Wallis called me in—"

"Wallis! Boy, you're coming up in the world, Gabriel."

"Wallis had talked with Hawks at some length, Dutch. They both feel very strongly that Gary Cooper should play Felipe."

Did I hear Dutch catch his breath, or was it a pre-electronic rale somewhere between Hollywood and Malibu? Seconds went by before he said, "So. It wasn't entirely unexpected, was it? Now I guess we go back to the drawing board."

"Maybe we don't. I think Wallis might have us over a barrel. They plan to do the picture with my participation or without. Wallis says it's Warners' property and Warners has the lawyers to back that up."

"Well, come *on*, Gabriel," Dutch's voice conveyed camaraderie and an intimation of anger. "We're not going to let them intimidate us, are we? We're clearly in the right, legally, aren't we?"

"I think we are, Dutch. But it could take years to find out. Warners might go ahead and make the movie in the meantime, or at best neither of us could make it. And Wallis made it pretty clear I'd be without a job. Maybe you, too."

"So you're going to let them do it?"

"It may just be for the best, Dutch. I know I promised you the part, and I know how much it means to you, but this could be a blessing in disguise. Wallis said there are going to be parts for you, important parts. He said you're a talented actor, but they want Cooper as Felipe."

"Gabriel, for crying out loud, I've got a lot riding on this. I hope you realize that's the end of it for Jane and me. She kept telling me something like this was in store. She kept telling me what an idiot I was to put my faith in some stupid, pie-in-the-sky idea, and I kept telling her you weren't just some fellow who could write a good script, you had *integrity* . . ."

"I'd like to think I still do, Dutch. I'd like to think we can get past this. I'm serious when I say that my first priority is to write something else for you, something just as good as Felipe . . ." Did I hear the line go dead? I said, "Dutch, are you there?" And the only response was the whine of a primeval dial tone.

I looked at Lorna, who had been at my side during the entire conversation. "He hung up." I replaced the receiver and put the phone back in its niche.

"You did a good job," she said. "You couldn't have put it any better. He'll see the light."

"I hope so." It was little consolation that once again I seemed to be doing an excellent job of throwing Ronald Reagan's life off track in ways I hadn't intended. In September of 1938 he wasn't supposed to be an angry young man on the verge of losing the first great love of his life. But if Jasper Hudnut were here to advise me at this point, surely he'd be telling me to leave well enough alone.

36

For the first time since I had begun sharing her bed, Lorna did not sleep through the night. When she did sleep it was with an aberrational restlessness. I hardly slept at all. At odd intervals we would have brief conversations. "Gabriel? Do you suppose I shouldn't drive my car at all? Or maybe just not in December. Do you think we could arrange it so we go away for the whole month?" And I soothed in response.

"Gabriel? Are you awake? Look, do you suppose it's possible, if somehow you were to establish yourself as some sort of psychic . . . I mean, you're a responsible member of society, you're about to be a well-known writer. I guess it wouldn't even have to be as a psychic, but if somehow you could *predict* something you know is going to happen, just to get people's attention. Then when you've got some credibility, maybe you could warn people about awful things. At first they wouldn't do anything, but after a while, wouldn't they *have* to?" And I responded neutrally, thinking that no, they wouldn't have to, telling Lorna that it was certainly something to consider. I'd had these fantasies, God knows. Pearl Harbor was just over two years away. Auschwitz had already been conceived, was perhaps even under construction, as we lay in bed. I would always tell myself that I was not here to attend to those things. But then, who was to say I wasn't? Hudnut believed he'd been given access to the machine to save the nation from Ronald Reagan's presidency. Was it possible that I, through Hudnut, had been given access to the machine to save the world from far worse atrocities? The conclusion I invariably reached— perhaps just because it was comfortable—was that these were wheels set in motion either so long ago or simply so inexorably that they could not be stopped.

— —

We sat groggily across from each other at the kitchen table. I said, "I shouldn't have told you any of this, should I?"

She wore her bathrobe. Her feet were bare, her hair still sleep-mussed. She did not have to go to work this morning. She said, "It's probably better you did. You're probably right: I'm not going to die. I don't think I'm going to stop worrying about it altogether. And I'm very concerned about what all this means. About what you might have the power to do."

— —

I drove to Burbank under a warm morning sun, the clear blue sky of the coast gradually giving way to haze as I got deeper into the valley. Lorna's words kept rambling through my mind: *What I might have the power to do.* It was a turn I hadn't anticipated. I should have expected that Lorna would concentrate on imminent horrors. Even if Hudnut was right, if Reagan was one of the great evil figures of the twentieth century, Lorna (or anyone else from 1938) couldn't begin to understand the events or the significance of his reign. Nor at this point in her education did she know much about the immediate future, other than that the war just around the corner wasn't going to be an easy one. But it seemed pretty obvious that I was going to be telling her a lot more in the days to come, and that as a result our life together would soon undergo some major changes. Not for long would the hot young screenwriter and the newly emerged movie star share their fan-magazine idyll.

Were it not for the cloud of apprehension that never drifted too far from my head, the morning might have been characterized as one of the best of my life. I met again with Wallis, and informed him that the plan—Howard Hawks to direct *Operation: Rescue,* starring Gary Cooper and Lorna Fairchild, my salary to be increased as previously specified—was fine with me providing he give me his solemn oath that my next project would be an A picture for Ronald Reagan. Wallis did not entirely appreciate my demand. From his tone of voice it was clear he did not cotton to being told what to do by a new kid, a writer at that. He had a proviso as well: he would agree to my "request" as long as I kept it quiet, as long as I did not tell the "other writers" that I'd struck such a deal, lest all of a sudden they start demanding starring roles for their own actor friends. I did not imagine that too many of my fellow writers had actor friends, and I certainly would not have told any of them about this arrangement for fear of being shunned as the scenarist equivalent of a teacher's pet.

I left with a handshake and the promise that contracts would soon be drawn up. Reentering my office, I noticed what was unmistakably a script on the floor in the corner of the room. Indeed, it was my missing copy of *Operation: Rescue*. It had lain precisely where I might not have seen it when searching for it the previous afternoon. But how had it found its way to the floor, to that corner? And why had I not noticed it when I first entered the office this morning? As I riffled through the pages, relieved but puzzled, my telephone rang. It was Hawks, who had just spoken to Wallis, he said, who had given him the good news. He very much looked forward to making *Operation: Rescue*, which was going to be a hell of a picture. While he admired my steadfastness in standing by my friend, I had to know that I'd ultimately made the proper decision, because *Rescue* was not just going to have better box office with Cooper, it was going to be a much better picture. A great picture.

Today it was Dutch who didn't appear at the commissary. I decided to take a long lunch, and drove to a very pleasant café I knew half a mile away. At a nearby wine shop I found two bottles of 1933 Chassagne-Montrachet for five dollars apiece. Back at the lot, I walked to the *Murder Plane* set, where I was told that Dutch hadn't shown up, hadn't even called in until noon. This, it was added, was very much unlike Dutch, generally the first actor on the set. Worse, since Dutch was in virtually every scene, his absence had caused a complete cessation of shooting.

From my office I called Dutch's apartment, but got no answer. I called Lorna and woke her from a nap. Was she depressed, or just groggy? Her mood improved audibly as I recounted the meeting with Wallis, the call from Hawks. I told her about Dutch's unexcused absence, asked her if she'd mind coming over and trying to explain the situation to Bryan Foy, for whom she'd worked. (Warners' entire second-line operation was known as the "Foy Unit," in honor of the man in charge of all B pictures.) And perhaps she might try to reach Jane Wyman, who was on loan to MGM? She'd see what she could do, she said.

— • —

At quarter past three there was a knock on my door. A good two hours had passed since my conversation with Lorna, time enough for her to have completed both missions. "Come in," I said, and the open door revealed not Lorna but large, florid, ominous Bill Wadsworth.

He seemed in good spirits. "How are you doing, Gabriel?"

"Just fine, Bill. But busy. No time to socialize."

He took several deliberate steps into my cubicle, toward my desk. "I'll say you're doing fine. I hear you and Hal Wallis are tight as ticks."

"How do you hear that, Bill?"

"Oh, you know, through the grapevine. I hear you're doing a Spanish Civil War picture."

I wondered where Wadsworth was getting his information. I supposed it wasn't all that unusual for news of a big deal to have traveled from Wallis's office to his in a matter of hours, but still it was annoying. I said, "What are you working on, Bill?"

"I've been doing some touch-up work on *Nancy Drew, Reporter*. Not exactly in your league, but it's not a bad little picture. It's a living, anyway." Wadsworth sat down in my extra chair. "Say, Gabriel, I'd guess you probably haven't given much thought to that discussion we had a couple of weeks ago."

"No, I've given it some thought. I thought about calling the police and having them arrest your man the next time he sneaks into the Colony."

Wadsworth smiled in the manner of a poker player holding a well-concealed hand. "But you didn't, did you? I wonder why."

"This is so stupid, Bill," I said. "This intrigue. I didn't because it would have been messy. Embarrassing. Why don't we forget about all this nonsense and live our lives? If you keep pushing me, I'll have to go to the police."

Wadsworth's smile suggested delusion more than the slyness I assumed he intended to connote. Before he could speak, there was another knock at my door—and indeed it was Lorna who entered this time, wearing her white shorts, as if she had in fact jumped into her car the instant she'd hung up the phone. I was not altogether sure how to feel about her arrival at this juncture.

"Oh, excuse me," she said. "Hello, Bill. Am I interrupting something?"

"Not at all," I said. Wadsworth got to his feet; Lorna met him halfway, and they engaged in a stiff little embrace. He offered her the straight-backed chair he'd just vacated; she declined, and both of them stood in front of my desk like lawyers before the bench.

"Really," Lorna said, "if you boys were in the middle of something, I'm sure I could occupy myself elsewhere for a while."

"That's not necessary," I said. This was the first time there had been more than two people in my office, the first time anyone with visibly sunburned knees had been in my office. "I think Bill was just about to leave."

"On the contrary," Wadsworth said, "Gabriel was just trying to get rid of me." He shifted his attention from me to Lorna. "He threatened to call the police. I called his bluff. I don't think a man in Gabriel's position is very likely to call the police."

Lorna looked at me. "Am I missing something? Why would you call the police?"

"Bill hired a private detective to follow me. He's the man Sally tried to speak to when she saw him sitting outside the house."

"No!" Lorna said. She gave Wadsworth as withering a look as I'm sure he ever received. "And I suppose he's the one who stole Charlie's camera?"

I saw no reason to disabuse her of that. Wadsworth said, "Let's hold on a second here. I don't think a man in Gabriel's position should be flinging accusations about penny-ante stuff when he's—"

Lorna interrupted him. "What exactly do you mean by 'a man in Gabriel's position'?"

"Lorna, darling, for God's sake, this is a man who doesn't exist! Never went to the school he claimed to, never worked at the job he claimed to. A man with no background, no history, who hangs around racetracks with disreputable foreigners . . ."

Lorna had quickly reached a stage of icy fury. "So what, Bill?"

"Well, he's definitely hiding something. And I don't think it's too much of a jump to say he's some kind of agent, probably a Communist."

She made a derisive noise, took a step closer to Wadsworth so she stood about eighteen inches from him. "You're such an idiot, Bill. Gabriel's no more a Communist than you're Mussolini."

Wadsworth stood his ground. "I happen to have considerable admiration for Mussolini."

"And you deserve each other," Lorna said.

"Bill," I said, "I think it's time for you to go."

Lorna continued speaking to Wadsworth. "For Italy's sake, I hope Mussolini's got more deductive power than you do."

"What exactly do *you* mean by that?" Wadsworth said.

"That you couldn't be barking up a wronger tree about Gabriel. If only you *knew*—"

I said, "Enough!"

Wadsworth said, "If only I knew what?"

I stood up, demicircumnavigated my desk, and pushed Wadsworth toward the door. "Get out of here, Bill."

He glared down at me. "Don't you touch me."

"Leave," I said, "and I won't have to."

Wadsworth made an attenuated bow in our direction and pointed a finger at me. He said, "I'm not done with you," and departed, slamming the door rather vigorously this time.

Lorna put her arms around my waist. "I wasn't going to tell him anything."

I reciprocated. "I didn't think you were. It's just that at this point, even implying that there's something unusual about me might set him off, make him more obsessive . . ."

"But what can he do?"

"Nothing, I'm sure. Make trouble."

"Maybe you *should* go to the police."

"Maybe I should."

Lorna let go of me, sat in my extra chair. "You mustn't worry too much about him, Gabriel. He's all bluster."

I sat on the edge of my desk. "Did you reach Jane?"

"I did. I called MGM and told them it was an emergency. She was annoyed at first, but she wasn't unfriendly at all. She's pretty much fed up with Dutch, I'd say, and she doesn't have a very high opinion of you, but she was perfectly willing to talk to me. She said Dutch called her around seven last night, sounding pretty awful, and as if he might have had a couple of drinks. She thinks that's your fault, incidentally. Dutch told her he never had a taste for wine before he met you, but you've introduced him to some of the finer things. Anyway, he told her she'd been right all along about his not getting the part. He kept apologizing and saying he wanted to see her, and she told him she was busy, she'd see him sometime later."

I'd seen Dutch consume more than an ounce or two of alcohol only twice—during his premortal, wiped-off-the-slate evening on Catalina, and the night we rehearsed *Operation: Rescue* in Malibu. I had never intended to turn him into a boozer.

Lorna continued. "Jane said his father's had a drinking problem. Maybe he's even a genuine dipso. It's something Dutch has expressed concern about, that it might run in the family. But the odd thing is how he happened to be drinking—"

"Wait," I said. "Did you get a chance to speak to Bryan Foy? Does Dutch still have a job?"

"No. He'd left for the day. About five minutes before I got there, they told me. But Gabriel, the strangest thing happened. I decided to stop off at the Montecito on my way here. If Dutch was ignoring the phone, maybe he'd answer the doorbell. I got to the building entrance, and there was this funny little man staring at me. He said, 'Aren't you Lorna?' and I said, 'Yes, but who are you?' "

This did not strike me as a felicitous turn. I said, "Jean-Baptiste."

"Why didn't you mention him yesterday?"

"Actually, I alluded to him. When I said Jasper had been wrong about the machine being left for him to find. When I said I didn't want to make things too confusing for you."

"But we had the most interesting conversation, Gabriel." Her tone was completely ingenuous, and animated. As much as I dreaded hearing the details, I was heartened by her recovery from yesterday's terrible combination of bewilderment and melancholy. "He was sort of . . . cautious at first. He said Dutch had just gone out. He told me you and he were old friends, and he'd seen us together. Then he said he didn't suppose you really considered him a friend, but he valued your acquaintance very much. He wondered how much I knew about you, and I told him I knew a great deal. He asked me if I knew that you and he had an interest in common . . ."

Shall I summarize? Shall I say that as obstreperous as Jean-Baptiste had invariably been with me, he evidently had the ability to charm women, or at least to charm Lorna? That by the end of their conversation Lorna believed she'd been talking to an earnest young political activist from an unspecified point in the future? That Jean-Baptiste had convinced her that while the time machine technically belonged to him, he didn't object to my using it, as long as I'd return it one day soon? *That Jean-Baptiste had showed up at Dutch's apartment with a couple of bottles of good French wine, and the two of them—the twenty-second-century French punk and the disconsolate young actor—had stayed up until four in the morning swapping stories?*

Whatever trepidation I'd felt during Wadsworth's visit was inconsequential next to this. I could be virtually certain that by now Jean-Baptiste had concluded Dutch Reagan was indeed the younger version of Ronald Reagan. But what was Jean-Baptiste's game? I could pretty much discount the possibility he was just looking for a pal. Most likely he was cultivating Dutch to gain some leverage against me. But what sort? And perhaps the most pertinent question: what did he imagine *I* wanted with Dutch?

I said, "You wouldn't happen to know whether Jean-Baptiste told Dutch where he'd come from?"

"No," Lorna replied. "He was clear about that. He said Dutch thinks he's just an out-of-work French actor in Hollywood. He says Dutch is going to try to find him some work."

"Lorna," I said, "my darling, my dearest, I have to make something as clear as possible. Jean-Baptiste is someone you want to do your very best to avoid. He's a dangerous man. He's extremely smart. He stole two time machines that must have been very heavily guarded. At best he's a sociopath—"

She broke in, "He says you know almost nothing about him."

"Not for lack of trying."

"Well, he was perfectly forthcoming with me."

"Because he's trying to use you to get to me."

"For what? What does he want?"

"He wants the machine, for one thing. And he wants me to give him my computer, my little television, so he can make lots of money at the racetrack—"

"But that's what you use it for."

"On a small scale, for God's sake. Jean-Baptiste would probably own Santa Anita inside of a few weeks."

"What about the machine? Why don't you give it back to him?"

"I've told him I'll give it back the first of the year. I've told him I need to have it in December. I haven't told him why." It did not take her long to capture my reference; once again I saw the significance of something I'd said cast a pall upon her features.

37

On my way back to Malibu I stopped at the Montecito and pressed Dutch's buzzer, off and on, for fifteen minutes. There was no sign of him—or, for that matter, of Jean-Baptiste.

Dutch didn't come to work Wednesday morning. I reported this to Lorna, who drove to the Montecito around noon and experienced the same futility I had with the buzzer. But she went a step further. She buzzed the building manager, who came to the front door, and explained the situation to him. She had no trouble at all convincing the manager to let her into Dutch's apartment. Dutch was not there. The place showed few signs of a bacchanal or even a lonely binge. There were, to be sure, two empty wine bottles, but they had been carefully deposited—along with two banana skins and an empty pork-and-beans can—in the kitchen trash. There was a vaguely unpleasant odor in the bathroom, which Lorna guessed might have been the vestiges of vomit. The bed was not made, nor was it a mess. Everything else—clothing, laundry, family pictures, foodstuffs, Bible—seemed in its place. Lorna told me that evening, "I realized when I got out of there that I'd been breathing through my mouth the whole time I was there. It wasn't that it smelled so bad, except for the bathroom. It was kind of stuffy, but mainly, I think it's that it was . . . not seedy so much as déclassé."

When Dutch did turn up it was at our door. Lorna and I were both sound asleep at two in the morning; Dutch said he'd begun knocking, ended up pounding, at the door for half an hour. I was in my underwear and Dutch was a mess. He was bleary-eyed, with a two-day growth of beard; the odor of alcohol was faint, not nearly as potent as the smell of stale sweat. I invited him in and poked my head out the door. I was enveloped by darkness and silence, so Dutch hadn't pounded long or hard enough to wake the neighbors. Dutch's Nash, I noted, was nowhere to be seen.

"How did you get here?"

"Drove. But I ran out of gas a few miles back. By the time I realized the tank was almost empty I was in no-man's-land. You know how it is when the last station's seven or eight miles back and the next one's seven or eight miles ahead. Anyway, I had a good walk. Did some thinking. Boy, what a couple of days I've had."

Barefoot, I led him into the living room. Dutch wore khaki pants, a grimy white shirt, and a slightly crumpled fedora. He flopped onto the couch. "God, what a day. What a couple of days."

"I understand you ran into Jean-Baptiste."

"Did I ever. More like he ran into me." Dutch performed a mild double take. "Wait a minute—how did *you* know we were together?"

"Lorna went looking for you yesterday—Tuesday—afternoon. Jean-Baptiste saw her outside your building."

"I didn't even know they'd met."

"They hadn't until then. Jean-Baptiste said you'd gone out."

"Out?" Dutch chuckled. "Out like a light. I mentioned that I liked that French wine, so he showed up with a couple of bottles. Not as good as the stuff you've given me, but not bad."

"Hold on," I said. "How did you and he hook up in the first place?"

"After you and I talked on the phone Monday night. I was in pretty bad shape, I guess. Went out for a walk and there was this little guy who looked kind of familiar, but I sure couldn't place him. He said, 'Dutch?' and introduced himself, said he just happened to be wandering around the neighborhood. He invited me for a drink, anyway, and we went to this little place on Hollywood Boulevard. I asked if they had Château-something Sauterne, and the bartender just gave me a look. So I had a ginger ale, and we sat there talking for an hour or so. J-B seemed like a pretty decent fellow. Cheered me up. Then I went home and listened to 'Battle of the Sexes' on the radio, and the next thing you know, there he is with the wine."

"You didn't think that was a little unusual?"

"Sure I did. But I'm not going to turn a guy away. If I'd *known*, of course. We must've talked till four in the morning, and I just conked out. He promised he'd wake me at six, but I was out till noon. Then I staggered around for a while, called Brynie Foy, and went back to bed."

What had I done? What dismal state of mind had I imposed upon Dutch so he'd stay up all night with the likes of Jean-Baptiste? And what could they possibly have found to talk about? "You name it," Dutch said. "I hadn't realized J-B was an actor, for instance. Not bad at all. He did some classical stuff for me, in French, of course, and he does this terrific impression of Jimmy Cagney, with that French accent it's a scream."

"What else?"

"Well, we talked about you a lot. I told him all about *Felipe*, how you'd written the part for me and now this big-shot director wants to do it with Gary Cooper. I said I guessed when everything was said and done you did the right thing. I mean, how can you turn down an opportunity like that? I said you'd promised to do another picture with me, and J-B kind of laughed. He said I shouldn't trust you as far as I can throw you, words to that effect. He said you'd run some big double cross on him, but he wouldn't elaborate. Then the next minute he was going on about how he admired you and he wondered why you didn't like him."

"Did he offer any theories?"

"A few, at one point or another. Evidently there's a piece of property somewhere he feels belongs to him, and that bothers you. Then there's some business about your feeling guilty because a friend of his died, and you were responsible in some way. But what he kept coming back to was that he was a better artist than you, and you knew it, and you hated him for it."

In a scary way, this was quite entertaining—listening to Dutch, earnest and affable as always, bedraggled for perhaps the first time in his life, describe an encounter with a brilliant madman from another country and another century. Beyond that there were the elements of an excellent puzzle, as I tried to determine whether there was any significance to Jean-Baptiste's fabrications as filtered through Dutch's narrative.

Jean-Baptiste had been on his way out for more wine when Lorna arrived. When he returned he roused his new pal Dutch and coaxed him into taking a drive. They headed east in Dutch's Nash, sipping burgundy, taking turns driving. Dutch decided around Bakersfield—

after a quart or so of wine—that he should quit the movie business and return to the Midwest, get back into radio. Jean-Baptiste was asleep at the time, and didn't wake up until they were well into the Mojave Desert. He was furious, and accused Dutch of being in league with me, of driving him out into the desert to get rid of him, or kill him. Dutch assured him he was doing nothing of the kind, and Jean-Baptiste ordered him to turn the car around. Dutch pointed out that it was 3 A.M., they had a quarter tank of gas, and the nearest westward civilization was a hundred miles back. So they pressed on to Needles, just west of the Colorado River and Arizona. Jean-Baptiste wondered why the town had been named "Needless."

After filling the Nash's tank they went for coffee to the adjoining diner, and here Jean-Baptiste, in Dutch's words, "got a little loony." He began interrogating Dutch as to our relationship. Didn't Dutch think it was peculiar that someone like me—a world traveler, something of an intellectual—would be interested in someone like him, a second-rate actor from the provinces? Dutch let this pass, pointed out that we had major interests in common, and suggested that Jean-Baptiste and I were a far unlikelier pair by his estimation—whereupon Jean-Baptiste became all the more hostile and aggressive. He told Dutch that his intention in the first place had been to forge some sort of arrangement. He foresaw a great future for Dutch, he said, but only if Dutch kept his distance from me, as I would be nothing but a source of malevolence and doom. He had intended to offer to protect Dutch from me—for future considerations—but now that Dutch had insulted him, he was reconsidering.

At that, Jean-Baptiste stood up and headed for the men's room. And Dutch, sobered up and very much put off by Jean-Baptiste's sudden change of character, paid the check, left the diner, and returned solo to Los Angeles. "They kept announcing that Cubs score on the radio. Hartnett hits the homer with two out in the ninth, they win six-five, they take over first place. I had to celebrate that with somebody. And I figured I was going to get here around ten. So that's one reason I'm here. Also I wanted to apologize for Monday night. I wanted to make sure we're still friends. And I wanted to warn you that J-B's off his rocker."

"I'm the one who should be apologizing," I said. "Of course we're still friends. Thanks for the warning. And let's get some sleep. Let's make sure you have a job tomorrow." I found him a pillow and a blanket; I went upstairs to Lorna, who slept like a baby. Before drifting off myself, I treasured the image of an irascible, displaced French punk trying to find his way back from the Mojave.

———

I overslept. I had not set the alarm clock, but that should not have been a factor because I customarily operated without one and almost invariably awoke within five minutes of seven o'clock. Having a two-hour chunk extracted from my slumber by Dutch's arrival and subsequent performance could serve as an excuse, but similar interruptions in the past had not thrown me out of my rhythm. God knows how long I might have slept had Lorna not arisen at ten to prepare for a noon meeting with Michael Curtiz and found me unconscious next to her. At first she assumed I'd forgotten to tell her about my morning off; when she discovered Dutch comatose on the couch, she figured something might be awry.

I ate what little breakfast I could ingest while Dutch struggled to make himself presentable. He shaved and managed to fit into a shirt and a jacket of mine, but had to wear his own rumpled trousers. It was ten-thirty before we got going. Halfway to Santa Monica, on a bright and beautiful morning neither of us could appreciate, Dutch pointed out his Nash on the side of the road. We reached the studio at ten after eleven. Dutch trudged off toward the *Murder Plane* set, while I headed for my cubicle.

The remainder of the morning was uneventful. That Dutch had not shown up at my door seemed to fit the no-news-is-good-news category. I had just returned from a solitary lunch when I got a call from Bernie Wiseman, nominally still my boss. "Gabriel," he said, "J.L. wants to see you right away."

"Jack Warner? What about, Bernie? Do you know?"

"All I know is, I've got a message to tell you J.L. wants to see you right away. I'd suggest you get your ass over there. And Gabriel—will you get the goddamn boat out of my garage?"

What did I infer from Wiseman's curt tone? That I was slipping away from him, that I had graduated from meetings with Hawks and Wallis to an audience with the big boss.

———

Warner was not alone in his office. As I entered, there were two Holly-wood legends before me: J.L. behind his desk, his expression omi-nously sour, and my chum Hal Wallis, equally grim of visage, sitting in a leather-upholstered armchair beside Warner's desk. Wallis said, "Come on in, Gabriel." The office was vast, its carpet deep and plush. I traversed it as if slogging through a swamp, my eyes on the boss, who continued to glare at me with a malevolence that mystified and unnerved me. I stopped three feet in front of the desk, Warner before me, Wallis to my left.

Wallis said, "Have a seat, please." There was next to me a chair, done in cloth, considerably less elegant than the one Wallis occupied but much nicer than the guest chair in my own office. I sat. Wallis said, "This is Mr. Warner. I don't know whether you've met."

As if it could have been anyone else. "We haven't met," I said, and resisted adding that I suspected I would soon regret that we had. Warner's glower was unrelenting. He was a small man, on the chubby side, balding, with a thin mustache. He wore a blue suit that looked extremely expensive. Wallis said, "Gabriel, some things have come to our attention."

What things could these be, I wondered. How could anyone have figured out I'd stolen *Four O'Clock* from the future?

Jack Warner said, "Who the hell do you think you are, coming in here and trying to pull crap like this?"

I said, "I'm afraid I don't know what you're talking about." I was confident that I was not about to lose my composure.

Wallis resumed, "Regarding your script, *Operation: Rescue*—"

Warner interrupted him. "What do you think we are? A bunch of idiots? Bunch of born-yesterday slobs?"

I was beginning to feel like a spectator at some sort of nightmar-ishly surreal tennis match, turning now to my left as Wallis struck another lob: "We've discovered that there are certain parallels between one of your central characters and a real-life personage . . ." And turning back as Jack Warner volleyed: "You think we would make a picture about some Communist fairy?"

And everything became suddenly clear. I said, "This is Bill Wadsworth's doing, isn't it?" Obviously there would be no response from Warner. I directed my entreaty to Wallis. "You have to understand, this is a man who's very bitter. He has absolutely no grounds—"

Warner drowned me out: "I'll tell you who has grounds, kiddo. *I've* got grounds to fire you! Kick you off this lot! We're on the verge of signing contracts! We're starting the publicity on this! We're about to sign Howard Hawks, for Christ's sake, for your little piece-of-shit propaganda. Not just a *Communist*, for Christ's sake, but a fag to boot! You want me to be the laughingstock of pictures? You want pickets in front of every Warner Brothers theater from here to Manhattan?"

Warner paused, eyes bulging, face flushed. I said, "There are certain similarities, yes. But I had no intention whatsoever . . ."

I had failed to recognize that his pause was only the eye of the hurricane. Warner's voice gained ten decibels: "I've got a mind to call in the FBI on you, buster! There's plenty about you that's fishy enough to interest them! I'll never let you work again in this town, and they'll see to it that you never work again in this country!"

I got to my feet. I turned to Wallis, who was clearly not as emotionally affected by all this as his boss. "Could I speak to you later?"

He shrugged. "I'm afraid not. I think it would be a good idea if you cleaned out your office."

On my way out, I heard Warner say to Wallis, "Goddamn college boys will be the death of me."

I was furious at Wadsworth for being such a vindictive sap, equally furious at Jack Warner for being a gullible political ignoramus, most furious at myself for not having anticipated Wadsworth's moves. On the short walk from Warner's office to my own I ran through the usual postconfrontation recriminations, decided I had at least done nothing to be ashamed of in Warner's office, and moved somewhat shakily on to strategy. The first recourse that came to mind was the obvious one: I could undo everything inside a couple of hours. I could get in my Buick, drive to Beverly Hills, enter the Wiseman garage by hook or by crook, grab the machine, and haul it to Malibu. But how far back would I travel? I could retrogress a few days, be more careful with my copy of the script, keep it from Wadsworth's eyes. That wouldn't work. Wadsworth would learn the story eventually, and surely reveal the García Lorca connection as soon as he knew it. I could return to the beginning of September, rewrite the script so the Pablo character bore absolutely no resemblance to García Lorca, and proceed exactly as before. I could retrogress to late August, either not attend Charles's party or go but mention nothing about my movie to Howard Hawks, then stick to the original plan of producing it myself, with Dutch as Felipe.

Entering the writers' building, I thought: *What about the headache?* What if the headache that followed this retrogression were exponentially worse than the last one? What if it put me in the hospital for a month? What if it killed me?

Twenty feet from my office door, I thought: If I do go back, if I choose any of these stratagems, Lorna would revert to the state of ignorance that preceded my great confession, which would make things a lot easier for us.

Mere steps from my door, I thought: Do I even *need* to go back? Wouldn't the principled thing, the courageous thing, be to pick up the pieces from this moment—to fight the system, make *Operation: Rescue* with Dutch, perhaps even with Hawks, if he were still willing to do it as an independent production?

Steeped in indecision, I opened the door and was immediately conscious of someone sitting at my desk. For the briefest of moments I imagined it was Wadsworth, there to gloat. Would that it had been. But no—it was Dutch, accompanied by one of the bottles of Chassagne-Montrachet I'd bought Tuesday afternoon. He gave me a good-natured grin and said, "Hey, Gabriel, how're you doing?"

I snatched the Montrachet off my desk. Dutch had consumed just more than half of it, straight from the bottle. "That's great stuff," he said.

"You're damned right it is," I said. I set the wine down out of his reach. "Dutch, look—I'm not doing so well. I just got fired. How long have you been here?"

"Jesus," Dutch said. "*You* got fired? Hey, so did I!"

"Are you serious?"

Dutch stood up, a little wobbly. "Sure as hell am! Went down to talk to Brynie Foy. I was so damn apologetic, I mean sincere and promising I'd never do it again, telling him I'd just been through a really tough time. It was true, after all. He gave me a cold-blooded look, like I was some kind of bug you'd step on, told me I'd screwed up three days of shooting, they'd kicked me off the picture, and that was that. Said he runs a clockwork operation, there's no room for prima donnas."

"Dutch," I said, "did Foy just fire you from *Murder Plane*, or were you fired altogether?"

"Altogether." He managed a sad smile. "Warners terminated my contract. I get some kind of severance pay, I think. Say, Gabriel, since I don't exactly have any responsibilities for the rest of the day, how about passing back that bottle?"

"Not a chance," I said, and at that instant there was a sharp rap at my door. Lorna or Wadsworth, I guessed. The lady or the tiger. I turned and opened the door, to my great relief beheld Lorna. She said, "My God, I'm glad you're here." We embraced. She said, "Did you hear?"

"Dutch told me he'd been fired. I guess it's not all that surprising. Foy's a nice guy, but he's got a business to run."

Lorna shook her head. "Foy kicked him off the picture, Gabriel, but it wasn't Foy who fired him."

"Foy told you that?"

"He said the order came from on high. I kept asking him what he meant by 'on high,' but he wouldn't tell me."

"I've got an idea," I said. "Because Jack Warner just fired me."

She jerked back her head in astonishment. "No!"

"You were right about our friend Bill," I said. "He stole my copy of the script, figured out the García Lorca angle, and told Warner I was a Communist agent. He must have included Dutch in the plot."

"And Warner *believed* him?"

"Apparently so. Are you sure you've still got a job? They might be thinking about birds of a feather . . ."

"And I might just quit," Lorna said.

"No," I said. "That's the last thing you should do."

Dutch, who had been observing us from behind my desk, said, "Hey, why *doesn't* she quit? Then we could all make *Felipe*."

Lorna said, "That's not such a bad idea, Gabriel."

It wasn't at that, and it would serve Warner Brothers right if their budding star left them in the lurch. But would they care? Wouldn't Bernie Wiseman just plug Ann Sheridan into *Four O'Clock*? And if they did care, wouldn't they sue Lorna into tiny pieces? I said, "Let's not get carried away. There's no reason you should jeopardize your career. If it works out that we can all do *Operation: Rescue*, wonderful. Maybe *Four O'Clock* could even give you some leverage."

Dutch said, "But what the hell am *I* going to do in the meantime?"

"Sober up, for one thing."

Dutch said, "What I'd like to do right now is finish that wine. I've already been fired. Who gives a damn if I have a few drinks?"

"Look," I said, "you've got to pick up your car and drive it back to Hollywood. I don't want you killing yourself, or someone else. For now, why don't we forget about the wine? Why don't we forget about Warner Brothers? It's a beautiful day. Let's go back to Malibu. We could stop at Dutch's apartment on the way. Let's change our clothes, go out and have a swell dinner somewhere, and talk about the future."

There was no argument.

38

The trip from the studio to Dutch's apartment was one of those drives that by 1994 had become anywhere from extremely unpleasant to virtually impossible. Did one choose to stay on clogged city arteries, or did one elect the Hollywood Freeway and the potential of utter immobility? But in 1938 it was a piece of cake, and a delectable one at that: skirting Forest Lawn on Barham Boulevard, up through the hills to Cahuenga Boulevard, then south on precisely the route the freeway would take, past the reservoir and then the great stretch (much greater then) of greenery around the Hollywood Bowl.

I started out in the lead, Dutch in my passenger seat, and Lorna seemed content to follow. I imagined that was one propitious result of my revelations: although her accident had not occurred until December of the 1938 I learned about in my travels, why tempt fate? So went my thinking until—a couple of miles from the Bowl—I got behind a slow-moving truck and was startled to see Lorna's little SS whiz by us both on the right.

There ensued an extended semi-chase. I didn't want her to get too far ahead because, as adeptly as she drove, she did have a tendency to start thinking about something else and forget where she was going. So as she darted in and out of traffic I stayed a respectable distance behind, caught up at stoplights, made the occasional aggressive move myself, and never lost her.

In the cozy afternoon sun we drove with our respective tops down. At one point, when Lorna eased past a big truck by squeezing— barely—between its bulk and the sidewalk, Dutch said, "You're worried about me killing myself when I've had a few drinks. I'd say Lorna's more of a problem when she's sober."

A block later, I had to get by the same truck, but there was room on the left by now. Dutch held down his fedora as I accelerated. I said, "She takes chances, but she knows what she's doing. She's a hell of a driver."

"I think I could've been too if I had the eyesight," Dutch said. "I've got pretty darn good coordination. I just can't see a damn thing. These glasses are all right for some stuff, but I can never tell how far away things are."

"Maybe you need a new prescription."

"Could be. I got these back in Des Moines."

We reached the park around the Bowl, on whose periphery there was a sort of sporting cavalcade—adjacent games of football, soccer, and baseball, several of each, as far as the eye could see. At the top of a little rise I noted that some two hundred yards ahead of us there had been some kind of minor accident: a couple of cars stood at odd angles, and behind them both southbound lanes were stopped. Lorna had evidently taken notice of this as well; she had pulled to the left, into the uninhabited outer northbound lane, at about thirty miles per hour, apparently intending to cruise by the stalled traffic and the accident, then cut back into southbound lanes.

I remember thinking this was a maneuver that would leave her on her own, one that I did not intend to imitate. I recall that Dutch had been discussing the magic nature of California seasons—how on a warm late September afternoon these kids could be playing football and baseball with equal propriety, not to mention soccer, whereupon he had gone off into a tipsy speculation on whether he might in different circumstances have been destined to be a great soccer player like Felipe, instead of a second-string lineman for a small college in Illinois.

My attention, if I might understate, was divided. I was watching Lorna with more than a little agitation; I was braking the Buick, preparing to take my place at the back of the line; I was listening to Dutch, thinking how marvelously absurd it was that he should fantasize about all these things he could have been, sitting here next to me, who was nigh on to preventing him from becoming what he should be, which was something far grander than any of his fantasies.

This is all to say that I was paying no attention, none at all, to the rearview mirror. So I was startled when a car flew by on the left, its driver evidently intent on duplicating Lorna's maneuver. "Boy," said

Dutch, "another crazy one." The car, a black sedan, appeared to be gaining speed rapidly as it moved away from us. Not three seconds after his previous sentence, Dutch spoke again. "Hey, I recognize that car! Isn't that your friend J-B?"

God, could it be? I had never made a definitive sighting of Jean-Baptiste's car, knew only that it was a black Chevrolet, five or six years old. If he had been following us, why would he now so ostentatiously have pulled ahead? Had he suddenly remembered an urgent appointment? Or was this in fact not Jean-Baptiste, but Wadsworth's detective? That confusion had occurred before. The possibility I was avoiding was that Jean-Baptiste had inexplicably, unfathomably decided to do harm to Lorna. But surely there was no way the black Chevrolet would even catch up to the little SS, which had a hundred-yard lead.

As the Buick came to a complete halt, I watched in rising horror as Lorna quite perversely slowed down. Perhaps she was doing so in anticipation of the intersection just beyond the accident, or to see if anyone needed help, or simply to have a good look at damage done. Whatever the case, she had cut her speed by half and from my excellent vantage point I could see the huge Chevrolet bearing down on her.

"What d'you suppose he's up to?" Dutch said, a touch of apprehension in his voice.

I turned the wheel sharply left, pulled the Buick into the northbound lane, pressed the accelerator to the floor. Lorna was past the accident now, and the SS had picked up speed, but the Chevrolet was no more than sixty or seventy feet behind her. Irrationally, I pounded my horn, as if Lorna could hear or would take notice if she did. Drivers gestured angrily as Dutch and I roared by. Lorna was moving gradually back into the southbound lanes; I guessed that if the Chevrolet ran full force into the rear of the SS it would send the little topless car hurtling over the curb, whereupon Lorna would at best be propelled through the windshield.

Just as we passed the accident, the Chevrolet caught the SS. The big car cruised alongside the little one for a second, and I imagined that my fears had been groundless, preposterous. Then the Chevrolet swerved into the southbound lane occupied by the SS. "Good God," Dutch shouted, "he's trying to kill her!"

Contact was made. The SS lurched to the right and began fishtailing. The Chevrolet proceeded straight ahead as if it had run over something insignificant. In retrospect I cannot say with precision how far we were behind the collision—fifty yards, seventy-five, a hundred. I could swear that I felt my heart stop, and I know I vowed that Jean-Baptiste, lunatic or not, would not go unpunished.

The little sports car came within inches of hitting the curb on the right side of the highway; had it done so, still traveling at considerable speed, it would certainly have flipped over. But Lorna corrected, only to have the SS swerve back into the northbound lanes, now occupied by a cluster of cars coming toward her. Had it not been for the opposing traffic, I think she would have pulled out of it unscathed. As it was, she was denied the option of straightening out and staying on the road, was forced to keep going into the park.

She hit the curb head-on. The SS became airborne but stayed level. It hit the ground rear wheels first, skidded twenty feet on dry grass, and stopped at the edge of a soccer game.

"Wow!" Dutch said. "How in hell did she manage that?"

I waited for the procession to pass, pulled across the northbound lanes, and eased the Buick up on the grass. Dutch said, "You want me to go ahead and try to catch him?"

"No," I said, getting out of the car, taking the ignition key. "We're all right. Everything's all right."

Dutch raced up the slight incline and got to Lorna first; I arrived four or five seconds later. She was surrounded by curious, uniformed soccer players, who chatted among themselves in Spanish. She was trembling, breathing heavily, telling Dutch she wasn't hurt. I opened the door of the SS and helped her out, sitting her down on the grass. An athletically built Hispanic man about Dutch's height and age said to him, "She's all right? She ain't hurt?"

"She's fine," Dutch replied.

I crouched next to Lorna on the grass. "That was amazing."

"What?"

"What you did."

"Almost getting myself killed?"

"The way you reacted. The way you didn't get yourself killed."

Dutch said to the soccer player, "See? She's hunky-dory. Hey, do you fellows need another player?"

The Hispanic man shook his head. The ball was at his feet; Dutch picked it up and drop-kicked it about eighty feet straight up. Had he meant to do that? It was impressive, in any case. Upon its descent the ball was caught by another player, who grinned and flipped it back to Dutch.

Lorna said, "All I remember is seeing that car come out of nowhere and . . . *whack!* I think I'll be all right in a minute."

I touched her forehead, which seemed unnaturally cool. Was she in shock? Did she know it was Jean-Baptiste who'd tried to murder her? Should she be permitted to drive home? Was the SS even ambulatory?

Dutch, who appreciated an audience, gave the soccer ball another prodigious vertical punt, to the amusement of the assembled players. There was a scramble to catch the ball this time, and the winner, a short and wiry copper-skinned man, elected to put on a little show of his own. He flipped the ball in the air, bounced it straight up off his head, caught it so it wedged between his toes and his lower shin, elevated it again, and proceeded to carom it off various upper body parts—shoulders, elbows, chin, nose—never using his hands. He let the ball drop and did a little dribbling routine, a sleight-of-foot that lasted about a minute and ended with a backward kick that sent the ball lazily toward Dutch's midsection.

Half-drunk as he was, Dutch caught the ball one-handed, then cradled it so he could applaud the performer. The rest of the players had doubtless seen the act before and stood impassively. It was about time to resume the game. Dutch spoke to his original correspondent, "Do you need another player?"

The man shook his head. "We have two teams. We have a game."

"I know that," Dutch said. "Would you mind another player?"

Lorna said to me, "He doesn't know how to play, does he?"

I said, "Dutch, I think he's saying it's an official game of some sort. They're not just fooling around."

Dutch let the ball drop, kicked it with his right foot three or four feet in the wrong direction, toward the road. He trotted after it, kicked it laterally with his left foot. Perhaps he was hoping the players would chase him, that he would somehow be absorbed into the game. There were murmurings from the crowd, words I understood, like *gringo* and *borracho.* I called out, "Dutch, bring back the ball, for God's sake."

But he continued to play his own game, kicking the ball in a direction fairly parallel to Cahuenga Boulevard, wandering farther from the assembled players, among whom there was now much annoyed conversation. After a minute or so, the performer set out in Dutch's direction, loping after him until he mimicked Dutch's shadow, this dark little figure moving parallel to the tall, ungainly North American. With the deftest of moves the soccer player extended his left foot ever so briefly in front of Dutch's right, so Dutch went tumbling to the grass while his antagonist never even broke stride.

Where was the ball?

Underneath Dutch, evidently. Lorna said, "Go see if he's all right." I said, "Are *you* all right?" She said, "I'm fine."

I hastened to Dutch's side. The performer greeted me with a shrug. Dutch was struggling to breathe, and I realized immediately that he'd fallen on the ball and had the wind knocked out of him. Nothing serious. I said to the performer, "*Está bien. No hay problema.*" And he replied, "Please, the ball."

Dutch rolled off it, clutched it, got to his knees, gave me a big smile. "That's always scary. You think you're never going to breathe again." His glasses were askew; he took them off and handed them up to me. He said, "Is that left lens cracked?"

"No. But they're a little bent. Probably fixable." I stood above him. "They want the ball, Dutch. Let's get out of here."

He stood up, holding the ball. The performer extended his hands for it, but Dutch ignored him. He set up for a kick. I assumed his plan was simply to send the ball back to the crowd of players near the SS, but he let loose with another mighty punt, evidently intending to break his previous altitude record.

He had caught it wrong, however—kicked it off the top of his foot instead of the toe, so instead of going straight up it went up and backward. I watched the ball soar toward the road; at its apogee it appeared to get a little push from the wind, negating any doubt there might have been about its destination. I watched the ball; I watched Dutch watching the ball, watched the performer watching the ball. The two men broke almost simultaneously into pursuit. The ball landed exactly in the middle of Cahuenga Boulevard and took a prolific bounce toward the southbound lanes.

The performer was fast and sober, Dutch drunk and blind as a bat, but Dutch was a competitor. Where grass met pavement, the performer slowed cautiously while Dutch seemed to accelerate, nearly catching up. There was no northbound traffic. The ball's second bounce carried it to the edge of the southbound lanes. Midway across the road, the performer came to an abrupt stop. What had he seen? From where I stood, only about fifty feet of the southbound lanes were visible; the accident and the traffic behind it were just out of sight. I felt a shudder of foreboding.

The ball had come to rest just beyond the curb, so Dutch was perhaps thirty feet from his goal when the car first came into view and I shouted his name. He did not respond. In the next instant I realized that the car, coming quite irrationally fast, was a black sedan, a Chevrolet, and now I called Dutch's name in as loud a voice as I had ever managed, hoping that if he heard me he would take notice of the car and dive for the roadside. The performer, having taken several backward steps in my direction, also yelled at Dutch, but neither of us could break through his absolute concentration on the soccer ball.

Hoping against hope that this could be some other black Chevrolet, whose drunk or absent-minded driver might at the last second avert impact, I shifted my attention the following instant back to the car, and made the incontrovertible identification of its driver. I thought: *Is he doing this for my benefit, or because Dutch left him stranded in the desert?*

I will spare you details of the collision. Suffice it to say that Jean-Baptiste was driving at least forty miles per hour when he hit Dutch and no one, not the hugest first-string lineman, could have bested that Chevrolet's grille.

I was first to reach Dutch after the performer, who simply said, "Dead." I checked for a pulse, found none. The performer said, "He crazy? Why he want to be crazy? We just want to play football." Most of the soccer players convened around Dutch's corpse. I crossed Cahuenga and rejoined Lorna, who said, "He's dead, isn't he?" I replied that he was. I said, "It was Jean-Baptiste. First he tried for you. Then he got Dutch."

She looked at me in horror. "That was Jean-Baptiste who tried to run me off the road? Why would he have done that?"

"I'm not sure. I can only guess."

I was not far into my guessing before the police arrived. A motorcycle officer had shown up to direct traffic around the accident up the road; one of the soccer players alerted him to the fatality down the road. The officer, a tall, stout man with a dissipated cast, was intrigued by the presence of Lorna's car on the grass, mine on the sidewalk, and briefly quite suspicious that we were somehow involved in the pedestrian death. A cursory investigation showed that our vehicles had hit no one. He wondered why the dead man, our friend, had been playing ball with "a bunch of Mexicans." We explained, evidently to his satisfaction. I described the car that had struck Dutch.

"Did you get a look at the driver?"

I stole a glance at Lorna; she moved her lips ever so slightly—telling me, I thought, that this was up to me. I said, "A man about thirty. Short dark hair." Lorna said nothing.

The policeman said, "All right. We'll put that on the radio right away. And as for you . . ." He looked impassively at Lorna. ". . . I should cite you for reckless driving, but since it's your friend that got killed, I guess you've got enough problems."

Delicately put, I thought.

We waited for the ambulance to pick up Dutch's body. Lorna said, "Shouldn't we do something? Shouldn't we call the studio? Shouldn't we try to get in touch with his parents?" I held her. I kept holding her. On this hot afternoon her skin still seemed unusually cool. She said, "Why didn't you tell them it was Jean-Baptiste?"

"It's complicated." Her expression indicated I would not get off so easily. "If I'd told the police I knew him, I would have had to explain an awful lot."

"You would?"

"At some point, yes."

"I think I understand," Lorna said. "You're going to use the machine again, aren't you?"

39

She convinced me that she was capable of driving, and it turned out she was right. I followed her back to Malibu, and she never exceeded the speed limit, never made an aggressive move. We passed Dutch's Nash sitting forlorn on the shoulder of the highway in Santa Monica. It had been there with its top down seventeen hours, give or take, without being vandalized or towed away. It could remain untouched another seventeen hours, or seventeen days, I imagined.

At the house, she said, "Tell me what you'd do."

"I'd get on the machine. I'd set it to go back a specific amount of time. Jasper seems to have fixed the controls so they work perfectly. In a flash I'd be there."

"And everything's back the way it was? So Dutch not only wouldn't be dead, he wouldn't be fired. You wouldn't be fired."

"Exactly."

"It seems so . . . unnatural," Lorna said. "It seems like cheating. Things didn't turn out right this time around, so I'll just go back and change them."

"It could be used improperly," I said. "I don't think I've done that. I've been here since March and I've used the machine just once, when Dutch died the first time . . ."

"And you got that headache. I thought *you* were going to die. What if that happens again?"

"The thought has occurred to me. There are all sorts of possible reasons for the headache. The first three times I used the machine— two little experiments and then the trip here—I felt euphoric after- ward. I felt wonderful. Then in less than two days I went to 1984 and all the way back here. The most obvious explanation is that after a forty-six-year trip I should have waited longer before using the machine again. Now it's been almost six months."

"But you're just guessing, Gabriel. Really, you have no idea what to expect, do you?"

"I don't. But Dutch is *dead*, for God's sake, and it's my fault. If I killed him, shouldn't I unkill him?"

"I'm not sure," Lorna said. "If he keeps dying, then maybe he's supposed to die. Maybe it's inevitable."

"But it didn't happen the first time around."

"Maybe once things are changed, it's impossible to change them back. Maybe the fact that you've intruded on Dutch's life means that he's destined to die no matter how many times you go back."

It was an extremely tempting notion. If I could come to terms with my conscience, I would have fulfilled my promise to Hudnut. Ronald Reagan would have ceased to exist on September 29, 1938, and history be damned. I could live out my own life with Lorna. I could call Howard Hawks tomorrow, see if he and Gary Cooper were still interested in *Operation: Rescue*, as an independent production or for some other studio. "Maybe you're right," I said.

"Or maybe I'm not," Lorna replied. "I don't know what to think."

I called Bernie Wiseman at home. He did not mention Dutch, so I felt no obligation to do so. How odd that would seem if the newspapers mentioned me as an eyewitness, but surely they wouldn't. Even if they did, if I retrogressed that too would be irrelevant. I got to Beverly Hills at six-thirty, once again squeezed the machine into the Buick, got back to Malibu at quarter to eight, stashed the A-4 back in its old, longtime home in the garage.

The "swell" dinner we were going to have with Dutch turned into left-over chicken. We finished one bottle of Châteauneuf-du-Pape, got through a third of another. Still, neither of us could sleep. Invariably when I drifted off I would be awakened by the intrusion of some violent image into my unconscious, or by Lorna turning over in bed as if she had just flipped an invisible opponent in a private wrestling match. We carried on a fragmented conversation throughout the night.

"If you did use the machine," she asked me at one or two in the morning, "how far back would you go?"

"I'm not sure. I've been thinking about the day I told Wiseman I couldn't do the picture unless Dutch played Felipe. I hadn't met Hawks, I hadn't written the script. I'd already promised the part to Dutch, but he hadn't become so attached to the character. I could have the same conversation with Wiseman, up to the point that he laughs at my suggestion of Dutch. Then I give in. But I give in on the condition that I can write a movie for Dutch in the future. Then I report all that to Dutch, who's obviously affected by it, but not nearly as much as if I let it get as far as it did."

Lorna wondered why I needed to go so far back. Why couldn't I just return to the night of the party, meet Hawks, neglect to mention my idea to him? Then, the next time Wiseman brought the subject up, I could tell him I'd changed my mind, that as far as I was concerned Edward G. Robinson could play Felipe. I told Lorna this struck me as a fine alternative.

Much later, she said, "If you go back, if you do either of those things we were talking about before, I wouldn't know about any of this, would I?"

"No. Everything that occurred after that point would be erased. You'd have no knowledge of it."

She was silent for so long that I assumed, or I hoped, she'd gone to sleep. Then she said, "We wouldn't have had our conversation. I wouldn't know about you."

"I'd have to tell you again."

"Would you?"

I'd been fantasizing about how much easier things would be if she *didn't* know. "Of course I would."

"But if everything went perfectly, you wouldn't need to."

All of this had occurred to me, of course. I said, "I'd still have Bill to worry about. All the Princeton nonsense."

"That's true," she said.

A great deal later, she said, "Gabriel, the same way this all seemed so preposterous that first night you told me, now I can't imagine that you're going to *obliterate* a period of time we lived together. It makes my skin crawl."

"I don't have to do it," I said. "But I think I should. I think both of us are going to feel lousy about Dutch forever."

"What if he just dies again?"

"Then we'll let it lie. We could agree to that. If Dutch dies again, I won't go back again. We could agree that this is the last time."

She was silent for an extended moment. "But I wouldn't *know* we'd made that agreement. That would be erased, too."

"I'd have to tell you that as well, when I told you about me and the machine."

"But would it make any sense to me, out of context?"

"I don't know. I can't be sure."

A minute went by, and another. "What about me, Gabriel? What if I die in December?"

"Why do you even ask? Of course I'll go back."

"Again and again? If I'm just not supposed to live?"

"It's not as if you're *doomed*, for God's sake. That's just superstition, just nonsense."

But wasn't there a huge flaw in my reasoning, if I could accept the possibility of inevitable short-term death for Dutch, but not for Lorna? Through the next silence I anticipated such a reponse. But when she spoke she said, "I don't want you to go. All this frightens me, and I don't want you to go."

"Then I won't go," I replied.

Just after sunrise, Lorna fell into a deep slumber. I too must have gone to sleep at some point, because all of a sudden the alarm clock read eight-thirty. I felt neither refreshed nor as if there were any prospect for further sleep. I got dressed, went downstairs, found the *Times* outside the front door. The banner headline read: FOUR-POWER PEACE PACT SIGNED. Britain, France, Germany, and Italy were the signatories; the Sudetenland was ceded to Hitler. What else? Errol Flynn had been stricken with a severe respiratory illness; his temperature for the past several days had fluctuated between 101 and 104; he might be forced to sit out the western *Four O'Clock*; a copy of the script had been sent to Cary Grant. In Chicago, the Cubs had beaten the Pirates, 10–1, to sweep their three-game series and assume a one-and-a-half-game lead. Dutch would have been pleased, might yet be. And ah, Dutch—on page three of the second section sat the one-column story about a hit-and-run fatality on Cahuenga Boulevard, the victim's identity being withheld pending notification of next of kin.

I had an urge, a strong one, to get on the machine that minute, set it to take me back a month, and let the chips fall where they may. I'd promised Lorna I wouldn't leave against her wishes, but if I went she'd never know that.

I couldn't bring myself to do it.

I made myself some toast, spread marmalade on it, barely got it down while finishing the paper. What was I going to do with myself until Lorna arose? I remembered my Del Mar winnings. Was my roll of cash still in the night table, or had Wadsworth somehow made off with it as well?

Upstairs, Lorna slept on her side, motionless and angelic. The money was precisely where I'd left it, although the roll seemed a mite less thick than before. But how many weeks had it been since I'd touched it? And was there any sense to putting it in the bank *now*? If I used the machine, the money would zip right back into its drawer. On the other hand, I had nothing better to do, and there was still a strong possibility I wouldn't use the machine.

I put on a jacket and tie and drove into Santa Monica, stopped at the Bank of America on Third Street, just off Santa Monica Boulevard. In my original era I had denied this concern my business for a variety of political reasons; whatever those sins were, they wouldn't be committed in the next quarter century, so I reckoned it was all right to take my money there now.

In the car, discreetly, I counted to 18,560. I'd cleared just about twenty thousand, but handed over five hundred to Jean-Baptiste. Still, that left me nearly a thousand short. I counted again, same result. This confounded me sufficiently so that I chose not to enter the bank.

Dead tired but full of nervous energy, I drove around Santa Monica without strategy, doing errands. I picked up cleaning, bought wine, filled the Buick's tank, bought a good-looking chicken at the butcher shop, bought some beans and some artichokes, all of this using minuscule fractions of my bankroll. At the Laurie Smith Grocery on Fourth Street, my last stop, I stuffed change from a twenty into my right pants pocket, which was home as well to the mother lode. I removed the latter and—subtly as possible—shifted it to the vest pocket of my jacket, where I felt a slight obstruction, a newspaper clipping. In the car, I unfolded it and read the headline: ACTOR DROWNS OFF CATALINA. I hadn't worn the jacket since that day, that extraneous twentieth of March. Wasn't this all too funny?

Lorna was up, sitting cross-legged on the porch swing with a glass of orange juice. She told me she'd called Information for Dutch's parents' number. She'd been about to call them, wondering what exactly she was going to say, when she decided she'd been wrong. "Even if he is just going to die again," she said, "it's not for us to decide that he shouldn't have another chance, is it?"

"I wouldn't say so."

"I mean, you could really argue either way, couldn't you? You could say that it's not right for us to defy nature and bring him back, but then you could say, with just as much merit, it's not for us to deprive him of another chance if it's in our power to provide it. Especially because he'd still be alive if it hadn't been for us."

"For me," I said.

"I had a part in it."

"Not a very big part. I don't think it's something that should be on your conscience."

"Whether it should be or not, it's there."

I sat down next to her, put my right arm around her as the swing pitched in clumsy reaction. I said, "I'll go back, then?"

"I wish you didn't have to. I don't want you risking your life."

"I won't be."

"But you don't *know* that, do you?"

"I'm awfully sure. Positive."

"So you'll just go in the garage, sit on that thing, turn the dials, and you'll disappear, and I'll be none the wiser. Then in no time at all you'll reappear somewhere—"

"In exactly the same place."

"In the garage, but somewhere else in time, and no one will notice that you've just sort of dropped in—"

"No more than you did last time. The question is, how far back do I go?"

She considered. The swing creaked gently; the ocean, not a hundred feet away, lapped softly. Lorna said, "Just far enough to bring Dutch back."

"Then there'd be a good chance everything would just happen all over again. I should go back at least to last Monday, last weekend to be safe. I should tell Wallis to go to hell, then I can call Dutch and tell him about it."

"No. That was before you told me everything. I don't want to have to go through that again. Couldn't you just go back to that night, before Dutch called?"

"Aren't we doing this so Dutch can live? If I go back too far, I can always tell you everything again. If I don't go back far enough, he's just going to start the same cycle."

After a while, Lorna said, "You're right."

I kissed her. "Do I go now?"

"You don't have to go right away, do you? Couldn't we have some lunch? Couldn't we make love one more time?"

Indeed, there seemed no reason whatsoever for me to go right away. On the other hand, it wasn't as if I'd be going away, leaving Lorna behind. I'd simply be rejoining her back on September 20, or thereabouts.

On the way to Venice there yet again was Dutch's Nash, sitting on the roadside awaiting a master who was not to return. This, too, would be undone. Our destination, of course, was Jack's, where we'd had our first dinner, where we'd then celebrated Lorna's being on the verge of getting the part in *Four O'Clock*. What a pity it was that our senti-mental choice had such miserable food. I couldn't even afford to wash down my soggy rigatoni with a decent bottle of wine. Exhausted as I was, I'd need to be fairly alert when I got where I was going in an hour or two. Lorna, who was under no such constraints, had ordered a half bottle of Chianti Classico. When I asked Lorna how her osso bucco was, she said, "Forgettable."

I laughed. She said, "What's funny?"

"It couldn't be much more forgettable. Even if this were the great-est meal you've ever had, you'd still be about to forget it."

"My God, that's right. Everything I've done in the last ten days is about to be erased. Everything I do in the next hour. I could take my clothes off and run around the restaurant. I could hit the waiter with a saucer."

"Not while I'm here," I said.

"You could tell me things, Gabriel. You could tell me things I don't want to know, because I'm not going to know them. When does the war start?"

"I'm not going to talk about the war."

"Why not? I'm not going to remember it."

"Because you're not going to feel like making love if I do."

"Then don't." Her giddiness was interrupted only briefly. "But tell me something else. Tell me something about 1994."

I thought for a bit. "The best cars are Japanese. Leningrad has been renamed Saint Petersburg. Most people have machines that answer their telephones when they're not home. Almost everyone has a television, or several televisions, and a machine that records television programs and plays them back at your leisure. There are lots of angry, unstable countries with weapons that could end the world pretty fast. It's fashionable for young men to wear baseball caps backwards, and young women to have rings in their noses. Negroes are called African-Americans, and African-American men tend to shave their heads. It's not permitted to smoke in most public places. Men have walked on the the moon, but no one cares about that too much. Newspapers and candy bars cost fifty cents. You can fly from Los Angeles to New York in five hours, but the food is terrible."

"Are there cures for all the worst diseases?"

"Some. Not cancer. And there are some horrible new diseases that outperform a lot of the old ones."

"Do people still go to the movies?"

"Not quite as much, but Hollywood's still going strong."

"And Jasper's a famous scientist?"

"Not famous, really. Well, maybe in 1984 he is, in the future where Dutch doesn't become president. But in the one where Dutch does, Jasper's just kind of a brilliant eccentric."

She paused, as if standing before a vast banquet table with lots of mysterious food. She said, "Is 1994 terrible?"

"No, it isn't terrible. I remember, when I was a boy in the late fifties and early sixties, there was a notion that technology was something that would make our lives much easier. There were little films, shorts shown before movies, about kitchens in which everything would be done automatically, and vacuum cleaners that would find their own way around these lovely modern houses, and cars that could be programmed to drive you home while you slept in the back seat . . ."

"And those things didn't happen?"

"No, most of them did, or they will. But the part about technology making our lives easier was wrong. It made our lives a lot more complicated, because there was so much more to do. And because there was so much more to *know*. I mean, at this very moment in 1938, there are probably hundreds of gruesome things happening all around the world, but we don't know about them. As far as we're concerned they haven't happened. That's what's so terrible about 1994. Technology has gone nuts and come up with all these marvelous ways of telling us exactly what's happening ten thousand miles away, but human nature hasn't improved a bit. So we get instant access to mass murders in Nebraska and tribal massacres in Africa, and there's still not a damned thing we can do about it."

The waiter brought our check. I reached for my cash and felt the newspaper clipping again. I offered it to Lorna. "Here's a souvenir," I said.

She unfolded it as I had several hours earlier. Her expression contained pain and puzzlement as she read. She said, "Isn't this from a day that was erased, so it never took place? Why didn't the newspaper story disappear along with everything else?"

"Because I had it. It was in my pocket when I used the machine."

"And what now? Will it disappear when you go back this time?"

"I have no idea," I said. "Jasper's got the manual, and he's fifty-six years from here."

40

It seemed to me—or perhaps it only seems to me in retrospect—that there was an element of melancholy in our lovemaking, as if we were in fact about to part for an extended period. To be sure, both of us were tired, and a friend had just been killed, if only temporarily. I lay supine, Lorna on her side, her head on my chest. I said, "Don't let me fall asleep."

"Why not?"

"Because I've got a feeling I should get going."

"Why? What difference does it make when you go? Won't it be better if you've had some sleep when you get there?"

She didn't have to twist my arm.

The next thing I knew, she was shaking me awake. My first perception was that it was still broad daylight. I said, "What's the matter?"

Lorna stood over me, wearing only her unbuttoned shirt. "Charles and Sally are here. And the kids. I completely forgot."

"I thought they were coming tomorrow."

"I know. They called yesterday. With everything going on, I completely forgot."

I was confused by Lorna's state of agitation. "But what's the problem? They know we sleep together."

"The machine. Don't you want to use the machine?"

"Is something wrong with it?"

"No, Gabriel. They're *here*! Don't we have to figure out some way to get rid of them?"

I sat up. "No. It's fine. I could tell them: Look, I'm from fifty years in the future and this is my time machine, and they wouldn't remember anything."

She sat down. "Oh, God, I keep forgetting that part." She laughed.

Lorna preceded me downstairs, then reappeared just as I was about to descend. "Gabriel, Charles says he has to talk to you about something extremely serious." This was not good timing, and given the circumstances it was within the bounds of reason for me to tell Charles to go to hell. But Charles had been more than fair to me, had accommodated me in more ways than one.

I met him in the living room, where it was the just the two of us. He was uncharacteristically ill at ease, making compulsive steeples with his fingers. Had he had some sort of unsettling encounter with Jean-Baptiste?

He reached for a little brown envelope on the sofa arm, and handed it to me. "These are a gift from Charlie, for you and Lorna."

I looked inside and saw several photographs. "Snapshots from the party," Charles said. "Some quite good ones, I'd say." I had a quick peek: Lorna and Hawks in the house; Lorna, Hawks, and me on the porch; Lorna, Hawks, and Charles on the edge of the sand. "Very nice," I said. "He's got some talent."

Charles cleared his throat. "There's another matter, Gabriel," he began earnestly. "Could you tell me whether you might be missing a large sum of money?"

I was relieved, and surprised to the point that I almost answered in the negative. When I finally spoke I blurted out, "About a thousand dollars?"

Charles blanched. "Oh boy." He stared at the floor. "He's spent a hundred of it, then." Charles took a step toward me, reached in his pocket, brought out cash, extended it to me. "Nine hundred," he said. "I'm terribly sorry, Gabriel. He's fundamentally a good boy, I'm convinced. He just can't resist temptation."

I dropped the photos, took the money, stuffed it in my own pocket, where it rejoined its extended family. "And I could be wrong about the thousand, Charles. It might only have been nine-twenty, nine-thirty . . ."

Charles looked sadly into my eyes. "I assure you, this won't happen again."

Lorna was in the kitchen with Sally. We all chatted briefly, then Lorna and I sidled into the garage. There was a conspicuous absence, you might say. The Hudnut Packard was there, but not my machine. "Jesus!" I said, and Lorna let out a gasp. I checked for the laptop: still in its hiding place. Lorna hastened back to the kitchen; I followed, got there just as Sally was replying to Lorna's question about Gabriel's boat. "Oh," she exclaimed, "Charlie! He's jumped the gun. He and Charles built something. They spent hours on it. An adapter so they could fit an outboard motor on that boat, I think. But Charlie wasn't supposed to do anything until we asked your permission . . ."

I was already out the porch door when Sally finished her sentence. I sprinted along the beach, wondering about the effects of saltwater on twenty-second-century plastics and their attendant electronics. There were children, many of them, down by the water, which at low tide was quite far away. Charlie had required not just his two little brothers but several older, bulkier boys to drag the machine and the outboard all the way here. No doubt they had been planning this little experiment for weeks.

I skidded to a stop like a cartoon character. The machine was listing thirty degrees in three feet of water. Charlie, already looking contrite, said, "We can't get it to stay upright."

Fully dressed, I waded in, grabbed my machine. Making an effort to keep my voice level, I said, "Let's get this back to the garage, Charlie."

The other boys, siblings and friends alike, stood gawking at the grown man in shoes and socks in water up to his waist. Charlie said, "I don't think it *is* a boat. It barely floats without the motor. With the motor, it would just flop over on its stern."

"Charlie," I said, "you're a little thief, and this boat's going to be back in the garage in five minutes."

He gave me an insolently questioning look, as if wondering whether to ask what kind of trouble I could provide, but that proved to be the extent of his defiance. Charlie and I and one big boy dragged the machine up the beach, the other children trailing. I heard this exchange en route:

"Who is he?"

"He's screwing our cousin Lorna. She's in pictures."

Lorna herself met us twenty feet from the house. She trotted alongside. "Is it all right?"

"I don't know. I'll just have to find out."

"Are you sure? Is it safe?"

"I don't know. I can't exactly take it in for a diagnostic checkup."

The boys seemed impressed, not least by this splendid jargon. We hauled the machine into the garage, past the Packard to its customary place, and set it down easy. I said, "Okay, now get the hell out of here." They scurried away. Charlie, last to go, gave me a stare more hurt than malevolent.

I checked the dials. There was sand on everything. Lorna raced to the kitchen and returned with rags. We dried and polished. Charles poked his head in. "Anything I can do? Sally told me what the boys did. If anything's wrong, Gabriel, if there's any damage, please hold me responsible."

I said, "Don't worry about it, Charles, please."

"One more thing, and then I'll leave you alone." He took several steps into the garage and extended a charred envelope. "I'm afraid Charlie's just set fire to your pictures. I've still got the negatives, so . . ."

I took the envelope and stuck it in the side pocket of my jacket. "Good," I said. "Fine."

Charles nodded, bowed, backed through the door. I turned to Lorna. "Obviously I can't keep this here anymore. I've got to store it again."

She said, "You mean now?"

"Well, soon. When I get where I'm going, ten days ago. So this doesn't happen again, the next time today occurs."

"Gabriel, wait a minute. I'm not at all sure it's a good idea to use this machine now. If someone had just driven a car into the ocean, for instance . . ."

"It's not a car. And what choice do I have?"

"Couldn't you try taking it back a really short time? An hour or two? You could see if it's working, and then at least I'd know what was going on."

"Whatever the risks are, I'm sure they apply just as much to a two-hour trip as a ten-day trip. Let's just get it over with."

"Aren't you going to change your clothes? You're soaking wet."

"Look, if I change my clothes now, I have to parade in front of Charles and Sally, who are probably already thinking I'm some kind of obsessive lunatic. Why don't I just go back and change when I get there? It's still a matter of walking up the same stairs." I sat down on the machine.

"I don't feel good about this," Lorna said.

"There's nothing to worry about," I said. She moved closer to me and I put my arms somewhat awkwardly around her waist, my head between her breasts. She knelt to kiss me, and I said, "If something does happen to me, promise me you'll drive safely."

"I will."

"I mean it. I love you very much."

"Wait," she said. "Where's that little machine, the typewriter with the television screen?"

"Behind the boxes over there." Lorna retrieved the computer and handed it to me. I said, "I don't need this."

"I don't want it left here," she said. I realized there was no point arguing. She said, "Promise me again you're going to tell me every-thing."

I set the dials. "I promise."

"I love you, Gabriel," she said. "Be careful."

I pressed the "go" button.

—▪—

It was daylight; it was warm. The Packard was gone. What could I con-clude from that? I had retrogressed more than a few hours, and not to a weekend when the car would have been parked here. How was I? I felt neither the incipient elation of my first four trips nor the nascent headache of my fifth. I descended from the machine and began the tentative journey I'd made twice before, out of the garage, toward the kitchen. Did I hear voices in the dining room?

The kitchen was empty, but there was considerable evidence of food preparation. Had I missed my mark? There had been no big meal at the house in late September. There were definitely voices in the dining room. I stood motionless in the kitchen, listening to Lorna's laugh. Filled with relief and confidence, I opened the door to the din-ing room.

Its occupants were as astonished to see me as I them. There was something quite harrowingly dreamlike about this moment—all these semi-familiar faces, everyone examining me. I had no trouble recog-nizing Lorna. I did a sort of double take when I determined that the very tall man who could have been Jasper Hudnut at age forty was most probably Edgar Hudnut, and thus the boy two seats away from him must have been Jasper. The woman next to Edgar would be Grace, I reasoned, the two adults around Lorna her parents, these

382

other children Jasper's siblings. My instinct, born of exhaustion, disorientation, and perhaps something quite atavistic, was to head straight for Lorna. But of course she didn't know me from Adam.

No one had moved an inch. Edgar Hudnut said, "Can I help you, sir? Have you had some problem with your boat?"

With my *boat?* Ah, yes: my trousers were wet and I was covered with sand. I said, "This may seem like a strange question, but would the year be 1934?"

"1935," Edgar replied. Grace shifted uneasily. Lorna was twenty, about to be a senior at Smith. What was Dutch doing? Re-creating Cub games in Des Moines? Was there any point, any future as it were, to my staying here?

"Boat trouble, yes," I said. "Terribly sorry to barge in on you." Did I giggle a bit as I recognized my unintended pun? My strong urge was to take Lorna aside, to try to explain things to her. But I realized at once it was an idiotic notion.

"Can we help you?" Edgar repeated.

"No, that's all right. I can see myself out." I'd just dropped in to ask what year it was. I waved good-bye, made my way back into the garage, calculating as I walked. What had gone wrong? The saltwater, obviously. The control panel was mechanical and delicate, perhaps even a good dose of humidity had thrown it out of whack. I'd set the controls to go back ten days, had in fact gone back three years. Did that mean I should now tell the machine to go forward ten days in order to advance three years? Unfortunately, I had no time to think things through. Soon the garage would be crawling with Hudnuts.

What was there to lose if I took the conservative route? At worst, I'd encounter the same crowd ten days from now. I sat on the machine, the computer resting on my legs, set the dials, and hesitated. Perhaps there *was* something to lose: if I set the controls to go forward ten days and in fact went forward ten days, what would my *next* move be? Another ten-day venture? How many of those before the headache struck?

There was a tall child in the doorway. "What are you doing?" he asked.

I said, "You're Jasper, aren't you?"

"How did you know that?"

"It's a long story."

"What's that thing?"

"Another long story."

"How about the little case next to it?"

"It's a very smart little typewriter."

He walked into the garage, past me, stopped at the machine. At thirteen, he was perhaps two inches shorter than I. "When you asked what year it was, I figured you were either crazy or from another time. You don't act crazy. I suppose you could have been an amnesiac, but that would be a bit far-fetched."

"More far-fetched than being from another time?"

"Under the circumstances, yes. I don't know a great deal about amnesia, but I imagine there'd be some physical indications. On the other hand, none of us know you, and you appear to know us, or at least me." He was examining the dials. "Where did you come from?"

Was there any reason not to tell him? If so, I couldn't imagine what it was. "Most recently, 1938. I was trying to go back ten days, and I seem to have come back three years instead. What's the date?"

"It's July twenty-third."

"Three years and two months, then. Anyway, my guess is that the control panel was damaged when some kids took the machine into the ocean. Your cousin Charlie, actually."

Young Jasper's eyebrows raised in coordination with the corners of his mouth. "Really? In 1938? This is all kind of swell. Do you mind if I have a look at it?"

"Aren't your parents going to be concerned about you?"

"No. I told them I was going out for a walk. They're pretty eccentric, anyway. Where's this machine from? What year?"

"Early twenty-second century."

"You too? Does it belong to you? Does everybody have one?"

"No, I'm just borrowing it. I'm from this century and I'm afraid I don't know a great deal about it."

I showed him how his older self had pried the cover off the control panel. He took a toolbox from a shelf above us and had the cover off in no time. "You're right," he said. "It's all wet in here. And why do you suppose they'd have mechanical controls when the rest of it, the heart of the machine, is something much more advanced?"

"It's French," I said.

Jasper used his handkerchief to soak up droplets of moisture. He lowered his head toward the corners of the panel and blew, then daubed again with the handkerchief. He replaced the cover. "It's dry now. Nothing's broken or bent. I'd say it's ready to go. You wouldn't let me give it a try, would you?"

"I don't think that would be a good idea right now," I said.

It appeared I didn't need to explain. Jasper said, "Do you mind if I set the controls?"

"Be my guest," I said.

He moved through the dials as if finding familiar stations on a radio. "So . . . 1938, and then . . . September . . . and the specific date would be . . ."

"The twentieth."

"The twentieth. And then . . . this button here, I'd guess, is the ignition, or whatever you call it."

"Right on the money," I said, whereupon Jasper pressed the button in question, and disappeared.

— —

Now came that familiar light-headedness, a taste of it anyway. My mind was in high gear already, working on contingent strategies. If thirteen-year-old Jasper had been as successful as his sixty-year-old self at regulating the control panel, I would be on secure ground. Stick to my guns with Hawks, tell Wallis no deal, let the chips fall where they may. If I'd arrived earlier than September 20, adjust accordingly. If I'd arrived somewhere between the twentieth and the thirtieth (my departure point), the trip might have been a waste. If I'd arrived *later* than the thirtieth, well . . . that could prove interesting. What would it mean if, say, a week had gone by without me? Would it still, somehow, be seamless?

I stepped down from the machine, and had a horrible thought. When I'd searched for evidence of myself in 1984 I'd found none; it was as if I'd never existed. Hudnut's timeline explanation would have been comforting had I believed it for a minute. I didn't, alas, and I strongly suspected that when I retrogressed from 1994 to 1938, I had wiped my life off the books; its forty-two years existed only in my own memory. Was this theoretically possible? I was in no position to check with the experts, and my gravest fear was that I'd just done it again.

I prayed I was wrong, but if there was any consistency to all of this, by traveling back past the point of my first meeting with Lorna I'd erased myself from her consciousness. If she remembered me at all she would recall the man with wet pants and a charred envelope protruding from his pocket who walked in on family dinner in July 1935. I'd also expunged everything else: my work at Warners, *Four O'Clock*, *Operation: Rescue*, and everything that had transpired between me and Dutch. Ronald Reagan's life was back on its original course. I'd have to start from scratch.

A second thought more horrible than the first: if it were later than December, would Lorna not have died as scheduled in her traffic accident? No, I realized—but only because she wouldn't have made it that far. I would not have been around to keep her away from the Roosevelt Highway landslide in February. If young Jasper had sent me anywhere later than February 28, 1938, Lorna was dead once more.

My heart thudding in grim anticipation, I surveyed the garage: things were not the same. There were fewer boxes; the place had been organized, rearranged; the children's bicycles were missing. I entered the house. The kitchen looked much as it had. The dining room had sprouted a lone row of photographs; I dared not look at them, for fear they would show me what I didn't want to see. There was still a telephone in the nook by the front door, but it was the sort I remembered from the early days of my own childhood: heavy plastic base with dial, receiver with mouthpiece and earpiece. In the drawer beneath the phone was something that hadn't been there when I left: a telephone book. It was the Santa Monica City Directory and it bore fateful, confirming numerals—1952.

Now awash in a sea of apprehension, trying to forestall utter panic, I reentered the garage, seized the laptop, and took my seat on the machine. I set the dials very carefully, my target now mid-February, 1938. I held my breath and pressed the "go" button, but nothing happened. I went through the process again, painstakingly. Still nothing. Again and again, to no avail.

What now? It wasn't as if I could call a tow truck and have the machine tuned up, overhauled, recharged. But if it wouldn't take me backward, perhaps it could still take me forward. To 1994? No, better to 1984, to that friendlier, beneficent Hudnut and the lovely Annabel—although quite possibly I had succeeded even in destroying that union. Unless Hudnut's timeline theory were somehow to prevail, Reagan's survival meant Orlando for Annabel and obscurity for Hudnut. But surely he would still possess the expertise to return me to 1938.

I set the controls for November 1984, pressed the "go" button. And nothing happened. I repeated *this* process ten or twelve times, and still I remained inert, static, fourteen years past one home, thirty-two short of the other. Whatever was equivalent in time machine terms to running out of gas, this machine had done it.

Time on
My Hands

I spent much of that night wandering around the house, as if searching for a ghost or two. Despite lack of sleep, I began to think fairly clearly. In the early morning, by telephone, I determined that the date was February 12. Later, after I'd helped myself to a can of beans in the kitchen, I called the long-distance operator and asked her to connect me to a Jasper Hudnut in Corvallis, Oregon. After several minutes she informed me there was no Jasper Hudnut listed in Corvallis. I asked her to connect me to Oregon State University.

Jasper Hudnut was not a member of the physics department, was nowhere on the faculty. This gave me hope, in an odd way. Wasn't it a confirmation of the timeline theory? Why, otherwise, would Hudnut's career have taken a different turn? If so, maybe Lorna was alive, perhaps even nearby. She would be thirty-seven. Then I thought: If I had encountered a time traveler when I was thirteen, would I have wanted to be an assistant professor of physics at Oregon State University?

I took inventory. In my pants pocket I had nearly twenty thousand dollars, worth almost as much in 1952 as it had been in 1938. In my wallet was a newspaper clipping announcing the emergence of Lorna Fairchild in a western called *Four O'Clock*.

I took a taxi into Santa Monica and bought a 1949 Ford pickup for $375. I drove the truck back to Malibu, managed to get the machine onto its bed, drove back to Santa Monica, rented a house two blocks from my former, future one for $200 a month, stashed the machine in its garage. I wondered what to do.

Ronald Reagan had just finished *Hong Kong* for Paramount. Later this year he would return to Warners and portray Grover Cleveland Alexander—the pitcher, not the president—in *The Winning Team*. He was about to marry Nancy Davis. He had just turned forty-one, was no longer a starry-eyed liberal. Here in the year of my birth, I would soon be forty-three.

Saturday morning, I called the house. Would anyone be there on a rainy weekend in February? Charles answered the telephone. I identified myself as a childhood friend of Jasper's newly moved to the West Coast. Charles thought it interesting I would have this number, and I explained that Jasper had often spoken fondly of a summer house in Malibu. It was my only lead.

Well, Charles said, it happened that Jasper was out of town, out of the country, actually. He was on sabbatical, spending a year in Australia, due to return in July. It was my intention to ask on sabbatical from where, to pose all sorts of follow-up questions, but I was compelled instead to say, "I wonder . . . Jasper used to talk about a cousin who was an actress. Her name was Lorna, I believe. I wonder . . ."

"Oh, my gosh," Charles replied. "Poor Lorna. She's been dead, let's see, just about fourteen years now."

I knew, but I was overcome just the same, managed to thank Charles hastily before hanging up.

I tried to remember if Hudnut had ever said *when* in 1952 he'd found that first time machine in the Oregon wilderness. A long shot was better than none at all, I decided. I sacrificed a month's rent and my deposit, drove the pickup and the machine to Corvallis, got myself a cabin in the woods.

As I said at the start, I've got time on my hands. I've been here three months, spending my days traveling carefully planned grids through the woods, my nights working on this little saga. As if I were a homesick exile in a preelectronic age, my aspirations, my waking and sleeping dreams, all concern a place I cannot reach, in any sense. It is my intention to return to Southern California in June, anticipating Hudnut, unless by chance I find that other machine first, in which case I will head immediately back to 1938.

Is Jean-Baptiste still there? Is the man who precipitated my final, disastrous trip still wandering around 1938? Is he looking for me? Were his actions as unfocused and anarchic as they seemed, or was there something much more sophisticated at work, something I was unable to see? His motives aside, I find myself obsessed by the paradox Jean-Baptiste presents. I had come to take for granted that there remained no trace of me in the consciousness of everyone I knew in 1938. And yet I assume that Jean-Baptiste remembers me quite well. If he is in 1938, then, perhaps his own alien presence has kept everything as it would have been had I stayed. Lorna lives. That existence progresses in parallel to this. One day soon I will find a print of the *Four O'Clock* I wrote.

But better that I get back there myself.

It is my intention to leave this disk in a safe deposit box, with orders that it be delivered January 1, 1994, to Jasper Hudnut in Malibu.

In August 1993, Frank C. Chapman, federal regulator in charge of the disposition of assets of the First Republican Savings and Loan Association of Clara Vista, California, contacted me regarding the contents of a safe deposit box. First Republican had failed approximately six years earlier, when bank examiners discovered that 30 percent of its loan portfolio consisted of grossly inflated real estate collateral.

Mr. Chapman informed me that the safe deposit box in question was one of 880 on First Republican's premises. Most of the boxes had been emptied of their contents by customers during the early stages of First Republican's difficulties. First Republican and then federal authorities had both made (in Mr. Chapman's words) "every effort" to locate registered owners (or their relatives) of the remaining boxes.

In the case of box #112, First Republican officers had initially tried to contact one Gabriel Prince, who had rented the box on June 8, 1952. Failing that, they had searched for one Jasper Hudnut—as per instructions left by Mr. Prince in 1952—again to no avail. The contents of box #112, now legally property of the State of California, would doubtless have been discarded or forgotten but for the efforts of Mr. Chapman, who felt they might have some historical value.

Mr. Chapman was also intrigued by the fact that box #112, which according to First Republican's extensive and comprehensive records had been untouched between 1952 and its forcible opening in 1989, contained an artifact that had not come into existence until the mid-1980s, a 3 1/2-inch computer diskette, as well as several photographs taken in the mid-1980s and several more that appear to date from the late 1980s or early 1990s.

In the three years since Mr. Chapman's call, my colleagues and I have dealt with these puzzles and others. The simplest explanation for the presence of anachronistic objects in box #112 is the occurrence of a break-in. While some intrusion may have taken place between 1952 and 1989—it has been suggested that the locksmith himself was in a position to secrete items as inconspicuous as these—the chances of a substitution having been made between 1989 and 1993 (when the contents of box #112 were in Mr. Chapman's possession) are quite slim. And the likelihood of any such event since August 1993, when the diskette and the photographs were delivered to my department, is nonexistent.

If indeed everything is as it seems, and this diskette and these photographs truly were stored in box #112 on June 8, 1952, then we are dealing with a phenomenon. Even if some skullduggery occurred between 1952 and 1987, I would ask the most skeptical reader to consider the following:

- The diskette in question is of the high density (1.44 megabyte) type, a variety that did not come into popular use until the late 1980s and would almost certainly not have been available in 1987, when box #112 was opened.
- The content of the diskette (the text you have just read) was written in a word-processing application[1] that did not exist until late 1993, or six years after the diskette was removed from box #112.
- The thirty-seven photographs[2] found in box #112 comprise three images from the mid-1980s, three from the early or mid-1990s, and thirty-one from the late 1930s. The foremost experts in the field[3] have confirmed that the three groups of photographs are "of the same approximate physical age," that all thirty-seven photographs were "taken within five years of each other," and that the photographic stock of the earlier pictures is consistent with their age: in other words, those photographs are not new prints made from old negatives.

Was there a Gabriel Prince? There is no record of his birth in Old Saybrook, Connecticut, no record of his attendance at Princeton Univer-

---

[1]WordPerfect 6.0.

[2]The photographs have caused my department great frustration. Of the thirty-seven left in box #112 we have chosen twenty-five to accompany the text, having judged the other twelve redundant. We have placed them where they seemed most relevant to the text. By and large, the photographs do not seem an attempt to provide proof of the events of the text so much as an effort to illustrate it. (An exception, perhaps inadvertant, is included below.)

[3]Lucitron Laboratories of El Cajon, California.

sity. Greenglass Enterprises has published four editions of *Entrée to Paris* since 1985, but has never heard of Gabriel Prince. Warner Brothers has never employed a writer named Gabriel Prince.

Warner Brothers did employ a contract actress named Lorna Fairchild between June 1937 and February 1938, when she was killed in a landslide on the Roosevelt Highway in Santa Monica, California. Miss Fairchild was third-billed in a B comedy called *Love on a Shoestring*, which was released in December 1937. (There appear to be no surviving copies of *Love on a Shoestring*, nor of any of the films in which Miss Fairchild had smaller parts.)

William Watson Wadsworth, known as Bill Wadsworth, worked as a screenwriter at Warner Brothers until his death in 1950.

Jasper Hudnut, too, is a person of record, although my department has fared no better than Mr. Chapman in finding him. Jasper Hudnut, who would be seventy-two years old at the time of this writing, has led what his cousin Charles Hudnut Jr. describes as "a vagabond life." He has been associated with none of the universities cited in the text, nor with the Max Planck Institute.

Charles Hudnut Jr., who at sixty-eight is the sales manager of a luxury automobile dealership in Laguna Beach, California, agreed in 1994 to read the diskette's text, and subsequently spoke to my department at length. Charles Hudnut had no recollection of Gabriel Prince. His cousin Lorna Fairchild did occupy the family house at the Malibu Colony in 1937–38, he told us, but lived there alone. The section of the text that purported to occur in 1984 he characterized as "pure fantasy." Was there anything about the text as a whole that rang true? Descriptions of the house and the Hudnut family, as far as they went, were accurate. And, Charles Hudnut said, he did recall the brief interruption of a family dinner during the summer of 1935 or 1936 by "a fellow with wet trouser legs who stood there for a couple of minutes and said some crazy things." Charles Hudnut suggested that his cousin Jasper Hudnut was "probably responsible" for the text and the photographs. "It is just the sort of elaborate prank that Jasper has always loved."

A bright young woman in my department came up with the idea of searching academic databases for the first name "Annabel." We found a single occurrence: an associate professor of mathematics at the University of Toronto, named Annabel Hotaling.

Mrs. Hotaling told us on the telephone that her maiden name had been Kinnamon, that she had done graduate work at the University of Wisconsin, and been elected president of the local SDS chapter a month before the mathematics building was bombed, and gone on to teach at the California Polytechnic Institute at San Luis Obispo, from which she was fired in 1973. She had moved to Canada shortly thereafter—first to Winnipeg, Manitoba, and then to Toronto.

I personally flew to Toronto to interview Mrs. Hotaling. She is a handsome woman of fifty-two, married to a university administrator, with two teenage boys. She bears a striking resemblance to the photograph of Annabel Hudnut included in the preceding text. As I had expected, she had never heard of Jasper Hudnut or Gabriel Prince. When I showed her the photograph she reacted with surprise and curiosity. At first, she said, she had presumed it to be a picture of herself at approximately age forty. Her second perception was that the woman in the picture wore completely unfamiliar clothing, and the room in which she stood was a room Annabel herself had never occupied, which led her to believe she was looking at someone who could be her identical twin. But, she added, identifying a figurine clearly visible in the back of the room, "that is without question my Buddha."

My department finds itself now, for all intents and purposes, at a dead end. I have barely scratched the surface of our efforts in the above, electing to summarize only the research and inquiries that have produced results of some relevance. We have of course shown the text, or offered it, to a number of prominent physicists, without much in the way of enthusiastic reception.

Whether Gabriel Prince traveled in time, or whether he even existed, is something I fear we will never know.

Raymond V. Johnson, Ph.D.
Southland Historical Institute
Santa Ynez, California
September 1996

PHOTO CREDITS

page 16: Brian Yarvin/The Image Works

page 25: Carol Walter

page 67: *Brother Rat*/Warner Bros., 1938/Turner Entertainment

page 77: *Jaguar: The Complete Works*, page 21.

page 92: Courtesy of the Santa Monica Public Library

page 94: Ernest Marquez Collection

page 101: Archive Photos

page 119: Culver Pictures, Inc./Ken Asplund/Stella Associates

page 128: Courtesy of the Santa Monica Public Library

page 143: *King of the Underworld*/Warner Bros., 1938/Turner Entertainment

page 150: Courtesy of the Catalina Island Museum

page 152: Courtesy of the Catalina Island Museum

page 153: Courtesy of the Catalina Island Museum

page 155: Courtesy of the Catalina Island Museum

page 207: Don Heiny/Stella Associates

page 208: Don Heiny/Stella Associates

page 253: *Girls on Probation*/Warner Bros., 1938/Turner Entertainment

page 255: Ernest Marquez Collection

page 261: *Brother Rat*/Warner Bros., 1938/Turner Entertainment

page 290: Don Heiny/Stella Associates

page 308: *Secret Service of the Air*/Warner Bros., 1938/Turner Entertainment

page 333: Carol Walter

page 391: FPG International

page 396: Don Heiny/Stella Associates

page 397: Archive Photos